Andrew Pastor lives in Drimpton,
365 days a year if he can and is i
He has written several books of
community plays, pantomimes ai
include:

Village Voices: Local Lives
Village Voices: Farming Families
Village Voices: The Nameless Stream
Who Were We?
Panto: The Manual

His most recent book is **Something of the Marvellous**.
Written in collaboration with Lancashire illustrator Patricia
Barrett, it invites readers to join them in their respective
gardens and local landscapes to move with them through
the unexpected pleasures of British Summer Time during
2020 – a year like no other, a year of pandemic and
lockdown – when the world outdoors called more loudly
than ever, and we all of us looked for ways to break free.

Making Waves

by

Andrew Pastor

First published 2023
© Andrew Pastor 2023
Andrew Pastor has asserted his rights under Copyright Designs & Patents Act 1988 to be identified as the author of this book

ISBN Number: 9798374590487

Cover and design by: Peter Marriage

Printed by Amazon

This is a work of fiction. Any similarity to a real time and place is intentional, though not everything here is as it was. All characters, save those in the public domain, are fictional and any resemblance to actual persons, living or dead is coincidental.

Leading characters and their families

Bluebell, a gentleman of the road

Amanda Clark, aged 11
John Clark, her brother, aged 14
Mr and Mrs Clark, their parents

Mr Hugh Dinsdale, CND activist
Miss Josephine Brooks, his friend and fellow CND activist

Mr Eric Dring, schoolteacher
Mrs Mabel Dring, his wife
Dickie, her dachshund

Mr Harold Newcombe, Headmaster of Dawlish County Junior School
Mrs Dierdre Newcombe, his wife

Susan Pearse, aged 11
Mrs Pearse, her mother
Ginger, their old cat

Mr Osbert Phipps, draper
Mrs Grace Phipps, his wife

Mrs Kay Trent, Dawlish Violets Queen
Mr Tom Trent, her husband

Supporting characters and their families

Mr Vernon Barry, member of Dawlish Repertory Company
Adrian Barry, his son, aged 11

Mrs Mary Bonfield, schoolteacher
Mr Leonard Bonfield, her husband

Peter Brace, aged 11

Miss Helen Bray, prompter for "Our Town"
Mr Philip Bray, her brother, member of Dawlish Repertory Company

Mr Brewster, councillor
Mrs Brewster, his wife

Mr Charles Burch, producer of "Our Town"

Henry Carey, sound effects for "Our Town"
Mr Carey, his father
Mrs Win Carey, his mother

Mr Arthur Drummond, councillor
Mrs Drummond, his wife
Miss Hilary Drummond, their daughter

Miss Linda Eaves, town librarian

Thomas Fowler, aged 11

Miss Rita Gordon, schoolteacher

Miss Monica Hardman, beauty pageant contestant
Mrs Hardman, her mother

Mr Jim Harvey, farmer
Mrs Cissie Harvey, his wife

Mr Malcolm Hill, stage manager for "Our Town"

Mrs Mavis Jackson, the Prettiest Grandmother

Mr Haywood, fish & chip shop owner
Mrs Haywood, his wife

Miss Hilton, schoolteacher

Mr Stan Holman, councillor

Mr Jack Liddell, odd job man
Young Liddell, his son, aged 15

Mr Ted Lowe, Chairman of Dawlish Town Council
Mrs Vera Lowe, his wife

Mrs MacAskill, WRVS
Miss Wilkes, her friend

Mr Nelson, travel agent
Mrs Nelson, his wife

Mrs Owen, hairdresser
Miss Betty Owen, her daughter, hairdresser
Chris Owen, her son, member of Dawlish Repertory Company
Mr George Owen, her husband

Mr Alan Patterson, member of Dawlish Repertory Company
Derek Patterson, his son, aged 11

Reporter from the "Dawlish Gazette"

Mrs Rudge, corsetiere

Mrs Speller, café proprietor

Mr George Stephens, councillor
Mrs Stephens, his wife

Mrs Christine Thompson, schoolteacher

Timothy Unwin, aged 11

The Vicar of St Gregory's Church

Clive Webster, aged 11
Wendy Wetherall, aged 11

Extras, walk-ons and non-speaking parts
Mr Bennington, CND speaker
Mr Billy Burrowes, from Rita Gordon's past
Nicholas Collier, aged 11

Mr Richard Cornall, from Rita Gordon's past
Miss Betty Crabb, from Rita Gordon's past
Vernon and Daphne Croxley, dance teachers
Mrs Dewhurst, former hairdresser
"Dulcetto", Austrian dulcimer player
Mrs Doris Hall, monologuist
Miss Helen Gibbons, beauty pageant contestant
Miss Jenkins, Sunday School teacher
Jimmy, Helen Bray's boyfriend
Mrs Keeley, from The Royal Hotel
Mr Lennox, member of Dawlish Repertory Company
Mr Len McCarthy, manager of The Royal Hotel
Ann Mortimer, aged 11
"Mystery of The Mind", mind reader
Paulo, barman
Miss Simone Scott, beauty pageant contestant
Mrs Scott, her mother
Mr Spicer, Osbert Phipps's former teacher
Sylvia & Peggy, from Mrs Lowe's past
Mr Alfred Tremlett, from Rita Gordon's past
Mr Roland Tubbs, treasurer of the Bowls Club
Mr Tucker, gardener
Dr Wallis, GP
Steven and Tom Webster, children
Mrs Sandra West, beauty pageant contestant
Mavis Whittaker, from Mabel Dring's past
Bernard Williamson, member of Dawlish Repertory Company
plus
various parents, aunts, uncles and grandparents
numerous children, uncounted townspeople
musicians and entertainers, crowds of tourists
council workers, policemen
black swans, cats

and
featuring real-life ballet dancers
and many others from the world beyond Dawlish

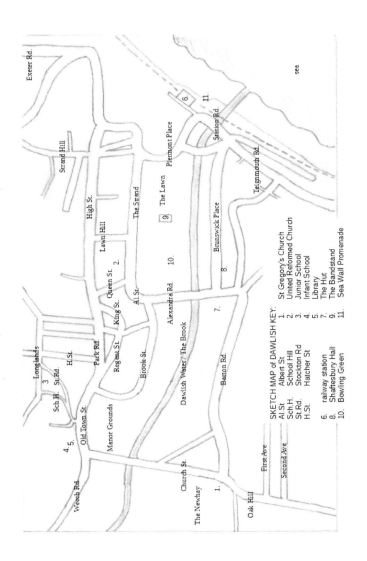

SKETCH MAP of DAWLISH KEY:
Al.St.   Albert St
Sch.H.   School Hill
St.Rd.   Stockton Rd
H.St.   Hatcher St

6.   railway station
8.   Shaftesbury Hall
10.   Bowling Green

1.   St Gregory's Church
2.   United Reformed Church
3.   Junior School
4.   Infant School
5.   Library
7.   The Hut
9.   The Bandstand
11.   Sea Wall Promenade

DAWLISH TOWN CENTRE

Contents

ACT ONE
1958

ACT TWO
1958

ACT THREE
1958

EPILOGUE
1988

> **'I Know What I Like'**
>
> *Gilbert Harding presents the type of entertainment which gives him pleasure and which he hopes will please you.*
> **BBC TV: Friday May 30th 1958**

> **'Dead or Alive?'**
>
> *Do mass selling, mass journalism and mass entertainment enfeeble our society? Are the readers of our popular press, the audience of television, a vast silent mass?'*
> **The Home Service: Wednesday July 30th 1958**

All programmes referenced in **MAKING WAVES** were broadcast on television and radio through 1958, and would have played in millions of homes, providing a sound and picture-scape for life.

There were two TV channels, BBC and ITV. BBC Radio broadcast on the Light Programme, the Home Service, the Third Programme and Network Three.

ACT ONE

WHIT MONDAY, MAY 26th 1958

'The Big Gamble' – documentary
With eternal optimism millions of people every summer flock to the British holiday resorts. They take 'The Big Gamble' with the weather and, on the whole, enjoy themselves. - BBC TV

In Town

On board the Royal Coach with its floral garlands and bunting Princess Warren Crocus is smiling and waving with gusto. In Amanda Clark's mind's eye, for she is a young princess this year, flowers are raining down as she takes her umpteenth curtain call in the company of Dawlish's very own John Gilpin. *The* John Gilpin. None other. Having invited her to dance with the Festival Ballet in New York, she has taken the city by storm. Amanda's Mum and Dad wave from their vantage point in front of the United Reformed Church on The Strand, its towering spire pointing up into the watery blue sky. Amanda beams. She charms. She loves America.

Susan Pearse, Princess Holcombe Anemone, isn't about to let her best friend down.

The boys of the Towing Party, looking spick and span in white shirts and dark grey shorts, pull the Royal Coach on passed the crowds filling the pavement below the awnings in front of shops and cafés all the way until they reach Sampson's Estate Agents & Auctioneers. Here, Councillors Drummond and Stephens – in the case of Councillor Drummond reliving his period of National Service as ground crew in the RAF – between them guide the Towing Party across The Strand and on to the grassy expanse of The Lawn. There is a moment of concern when a wheel judders sending the Royal Party swaying, but Amanda simply laughs. Her happiness is beyond words.

*

'Whoa!' calls Mr Newcombe, the Headmaster at the Junior School, today in his position as Master of Ceremonies, complete with an outsized bunch of violets pinned to his blazer lapel.

The Towing Party halts in front of more crowds by the bandstand near the Bowling Green and the Royal Coach whoas. Councillors Drummond and Stephens share a nod; they can relax.

Mr Newcombe steps forward and hands down the Violets Queen. Amanda and Susan sort themselves out with a bit of encouragement from Mrs Stephens, Brown Owl of the town's Brownie pack. Mrs Kay Trent's ash blonde BeeHive almost torpedoes the bunting, but she is quite regal enough not to flap. In no time at all the party has assembled.

'Your Majesty.' Mr Newcombe makes a formal bow to the soon-to-be crowned Violets Queen. Not to be outdone Mrs Trent nods back. The crowd likes that. 'Princesses.' And again Mr Newcombe bows. Susan nearly giggles. Not Amanda. She smiles like a young Princess Anne. 'Councillors, Ladies, Gentlemen, boys and girls.' He pauses to take a theatrical breath, as usual. He makes no bones about it. He sticks to the winning formula when it comes to public functions. The crowd appreciates it.

*

From the very back of the crowd Mr Phipps is urged by his wife to comment. 'Well?'

He pauses as long as possible. 'White dresses. Pleated bodices. Mauve shot taffeta capes decorated with gold braid. White head-dresses.' Mr Phipps isn't done yet. 'The queen's in white nylon over taffeta with a pleated bodice and a stand-up collar. Very full skirt. And the cloak's in violet velour, with gold braid.'

Mr Phipps, Draper, is not a person to get velour confused with velvet. Taller than the average he has seen more than enough. He turns away from the rear of the crowd and strides off. Mrs Phipps has seen nothing.

The tannoy speaks, screwing Mrs Lowe's voice into a harsher key. 'It is with great pleasure that I crown you the Dawlish Violets Queen for 1958.'

With those few words Mrs Lowe slips a dignified tiara of diamonte into the BeeHive of Mrs Trent to be embedded some inches above her head. The new queen waves royally and the crowd cheers.

'Osbert, why did you hurry off like that?' Grace Phipps is breathless. Her husband slows, but only a little. 'Did the queen look lovely?' He sidesteps a small child. Grace supplies her own confirmation. 'I'm sure she must have done.'

'Yes, dear.' And Osbert crosses Piermont. He has said all he means to say. Grace looks about her for inspiration. The Lawn is full of activity. Flags flying. Displays of summer colour provided by Parks and Gardens. All as it should be. Grace now follows to where Osbert has turned to Hopkins' window. Excursions to Clovelly and Bodmin are advertised. His reflection shows a man in his 50s, wearing a brown jacket, brown trousers and brown brogue shoes, a white shirt and a brown knitted tie. It is a weekend look he has had for years and very similar to what he wears during the working week at the shop.

'Mr Newcombe always gets things just right at these dos, doesn't he? It wouldn't be the same without him.'

'Do you think so, dear? I'm quite sure it would be.' Osbert reads about Weston-Super-Mare.

'He gives his time for nothing. Mr Newcombe. He gives his time free and for nothing.' Grace is finding that her new court shoes are pinching. A breeze causes her light blue belted cotton frock to flutter. She is glad she is wearing a cardigan.

Osbert moves to another notice. A mystery tour is scheduled for tomorrow morning starting at 8 o'clock, due back at 6pm. He doesn't like the idea of a mystery tour. He tries to picture himself on the coach, but can't. Osbert turns from the window and looks off into the distance. Grace has a sudden twinge in the back of her neck. She's been craning up at her husband too long.

Osbert pans slowly from left to right across the scene being played out in front of him across the road on The Lawn, with the Fair beyond, and further off to a good wedge of Dawlish stacked up behind Brunswick Terrace. He pulls back to focus on the nearer distance and views the citizenry of the town, together with holidaying visitors from all points north and east. The scent of pagan devilment is in the air.

Somewhere within the crowd, the Bonniest Baby is being cooed over and jiggled up and down, up and down till it gurgles or belches or bawls. That is not the half of it, not by a long chalk. The Happiest-Looking Girl is smiling her way inanely through the minutes as a judge peers. Happiest-Looking. It matters not a jot what is really going on inside. As long as on the surface all is grinning contentment, who cares? The Boy First To Eat A Bag Of Crisps is stuffing himself. The Lady Prettiest Below The Knee is being gaped at and encouraged to show just a little more. The Smartest Man is smug. The Men With Knobbliest Knees are mocked. The Prettiest Grandmother flirts ridiculously with The Manliest Grandfather as The Couples Most Like Each Other stroll hand-in-hand, parodying fidelity. Osbert slowly turns from the revelry. He has an itch, an inkling that the world is amiss.

Grace scans the same scene and smiles.

'The Grand Prize Raffle will be drawn in five minutes, Ladies and Gentlemen,' Mr Newcombe booms. 'This is your last chance to get your winning tickets, so, hurry, hurry!'

It is then for Grace Phipps that a penny drops. Heading their way are the Harveys, Jim and Cissie. Jim, twenty stone and then some. Cissie, skin and bone, not much of either.

'Hullo, you two,' beams Jim, and he pats his giant paunch like some proud gardener of a prize-winning marrow. 'Done the trick this year.'

Cissie Harvey nudges him. Her sharp elbow might puncture that enormous barrage balloon. 'He's a one,' trills Cissie. 'It's hard to credit, but I swear he swelled up even more when they announced we'd won and pinned these on.' She indicates the twin rosettes.

'I owe it all to her, of course,' and Jim squeezes his wife. 'All this,' and he thumps his gut, 'is her handiwork. Years of hard work coming up with three square meals a day have gone into it. And now it's paid off.' The Harveys dissolve into merriment. Another farming couple comes up. Jim's back is well slapped. When his milking cows win prizes it is no better than this.

The Harveys move off, heralded, it seems, every step of the way. The Contrasted Couple of 1958 leave the Contrasted Couple of 1951 in their wake. Now Grace Phipps knows full well why her husband had turned his back on the proceedings when he did. It is quite simple. He had no intention of being faced with a repeat of that earlier Fair when the Phippses took first prize. Toasted and cheered they'd been. Osbert had died.

*

'Did you see?' Amanda rushes up to Susan, her princess dress hitched up. 'Did you? Did you?' Susan feels rather foolish with her candy floss. 'You must've seen. You simply must've.' Susan looks about in the hope of catching whatever it is. 'You didn't, did you? How could you miss him?'

At last a clue. 'Who?'

'Who? Who? None other than....Robert Helpmann!' Her hands fly to her cheeks. 'That's who.'

Susan is caught with a mouthful of pink sticky stuff. 'No! But we saw him in "Coppelia" on television last night. He can't be in Dawlish now!'

Amanda's head refills with those magical images in black and white squeezed into the Pearse's TV set. Amanda had been Swanilda, the village girl captivated by Robert Helpmann's scary Dr Coppelia.

She re-emerges from her dancing day-dream and rolls her

eyes. 'For goodness sake Susan, that was recorded last year so of course he could be here today. And he is! Cross my heart and hope to die! He was over there between the tombola and the dodgems. He's won a goldfish, a yellowy-gold one, at that stall where you throw darts at playing cards. You know the one.' Susan nods. She knows the one. Yes, she knows the one all right. She really has to win one for herself. 'He was standing as near to me as... well, as near as... Stay there.' Amanda takes a step away, 'Don't you move.' She darts off, then straight away rushes back. 'As near as that!'

'No!'

'Yes! Honest to God!' That shocks Susan. In Sunday School Miss Jenkins says... 'He was, I tell you. As plain as day and twice as natural,' as Amanda's Mum is keen on saying. 'He was standing, very casual... In Second Position.'

That clinches it. Susan is impressed. Second Position. 'What did you do?'

'What do you mean?' Amanda is bobbing and weaving on the spot, seeing if the ballet dancer is still anywhere to be seen.

'Well, did you say anything to him?'

Amanda is dumbfounded. To the core. 'How?.. How could you?.. For Heaven's sake, Susan!.. It was ROBERT HELPMANN!' The name soars above the Fair. 'You don't just go up to someone like him.'

'Oh.' Susan wonders why not.

'You can't, you know. You just can't.' Amanda wrings the end of her sash round and round her hand. 'Besides, what could I have said?'

'You could've told him you've got his picture stuck up inside your wardrobe.'

'Shh!' In a trice Amanda checks every point of the compass for eavesdroppers. 'Susan Pearse! How could you? You swore you'd never tell!'

'But you could've said something.'

Amanda covers her face with her hands and her strangled sash. 'I couldn't. I just couldn't. I'd've died!' Her hands slide down dragging her face into ugliness. 'You don't seem to realise. That was...'

'Robert Helpmann.'

'Don't say it like that!'

'Like what?' Susan twiddles the candyfloss stick.

'Like... Like you just said it.'

This isn't getting them anywhere. There are so many things Susan hasn't done yet at the Fair. Besides, she isn't sure she can believe Amanda in spite of her crossing-her-heart and hoping-to-die. Susan, Amanda's Very Best Friend, doesn't have to think hard to remember twice before when Amanda has sworn blind she'd bumped into Margot Fonteyn herself – both times in Boots the Chemists by the Number Seven cosmetics. Now she eyes her friend carefully over the last threads of candyfloss. Amanda is re-running the near-encounter in her head, Susan can tell. She is hugging it to herself like a hot water bottle in the winter. She isn't about to let it cool. 'Look!'

'Where?' Amanda snaps out of her reverie ready to rush. 'Where?'

'There.' Susan points with the stick. 'It's your Mum and Dad.' They are making their way on to The Lawn led by a proud Mrs Clark, who is receiving kind words as she goes.

Amanda slumps.

'With your brother.'

Amanda slumps as far as it is possible to slump and still stay on her feet.

'Let's go and tell them about Robert Helpmann.'

Amanda fires a look at Susan. Could she be so... What is the word? She's read it. In a book. A book about Pavlova. Nigh-something. Nigh-eve. That is it! Susan offers her widest, most open smile. She could be. She could be. But Very Best Friend or no Very Best Friend, Susan must have things explained to her sometime soon. Or otherwise they could end up falling out.

*

An upstairs window on Oak Hill slides closed the last few inches muffling the noises of the Fair that carry across the town. Eyes, screwed up against the brightness, are streaming. An unscratchable itch lurks behind each eyeball. The Fair's carousel, though quieter, plays on the highly sensitized nerves and promises a new surge of headache. Its music is fuzzy in the ears, dull beyond the sounds of laboured breathing and swallowing. Pricklings gather in the nostrils. Breathing is becoming shallower. The mouth gulps in air. The tear ducts overflow, blinding, welling over the lower lids, especially the right eye. It is not good. It is everything but good. It is awful. It is hell. It is only the start of summer.

Eric Dring sneezes once, twice, gasps, sneezes twice more, spraying the window before blanketing his face in a handkerchief still damp from the last attack. A shaking hand draws the curtains together. His head is raw inside. His brain doesn't fit. His eyeballs rasp. His nose is swollen to bursting and tender as a wound. His mouth is dry. His tongue is not his own. His teeth throb. His throat is swallowing, swallowing, swallowing in spasm. His spirit is at zero. He clutches at the back of a chair as another attack bends him in two. Sneezes rattle the window, ricochet off the walls, disturb the dog downstairs, destroy the last shreds of his strength. Mr Dring is wrung out. His whole frame is as tight as the braces holding up his trousers. He can give no more. Yet still he sneezes. Nothing exists except The Sneeze. Each sneeze kills him a little more. Death has to be preferable to this. He turns a slow pirouette and slumps slowly onto his bed, sinking into the eiderdown. Why can't it swallow him up, put him out of his misery? This yearly struggle; his annual defeat.

He presses his face harder and harder through the

handkerchief. Eyes shut. Eyelids caked. Nose now blessedly blocked. Panting. Taking in gasps of stiffling air. He fancies he has all but used up the oxygen in his restricted supply and now is making do with what little is left, pumping it round and round. But he's stopped sneezing. Maybe. Perhaps. Don't relax. Not yet. Not yet. Not for another six weeks. Mr Dring calms. The attack is retreating. But, don't be fooled. He sits on the bed unmoving, not changing his pose, frozen, concentrating on his nose – the agent of his suffering. The pricklngs prickle less. He feels himself slowly surfacing, coming back from the brink.

When, after some five minutes, he hasn't sneezed again, he lowers the handkerchief and gingerly stirs. No secondary attack. Yet. After another minute, and, moving like a phantom, he pushes himself up into a standing position. He means to disturb the evil dust-charged, pollen-loaded air as little as possible. If only he could zoom away in the way of Dan Dare, he would. He'd escape the whole god-forsaken planet. Deep inside he swears in careful detail.

He coasts across the bedroom, sidestepping areas where he knows dust is lurking. With handkerchief back pressed hard against his face he makes his way along the landing, pushes open the door at the end. Across the linoleum, ignoring the apparitition in the mirror, he plugs the basin and turns on the coldwater tap. Hurry. He is impatient for relief. The basin fills. The last drips drip, plinking. He casts aside the sodden handkerchief, rolls up his shirt sleeves and with one hand either side of the rim lowers his ravaged face to the water. He pauses a second. Anticipation. Then he dips. Down. Deep. As far as his ears. The cold water bubbles, soothing his stinging eyes, cooling his blasted nose, lapping at his fevered brow. Bliss. Drowning must be a nice way to go, in spite of what people say.

*

'And that, Ladies and Gentlemen, concludes the Grand Draw. On behalf of the Cottage Hospital I'd like to thank you for your support. It only remains for me to remind you that this evening at The Hut the Musical Society will be presenting a concert of choruses, solos and duets with a special guest in the person of Mrs Doris Hall of Dawlish Warren whose monologues are a treat. Tickets are available at the door. Thank you all for coming, Ladies and Gentlemen. Goodbye.'

There is a smattering of applause, but most of the crowd started to move away when the last prize was claimed by Susan Pearse. Mr Newcombe switches off the microphone. Young Liddell is already dismantling the drum. 'Thank your father, won't you?'

'Right.' The youth doesn't bother looking up.

'And do you think he could oil it before we use it for the next draw?'

'Right.'

Councillors Stephens and Drummond are trying to dragoon enough volunteers to drag the Royal Coach off The Lawn. The Guard of Honour that had been the Towing Party has long since disbanded, vanishing into the Fair. One or two brylcreemed heads can be seen hurtling the dodgems about.

*

'He's not as nice as me, I hope.'

Kay Trent hurries on towards the car, taking off the tiara which is beginning to slip. The velvet and blinding white nylon announce her progress. 'Mr Newcombe shook my hand!' Surely that is all the explanation that is needed.

'He might look as though he's never had a … thought in his life. But I shall be keeping an eye on those roving hands of his.'

'It's not *his* hands I've got to worry about.' She slaps Tom's. 'He's just a nice man.'

'A Nice Man? Is that Animal, Vegetable or Mineral?' Tom unlocks the car door. Kay slips in, fingers crossed against the chances of getting grease on her royal outfit.

A knock at the passenger window and Kay looks out into the powdered face of Mrs MacAskill, who is clearly expecting the window to be wound down. '...and I know I speak for everyone when I say how well you handled yourself. Such poise is not seen so often these days. The way you managed the Grand Draw, which is never easy, even though I didn't win, but I'm accustomed to that, and I'm not blaming you in any way – it wouldn't be called a lottery if it wasn't one, would it? - you were in complete control, my dear, and I'm sure Mr Trent was very proud.' She ducks a little to address him.

'She was wonderful.' He pats Kay's knee.

'Indeed she was.'

Kay endures the praise. 'Do you know, Mrs MacAskill? I think I owe it all to "Andre and Roma".' She smoothes the BeeHive with a palm.

'Nonsense, my dear, don't belittle yourself. The town's just so pleased. Think, not so very long ago we none of us really knew you, and now you're our queen.' Kay longs to wind the window back up. 'Oh, there's been something I've been meaning to ask.' Tom smirks, but not for long. Mrs MacAskill almost dives through the open window. 'Mr Trent, I've been concerned for some time now on a technical matter, and I believe I would benefit from your opinion. It's radio waves and the like. Radio waves and especially television picture-signals, and now satellite what-have-you.

'Well, in short, I'm fairly convinced that none of them are good for us. Just to think of those waves passing through the air all the time, morning, noon and night can't be doing us any good whatsoever.'

'I don't really think I'm qualified to comment.'

'Not qualified?' Mrs MacAskill believes in certificates. 'Are you not a certified television engineer?'

'Well, yes...'

'Like I thought.' And she is completely satisfied. 'It is my belief that television pictures, ITV pictures especially with their commercial breaks, and radio programmes hanging in the air or flying straight through everybody are a root cause of so much that is wrong these days. There's all this noise. And nobody listens any more. As you deal with so many people face-to-face I'm wondering you haven't noticed.'

'It's all perfectly safe.' A medical man could not have bettered Tom. 'There's really nothing to get anxious about.'

'If there was,' Kay steps in, 'that new "Which?" magazine would have done a report on it.'

'But do we need it all?'

Kay goshes at the time, remembers she has washing on the line and Tom has a shelf to fix. This is news to him, but he starts the car and they both 'Goodbye'.

Mrs MacAskill stands for a moment before heading home for "The Archers" on the wireless. She and Miss Wilkes never miss "the everyday story of countryfolk".

The Trents drive on savouring their escape. 'What could have got into her?'

'Don't go getting involved, Kay. She's just another happy person in need of a minor problem to worry about.'

*

As the crowd thins it is almost time for Bluebell to make his slow way from the peace and relative quiet of The Newhay behind St Gregory's to hunt for cigarette ends.

***

At Home

'Choosing a Puppy'
A dog is above all a companion, and choosing one is an art. Stanley Dangerfield, chief steward of Cruft's Show suggests how to go about it. – Network Three

Dickie stirs when he hears the front door swing open over the coconut mat. He is hungry. He'll go welcome her. From the far end of the hallway he sees her, standing with her back to the door. She pauses. There are wireless sounds from upstairs. Mrs Dring pushes the door shut with her bottom. Dickie watches her turn to the hallstand. Off come the gloves which she deposits in the drawer, pleased to see the back of them. She shrugs off her coat, the navy and white one with the large square buttons, and hooks it on a bracket. She adjusts her frock and straightens the rucked sleeves of her cardigan. At last, off comes the hat with the brim. She places it on the small shelf for the time being, and eases some life back into her flattened hair. She faces herself in the small mirror. Mabel Dring looks back at Mabel Dring. For a moment, behind the closed front door, in the dim hallway, Mabel smiles at Mabel. "Well done," one silently says to the other with some weight. She is then aware of being watched. The smile is suppressed as she swings round, ready. In an instant the smile flashes back on. 'Ah, Dickie Wickie! Who's a naughty thing creeping up on Mummy like that. Come on.' She leans forwards, bare hands on her knees and pats. 'Come to Mummy. Mummy's got lots and lots to tell you.' She looks upstairs, but there are no sounds of movement. Mabel heads for the kitchen. Dickie is so hungry. He patters along the Marley tiles, his black tail curved up behind showing its feathers to full effect. 'Mummy's little boy! Mummy's little sausage!'

Mabel Dring closes the kitchen door, stoops and scoops Dickie up. Her black-and-tan parcel swoops up to her cheek, which he nuzzles and licks, offering Mabel a warm wetness. He tastes powder and rouge.

Mabel coos quietly, 'You'll never guess what's happened to Mummy today, Dickie. Never in a thousand years. No, not even then. Shall I tell you?' Dickie licks. 'Very well, because you ask your Mummy so nicely, I will. And while I tell you I'll get you your tea. Is your little tummy empty?' And she flips Dickie over to tickle the blotched skin of his smooth belly. His ears fold inside out and hang down. She pats, and it sounds like dough being slapped. 'Right, Dickie, enough of this. What's it to be? Some "Lassie" for my laddie? Or some "Pal" for my pal?' But she does not giggle. There's no need. Not with Dickie.

'Are you really hungry? Really and truly?' Dickie is all eyes. Mabel Dring does not want to resist. 'Very well, you little greedy guts, have the lot.' She spoons out the jellied meat which flops on to Dickie's dish. 'Mmm! Looks scrummy.' She pushes the dish under Dickie's waiting muzzle. 'Now don't bolt your food.' Dickie troughs.

Mabel sits herself on one of the two kitchen chairs. Her feet are not neatly resting together, nor are her knees. She leans forward, elbows on the table, the weight of her chest hanging in her brassiere, resting her head on her fists. She has big hands which look smaller in white crocheted gloves.

Dickie licks up the last morsel of meat. 'Are you ready now, Dickie?' He wonders if there might be more. Mabel looks up to the kitchen ceiling. The wireless is still on upstairs. Otherwise all is quiet. Mabel lowers her voice to a whisper. 'Mummy has won first prize in the Grand Draw!' She cannot believe what she is hearing herself say. 'And it's nothing less than a Holiday in Cherbourg! That's in France.'

Mabel bubbles. She lets the image of France can-can in the kitchen before going on. 'Miles away from here. Miles away. Simply miles.' She shifts her position. Her wedding ring was digging into her cheek, leaving a red dent. 'I'm to go by ship. In no time at all I'll be on The Continent. Luxury hotel. Eating off crisp white tablecloths with matching crockery. Everything elegant. Speaking French most likely. Bonjewer. That's good-day. Mercy bowcoo. That's thank-you-very-much. Oh, and O rivwar. That's goodbye. And more.'

Mabel's mind switches track. Still she whispers. 'And I'll have wine. White wine with fish. Red with meat. Van they call it. There's so much!' and she thrills at the muchness of it all. 'Of course, I'll need a new outfit to go in.' She visualises her blue and white coat, the hat with the brim and her white crocheted gloves going up in flames. 'Goes without saying. Something really me! A swishy skirt with an off-the-shoulder top.' She has good shoulders, not that anyone ever sees them. 'Some fancy slacks and a silk neckscarf. 20 denier stockings. Good Italian shoes. Perhaps I could run something up.' An explosion echoes upstairs followed by a moan. Eric has sneezed.

Mabel locks France away. She quietly stands and smothes her frock. She unbuttons her cardigan, removes it and folds it neatly over the back of the chair. From the larder door she unhooks her pinny and puts it on, tying it at the front.

Dickie is still waiting in hope. Mabel bends, picks up his dish, places it in the sink and runs water over it. Dickie gets the message. He patters off to doze. Mabel turns off the tap and looks at the dish, brim full. She glimpses her reflection and quickly swills the dish. Not now. No time for that now.

*

Now is time for tea. Caddies and cosies. Trays and tray cloths. Milk jugs and their beaded covers. Sugar in bowls. In pots across the town tea brews. Back among the trees in The Newhay Bluebell slurps from his old ex-Army tin mug, having drawn the very last drag from a fag.

*

'Twenty Questions'

Anona Winn, Joy Adamson, Kenneth Horne ask all the questions & Gilbert Harding knows some of the answers. – The Home Service

Grace Phipps sighs from the depths as she lowers herself on to the settee in the sitting room above the drapery shop on Queen Street. Having been on her feet for hours they are protesting. She pushes off her shoes and draws a foot up to massage it. As a joint cracks Osbert flips up his newspaper.

Grace pours out tea for two. She adjusts her roll-on where it has been digging in and slowly twiddles her toes. Another crack. She'll have to go to the chiropodist to have her feet seen to. She suffered with chilblains last winter till she all but wept. The shop could be like a fridge at times. 'Don't go letting your tea get cold.'

Osbert reaches for his cup. Grace takes a sip from hers, and eases the cushion a bit further into the crook of her back. 'What's on telly tonight? Is it "Take Your Pick"? Or "Double Your Money"?' Across the land Michael Miles and Hughie Green tinker with fortune each week. Hughie's jingle has lodged itself deep in countless heads and refrains at the slightest encouragement. *"Double Your Money and try to get rich. Double Your Money without any hitch. Double Your Money it's your lucky day. Double Your Money and take it away."* If only it was that simple.

Osbert is still reading, drinking in the print.

"What's in the paper?

'The Disarmament Debate,' he announces.

'Yes?' Grace waits. Is Osbert about to proceed?

'Which, in the opinion of our Mr Macmillan, is the most important subject we must attend to.'

Osbert Phipps turns the page, folding the knife edge crease. 'Unfortunately the debate isn't as simple as Mr Miles and his "Yes-No Interlude".' He makes an attempt at being Michael

Miles, a tall man much like Osbert, but with a New Zealand accent. 'Are nuclear armaments safe?... Er. No...Bong!' Osbert mimes striking an invisible gong sending the phantom contestant on his way. 'Next contestant, please.' Osbert's crossed leg begins to swing. 'Maybe if they presented the facts For and Against Doomsday with Michael Miles grinning his way through the facts and figures, then maybe, may-be Mr and Mrs Average would drag themselves away from the tensions of The Mystery Box and what it contains and address themselves to the theme of imminent destruction.' He takes a breath.

Grace sits in some shock. 'Oh.'

'Maybe. But I doubt it. I doubt it very much indeed.' He raises his tea. He needs it.

'I didn't realise.'

'You're not alone, dear.' Osbert manages a weak smile.

'I didn't realise you felt so strongly about it, Osbert. I mean, what do you think will happen? What do they say?' She waves at the paper. 'We're not heading for World War Three, are we?'

'No, dear. Well, not before "What's My Line?" which is on in a while.'

With that Osbert smiles again, finishes his cup of tea and turns to the Quick Crossword.

*

'Children's Hour'
The Magic of Pavlova – Ursula Rosebeare revives memories of the great ballerina and introduces some records of the music to which she danced. – The Home Service

Upstairs in Amanda's bedroom the wardrobe door is swung wide open. It was her Grandma's at one time. Now it is Amanda's and it is exactly what she needs. It is dark brown, with a big drawer for things at the bottom. Inside the top part there is a rail that pulls out. Facing Amanda from the back of the third shelf is Robert

Helpmann. On the inside of the open door is a near full-length mirror. When Amanda places a chair in front of it, it is perfect for barre work.

Susan is lying on Amanda's bed reading "The Four Marys of St Elmo's School" in "Bunty". She is aware she's not posh, but maybe she could be the scholarship girl, Mary Simpson.

The bath cubes Susan won in the Grand Draw are scenting the room. She is oblivious to the scratched recording of "The Nutcracker Suite" coming from the gramophone. It is one of a pile of 78s that like the wardrobe came from Amanda's Grandma.

Amanda stands in her underwear facing her reflection, toes turned out, hands on hips, shoulders back, chin up. She begins. She swings her arms, first one, then the other, then both. She imagines she has wings that reach the ceiling. They swoop up and then down. She concentrates on her hands, watching them in the mirror as they float out then back in to her heart. Hands like Margot Fonteyn has are her goal. Hands that ooze feeling. Wrists that make you cry. Amanda flicks and twists them. Then she works her way through her back and waist. Suppleness is everything. Suppleness and Poise. Last come her legs. She swings them one at a time. Lifts them out straight as high as she can in every direction. She stops.

It isn't the shakiness of her *grand battement*. Her eyes measure her reflection. Her shoulders sag. 'I'm a dwarf!'

Nothing.

'I said, I'm a dwarf.' She thumps a thigh. 'Oh, Susan, what can I do? I'm a dwarf!' She thumps herself harder. 'Don't you see? Worse, I'm a midget. Midgets are smaller than dwarfs, aren't they?'

Susan doesn't know, so keeps quiet.

'Doesn't matter anyway.' Amanda goes up on to the balls of her feet and straight away sinks back down. 'They're both short, dwarfs and midgets. They've both hardly got any legs at all.'

Susan pushes "Bunty" away. 'But you're not short.'

'I AM.' Amanda is not to be disagreed with in this.

'You aren't.' Susan sits up. 'You're not. Really you're not.'

'I am,' Amanda whimpers. 'There's no point in saying I'm not, 'cos I am.'

'You are not short!'

'I'm shorter than you.'

'Yes.' Susan can't argue with that. 'But I'm tall. I'm tall for my age. Everyone says that. Everyone says I'm tall for my age.'

'And everyone says I'm short.'

'They don't.'

'Do too.'

'Just because you're not as tall as I am, doesn't make you short.'

'Oh, yes? So what does it make me then?'

Susan is inspired, scholarship material. 'Normal.'

'Normal! But I can't be normal. Ballerinas aren't normal. They're long and leggy! No-one ever got to be a ballerina with legs like mine. No-one. Ever.'

'I'm sure there's nothing to worry about.'

'It's all right for you to say that. You and your long legs. Your legs which start up under your armpits and go on and on. It's all very well for you to say I've got nothing to worry about. I suppose I should be happy with them, should I?' She waggles a leg. 'I suppose I should say "Thank you very much".'

'Worrying won't make it any better.'

'You're getting to sound just like my Mum.' Amanda shoves the wardrobe door shut. Robert Helpmann disappears into the darkness. 'It's not fair. There's you with marvellous ballerina legs and you don't care tuppence for ballet. And there's me with legs like… like….'

'A duck?' It just slips out.

'What?!'

'Sorry.' Susan grabs "Bunty" back.

'What did you say?'

'Nothing.'

'Like a duck!' She kicks the mattress. 'You see. I AM short. I'm short, short, short! Oh, it isn't fair.' Amanda is on the edge of tears.

'Look, you'll grow. Your legs'll grow. You're only just eleven.'

'So are you. You're only eleven, too, and look at your giraffe legs!'

'That's not the point.'

'Oh, so it's not the point, is it? Then what is the point, Longlegs?'

Susan is not going to get cross. 'The point is that you'll grow. Your legs'll grow. It's only natural.'

'Midgets' legs don't grow, do they? Their legs stay short. So why should mine grow? I bet the best friends of midgets and dwarfs – that's if they have any really good friends – keep telling them not to worry, one day they'll wake up with nice long legs. Well, they don't, do they? They go through life with legs not touching the floor when they sit down. They spend their lives being made fun of. I mean, you see them at the Circus. That's probably what'll happen to me. I'll have to join the Circus, and you know I hate sawdust.'

'I never knew you didn't like sawdust.'

'Well, now you do!' Amanda rolls her head to the ceiling the better to moan. 'Ohhh!' And she yanks at her hair.

'You know you're not as short as you used to be.' Amanda doesn't yank quite so hard. 'You used to be much shorter.' Amanda has no answer for that. 'Yes, it's true, isn't it? You used to be tiny. You didn't use to come up to my elbow. Honest. Now, come over here.' Susan hops up off the bed. 'Stand next to me. Stand up straight.'

'You, too.'

'I am.' They stand and Susan measures with her hand. 'See? You come up to here. Almost to my shoulder. You are growing, see? It's just that you're not aware of it, 'cos everyone else is growing, too.'

'But I've still got such a long way to go!'

'Maybe you're going to be a late developer.' Susan plonks herself back on the eiderdown.

'A what?'

'One of those people who don't do their growing till they're older.'

'But I can't wait forever. I've got to have long legs. If I don't have long legs, I might as well give up ballet now.' That thought throws Amanda on to the bed, bouncing Susan. 'I can't live with short legs. I can't. I really can't. I'd rather die! There's no point in having long legs when I'm old like my Mum. I need them now... or at least soon.'

''Manda, think of all those poor people in the world who don't have any legs.' Miss Jenkins would be proud of that, thinks Susan. She must remember to tell her next Sunday.

'Yes, but they don't have to be ballerinas.'

'Have to be?'

'Yes! Have to be! Have to be!'

'And you have to be?'

'YES!' The tears come. Susan hates scenes. She starts to move. 'Don't go!'

'But it must be time.' She picks "Bunty" up.

'Just five more minutes. Please!' Amanda screws a wodge of eiderdown.

'But...'

'Please, Susan. Please!' Susan sits back on the edge of the bed. 'You're my Very Best Friend. You must help me. It's SO important.'

'What can I do?'

Amanda hunkers close to Susan. 'Tell me your secret.'

Susan fears Amanda might have heard something about Ann Mortimer's skipping rope. 'What secret?'

'The secret.' And Amanda's eyebrows jump. 'The one that helps make you grow.'

Susan tries to get things straight. 'I... I don't have a secret.'

'Oh, Susan, you do. You do!' Amanda nods while Susan thinks about it. 'You must do. It's obvious if you think about it. Your Dad's not tall. Your Mum isn't tall either. What's more, your sister is shorter than me.'

'But she's only eight.' That gets Susan a sharp look.

'So there must be something. It could be what they give you to eat. Or what you do.'

'Susan!' Mrs Clark calls upstairs. 'Your mother says your tea's ready.'

Susan stands up to go.

Amanda springs up. 'Look, Susan, you are my Very Best Friend, aren't you?'

'Course I am.'

'Susan!' Mrs Clark again. 'Did you hear?'

'Yes, Mrs Clark. Coming!' She snatches up the bath cubes.

'And you do see how important ballet is?' Susan nods. 'I knew I could count on you.' Susan feels she has missed something. 'That's what best friends are for.'

Susan opens the bedroom door. Has she agreed to something? She can't be sure. As she goes downstairs "The Nutcracker Suite" starts up again.

*

'Ask Me Another'

A General Knowledge contest. Each week a new team of challengers compete against members of the general public who in successive years have won the annual 'Brain of Britain' contest. – Chairman, Franklin Engelman – BBC TV

Grace comes back from taking the tray to the kitchen. Osbert ticks off another clue as done. She stands behind the settee straightening the antimacassar, not that Osbert believes in hair oil.

'Going well?

'Hm?'

'You seem to be going well.'

'It's the Quick one.'

'Nearly finished then?'

Osbert looks up. 'Dear?'

'It can wait. It's all right. Go ahead and finish.' Grace goes to the sideboard to get out her knitting. She is aware of Osbert watching. 'No, you finish. If you're close to finishing, I can wait.'

Osbert puts the paper down. Grace turns with her knitting clutched to her chest. 'Have you seen my other glasses? For my knitting.' She makes it clear she's noticed the paper pushed to one side. 'I've been thinking about what you were saying. About Macmillan and that.'

'It was only a for-instance, dear.'

'A for-instance of what?' She teases at the corner of the nearest cushion before sitting. 'What does the paper say is going to happen?'

Osbert retrieves the folded paper and turns it in his hands. 'The Disarmament Debate is an example. It's just one aspect.'

'Of what?.

'Oh... the whole thing.'

'What whole thing?'

'What I'm saying is that the Debate is just a part of... everything,

'Which is?'

'Oh... People... The World... All of it, really.' A balloon was rapidly inflating in Osbert's mind, a balloon he hadn't known was there until it started to fill.

Grace sits waiting for him. He flips his paper up again. 'Oh, no, you don't. You can't stop there. Talk to me, Osbert. Explain it to me. Please, I want to know. I want to understand what's wrong.'

Osbert Phipps looks across at his wife at the same time as he peers at his own dim ideas. 'What's the point?'

'What is that supposed to mean?'

'Dear, there's nothing you or I can do about it.' But the balloon keeps swelling.

'Then, why be so bothered that Mr and Mrs Average aren't doing whatever it is you want them to do?'

'It must be nearly time for "What's My Line?"', and he stands up. If only he could jab the balloon with a nice sharp pin before it gets much bigger. Then he would settle happily to watch the panel making some poor unfortunate squirm, some toothpaste tube filler with an obvious mime, or...

'Don't switch it on, dear. Please.' Grace throws out a restraining hand from the settee. 'Sit down.' The paper dangles from his hands as he is marooned on the rug. 'Besides, it's still not on for a while.' He sits back down. Isobel Barnett, Josephine Douglas, Frank Muir and Denis Norden are still in make-up having the shine taken off their familiar faces.

'Now, Osbert, it may be hard to explain, and I may not be the brightest when it comes to politics and the like, but I really want to try and understand.'

Osbert presses the paper's edges, running it between finger and thumb, and pushes it down by the cushion. He looks at the inner balloon shining redly now. 'It's just that things are changing, Grace.'

Grace stares at him as if through binoculars. She is determined to bring him up close.

'The world is changing.' His eyebrows shrug. 'That is it. The world is changing. You only have to look around you for proof... I don't just mean newfangled gadgets and appliances and all those things; the price of a pint of milk. Though that's about as far as most people look. And then they moan that it didn't use to be like this. Then they switch on their TVs and wonder how they'd ever got by without "Emergency Ward 10".' Osbert briefly wonders if there was a medicine that could cure his concerns. 'But it's not that.' He pulls at an earlobe. 'Don't get me wrong. I'm not saying we must try and put the clocks back. Everybody who wants a job has got one, and if you go down sick, you can call in the doctor. That is all very well and good. It really is. But what's the point of it all if at the end of the day you're living as comfortable as Larry just so you can be blown to Kingdom come?'

Osbert's hands are beginning to move in unaccustomed spirals in the air, miming something to mislead the panel, to keep them all guessing. Is this what he thinks? He ploughs on. It is sounding good.

'Think of Sputnik. I mean, where's that going to lead us?' Grace holds her breath. A memory of school ignorance about to be revealed. Osbert saves her. 'God alone knows.' So she was correct. Not knowing was all right. 'But, no sooner have we got a glorified wireless orbiting the earth, then, hey presto!, there's a dog going around, up there, over our heads.' Grace involuntarily glances up at the ceiling. 'If we can toss animals like that up into space, what'll we be sending up next, and what's more, why?'

The questions hang in the living room.

'It's all very well what the scientists say. Every day brings something new. Not just for us either. It really is just as new for them. Each day they're saying that they've broken new bounds. What they mean is that they're just as much in the dark as you and me. And while they are meddling we're meant to sleep soundly at night. It's all going to lead Lord-knows-where.' Osbert leans forward intending to fix his ideas. '"Trust us", they say. "We're moving into a new era. The Age of Technology."' In spite of the tea Osbert's mouth is feeling dry. 'Everything is technological. Techno-logical this. Techno-logical that. But where is the logic? What the dickens does it mean? Technological.' He lets the word run through his head a few times. It sinks like lead.

Grace is spell-bound. She has never thought.

'Look where scientists have got us so far. Think of the

horrible things we were able to do during The War. Before you could snap your fingers the Yanks were dropping atomic bombs on Japan, roasting thousands of people. Thousands. People just like us, burned to a crisp. Leaving only sooty stains on the streets.'

The teacup slips on the saucer in Grace's hands.

'But people aren't thinking like that. They think the world is still the chummy place it's always been. They go to Fairs like they've always done. Each year they crown a Violets Queen, compete in knobbly knees contests like they've always done, and claim that it only goes to show that in spite of everything all's well with the world. But it isn't. It isn't. It's fine having a refrigerator on twenty-four monthly installments, but who's to say you're going to be around to use it.'

Grace continues to sit, perched, her teacup at a precarious angle on the saucer in her lap. Why hadn't he warned her that there'd be so much to take in? Osbert should've warned her. And it is all important. Surely it's important? Of course, it is. And now he's stopped, the words are fading. She makes a grab at as many of them as she can, but like bubbles most burst before she can take hold. The feelings though still hang in the air like smoke. The feelings she can handle. Osbert hasn't beaten about the bush. He's shared his thoughts. The cup slides.

'Careful.' Osbert warns as Grace steadies it just in time. He's been watching.

'Thank you.' Osbert nods. 'No, I mean thank you for telling me everything. There's so much... I never thought...' Grace smiles an apology. 'What can we do?'

'There you have it.' He pats the paper on his knees. 'Letters to the "Dawlish Gazette"? Posters in the shop window? Walk up and down Marine Parade wearing a sandwich board, "The End of The World is Nigh" ?' He almost laughs.

'Please, Osbert, don't. Don't.'

'No... But there it is. It's all very well us feeling something is seriously wrong, but... I'm just a draper, selling chintz by the yard, sateen and cotton prints, printed rayons and haberdashery.' He'd fox the panel completely. Here's betting Isobel Barnett would say, "Well I never!" after Gilbert Harding had counted them out. Osbert tries a smile, '"Good morning, madam, can I interest you in the End of the World?" I don't think that'd go down well, do you, dear?'

Grace fixes one of the plaster heads on the wall with a glazed stare. The negress beams back. Knick-knacks are privy to so much. Grace needs inspiration. The clock on the mantelpiece whirs and stops. It is getting ready to strike the hour.

Osbert glances up. 'I'd best go down to the shop. I need to price the items in the sale. Those hats for one thing.'

Is the negress keeping something to herself? Grace is unaware of tracking the loop of the one wire earring the head wears. 'Right. Sorry I was miles away. Do you need some help?'

'No. No. You rest your feet. We can't have your arches falling, can we?' It is a wisecrack. What an evening!

Osbert leaves the room. Grace listens to his slow footsteps descending the stairs to the shop. She needs to think. When the clock chimes she is doing just that.

*

'Sunday Night Theatre presents The Frog.'
The fight of the authorities against a man known to the outside world only as 'The Frog' – a man who is sworn to wreck the country's prosperity. - BBC TV

Eric Dring, who keeps classes of Top Juniors in thrall, sits facing his wife.

That is not quite true. It's not possible to say what Mabel's husband is facing exactly. Perhaps he is just trying to get a bead on the sugar bowl. Sitting across the kitchen table from her, his shoulders bowing towards his chest, tightening with each wheeze, he is a crumpled handkerchief and a pair of red ears. His ears always redden when he is under stress. Stress. He is usually to be found under it, in one of its many guises. By his teaplate humps another saturated hankie put out to dry, a little. What was free-flowing goo only an hour ago has caked, creating an airtight seal to his nasal passage and lungs. His nose feels as if it has been dragged along a gravel path.

Mabel pushes the tin of Peak Frean Assorted biscuits a bit nearer, inviting Eric to take one. A taunt of sorts. She is sure he won't want one. She is correct. He makes no move. A biscuit is out of the question. He is on the rack. But, so is Mabel.

Then, it happens. Not for the first time. When was that? The first time. She can't recall. Some time back. Years maybe. But here he is again – a frog. A dead frog. Pickled in that evil-smelling stuff called... Oh it doesn't matter what it is called. Her husband is a dead frog. That is more important, surely? What can it mean? It has to mean something. Everything means something these days. "People's Friend" is always saying that things like this, like seeing your husband as a dead frog for instance, means something. But what? She doesn't want to know, does she. Does she?

Formaldehyde! That's it. That is the foul-smelling stuff. That is the stuff they pickle dead things in. They had it at school. Jars with dead things crammed in, folded up, pressing against the glass walls. Pushing out as the glass pushed in. And now she can smell it. Here in the kitchen she can smell it. She pushes away her half-eaten custard cream. Her husband is this frog, and she... she is pinning down its slimy scrawny body with pins, with hat pins, with sharp shiny no-nonsense hat pins. She is pinning down her husband's pale, unnaturally hairy body. How can such a pale thin man have so much body hair? She is pinning him down with hat pins, with skewers, with knitting needles, with the metal spokes of a bicycle wheel. That shocks her. Her husband isn't a frog. But he is. He is!

The frog sneezes. Eric sneezes.

'Bless you.' With a final stab to make quite sure her husband doesn't move, cannot move, would never move, Mabel gives her blessing.

*

'Opportunity Knocks'

The television talent-spotting show presented by Hughie Green – ABC TV

In the shop's yellow light, yellowed by the blinds, Osbert Phipps leans by the till sifting through "Sale" notices. He has clearly surprised himself. Running and re-running through his head are the half-remembered snippets of what he's only recently said upstairs. Phrases flare again with almost as much novelty as when he first heard them shoot into life. He had honestly not had the slightest idea he was going to say what in the event he had said. Because of that, he is left with doubts. He feels that during those moments upstairs, he managed to say something. Something that is now fading. Getting dimmer with each attempt he makes to snatch at the meaning of it all. For a minute or so he'd been blessed with words. He'd been impressive. Impressive is not too strong a word. He'd gone beyond himself. And he'd meant every word of it. Hadn't he? The trouble is that it was all so new. It'd just come. Sort of Vesuvius. Just, whoosh!, and there it had been, hanging, blazing in the air above his head. Thoughts made flesh.

The door at the back of the shop opens. 'How are you getting on, dear?' Osbert looks up from far away. 'I was thinking of getting supper. I was thinking of having an early supper. What would you like?'

Osbert scans the shop. 'I've still got a lot to do.' He re-scans.

Even the dust waits.

'Would you like a nice chop?'

'There are the hats in the window. I've still not priced them.'

45

The rubber band he didn't know he was twiddling with snaps.

'Can I help? I'd like to help. Tell me what to do and I'd have it done in a jiffy.'

'It's all right.' He needs the shop to himself. 'A chop would be fine.'

'There's the steak and kidney pie from yesterday, if you'd prefer.'

'Fine.'

'Or I could do some plaice in breadcrumbs. I've got some lovely pieces of plaice. We were going to have them tomorrow. I know how much you like it.'

'Anything. Anything at all.'

'I'll do the chops then, shall I?'

'Good.'

Osbert moves away from the counter towards the window and slides back the partition so that he can climb in. Grace watches as he removes his slippers. She gave him those Arran socks last Christmas. For a while Osbert stoops, as still as the headless torso modelling a yachting blazer. Osbert prides himself on his window displays. Touches like the pale cravat that covers the dummy's sawn-off neck are missing in the displays of other shops.

He casts what he likes to think of as an artist's eye over the array before tip-toeing through the stock. One by one he places or pins the "Sale" signs where they'll best catch attention. Two remain. He is in a bit of a quandary. He straightens up as far as he is able and views the overall effect.

'Dear, how about putting one by the corsets?' Grace cannot return upstairs. She still wants to help somehow. She owes her husband.

'Don't you think that'd be a bit cheap.'

'Isn't that the whole point of a sale?' Grace glows. The unexpected pleasure of making a funny remark.

'I didn't mean that – (Please, let him see it was a joke!) - but, of corset just might work.'

Grace pauses in disbelief. Has he? Have her ears deceived her? One sign is left. Grace's heart is racing. Today, anything is possible. And then he turns. Osbert turns from the window. He faces his wife and sees that he's nonplussed her. It is clear. As clear as day. No two ways about it. Grace looks. She cannot believe her eyes. Speechless, she is. For under his chin, neatly fixed to the knot of his tie, the last red sign announces "Sale". Grace fiddles with her pinny and stares.

'And now I'm peckish, dear.' With that Osbert Phipps steps from the window, his showcase.

The bolts of material stacked on their shelves, among them the Celanese jersey and the Osmalaine, are in danger of rocketing away. Grace senses them quiver, wanting to festoon the event; for it is an event. The Fair was a small dull thing by comparison. She puts out a hand to steady herself. A display of buttons sways. Should she turn and lead the way upstairs? Should she take a step, just one, towards her husband? Can she bear it? Is this evening so fragile that it cannot be handled? Dare she do something? Do what? Do those things that women called Claire or Fiona do in "Woman's Own". Express in one all-knowing, all-caring look all the love she feels. Love! She almost says it. Thinking it threatens the buttons with instant calamity. The stand sways further. Well, dare she?

'Pork chops it is!'

For pity's sake what is she saying? This thought befuddles her. Women like Charity or Felicity never talk about cuts of meat at times like these. Why, she asks herself, is she standing in a darkening shop with an itch inside her roll-on blurting out things like "Best End of Neck"? That freezes her blood. Thank the Lord she'd not said that! It is a small mercy she'd not thought of making lamb casserole.

'Pork chops. With apple sauce.' Osbert picks off a stray thread from his trousers.

Grace closes her eyes tight. Is this what she's seen in the man, this too-tall man? 'And for afters?' she asks, tempting fate.

'Af-ters?' Osbert stretches the word, like elastic. A pulse beats in Grace's throat. 'How about rhu-barb crum-ble?' He conjures pleasure. The "r's" roll around the shop. The "um's" hum on. Grace is afraid she has lost the power of speech. 'Hm?' Osbert tempts.

Grace treads water. 'With custard?'

'Oh, yes!' Osbert takes off. That's it. The buttons scatter. Like a colander of peas they fling themselves across the floor, rolling on and on, wheeling their hundred ways in search of inaccessible corners. Osbert dives to stem the flow, proclaiming, 'With custard AND cream!'

Grace sinks to her knees. 'No, dear,' Osbert raises a hand. 'I'll do this. I'll hunt the little devils down. You nip upstairs and get supper on the go.' Grace cannot possibly nip anywhere. Not to save her life. Her legs have quite gone. She's been brought low but not from any urge to help out. She's never known such... Whatever it is, she knows she's never known it. She crawls towards the counter.

'Look don't worry yourself with the stupid things, Grace. I've been meaning to move that stand since goodness-knows-when.'

By the counter Grace makes to pull herself up. With effort she manages the near impossible. Once standing she finds that in spite of herself her blood is still flowing, air is still being taken in and pushed out; her body is ticking over. That's a blessing. If any vital process had needed conscious effort, Grace would never have made it out of the shop. As it is, she does, sent on her way with a final ringing call for 'Custard AND cream!'

'Got you!' Osbert is not finished. He draws a pearlised button out of its hidey-hole and pauses. The yellow light in the shop is dimming as outside the sun sinks below the rooflines of the shop buildings across the road. He'll need to put the light on in order to keep searching. Instead he pulls his legs stiffly round and settles with his back to the counter. He brushes his knees. It is impossible to keep sand from the beach out of the place. His fingers roll the little button this way and that. It catches what light there is and speckles pink then grey.

Osbert pulls his knees up and places the button with deliberate care on the floor in between his slippered feet, equidistant from both. His elbows loop his knees, his hands loosely locked. 'Well? What does it mean? Answer me that. What does it all mean?' Like the shop the button has no idea. 'Poor Grace must think I've gone clean round the bend.' He catches sight of the "Sale" sign still fixed to his tie. He'd quite forgotten it. But he doesn't unpin it. Instead he turns it up towards him. It almost says "alaS". Not quite. But near enough. Does that mean something? After all. It is a sign.

He shifts his behind on the hard floor. 'Look, I've got to look at this rationally.' He tries, but nothing comes. Everything in the shop has its finger to its lips. Nothing makes to break the hush. 'I said all that... stuff, so... so..' but his waving hand is unable to claw the words from the darkening air.

The shop door suddenly rattles, scattering Osbert's feeble thoughts like so many buttons. He holds his breath. It's well past closing. Whoever it is will soon get the message and go away. Then the flap on the letterbox pops open. Surely whoever it is isn't going to peer in? Osbert desperately searches for an explanation should a prying eye catch him sitting on his own shop floor.

A package is pushed through. And whyever not? After all that is what a letterbox is for. Why should Osbert be so surprised? It is, however, the very last thing he expects.

Footsteps walk away. Osbert just watches the small brown parcel. He is quite prepared for it to burst into flames. It is one of those days when simple, everyday things don't happen. Packages, whatever else they might do, will certainly not contain innocent contents today. Osbert moves across on hands and knees. On the front is written his name. Nothing untoward in that. In the top left corner is written "Delivered by hand". Unarguably true. He slips a finger under an edge and rips; it is a paper bag folded over and stuck down. He tears the enclosed note accidentally. He homes in on the signature; Charles Burch. 'What's he doing writing to me?' Osbert asks aloud. He feels he is called upon to do so in the circumstances. He reads the note:

Dear Mr Phipps,

Let me come straight to the point. It has been a long, long time since you trod the boards, and I am hoping against hope that I shall be able to persuade you to come out of retirement. You have rested far too long in my opinion. I fondly recall your bravura performance as Lion in our "Midsummer Night's Dream", but that was nearly six years ago now!

As you no doubt know the Society is mounting "Our Town" by Thornton Wilder in the Festival at the end of June, and I think I have the perfect part for you. It is a wonderful cameo role, small but telling. It will not entail much rehearsal. The character is only in the First Act, so you will be able to be away by eight-fifteen, though it would be grand if you could be there for the Curtain.

The part is that of Professor Willard, who is described as a "rural savant". Now, doesn't that whet your appetite? I truly hope you will agree to take on the role.

I know it is a bit short notice, but I have been let down rather badly. Anyway, my fingers are crossed. Enclosed pleased find a copy of the play.

Regards,

Charles Burch, Producer 'Our Town'

PS: I will call round for your decision tomorrow.

Osbert's blood bubbles. Flattery is much like alcohol. Recalling "Lion" he misremembers. He overlooks much, and recalls the laughter. He rarely makes others laugh, but he had given a performance of craven bravery, delivered with a Welsh

lilt. Had it really been six years ago? 1952. Osbert feels a flush of
desire. A desire to review the programme in which his name
appeared, to flick through cast photos – him with that tail! He
could get up and find them. But he doesn't.

*

'Animal Attitudes'
Gerald Durrell describes some of the extraordinary aspects of animal life. - The Home Service

The last of the low evening sun streams into the living room at the
Drings' home on Oak Hill. Dickie is fidgeting in his sleep. His
black shiny lips flutter. His padded feet flick. Eric is slumped in
the armchair by the radio. His body lolling towards the machine.
His white flesh puckers. Through parted lips his dentures gleam.

From her chair at the other end of the fireside rug Mabel stares
at him. Should she use the phone? She could go to the window
and call out. But what would she shout? In fact, should she shout?
Should she scream? Perhaps. But she's never screamed, and she
isn't sure she can. On the other hand, maybe she ought to be
uncommonly calm. Shock does strange things and she would be in
shock. At least she would have to seem to be in shock. It would be
expected. If she didn't appear shocked, people would feel let
down. They might even become suspicious.

There is a tap, a single tap. Was it the knocker on the front
door? Has someone got wind of what she has done? Mabel waits
for a voice. A voice that will say something like, "I think you'd
better come along with me." A PC like "Dixon of Dock Green".

Then Mabel notices the blackness in her husband's mouth. His
upper denture has dropped. It has come adrift and percussed, just
the once, with the bottom set. It has come adrift. How very right.
How suitable. The set now rests on Eric's limp tongue, before
very slowly turning – encouraged by the tug of gravity – and

edges towards his throat.

Mabel waits. At last Eric gags and wakes choking on his denture which shoots clean out of his mouth.

Rarely can the casual observer – in this instance, Mabel – view a scientific truth dynamically proved before their very eyes in everyday life, but there now occurs a real-life presentation.

There is a physical Law which says, "For every action there is a reaction". That or something like it. Well, Eric's denture does it. That is, it provides a perfect example. Propelled by an inner force created by the constriction of his throat, with air expelled under extreme pressure from his lungs, aided by a rapid acceleration of his head forwards, it (ie: the denture) leaves the orifice (ie: the mouth) with velocity. Thence it inscribes an arc. It might even be a parabola – though that could well be a cone-shaped toy tossed about with a string stretched between two sticks, very popular in China. Even at times like these (not that there are many times like these) it is easy to go off at a tangent. Mabel endeavours to re-focus.

Back to the arc. Now the drag effect is coming into play as a combination of friction and gravity cause the said denture to both decelerate (ie: lose speed) and fall (ie: lose height).

Let it be noted that all this (not that in real time it has taken very long) has not occurred without some little noise. Indeed the initial gagging-choking-denture expulsion was quite explosive as is only to be expected. Anyway, be aware that Dickie is no longer asleep. Nothing else has changed though. The radio is still on.

Back to the denture. Still slowing. Still falling. Catching the light in a way not unlike that pearlised button in a draper's shop on Queen Street.

The denture or plate slows. It falls. It tumbles in flight. Then, demonstrating an unfathomable canine caprice, Dickie leaps up (a feat for a dachshund) and snaps the denture in mid-air. Heaven only knows his intention. A game? Something deeper? "People's Friend" has had nothing to say on such happenings, yet. Besides, who can penetrate the thought processes of a sausage-dog?

All this Mabel watches. It is being performed solely for her. Dickie scampers out of the room with his trophy. "For every action there will be a reaction" echoes slightly changed with suggested meaning.

As Dickie curls up to lick the interesting tastes, to gnaw at the pink and white, Eric is hunched double, clutching at his throat with one hand, holding his head with the other. He has seen Death, or so he thinks. This time it is certainly not the sugar bowl.

*

Elsewhere in a private spot under the trees in The Newhay on this Whit Monday evening Bluebell is sorting through his treasure trove of finds, fag ends among them.

*

'Anything you say, your Majesty,' and the Violets Queen's obedient servant takes her in his arms and kisses, a real passion-smacker, as Barry Alldis prepares to spin another disc from Radio Luxembourg. "Whether at home or on the highway, thanks for tuning my way…"

'Mind the hair.' The Violets Queen pushes away and grabs some air. 'Tom Trent, if you carry on like this, there's going to be trouble.'

'Your wish is my command,' Tom eagerly obeys. Her Lord in-Waiting is not inclined to wait.

*

Robert Helpmann is at this very moment on his way to Army Cadets.

***

THURSDAY, MAY 29th

'The Dilemma of Security' by Michael Howard

How 'secure' can any nation be? Can a state be armed for defence without appearing to threaten its neighbours? –
The Third Programme

Most thoughts have a very short life-span, to be compared with the lives of mayflies. They hatch. They take wing. They swarm. They are consumed. 'Thank you very much,' say the fish. A tempting idea to be resisted. Besides, what is the role of the fish in such an analogy? It is true that thoughts flit – being insubstantial entities. It's equally true that every so often a thought settles and refuses to be budged. Such a thought has taken Grace Phipps to the Library on Old Town Street.

'Good morning. Can I help you?'

Grace holds her shopping bag more tightly. She looks at the narrow wooden troughs filled with so many fingerworn cards. Her ignorance mushrooms. Grace steadies herself, 'The Bomb.'

Miss Eaves, the Librarian, leans back.

'I'm wondering if you have anything on The Bomb.'

Miss Eaves' beads click. 'Any particular bomb?' She has the habit of flaring her nostrils. This she now does.

'The Bomb,' Grace emphasises the capitals. 'You know?' She nods hopefully.

'Perhaps Wars and Warfare might be what you're after,' and Miss Eaves looks across her small library towards the mid 350s. Dawlish is Dewey Decimal.

'Maybe.' But Grace wonders if the Librarian is as much in the dark when it comes to annihilation as she is.

'We've The Bouncing Bomb,' Miss Eaves brightens. 'Barnes Wallis, The Dam Busters, you know?' Grace cannot help nodding again. 'Oh, and I'm sure we've got something on Anarchism,' adds the Librarian conspiratorially, if unsure in which direction to look. The 300s? Maybe Reference. But Miss Eaves doubts it. 'I could always call the Central Library in Exeter. They've got a lot of wars on their shelves. After all there've been so many.' Miss Eaves muses. 'All the way back as far as you could wish,' and she smiles.

Grace smiles, too. There are the sounds of children playing in the Infant School playground next door. 'Thank you.' This isn't helping Grace at all. She tries to back away.

'No?'

'Sorry. Sorry for bothering you.' She takes a step towards the door. 'But it's the atomical bomb I'm after.'

Miss Eaves almost charges the counter. 'Oh, that thing!' That fixes Grace to the spot. 'You know, you're in luck. We've got Neville Shute's "On The Beach".' The Librarian pauses for a response.

Grace oohs as required, not that she's heard of it, or him for that matter.

'The extermination of life on Earth brought about by a minor power.' Miss Eaves raises fingers to her lips. 'But I mustn't go spoiling it for you. If it's in, it's under F:SHU. That's if it's not out.'

'Fiction?' Even Miss Eaves picks up on Grace's lack of enthusiasm.

'Yes. But terribly real. I've heard nothing but good things said about it.' Grace half-turns. 'Over there,' Miss Eaves points. 'Third or fourth shelf down.'

Fiction, no matter how terrible or real it is is not what Grace has come for. Surely Fact is terrible enough. The truth doesn't need to be made more shocking. If she is going to find out for herself what the world is coming to, she'd rather have it straight. Grace feels like a good strong dose of eye-opening genuine honest-to-goodness, no-holds-barred suffering. But then, as Miss Eaves has said, "nothing but good things" have been said about the book, so maybe "On The Beach" is as good a place to start as any.

Grace runs her eyes over the shelves. F:SHU. Up goes her hand. Down comes "A Town Like Alice". Grace nearly drops the fraud as if burned. Quickly she goes to slip it back on the shelf, but the neighbouring novels are immediately uncooperative, swelling in their bindings to occupy the space, breathing in and flexing their spines, revelling in the newly-vacant inch-and-a-quarter.

Grace dumps her shopping bag. Already there is panic. No gentle build up. No fraying of the nerve endings strand by strand. As if all but sawn through, they are snapping even as she fumbles. She removes another book, another Neville Shute. Then another. How is it that Australia on the other side of the world has produced so much imagination in one man? With each withdrawal the remaining books expand within their jackets to fill the ever-growing space.

Isn't this another law? A Law of Nature made flesh. If not flesh, then glue and paper. If not Nature, then Divine. "And the Word was made Flesh, and the Flesh flexed itself, and lo the Void was made whole."

A pile of Shutes is building on the floor – "Round the Bend" on "Lonely Road" on "No Highway" on "Ruined City". Has the man got a thing about town planning? Grace wonders. All topped off by "Whatever Happened to The Corbetts"? Grace doesn't care; the Corbetts aren't real; they can go hang.

As these books cast themselves from the shelf, others by other authors lean inwards and collapse like so many slices of toast. Grace pauses. In the library-hush another volume slips to slap the woodwork. Grace feels the sting. It is "On The Beach". She dares not touch it. She doesn't ask herself why the book she's been looking for had hidden itself away among a series of Steinbecks. Mr Dring, arch conspiracy theorist, would be able to tell her if she knew him well enough to ask. She stares at the book in disbelief. Is it real? If she removes it, will it turn out to be the wrong book in the right dust jacket? A turncoat. Will the entire collection descend upon her head, an avalanche of make-believe to wipe her out with no St Bernard in sight?

Gingerly Grace lifts the book down. Nothing happens. Of course, nothing happens. This is after all a library. This is not the place for things to happen. Apparently the books have run out of tricks. They are all innocence, willing to be re-shelved with space to spare.

*

'The Limits of Science' by Magnus Pyke FRSE
We believe that science is a 'good thing'. Decades of successful scientific thinking have made us come to assume that everything is scientifically explicable. What then are the limits of science? - The Home Service

'Oh, you're reading that! What do you think of it?' The young man doesn't wait. Grace isn't about to answer. She has been struck dumb by his acne. 'Look. Is it all right if we both join you? I mean, you're not with anyone, are you.' This is no question. 'Mrs Speller? Two teas and a bath bun? What do you want?' A tall young woman with a pony tail shrugs and makes to speak, but is cut off. 'Make that two bath buns, Mrs Speller, and make sure they're today's.'

Mrs Speller rattles cups by way of reply. The grating of two chairs being pulled back covers any comment she makes.

'Don't you think it's such a deliberately terrible book? But it couldn't be anything else in the circumstances.' The man sits, his elbows hitting the table top even before his bottom has settled. As he talks he fingers one spot or another. He has a whole neckful to pick at. 'It makes me ruddy angry when I hear members of the industrial-military combine sound off about the winnability of nuclear war. By the way I'm Hugh Dinsdale. This is Josephine.'

'Josephine Brooks.' The pony tail swings and Miss Brooks smiles, giving Grace the encouragement to introduce herself, which she does.

Chit chat is not Hugh's style. 'Mrs Phipps, are you reassured by the likes of Montgomery?' He awaits an answer.

Grace has no idea, not even a hazy one. Montgomery? Montgomery Clift?

Hugh is not one to wait long. 'Old Monty might have been just the ticket for wholesale slaughter in the desert, chugging up and down across the sand dunes with his Rats,...' Grace has General Montgomery now placed, complete with beret,... 'but when it comes to The End of The World I'd rather trust the thinking of Russell, wouldn't you?'

Grace is sure Mr Dinsdale isn't thinking about Jane Russell. Hugh throws his friend a look before continuing in a strangled whine. ' "If we are attacked, we'll use nuclear weapons. Of course, we should ask the politicos first. But that might prove a bit tricky...' Hugh emphasises the weak "r" both times, '... in the circumstances. So, I'd use the Bomb first and ask afterwards." ' Josephine beams at his stiff-upper-lip.

Hugh switches back to himself.

'That in essence is what Monty recommends. Good, eh?' The impersonation? The message? Grace has got hold of the book. Can she make a run for it?

'Then there's Kruschev,' Josephine prompts. Grace's hand locks on the book.

'Then there is most definitely cuddly Kruschev and his "Ve'll bury you!"', delivered by Hugh in cod-Slav. 'There's no forgetting him.'

'And Dulles,' Josephine in her role as stooge puts in.

Grace is completely at sea. As a result she is quite unprepared for the Hollywood drawl.

' "The ability to get to the verge without getting into the war is the necessary art. If you are scared to get to the brink, you are lost." '

John Wayne? Isn't he really Marion Something-or-other?

Dulles has vanished. 'Art! I ask you. What do men like that think they're talking about? "If you're scared to get to the brink, you are lost". Well, I can tell you, Mrs Phipps, I'm bloody scared,...' The sworn word thrills Josephine. '...really bloody scared about getting to the brink `cos you can be certain that if we do get anywhere near it it'll be curtains for the lot of us. Lost for good. No coming back from Doomsday.'

'Two teas. Two bath buns.'

'Thanks, Mrs Speller.' She is dismissed. Hugh takes a slurp. 'You don't see too many people taking their holidays on Bikini, do you?' Grace is forced to shake her head. 'Not what you might call the number one sunspot destination, eh?' Hugh changes shape in an instant to re-emerge as a Voice for Grace to try and place. Someone from the Third Programme. Or maybe that nice young David Attenborough from "Zoo Quest" .

' "It's February 1954 and all the tropical birds and bugs and creepy crawlies are flying about in paradise, eating themselves silly, not giving a second thought to where the next leaf or seed is coming from, blissfully ignorant of The Schedule. One or two of them notice that pylon as a Good Thing, a suitable nest site, a vantage point, a launch pad. Little do they know. It is a launch pad all right. But not one with a future. A once and once only. A launch into oblivion is on offer. A one-way ticket to Nowhere" ' Hugh (or David) is magnetic. ' "The calendar flips over from February to March, as it has done since goodness-knows-when. Nothing to remark. No seasonal change. No inkling of catastrophe just around the corner, a day or two away. The birds continue their flitting here and there, making plans. The bugs and creepy crawlies continue their munching. Then. Flash. Bang. Boom. Goodbye Bikini. A little 15megaton farewell present to Life." ' Hugh sighs deeply. 'What do the powers that be proclaim? What do they come out with as the dust and the ashes balloon, as the particles of birds, bugs, creepy crawlies and much of Bikini vapourise into nothingness, radioactive nothingness?'

Josephine with her pony tail has waited for her cue with great patience. ' "We've got a bigger bang for our buck!" '

Hugh all but indicates the brilliance of his partner's timing. A pause. A measured pause. A moment of silence for the stupidity of all mankind. For the death of Bikini. For a sip of tea and a mouthful of bath bun.

Without warning Hugh re-ignites, 'Bikini gone? Yes. And No. Life there may have the last laugh. A grim one, mind you.'

'Yes.' Grace has spoken, but why? The two almost-strangers wait. 'We could all be burnt to a crisp.' Osbert echoes in her mind. 'Be just like stains on the streets.' It is Hugh's turn to feel at a loss. 'Like Japan. Like Hiroshima.' Grace's hands relax at last.

'True. Very true,' Josephine agrees. 'But I think Hugh was talking about something more insidious, weren't you?'

'I was. Not to say that what you say isn't a frightening possibility, Mrs Phipps.'

Grace is pleased. A frightening possibility. She could be right, Mr Dinsdale has said.

'But I was referring to a less spectacular end for us all. Less spectacular, but just as final. Bikini went boom, yes?'

'Oh, yes.' Grace is getting the hang of this.

'Gone, but not forgotten.'

Josephine smiles cheerlessly. She knows Hugh is about to get really serious.

'Bikini erupted like a sunrise,' he begins. 'A Japanese fishing boat that was 80odd miles away saw it happen. The fishermen thought the sun was rising, but on the wrong horizon. Two hours after the island died it drizzled back down in a dust storm of ash. Over the crew. Over their catch. They sailed for home. They sold their fish. Six months later, in spite of everything the doctors tried, the radio operator died of radiation poisoning.' Another quick swig of tea. 'But that isn't the end. Tests go on and Bikini continues to drizzle down on us, on everyone; as do bits of Australian desert and stretches of Siberia. Dosing us up on death, particle by radioactive particle. Unseen. Strontium 90 ticking away in our tea.' Hugh Dinsdale cannot pass up the opportunity to tap, tap, tap his cup.

'It's everywhere. It has already killed. Yet the Macmillans of this world, the Macmillans and the Eisenhowers say the hazards are negligible. Hah! In official reports on the efficiency of the damned things they talk about megadeaths. How can they think to trick us? How dare they think we are fooled?' Hugh pauses briefly. 'Because most of us want to be fooled, that's how.'

Osbert was right. The realisation blossoms in Grace.

'It's a weapon that kills with poison, how can its testing be safe? How?'

'Yes. How?' Grace sounds brave. 'I blame those men in white coats, those scientists.'

'Oh, no,' Josephine soon puts a stop to that. 'Most scientists are disarmers.'

'But, Josephine,' Hugh is quick to correct, 'that's just because they want to restore the good name of Physics. It's all very well protesting and being metaphorically martyred,' he turns to Grace, 'but they've tasted of the Tree of Knowledge. They've sinned and the knowledge can't be conveniently forgotten.'

'We can't go back to the Good Old Days,' Grace chips in.

'Exactly, Mrs Phipps. The world we have is a terrible one, but we mustn't be ostriches. We must face up to its horror, to an approaching Armageddon, and act.'

'That is why The Campaign for Nuclear Disarmament is so very important.' Josephine's fervour jiggles the table.

'We're not just talking about scrapping strategic weapons, we're telling Them that ordinary people demand the right to influence policy when it comes to our lives and deaths.

'You must join us, Mrs Phipps' Josephine implores.

'Pardon?'

'CND.' Self-explanatory, surely. 'If you care, you must.'

'I'm not sure I could.'

'Could? Could what?'

'Well, they march, don't they?'

'Stand up and be counted!'

'But, I voted Conservative. Don't you think it'd be wrong.'

Josephine can only shake her head, sending her pony tail swaying.

Hugh takes over. 'Please, Mrs Phipps. What are you saying? Listen to yourself. Just because H-bomb Harold is in favour and Winnie sounds off about "Our Bomb", it doesn't mean that you have to love the thing. We may not have many rights left, but an ordinary person still has the right to doubt, and to express it.'

Josephine flicks her pony tail. 'Are you in favour of atomic weapons, Mrs Phipps?' asked in such a nice way that even Grace sees through it.

'Well, no. No.' So much for the Yes-No Interlude.

Josephine's pony tail flicks again. 'When we tell you that in spite of all the talk about Disarmament not a single weapon has been abandoned, doesn't that make you a bit annoyed?'

'Yes, I suppose it does.' The Yes-No gong re-sounds.

'You suppose?'

'Well, if I thought about it, it probably would.' Grace has a stranglehold on her handbag.

'For goodness sake, Mrs Phipps, for the good of us all, think about it.' Josephine's pony tail lashes as she drives her point home.

Hugh Dinsdale sees Grace is on the ropes and mercilessly lobs another unpleasant query at her. 'Doesn't the blithe talk about thousands dying sicken you? When they talk about "acceptable" damage, they in fact mean tens of millions dead.'

Grace reels.

'Then, if or when it all falls to pieces and the Bombs drop, doesn't it upset you to be advised that the best thing you can do in your last four minutes on Earth is, - now you may find this a bit hard to credit, - to whitewash your windows?' Hugh sees that he has reeked havoc, and glows. A very palpable hit!

'Whitewash?' is all Grace can say.

'Whitewash! Roger Bannister, lucky man, could run a mile. Much good it'd do him, though. As for us, us ordinary types, all we can do is get out our brushes and splash on the whitewash. Inspiring isn't it? It makes you wonder which cretinous mandarin in Whitehall came up with that. Whitewash! What good can whitewash be? Are they telling us that if only the good people of Nagasaki or Hiroshima had had the foresight – not forgetting the four-minute warning – to have got in a sufficient quantity of unrationed whitewash and brushes, they could have avoided becoming the gruesome statistic that you mentioned earlier, Mrs Phipps? Whitewash. How admirably British.' Grace colours with shame. 'And, Mrs Phipps, if you're left pondering on your role in all this, let me tell you. You are to be one of the megadeaths. Just like me. Just like Josephine. Like Mrs Speller over there and everyone else.'

Grace notices odd anonymous shapes passing the café window. She thinks of Osbert. Osbert who's just flared into thought. Is it all going to be too late?

'We are the statistics waiting to be logged. If that's all right with you, there's really nothing more to be said. If, on the other hand, it's not all right with you and you're willing to be seen in the company of pacifists, like me and Josephine, and Trades Unionists, anarchists, concerned parents, rationalists, Canon Collins of St Paul's, Bertrand Russell, Edith Evans, Sir Julian Huxley, J B Priestley, Quakers, the warweary, and army veterans who've seen death close up, possibly like Mr Phipps?...' Both Hugh and Josephine let that hang a while before Grace nods.'...As well as angry young people like us, Mrs Phipps, who can imagine death close up...' Josephine's eyes are watering. '...In fact the whole Heinz 57 varieties of human kind... If you're willing, and you really care, then you have no alternative.' Hugh Dinsdale is adamant.

'You simply have to join us,' Josephine pleads.

'Anything else?' Mrs Speller is clearing away. Grace's tea is stone cold beneath a cloudy film of strontium-ised milk.

'Here, let me get you another.'

'No, Mr Dinsdale. I think I've had enough.'

'But you've hardly touched it.'

Grace stands. 'Thank you, but I must be going.' She snatches up her shopping bag.

'Why don't you come to our next meeting at The Hut? Next Tuesday evening at 7.30.'

Grace pushes her chair back under the table for neatness. 'It's so difficult, isn't it? It's so big. So big and complicated.' She has reached the safe door and opens it. Noises of Dawlish enter. Grace steps outside.

'Don't forget this!' Josephine is holding "On The Beach". She hurries to the door with it. Before Grace drops it in her shopping bag a line of blurb from the back cover hits her. "Just a story". It is too much.

Grace hurries away along The Strand, passing The Antique Shop with its window full of china. Perhaps a sight of the sea will help settle things. A few shops further down the road she slows, but definitely not to browse the comic postcards in their racks outside Boone's. Does she really care? Does she care enough to put in the effort that is needed? Hugh Dinsdale and Josephine Brooks must've put in a lot of hard work to become so aware. The idea of being aware of Facts, indisputable ones about horrors and disasters can be overpowering. To be frank, it is overpowering. The Facts make Grace squint. Awareness means handling things like Truth. Why is it that the whole business of thinking means facing up to really big things. Goodness only knows where Truth might lead. It could lead absolutely anywhere. Then how can anyone be sure when they have found it?

Grace walks on even more slowly, causing others to weave passed her, among them children eager to be building sandcastles. She is almost unaware that she has reached Piermont Place. It'll mean her reading. It'll mean a lot of reading. Reports. Serious articles in the broadsheets. Listening to debates on the radio and watching them, too. "Brains Trust", for a start, with all those professors. She'll have to catch up on so much, become familiar with names and dates, learn how to say long scientific-sounding words without stumbling. All that and so much more if she is going to be able to become aware and show that she's become aware. But why? Unless she is going to DO something with it, what good will being aware do? No, if she is going to educate herself, it has to lead somewhere. Education's meant to do that after all.

Grace has slowed further and stopped. She is outside W H Smiths. Rows of books. A window full of them. Among the light reads other books with pages and pages of ideas and opinions crying out to worm themselves into Grace's mind. In a flurry she steps off the pavement to cross towards the sea. Passing under the railway line she finds a place to sit down. Her brain is reeling, and she's not dabbled with any important thoughts at all yet. Only thinking about thinking.

Grace sits. In front of her the outgoing tide hushes as it heads away. "How am I going to handle the really big ideas if the very thought of thinking does this to me," Grace thinks.

*

'Woman's Hour'
'The Role of Woman to Be rather than to Do'   *A discussion between people of three continents* – The Light Programme

It is the first day back after the short Whitsun break at the County

Junior School and at last the hand on the Top Juniors' classroom clock crawls to 10.15. Sir closed his maths text book minutes ago.

'And where do you think you lot are going?' Amanda and others sink back on their seats. 'Right. For homework tonight finish off exercise C and do the first seven questions of exercise E on page 23. Got that? Make sure they're here on my desk first thing tomorrow morning.'

A look from Mr Dring tells the class that that is that. Yet, in spite of their youth, they are no match for the practised Dringaling who in spite of his allergy and blocked nose gets to the door a clear winner. He has it open and is off before the last of the desk lids has dropped and the scrum has formed.

God he needs a cigarette. God he needs a coffee. God he needs another lesson like he is in need of a bolt through the brain. How many weeks are left after the criminally short Whit break? Too bloody many. And no bloody breather. The long, long haul. Dragging himself for another year from Easter through to the end of time, as this year Summer term stretches clear into August. It should not be allowed. It goes against everything Eric Dring believes in, every rule in his unwritten rulebook.

He knew it was going to be a bad year way back last August when The Office sent out its yearly notification of Dates. He had looked at the memo for one thing and one thing only – when wouldn't he be in school. When would he be out, away from It All. Away from the Sandras, Clives, Pauls, Helens and Margarets, who fill his term-time waking hours with Hell. Peopled by pupils intent on his demise. Plotting his destruction with innocent unplanned ease. Conspiring to jangle his nerves on a daily basis. Teasing him to the brink of a breakdown. What they come up with is hard to credit. Give them sets of compasses in a geometry class and the opportunity is too good to miss. Earlier in the year it was Peter Brace who succeeded in skewering his knees together. It is a proven verifiable fact that the legs of sitting boys shoot together when an object is dropped into their laps. It is just unfortunate when these objects have a sharp point. In the case of dividers, two sharp points. It was after the first pair of pinned knees that Eric Dring shelved geometry until the Christmas term of the Top Junior year. He'd not do it then if he could avoid it. Leave it to the Secondary Mod or the Grammars in Torquay to chance their arms (or legs). But, what with the 11-Plus coming in the Easter term, it had to be done.

'Sir. Sir.'

Eric Dring's hand is on the staffroom door. His cigarettes are on the other side.

He blinks his eyes shut. In his mind he throws a switch and a million volts flash and crackle. A whiff of ozone. So bracing. He then focuses on a Sheila or an Ann. The child is an unrecognised Lower Junior. It holds up its hand feeling that that might calm the glare in Dringaling's eye.

'Well?' Eric enunciates the single sound with chill precision.

'Please, Sir. Is Miss Hilton there, Sir?'

'What?' Eric's voice all but dries up.

'Miss, Sir. Is Miss there, Sir?'

It is as well for the child that Dringaling's hands are full. 'I do not know.' He quietly smiles a strained smile.

The child has the wit to take a step backwards.

'As of yet I have not been into the staffroom, though I would dearly love to do so. You may not have noticed but the door, this door...' and he rattles the handle, '... is closed and I remain on the outside of it. I have numerous powers, but the ability to see through solid objects hasn't been granted me...'

'What is it?' Miss Hilton has opened the staffroom door with a flourish.

With a sweep Eric Dring veers from the child to the refuge of the staffroom. 'It's for you,' and Eric heads for his ciggies.

'Miss. It's Janet. She's had an accident with her knickers.'

The door is shut. Enough is more than enough. Eric has grabbed his Players and now heads for the sink where the Baby

Burco sits steaming. The assembled staff are variously hunting for two sets of exercise books, a box of chalks, a games whistle and a red pen. Teachers are commenting on The State of The Economy, Art, High Finance and Morality; that is Hire Purchase, Denis Lotis, ERNIE, and Brigitte Bardot. They are sitting in a range of cardigans, practical skirts and shiny suits. Eric Dring carries his coffee to his corner, lights up, and only then notices An Absence. 'Mary, where's Rita?'

Mary Bonfield looks up from her knitting pattern in that way that Eric has come to know and dread.

'Not again! Don't tell me.'

'Very well, I won't.'

'Sainted Aunt! It cannot be a month since the last time.'

'It's her teeth.'

'It's not started to affect her teeth, has it?' His coffee splashes as he sits, adding another stain to his jacket. 'It therefore means that her band of charmers will be combined with my sweet cherubs, hm?'

'For "Music and Movement".' Mary confirms with the hint of a smile directed at fellow teacher, Christine Thompson.

'Dear God! Here I am daily at death's door, and Saint Rita, that martyr to monthly disorders and the rest, takes another week's R and R. How is she to know I'm not in the direst distress? Can I for one moment believe she checked the pollen count before crying off?'

'Low today?' Mrs Thompson looks up from untangling raffia.

'You may have noticed, Christine, that I've discarded the oxygen cylinder and am presently breathing almost normally. But why should I expect sympathy and understanding?' His voice rises.

But as far as the staff are concerned, it is just Eric being Eric. Besides, it's Break.

'As long as I'm warm and upright. As long as I can stagger to a classroom, why should anyone care?' He pauses. 'Pardon? Did I hear anyone protest?... No? I didn't think so.'

'You've got the key to the cupboard?' queries Mary as she counts stitches.

'I only hope that whoever last used the tape recorder rewound it and didn't leave the ruddy stuff like so much spaghetti.' The threat lifts off to quickly settle, unheeded.

Mary gets to the end of a row. 'Be prepared to be a leaf.' Eric demonstrates blank pain. 'A fragile little leaf carried on the Autumn winds, piled into heaps for children to kick about. A golden leaf shining proudly in the sunlight or drifting on the dappled water of a rushing stream.'

'Oh, spare me! The thought of fifty-five pairs...'

'Fifty-four.'

'...stomping about, kicking up clouds of dust and making enough noise to waken the dead makes me want to do the most unpleasant things imagineable to Joyce Grenfell. As for Uncle Sandy at his organ, if I ever run into that jovial gent oozing his sickening niceness, I shall fix him with my steeliest look and strangle him with the aid of Muffin the Mule.'

'You could always tell them to take off their shoes.'

'Watch it, Christine.' She holds up the book she is about to mark by way of making peace. 'I have no need for anyone's bright ideas. I have even less need for ideas that would prove lethal. I ask you to think, but not for too long – I'm not completely without an ounce of human kindness, much as it may be put about that I am – just think what 35 minutes in the company of fifty-four pairs of unwashed and sweaty nine-, ten- and eleven-year-old feet trying their damnedest to be prancing like Autumn leaves would be like.' Eric splutters and wipes his dripping nose. 'Words like "noxious" and "reek" come to mind.'

'Pestilential?'

'That's it, Mary. The very word.'

'Well, take them outside and play rounders.'

'Who said that?' Eric looks about as if unsure of where

Christine is sitting. 'Hah! I might've guessed, Mrs Jolly-Hockey-Sticks!'

The women in the staffroom share a meaningful look which Eric picks up on.

'My idea of education might well be described as being out of the Ark. But I'll have you know that those inside the Ark survived to see another day. I have no intention whatsoever of allowing the rising waters of Junior Two and Three to wash over me and carry me off. The very thought of that mob armed with sticks and balls, given free rein to lay about them in the name of sport is not one I mean to encourage. You've seen "Blue Murder at St Trinian's" at The Scala, I suppose?'

Heads nod.

'I hear it's closing. Mr Lewis's company can't afford the necessary repair work.

'Is that true, Christine?'

'Fraid so.'

Eric Dring raises his voice before memories of evenings spent at The Scala threaten to smother his grievance. 'Very well. If we have to be leaves, so be it. But I tell you here and now, before a panel of my peers, that in my opinion the time would be far better spent reciting timestables.' A swig of coffee.

'Now Christine, aren't you supposed to be on playground duty with the Headmaster?' Eric beams as Mrs Thompson abandons her marking and heads for the door at speed.

*

'Six Wonderful Girls...'
...who will dance, sing and otherwise entertain you. – BBC TV

'Stop doing that, Amanda. It's not right.'

'Says who?'

'Says Miss Jenkins at Sunday School.'

She's never done a handstand in her life.'

'That proves that doing handstands against the playground wall and showing what you shouldn't to everyone is wrong.'

Amanda looks about in her upside-down world. She can see most of the goings-on going on at playtime. Boys climbing the coke heap. Girls skipping, Boys playing football. Girls arm-in-arm. Boys with marbles, with paper planes, tearing around after each other. Girls chasing around after the boys, certain boys, two boys especially; one with longish blondish hair and a way of making you laugh; the other with nothing special, but very chaseable all the same.

Upside-down the world looks different in a good way. Having perfect nursery-rhyme clouds way above your feet is really special. 'I'm dancing on air.'

Amanda does some fancy footwork against the wall, a series of beats and almost *entrechats*. 'Come on, Scaredy-cat, show us your knickers!'

'Amanda. Don't!'

'Come on, Susan,' Amanda's legs all-but blur as they scissor. 'Come on. Or aren't you wearing any?'

'Amanda Clark! You rude beast! How could you say such a wicked thing?' There is the threat of tears. 'I'll never help you now!'

'Help me?' Amanda tries an inverted *arabesque*.

'Never!' Amanda's legs come to rest. 'You don't remember, do you?'

'Remember what?' Amanda is not especially interested.

'Well, Miss Amandarovna, you said you wanted something. Something that I could do if I wanted to. You wanted me to tell you my special secret.'

'Oh, Miss No-Knickers, I know ALL about that skipping rope of Ann Mortimer's. That's nothing. I've known that for ages. Everyone knows that.'

'Do they? I don't care if you know that or if you don't know that. Besides, I'm not saying that what you say you know is right or wrong. That's not what I'm saying at all. That's not a secret worth having anyway. That is if it is a secret. No, I can think of a hundred secrets more worth having than any old secret about a stupid skipping rope.'

'Amanda Clark, get down from there!' Mr Newcombe doesn't need a microphone.

Amanda's arms have got tired and enough people have seen her so she can get down. 'So what is it, your special secret?' she asks looking up into Susan's flushed face.

Susan straightens and flicks her air. 'If you don't remember, I'm not going to tell you. It's just that I thought it was really important. I thought you said it was a matter of Life or Death. Perhaps I was wrong.'

With that Susan turns and races away to join in chasing the boy with the longish blondish hair who can make people laugh, and the bell rings too soon.

*

| **'For the Schools'** |
| *'Music and Movement'* – The Home Service |

The Leaf turns on and on, one leg whipping the other out and in to complete a circle. It is all very hard and done because it is so hard to do. The Leaf thinks *fouetté*. It has visions of pain, struggle and total dedication to Art. It carries its arms, the image of grace, before embarking on a *glissade*. Is the Leaf going down when it should be going up and vice-versa? It is tricky to master. Everyone says that. Amanda bets that even Ulanova struggles getting the rush of gliding steps correct.

Amanda The Leaf arches a foot until it hurts, her arms in *bras bas*, balances a little precariously and flings her head back dramatically. Then she remembers to cross herself. A little late, but never mind. Pavlova always did that. The music swells and she spins out further centre stage. Her *port de bras* oozes emotion. Though when the folding doors are folded back and the desks are shifted the floor area is a fair size, the presence of fifty-three others means that space is limited, making gestures all the more important.

A sudden *grand battement* winds Adrian Barry. But Amanda is no longer there. She is shivering in the icy winds that toss her along Theatre Street in Leningrad. Is there a hint of snow in the air? A lift would be grand or a promenade, but whatever partners offer themselves can only gallumph by, arms stuck out like scarecrows. Hopeless amateurs. No Gilpin here.

'Right. Leaves. Stop.' Even through the handkerchief clamped over his mouth, Mr Dring, though muffled, is clear in what he wants.

Amanda pirouettes a final time.

'That's enough!'

Amanda stands, her neck as swanlike as Odette, her feet in second position, her hands nested, elbows gently bowed.

'Is that it, Sir?' someone asks.

'Most definitely.' There is a rush. 'One moment! I didn't say you could go. I need someone to help put away.'

'Let me, Sir,' Amanda offers, raising an arm with such grace that Margot would have been in tears if she'd been lucky enough to see it.

'And one other. You.' Dringaling's finger pins Derek Patterson to the spot. 'The rest of you can go. Quietly,' he shouts.

Derek drifts across to the tape recorder and hangs there while Mr Dring blows his nose. Amanda has the floor to herself. "Midnight in Moscow" plays in her head. It isn't Leningrad, but that doesn't matter. She slowly turns her head to left and right wearing a prima ballerina smile, then swings her left leg out and back and descends with hardly any jerkiness at all into the lowest of low curtseys. She positively melts to the floor.

'I thought you said you were going to help.' Mr Dring is

trying with the hand not holding the hankie to remove the rewound spool.

Amanda looks up. There stands Derek unmoving. There is Mr Dring almost done. Amanda glows. 'Isn't Art simply wonderful, Sir?' That causes Eric Dring to pause. 'Isn't it really and truly the only thing in the whole wide world, Sir?'

Mr Dring prises up the spool and the inevitable happens. Derek Patterson chooses this moment to assist. The spool spills tape over both of them. Eric is beyond words. He doesn't even think to clip Derek's ear. Derek ducks though.

This is just another manifestation of The Universal Conspiracy Theory which Eric subscribes to. It had to happen. It wasn't Fate. Nothing like that. In Eric's experience there are no such things as chance happenings or inanimate objects. What others call soulless are anything but. They are instead to be marked down as having the most malicious and utterly destructive of animas. They furnish Eric Dring with the endless sequence of failures that blight his life.

Amanda springs up and twinkles after the rolling spool as it scoots across the floor. She is almost *sur les pointes*. Derek stands not breathing while Mr Dring views the unravelling reel, which try as she may, Amanda seems unable to halt. Mr Dring slowly turns on heel and toe so's not to lose sight of the reel inscribing as it is the largest of loops around the stranded pair. The tape ribbons out and out. Amanda briefly closes on it.

Mr Dring wants to warn her not to step on it, but finds he cannot.

What point would be served? He is certain she is going to step on it and it's going to be shredded like so much tickertape. He just knows.

Derek's hands dig deeper into his pockets. The reel is mesmerising. This could go on forever and not lose its attraction. Then with a volcanic sneeze the show ends. The quiet of the running reel with occasional gasps from Amanda is broken by Mr

Dring. And in that instant of heart-stopping noise Amanda swoops and retrieves the all-but empty errant reel. She holds it aloft, the image of a manic maypole dancer. The tape coiling and snaking away, floating here and there in drafts of air.

Now Eric thinks to clip Derek's ear, but he is out of reach. Besides, it is too late. It really wouldn't make matters any better. The tape has done its worst and won hands down.

As Amanda loops the trailing stuff over her arms, working her way by a circuitous route back to Mr Dring, he feels even more powerless if that was possible. His shattered spirit weakens further. Just when he wants to hurl the tape recorder out of the window, to smash the reel underfoot and tear the tape into confetti, he knows that he is going to have to cope. He is going to have to force back the titanic desire for vengeance and inch by painful inch rewind the cursed stuff, untwisting it as he goes with patience. In this the reel's victory is made perfect.

Amanda, garlanded in tape, offers the spool with outstretched hands. She almost bows her head. It is for her a ceremony. 'There', she says as she would do if she was handing over a bird she'd found with a damaged wing, and tips the reel gently into Mr Dring's hand, which is almost shaking.

'Art is just incredibly amazing, isn't it, Sir?' Mr Dring cranks his fragmented thoughts into gear and focuses on Amanda. 'I don't mean paint and paper, crayons and colouring-in. I mean, you know, the whole thing.' Eric is incapable of following her.

Amanda reaches out to him. 'Here, let me, Sir.' She takes back the reel and starts with great care to unwind herself. Eric can only watch and listen as Amanda slowly circuits the space ravelling as she goes.

'Doesn't it ever make you want to stop doing everyday things and devote yourself, Sir? `Cos I do. I really truly do. Some people are all right, I suppose, doing ordinary things. My Mum for a start. I'm pretty sure she's all right doing what she does. But I couldn't do just ordinary things, Sir. I couldn't. It's in me, you see. And when you have to do something, you have to do it, don't you, Sir? It doesn't matter what everybody else thinks. It's not like I'm telling everyone else what to do, so why should they try and tell me?' Amanda pauses to untangle an awkward piece of tape. 'What do you think, Sir? I mean, I am right, aren't I, Sir?' She craves an answer.

'Derek, take your hands out of your pockets.'

'If there wasn't Art and Dance and Music, Sir, where would we be?'

'Up the creek.'

'Or still swinging in the trees, if you ask me, Sir.'

'Now Derek, see if you can put this machine away without bringing the whole building crashing down.'

'Do you love Art, Sir?'

'Have you finished, Amanda?'

'Nearly. Don't you just love Art, Sir?'

'It goes on the second shelf, Derek.'

'Don't you, Sir?'

'Amanda, I ADORE it.'

'Oh, Sir, I knew you would. I just knew you had to.'

'Finished?'

A last hurried turn or two of the reel. 'Finished,' and Amanda hands over the reel for the second time.

'Now off you go.' Eric Dring makes to leave.

'What do you do, Sir?' He's brought up short. 'I do classical ballet. I'm going to be a ballerina. What do you do?'

'Me, Amanda? Me?' Eric knows full well what he'd like to do. 'Well, promise you won't tell.'

'Oh, yes, Sir!' This is about to be a moment for her diary, surely.

'Well, I used to be a pedagogue.'

'Really, Sir?' That sounds grand. It could be something foreign.

'Many years ago, though.'

'And now, Sir?'

'Now, Amanda, it's time for me to go to class.'

'Me, too, Sir.' Amanda hurries off, not forgetting to practise her elevation as she goes.

Eric Dring clumps off. Derek feels at last he might breathe properly.

'Derek Patterson, what are you doing there?' Mr Newcombe leans into the room.

'Been helping, Sir.'

'And now?'

'Just going, Sir.' Derek slinks away to the lavatories where he can have a few minutes to himself; maybe have a quiet read.

*

'Mainly For Women'
Cookery Club with Marguerite Patten - BBC TV

'Cherbourg is here. At the end of this pointy bit.' Mr Nelson, the travel agent, pushes a map across to Mrs Dring. 'There. See? It's the part of France that William the Conqueror came from. The Battle of Hastings. 1066 and all that. In fact, if you were staying for a bit longer you could go to Bayeux and see the famous tapestry, but there we are.' Mr Nelson's mouth is dry. He doesn't usually feel the need to talk so much. 'Then there are cathedrals and castles. And the food, Mrs Dring.'

Mr Nelson waits.

'I've heard about French food.'

Mr Nelson clutches at this first sign of real contact. 'Before you jump to any wrong conclusions, it's not all snails and frogs' legs.' Mr Nelson proceeds, unaware of the whiff of formaldehyde he has conjured up in the travel agency. 'I do hope you like your food. French food is an especial hobby horse of mine. Normandy food is no exception. And there's just so much of it. The regional speciality is *assiette de fruits de mer...*' At last, French. Mabel immediately wants more. 'It's a platter of seafood and shellfish. It's a visual and culinary delight. Crayfish, crab, several kinds of shrimp, oysters, clams, cockles, mussels and winkles. You do like seafood, Mrs Dring?' She smiles encouragement. 'There's *sole normande*, garnished with mussels, shrimps and field mushrooms, and *matelote à la normande*. Then there's *marmite dieppoise...*' Mabel's knees go a bit weak. '...This can consist of a mixture of turbot, sole, brill, mackerel, whiting, shrimp and crab again, all simmered in their own delicate juices to make a truly substantial half-stew, half-soup to which wonderfully thick, nutty, ivory cream is added.' Mr Nelson glances at the clock. Not long till lunch. 'It's all rather rich, and totally irresistible.' Mabel has no desire to resist. She is simmering. Jelly she is, wanting more.

'If a dish isn't cooked in cream, it's often poached in an honest rough cider. Ham, chicken, duck, rabbit and hare braised like this are quite unforgettable. Other than local cider there is also calvados, a mature fiery apple brandy to set the inner man or woman at complete ease. Oh, I almost forgot *agneau pré-salé...*' Taste buds liberally explode. Mabel tingles in expectant hush. 'Lamb fed on saltwater grasses. It's a Mont St Michel speciality. But, Mrs Dring, never fear, I know at least one restaurant in Cherbourg which serves it.' Mr Nelson beams. The Benefactor. Mabel almost blushes. The Supplicant.

'For dessert there's a whole array of pies, turnovers, pancakes and cakes almost all stuffed to the seams with apple.' There are parts of Mabel in danger of over-heating. 'And then, to finish off, there are the cheeses. Camembert. Pont-l'Évêque and Livarot. Extraordinary stuff. It may be true that Pont-l'Évêque never tastes quite as good as when eaten in or near the small village from which it takes its name, but you must try some.' Mabel makes her heartfelt promise to do just that.

'Now the meal wouldn't be French without wine. As it so happens Normandy produces no wine of its own.' Mr Nelson throws up a hand to forestall any worries. 'However, the Loire is right next door and that area can provide most reliable wines. Sancerre and Muscadet are just the thing with seafood. The rosés and soft reds of Chinon and Bourgeuil are versatile and could happily accompany the lamb, say.

'To complete the meal, the cheeses - those rich remarkable creations – call for a medium- to full-bodied red Bordeaux, Burgundy or Côte du Rhône.

'All in all a meal to satisfy, I think you'll agree. To satisfy both in eager anticipation and in grateful consumption.'

*

'Woman's Hour' with Marjorie Anderson

including 'A New Start': a wife speaks anonymously about her marriage – The Light Programme

---

As Eric pushes open the front door Mabel is swanning along the hall. '"Bonsoyer",' she trills. A glimpse of a tea-tray, before breezing out of sight. Mabel's mules flip-flop into the sitting room.

'What?' Eric calls, marooned on the coconut mat.

' "Bonsoyer". I said "bonsoyer",' Mabel calls from the sitting room where she has settled.

'My God,' Eric mutters to himself. His key is still in the door.

'It's French.'

'I know,' he almost shouts. His key is stuck.

'It means, "Good evening". "Good evening", in French.'

'I know. I said, I know.' The key will not budge.

Dickie patters down the hall.

'Is that you, Dickie? Come to Mummy. She's got a nice bicky for you,' Mabel clucks and coos.

Eric dumps his briefcase and yanks on the key with both hands.

'Can't you close the front door? It's blowing a gale in here.'

It is then that the key bends. Eric slams the door shut.

'Careful. You'll break it one of these days.'

"If only," he thinks. He swallows hard, stumbles over his briefcase, swears, pulls off his bicycle clips which he shoves in his jacket pocket and comes into the sitting room. 'What is... this?' His eyes accuse the tray.

'Afternoon tea. What does it look like?'

'It's not Sunday though, is it?' His lips cannot be thinner.

Mabel beams. 'Can't disagree with you on that. We can't disagree with Daddy about that, can we Dickie?' and she cuddles him, hard.

Eric slumps in his armchair. His feet are like concrete. Every fibre of his being sags at the same instant. 'Dear God!'

'Mon Dyou!' Mabel is mock serious, then chortles. 'That's...'

'Don't!'

'Don't what?'

'Don't... Just don't.'

'My, my, Dickie, but Daddy is a crosspatch today, isn't he? All I was going to say...'

'I know full well what you were going to say. I always know precisely what you are going to say. After all these years there's not a single thing you can come up with that I don't know you are going to say. You've already said every last thing you were going to say, so don't tell me what you were going to say because I already know!'

Mabel wriggles a little deeper into the cushions. 'Really?' She is not to be riled. 'So Clever Daddy knows everything that Silly Mummy says long before she say it, ness-sir-pa?'

'What is all this about?'

Mabel turns slowly to focus fully on Eric. 'Are you speaking to me? Mwa?'

'Why all the French?'

'But, forgive me, I thought you said you already knew...'

'Mabel!' Eric sounds a teacherly warning.

'There's not a single solitary thing that you don't know about me, you say, so you tell me what this is all about. I'm all ears. I'd be only too pleased to hear what you already know about all this... dear.' Mabel switches on a listening face. 'Go ahead. I'm ready and waiting.'

Eric notices that the mirror over the mantelpiece is askew. Is this one of those animated animas pointing towards an insight? Mirror – reflecting life. Askew – not on cue. Anyway Eric stares at it willing it to straighten itself and so provide him with some balance. He tries to dredge up a calm thought or two. 'I could do without this, you now. I really could.'

'What!' Mabel immediately warms to a game of intentional misunderstandings. 'How can you say that? My mother gave it to us!' She glows deep down. The game is off and running.

'What?' Eric is winded already, just the way he should be, thinks Mabel.

'Typical. Men! You've just not got one shred of consideration in your whole body, have you?

'What the devil are you on about?'

'Oh, so now you don't know what I'm saying. Changed your tune, haven't you?' She shares a look with the mirror.

'Do you have to...'

'Yes, I do! For the simple reason that if I don't, I'll turn my back and before I know it will be tossed out like that standard lamp Aunt Phyllis gave me.'

'But... But that was hideous.' Eric snatches at the subject like a drowning man.

Mabel is having such fun. 'That's not the point. It was mine and you threw it out.'

'You couldn't stand it. You must've said a thousand times how much you hated it. You only gave it house-room because you thought she'd leave you something in her will.'

'That's untrue! Dickie, don't you listen to the horrid, horrid man!' She covers his ears, then hisses, 'That's just not true!

And you know it isn't.'

'I don't know any such thing.'

'And now you want to get rid of my mother's mirror.'

The straw snaps. 'I what?!'

'Don't try and play the innocent with me, Eric Dring.'

'Dear God!'

'Mon Dyou.'

Game and first set to Mabel. She wafts the scent of her success across the sitting room by puffing up a cushion. She lets a skein of dust hang for a while, giving Eric a little time to get out his hankie, but not enough time to juggle his thoughts in an attempt to sort them out. The specimen is not going to be given the chance to wriggle clear of the aspic. 'You lay a hand on that mirror, and I shall never forgive you, Eric.'

'I have no intention of laying a hand on that ruddy mirror!'

'I'm glad to hear it.'

'I never had any intention of doing anything whatsoever to the damned thing!'

'So I should hope, and there's no need to swear.'

'Satisfied?'

'Perfectly.' And Mabel is. Yet it is too good to stop. 'Now we've sorted that out, there's one more thing I need to know.' Mabel pauses until she's caught Eric's eyes. 'What have you done with my wadding?' Cruel, but so effective. Eric's sagging nerves, fibres and what-have-you swoon. 'It's a straightforward enough question, Eric. What have you done with my cotton wool?'

Eric tries and fails to suppress an instant image of Rita and her Condition. Words refuse to come. A wave of guilt is above him waiting to crash. A veritable tsunami. 'But I haven't touched it.'

'I suppose it's got up and walked off all by itself, has it? Or maybe Dickie has snaffled my wongy and buried it. Hm?'

Eric can believe anything of Dickie. Any dog that as good as steals a man's denture from his mouth is not to be trusted. 'Look, dear.' Eric makes a valiant attempt to be reasonable.

Mabel at once realises that she has him all but beaten, 'Don't you "look, dear" me in that tone of voice!'

'What tone of voice?'

'Never mind what tone of voice. You know full well.' Eric is spinning. 'What I want to know here and now is when are you going to replace my cotton wool. You know how much I depend on it.'

Yet again the picture of Rita flashes up. Rita with her mountain of cotton wool unable to stem the flow. Eric wipes his damp hands on his armchair.

'I've told you before not to do that. It stains. Goodness only knows what's in your sweat, but it won't come out no matter how hard I rub it with 1001. You want to wipe your hands, use an old towel or something.'

Is this the same man who was talking with Amanda Clark about Art?

'I'm waiting for an answer.' So is Eric, although of a different question. 'When are you going to get me some new cotton wool?'

Eric looks at the wall clock. Twenty-to-five. The wave at last crashes. 'Now.' He gets up and after a long slow blink faces the mirror. His hands rise. Mabel is about to protest when she hides it with a cough. Eric gently straightens the mirror and leaves the room.

Game, Set and Match. Mabel hears the front door open. She flips Dickie on to his back and nuzzles his tight belly. 'Cherbourg is our secret Dickie, eh?'

'What did you say?'

'You still here? You'll miss the chemists.' Still the front door doesn't shut. 'What are you doing?'

There is a sharp smack followed by silence. 'What was that?... Eric, you still there?' Mabel tuts. Something else to sort out.

She plonks Dickie down on to the carpet, brushes a few hairs off her skirt, and goes out into the hall. The front door is open. Eric is standing outside resting a socked foot on the doorstep. In his right hand is his left shoe. Eric's head is craned back so's best to see the sky. The thumb of his left hand is gently stroking the thumb of his right.

Mabel flip-flops along the linoleum to the door. 'Now what's going on?' She then stands on something, something quite small but noticeable through her mules. Lifting her foot she sees a metal disc, possibly a coin. "See a penny, pick it up. All the day you'll have good luck." It is in fact the haft of a doorkey. Two and two are instantly put together. Mabel sees the lock. There glints the fractured metal of the key blade. She sees the black shoe in Eric's hand. She stares at her husband skywatching. 'Mon Dyou!' and she slams the door on him.

'My God!' Eric prays quietly on the doorstep.

***

'Amateur Theatre' – 'Across the Footlights'

*Questions submitted by an audience of amateur dramatic
societies from the Arts Centre, Bridgwater* – Network Three

Mr Phipps had walked the relatively short distance from Queen
Street along Old Town Street and arrived early at the Old Forge
where the Repertory Company holds rehearsals. On his way
Osbert had looked in at shop windows to see how fellow
shopkeepers are displaying their wares and if there is something
he could learn. Charles Burch had said 7.30, but Osbert had not
been able to stay at home running Professor Willard's lines any
longer.

At 7.15pm across town a train sounded both its arrival at the
station and that of Charles Burch from his grey Hillman Minx.
Just as well for Osbert had all but convinced himself to cry off.

Osbert is now sitting out front, clutching his French's copy of
"Our Town" while in a clear patch of floor, Harold Newcombe,
who is playing the role of the "Stage Manager", is scene-setting.
Malcolm Hill, from the National Provincial Bank, is the play's
actual stage manager, and Rita Gordon, from the Junior School
like Mr Newcombe, is in charge of props. She is perched on a
folding chair sat by a card table, ready to make notes as and when
needed.

'... "The first act shows a day in our town. The date is May 7,
1901, just before dawn..." ' There is a loud cock crow from what
passes as the wings. Out front there is some giggling. '... "Sky is
beginnin to show some streaks of light over in the East there, back
of our mountain...." '

'Let me stop you there, Harold. Remember you should move
across towards centre stage ready to stare up off left for the
morning star. And, Henry, the cock was a bit too raucous, OK?'

'Right you are,' and Henry Carey, makes a note.

'Fine. Right. Harold, pick it up from "Sky is beginnin' to show…" and don't forget the move.'

Harold backs away a few steps, focusses on his script, looks up, and sets off again. He maps out Main Street, Polish Town, all the local churches, the Post Office, Town Hall and stores, Banker Cartwright's big house and the Gibbs's home.

Osbert is so glad he isn't playing the "Stage Manager". So much to get wrong, but already Harold Newcombe is near word perfect.

… "This is our doctor's house – Doc Gibbs." ' Harold pauses and looks off towards Rita. Osbert can tell he's trying to signal something. Charles can tell, too.

Harold is diplomatic. 'Shouldn't the trellises come on now, Charles?'

'Sorry. Sorry, but they're not ready yet, Charles. Keep on falling over.' Rita is all apologies.

'Well, let's make do with a couple of chairs in the meantime.' Charles is keen to get on.

'Righty-ho.' Rita and Malcolm Hill bring them on. Why he's agreed to help out with the props, he's no idea. It isn't as if he doesn't have enough on his plate. But Rita had cornered him at the bank. They had been arranging a loan she was seeking, and in conversation after they had signed the necessary paperwork he'd not really been listening to what she'd been on about, and he had nodded his head when he shouldn't have done. So here he is. His wife hadn't exactly been understanding when he told her. And she is still not best pleased.

Once the chairs are in position Harold picks up on his own cue and guides Osbert further through the imagined world of Grover's Corners, New Hampshire. Henry conjures up the 5.45 for Boston with a sort-of train whistle and Harold at last steps aside to introduce the Gibbses and the Webbs.

Osbert is quickly caught up in it all. Even though this is the Old Forge and everyone has a script close to hand, the extended mime of household chores, the daily doings of ordinary folk is soothing. Doubts are quietened. Reality may be shelved, for the cast as for a future audience. Miss Hilton, from the Junior School, and Mrs Speller from the café are happy to be putting their own daily lives behind them, both now aproned to help them get into their roles as "Mrs Gibbs" and "Mrs Webb".

"Mrs Gibbs" grinds coffee, pumps water, slices bacon and cooks it, cuts bread and serves a pie. She sets the table, cracks eggs, puts away the milk. She pours coffee. She turns the eggs. She gets out plates. She pours a glass of milk. She goes into a cupboard and takes out corn. Outside she feeds the chickens. Osbert sees them. And she brushes her apron and curls a wisp of hair away. Her day is measured. Tidily outlined. Paced and purposeful.

All this while "Mrs Webb" shakes the grate, adds coal and turns the damper of her stove. She grinds coffee, too, and puts it on to boil. She mixes, rolls and cuts oatmeal. She pours milk. She clears away the dishes and sets them in the sink. She opens a cupboard and gets out a pair of bowls. Outside she picks beans and strings them. Life.

Time passes. Milk bottles rattle in their rack. The milkhorse whinnies. The whistle at the blanket factory blows. The school bell rings faraway. Chickens cluck and squabble. Rita, Malcolm and Henry are working well at the effects.

'... "Thank you very much, ladies. Now we'll skip a few hours..." '

'Thank you Harold.' Charles cuts in and moves forward. 'Very nice. Very nice indeed. That was just the ticket everyone.' Charles smiles at the faces of his cast, before quickly jotting down a note or two.

'Mr Phipps, it's good to have you on board,' Harold Newcombe comes over to Osbert. 'We were all worried we'd not find a "Professor Willard", you know.'

'Well, Harold, Osbert here has stepped into the breach and I know he'll be an admirable Professor.' Charles, with a hand on Osbert's shoulder ushers him towards the acting area.

'Will you be needing me again, Charles?'

'No, Chris, you can go. I'll need you Monday, though.'

'But…'

'I'll only be needing you for half-an-hour. OK?' Chris Owen nods. 'Keep working on the lines.' Charles now turns back to Osbert. 'Liked what you've seen so far?'

'Very much so.'

'We know it's about the past, turn of the century America, but it's got so much to say to us now. Simple, straightforward, resonant, so full of compassion.' Osbert agrees. 'Completely human.' Again Osbert agrees. 'Honest, that's the word.'

Charles leads them through the chairs and tables that mark out the homes of the Webbs and the Gibbses. 'Right, Osbert, shall we start?'

Osbert feels a stiffness invading his knees.

'Ready, Harold?'

Osbert doesn't doubt for an instant that Harold Newcombe is ready. He on the other hand is finding it hard to move.

'Now, Osbert, "Professor Willard" comes on from downstage right, that's over here. He's a nervous type, probably unused to addressing people in a public place. Definitely happiest with his books, don't you think?'

Osbert would agree if he could.

'If you go and wait over there, then, when you hear your cue wait a second or two before coming on. Head for centre stage front. All right? Fine. In your own time, Harold.' Charles heads back to his chair.

Harold Newcombe as "The Stage Manager" walks to centre stage consulting his script this time. If Osbert could notice, it might make him feel a little better.

'…"So I've asked Professor Willard of our State University to sketch in a few details of our past history here. Professor

Willard?"

A slight nod from Harold prises Osbert away from the spot on which he has all but taken root. He has instantly forgotten how to walk, though. His arms refuse to swing in time with his legs. His legs don't care to take him where he knows he needs to be. His feet have swollen, threatening to trip him at each step. He is finding it hard to judge distance. He bumps into a chair and stumbles over a floorboard. Somewhere Harold Newcombe is still acting. Somewhere else, deep down inside, Osbert knows he never can.

'…"Just a few brief notes, thank you Professor – unfortunately our time is limited." '

'Osbert, don't change a thing! You'll steal the show. Brilliant. I knew you were the man for it. Such a natural.' Charles's smile wraps itself around Osbert, whose script is damp in his hand, almost throttled. 'I loved the little touches. The hesitancy. The business with the hankie was a gem. As for the notes in the pocket, well, keep it all! All! I especially loved the way you didn't want to leave the stage when "The Stage Manager" said he'd heard enough.'

Osbert turns to Harold Newcombe. He is smiling, too. Miss Hilton feels he deserves a gold star. The little boy inside the tall man smiles to complete the picture. Why not? He was brilliant. Charles had said so.

It is just unfortunate that Osbert has no recollection of any of it.

*

| **'Friday Night is Music Night'** | The Light Programme |

Osbert swings along, his usual stoop barely noticeable. Inside, little bubbles of pleasure are popping. He turns corners without pausing. He crosses narrow roads without looking both ways.

What's more he is aware he is crossing roads without looking, and it makes him bubblier. His attention is anywhere but on the pavement beneath his feet. In this way he strides into Regent Street before swinging right into Town Tree Hill where he nimbly sidesteps a cat. At the end of the road by the grocers he turns sharply left into Albert Street. On he goes and the sounds of merriment coming from The White Hart add even more spring to his step. He cuts through the light and voices and fug spilling out on to the pavement. A cheer breaks out, but before Albert Street merges with The Strand the scent of fish and chips from Haywoods brings Osbert to a halt.

A brief delay and Osbert is off again. He crosses to The Lawn where the sweeps of coloured lights come into view; the low-slung chains that loop just above the surface of Dawlish Water as it heads for the sea, for which Osbert prefers the old name of The Brook.

For the first time in a long time "Burlington Bertie" pops into his head. The tune pom-poms as Osbert's strides lengthen. His spirits swoop and soar with each looped garland of lights. A slight movement of his head indicates the great upwelling of happiness within. A child on a swing couldn't be more content, more pleased with himself.

The mid-evening sky shades through all the deeper blues. Puddles of brightest green bloom in the trees. Within the silver waterway reflecting lamps flare.

Before his newspaper parcel has a chance to cool Osbert finds himself a bench beyond the Bowling Green. To make the evening truly perfect the bellringers would be practising. But Osbert is more than satisfied. The chips are crisp to the bite, then soft inside. The cod flakes apart in its shell of batter.

In a grease spot in the newspaper Osbert catches sight of the word "Spud". How right! He clears some chips away to reveal the report beneath. Not "Spud" but "Sputnik". Osbert reads: "Soon after Sputnik II was launched, Mr H E Morgan reported sighting it. Now he and his family have had an excellent view of it just before its disintegration. They saw Sputnik II at 8.15pm on Saturday 12th and at 7.50pm on Sunday 13th. It appeared over Haldon and passed to the NE of Dawlish, moving out over the sea. At its brightest, said Mr Morgan, it was almost as bright as Jupiter, but it grew fainter and disappeared into the Earth's shadow near the star Arcturus..." At that point the paper is torn.

Osbert tips back his head, the better to scan the heavens. Now there is Sputnik III passing this way, he thinks. Right over us. Bleeping and trilling its call signs, crackling through the static. Arcing the sky. Scoring and re-scoring a flickering wound with each and every orbit. Looping the loop on its journey to self-destruction.

Osbert slides a chip into his mouth. It is cold and greasy. He screws up what is left and drops it in the nearby waste basket.

*

'Come Dancing'
At the Sherwood Rooms, Nottingham. Master of Ceremonies Eric Morley – BBC TV

Grace puts down the book as Osbert comes into the room. It slips neatly into the space between hip and cushion. He has clearly decided to turn on the TV before entering. He negotiates the chicane of settee and coffee table, the tile-topped one, before stooping to swing open the cabinet door. Grace tucks the tail of her hankie up her cardigan sleeve. The TV warms up. Osbert looms in the growing glow as the grey brightens; the sound dragging itself up from silence.

"...for Home Counties North. They have been dancing together for almost three years. Brenda is a shop assistant and Colin works as an Inspector of Taxes. Brenda's dress is a spangled orange organdie with lemon satin motifs on a bodice decorated in golden rhinestones and sequins. Brenda designed and made her dress herself…" The military two-step sends the couple marching across the polished floor. Osbert backs from the TV to his armchair.

'Well? How did it go?' Grace asks once Osbert has settled himself. He notices the reflections of two small TVs in her glasses.

'Oh, you know, fine, I suppose. It's a fine play.'

'Yes, but did you remember your words?'

'Charles was letting people use their scripts.'

'But you knew your part, yes?'

Osbert smiles. 'I was fine, dear. Fine. It's not a very large part, Grace.'

'No, but that's not the point. It may not be a large part, but he's an important character.'

'Yes, well, anyway. Everything went well. I was fine.'

'Of course, you were. I bet you were better than fine. A lot better.'

'Well. Charles did say I was brilliant, not that…'

'You see? You see?' Grace needs him to see.

'But…'

'But nothing! He said you were brilliant, hm?' Osbert nods. 'There we are then. That's my point exactly.'

'But I'm not good. It's just that I wasn't awful.'

'Ooh, Osbert Phipps. I really don't know what I'm going to do with you, really I don't.' Grace fixes him with an over-the-glasses look. A Viennese waltz is now gliding across the dance floor. Osbert watches the couples sweep across the screen, patents flashing, elbows brittle, icy smiles. Grace watches him. His knees thrusting through his trousers, folded like a deckchair.

'Are you peckish?'

'Well…' Hopeful. In spite of the Fish and Chips.

'Poached eggs on toast? Would that do?'

Osbert is thinking of Welsh rarebit. 'Yes, but   there's no hurry,' he adds – a code he is sure Grace has never cracked.

Grace gets up. The book slides completely out of sight. 'If I don't do it now, it won't get done.'

Osbert recalls "Mrs Webb" and "Mrs Gibbs". The sitting room door swings shut.

*

Grace takes the empty plates out to the kitchen.

"...have been dancing together for more than twelve years. Sylvia's dress is in lilac tulle...." With a million sequins all sewn on by hand by her crippled grandmother in Bournemouth! That unbidden image strikes Osbert like the discovery of a slug on his supper plate. Instantly the music sours for him. Like having Sputnik crash-landing on your doorstep.

The TV picture starts to roll. Flip. Hold. Flip. Hold. Flip. Impeccable footwork skitters a few steps, then skyrockets out of sight to re-emerge a few steps further on.

'It's a bit late for tea,' Grace is at the door. 'How about a Nesquik?'

'Fine.'

Fine? He must stop saying that. How can everything be fine? Not so much a word, more a stopper. A plug to jam into every conversation. To put a stop to going further.

Osbert tries to adjusts the vertical hold, but gives up and switches the TV off. He backs away and sits. Chunks of his life slip out of focus. Blurred at the edges. A finger traces the cream meanderings in the nut-brown moquette. The three piece suite came from a flat they rented during the War. His finger traces on and on. Not for the first time. Nothing is ever for the first time, he thinks. Not at his age. His finger winds around and about the arms of the chair. The patterning leads on and on, over the edge to snake back. Going nowhere at all.

He is going to have to drop out of the play. He'd been too good. There is no way he can do it that well again.

SATURDAY MAY 31ˢᵗ

'Six-Five Special'

featuring Stanley Dale's National Skiffle Contest with The Demon Boys of Cardiff .v. The Woodlanders of Plymouth and The Johnny Spencer Group of Bristol – BBC TV

'You've got to try harder,' Amanda encourages, her voice showing some strain.

'Why?' moans Susan.

'Because you'll never be able to do it if you don't try.'

'But I don't want to. It's not me that wants to be a dancer.'

'A ballerina,' corrects Amanda.

The girls are lying face down side by side on Amanda's thin bedroom carpet. Amanda is forcing the soles of her own feet to touch. Not just her toes; heels, too. Susan has given up.

Amanda is resting her chin on the backs of her hands. A copy of "The Ballet Annual 1957" is propped up against a bed leg. John Gilpin has Marilyn Burr in his arms on a well-thumbed page. As Amanda reads she makes frequent checks that her hips and knees are still touching the floor. She is unaware of her likeness to a frog. But she wouldn't care if it improves her turn-out.

Susan rolls over on to her back and gently jiggles her knees. She wiggles her bottom a bit to make sure her hips are still in their sockets.

Yesterday evening Ulanova tightened the knot in Amanda's intentions. The girls saw the film of her dancing in "Romeo and Juliet" at The Hut. Ulanova in her costume like wisps of cloud had hung transfixed, borne on a breath. Now "The Ballet Annual" blurs. Ulanova was too beautiful for words. The love she had danced too much to hold in one heart.

'I've got to be a ballerina!' Tears trickle. 'I've got to be.'

Running feet thump upstairs taking them two at a time. A fist bangs on Amanda's bedroom door. 'Oh, Amanda,' her brother singsongs, 'your boyfriend, Little Johnny Hairpin, has been on the phone. He wants you to catch the next plane to New York.' Amanda's hands clench. John snuffles at the door. 'He knows how busy you are. But he's desperate.'

'Go a-Way!'

'Shall I tell him you're not able to go?' John waits. 'Shall I? Won't you even think about it?' John waits again. 'No? He'll be heart-broken, and you know how easy it is to break his lickle heart, don't oo?'

Amanda springs up. 'SHUT UP AND GO AWAY!' Her words shatter against the closed door like so much thrown crockery. 'I HATE YOU!' Her body is rigid. Her fists behind her, dumbells at the ends of locked arms, as if she will dive at the door or at her brother if he opens it.

Outside John grins, then loudly kisses the back of his hand again and again. Each kiss, the smack of a slap. 'That's from Johnny. He told me to tell you how much he MISSES you. How much he NEEDS you. How much he WANTS you...'

Amanda claps her hands over her ears.

As if he knows, John shouts, 'HOW MUCH HE LOVES AMANDA CLARK! T...R...U...E!!', before bursting into song: '"Don't you rock me daddy-o; don't you rock me, daddy-o; don't you rock me, daddy-o, don't you rock me daddy-o..."' John leaps across the landing brandishing his imaginary guitar, and slams into his own bedroom, where he checks his quiff in the mirror. Mission accomplished.

Amanda flings herself at her bed crushing the eiderdown. But no tears. Tears are for Art. Why can't her brother be dead? Why can't he die? In a horrible way. In the horriblest way. Boiled. Made to eat himself bit by bit. Her heart bounces in her chest, thumping and thudding. She scrunches up handfuls of eiderdown, pressing her knees as flat as they will go. 'He's an animal!' She turns quickly to Susan standing near the window. 'He is. An animal. My brother...' she spews up the word, 'is the worse kind of animal ever.' Susan is twiddling with the curtain. 'Why do there have to be people like him in the world?' Susan stays silent. 'Susan, why are there people as horrible as my brother? Why does God let it happen?'

That hits home, but still Susan stays quiet.

Amanda hunches up on her bed. 'Nobody likes people like that, do they? Nobody needs them. He never ever says anything nice. He just enjoys spoiling everything. He goes about being horrible all the time, so why doesn't God do something about it?'

Amanda prises out an answer.

'Maybe it's a test. Maybe God makes people like your brother to test the rest of us.' Susan leans against the glass, her nose pressed up to it, making misted patterns. 'I mean, if everybody was nice, it'd be too easy to get to Heaven.'

'But God lets them get away with it.'

'No, he doesn't.' Susan is edgy talking so matter-of-factly about Him.

'He does, too. There are loads and loads of horrible people. Think of the ones we know. Clive Webster for one.'

'Ann Mortimer.'

'Yes, and Nicholas Collier.'

'Thomas Fowler.'

'Wendy Wetherall.'

'She smells.'

'That's no excuse for being horrible.' Amanda lowers her voice a notch. 'And there's Old Dringaling.'

Susan swings away from the window. God is one thing, But Mr Dring is something else.

Amanda is not to be stopped. 'He might be alright sometimes, but you can't ever be sure when he's going to blow his top.' Susan feels the blade of fear in her throat. Amanda reflects. 'Of course he's quite probably loony.' Susan cannot swallow. 'Like when Thomas Jennings said his Grandma had put his Arithmetic exercise book in the launderette. I was sure Old Dringaling was going to kill him. He went that really funny colour.' Susan is trying very hard not to remember. She fails. 'And when he had that accident with the tape recorder, he was just like that cat you used to have. When you put it on its back and rubbed its tummy it went sort of lifeless, well that was how he was. Just like that. Lifeless.'

'Sort of a heart attack?' Susan wants to bite off her tongue as soon as she says it. Now she is in it, too.

'I don't know what was wrong with him, but he was just like your old cat.'

Both girls now picture Susan's Ginger. He scratched your ankles and was put to sleep at the same time Susan's mother got new curtains for their lounge.

'So anyway, there are these hundreds of horrible people, some of them really nasty, maybe even evil, going around doing whatever they want and God doesn't so much as lift a finger to stop them.'

Susan gives a half-hearted look of warning.

'Well, He doesn't. It's the truth.'

'Like I said, maybe He's testing us.'

'I don't need testing. I get enough tests at school as it is. And I don't need a horrible brother. If I'm going to be a ballerina, which I am, I don't need people like that. I'd've thought God could see that, 'cos He can see everything, and would do something about it. That's what I'd've thought. If He can, why doesn't He? Why doesn't He make an example of my brother for a start? A bolt of lightning, or something.'

Susan turns back to the window and looks down at the back garden where starlings are bickering, trying hard to block her ears.

'In the Bible God's always taking steps against evil doers. He's always making people see The Error of Their Ways. Well, my brother needs his errors seeing to!'

Susan speaks to her misty reflection. 'They won't get into Heaven.'

'Of course, they won't. I know that! But that's not going to happen to my brother for ages, is it? He can get away with anything till then,' and the pillow receives a sharp nudge from her elbow.

*

'Emergency Ward 10'
The work of Oxbridge General and the lives of the nurses and doctors there. - ATV

It is that time of a Saturday, lunchtime, the half-hour or forty-five minutes when the shops of Dawlish go quiet.

Osbert Phipps is standing with his hands splayed on the glass counter top. Underneath his spread of fingers are trays of zips, bodkins, darning and knitting needles, crochet hooks, press-studs, hooks and eyes, darning mushrooms, tape measures, sewing needles, safety and dressmakers' pins, ribbons and thimbles. Elastic coils in white, pink, blue and black, in quarter inch, half inch, three quarter inch and inch, in single strength, double strength and extra-double strength. Ideal for every eventuality, including, not that Osbert condones it, ideal for catapults, as many of the town's seagulls can readily confirm.

Behind him rank the rolls of material from cottons to serge, sateen to velvet, the plain and the patterned. The till rests at peace. Now is the time to plan how best to get out of "Our Town". Osbert had been brilliant Charles had said. But there is no way in a million years he can be brilliant again. He's not been at ease since his awareness of his brilliance sunk in. He isn't cut out for it. That is it in a nutshell. He does no do "brilliance". The business with the notes in his pocket so admired by Charles? Vanished as if it had never been. He'd been so good that the cast will surely line the wings nightly to view a moment of local theatre history in the making. The counter might sense Osbert sway at that.

Maybe he is just going to have to sicken, to go down with something. He is only half aware of the shop bell ringing.

'You're looking pleased with yourself, Mr Phipps.' Mrs MacAskill has materialised in front of him, hair tightly permed. A lady with a talent to pop up unannounced as Kay and Tom Trent found a few days ago at the time of Kay's coronation, and for being anywhere she might be useful. That is how she likes to see it. 'Yes, I must say that it's not too often I call in here to find you looking so hearty.'

In a trice Osbert folds double, clutches his side and lets out a mew. It takes a very special pain to make a grown man mew.

Mrs MacAskill is round the counter before Osbert has the chance to think. His body has taken over. Folding up like some clothes horse has surprised Osbert more than Mrs MacAskill. A leading volunteer in the WRVS is hard to surprise. His head is between his knees, thrust there by Mrs MacAskill. She drags over the counter stool with the hand that isn't pressing down on the back of Osbert's neck, muttering encouragement and clinical cooings.

'Now, Mr Phipps, sit yourself down. Tell me, where does it hurt? Is it your heart?'

Osbert is clutching at a place somewhere east of a kidney. He shakes his head. As much as he can without rattling it against his knees. He now makes recovering noises, but finds the downward pressure on his neck from Mrs MacAskill's hand unwavering. She is really surprisingly strong for such a slight woman. Here is a stalwart of the War years at Marks & Sparks after all, Head Office, no less. She kept whole departments under her thumb in her time.

Osbert makes smacking noises with his lips.

'Would you like a glass of water?'

The patient does not need to answer. Mrs MacAskill nips behind the curtain to the cubbyhole where there is a sink. How she knows it is there is something Osbert will only come to think about later. He peers under his arm at the swinging curtain before straightening up.

When Mrs MacAskill returns with the water Osbert is gently probing an area best called abdominal. That action manages more than anything Osbert might say to keep Mrs MacAskill at a distance. 'Water,' she announces unnecessarily.

Osbert takes the glass and sips. Mrs MacAskill removes herself to the customer's side of the counter. 'You don't look too good, you know. I hope you're not going to go rushing round this afternoon.'

'Needs must, Mrs MacAskill,' delivered with a martyred look.

'Promise me that you're going to take it easy. I couldn't face your wife if for any reason anything serious was the matter and I hadn't done anything about it.'

'Mrs MacAskill, don't go worrying yourself on my account,' Osbert pats his stomach. 'Probably just something I've eaten. Now let me see to whatever it was that brought you in.'

Osbert Phipps, Draper, slips into smooth-running gear, a role he could play in his sleep, shelving (for the time being) Osbert Phipps, Invalid. An illness is just what the actor ordered.

'If you're really quite sure, Mr Phipps, I need two yards of the narrowest white elastic you have.'

Osbert is already sliding open the door to the counter cabinet. 'This is the very best.' He hands Mrs MacAskill the end of a roll which he unwinds. 'High quality. Long lasting. Double strength. Fourpence a foot.' And as he patters he briefly catches sight of Mrs MacAskill not repairing her underwear for that would be a most unprofessional thought, but taking potshots with her catapult. 'I've never heard of it snapping.' And he warms, having given another well-rounded performance, this time to an audience of one who would never manage to keep his "spasm" to herself. Farewell, "Professor Willard".

*

For The Schools: 'Early Stages in French'

A programme in simple French in which listeners are invited to take part : 'Seine: un nouveau client' – The Light Programme

"*Un café, s'il vous plaît.*"

'Ern ka-fay, seel voo play.'

Dickie is lying with his back to the paint-by-numbers firescreen that masks the grate each summertime. A waterwheel slops its solid doses of 12, 57, 29 and 8 from stream to shute.

"*Oui. Tout de suite, madame.*"

'Wee. Tood sweet, madam.'

Dickie's ears spreadeagle on the rug. Their colours clash marvellously. Dickie's colour-blind.

"*Ah, Henri. Comment allez-vous?*"

'Ah, Arn-ree. Common tally voo?'

Dickie is concentrating nearly as much as Mabel. But his attention is not on the French, but on the plate on the table. Still not cleared away. He is willing her to think of him.

"*Très bien, merci. Et vous?*"

'Tray bien, mare see. Ay voo?'

The fat stripped from the boiled ham congeals a little more. A trickle of slobber wets the rug.

"*Pas mal. Asseyez-vous un moment. Je vous en prie.*"

'Pa mall. Ah-say-yay-voos ern mommon. Zhur… zhur… zhur…' Mabel's finger desperately scans the page.

"*Garçon! Un autre café, s'il vous plaît.*"

'Hang on. Just a sec. Oh, Garson, Ern otra ka-fay…'

"*Voilà, madame.*"

'…seel voo play. Um…'

"*Quel bon café, n'est-ce-pas?*"

'Stop,' she pleads. 'I'm not ready.' The disc keeps turning. 'Vwa-lar…'

"*Garçon, l'addition, s'il vous plaît.*"

'Stop!' Mabel fumbles with the record player.

"*Voilà mad…*" and the French voice is sliced into silence as the needle is whisked away.

Upstairs in the boxroom Eric pauses, paintbrush in one hand, grenadier in the other. The diorama is half-finished or half-started. The sudden onset of peace downstairs hangs in the air. Is it the real thing or just a temporary lull in weekend hostilities? Eric is not one to be fooled so easily. For Pete's sake, if there is anyone aware of the tricks and ploys of humanity, it is him, Eric Dring, Schoolmaster and Husband. Trained in the toughest of schools, tutored by experts – Mabel Dring née Nicholson, and year after year of Top Juniors.

"*Un café, s'il vous plaît.*"

'Ern ka-fay, seel voo play.'

The muffled chanting resumes, rising and falling. Religious responses.

Eric returns to the delicate work of putting in the details of the grenadier's uniform, a perfect copy of that worn during the Peninsular Campaign when the British with their continental allies during the Napoleonic Wars trooped victoriously through Spain, spreading dismay among the Frogs and doing such things as Eric would love to be able to do. Forcing the enemy to its knees, to capitulate. Extorting promises. Demanding satisfaction, and getting it. Living magnificently. His lips whiten at the "if only" of it all.

With each careful brushstroke Eric muses on carnage. Cannons boom. Muskets crack. Horses scream. Flags are tattered. Bodies are flung apart. At these times Eric is at his calmest. The pure chance occurences of death in battle support his view of life.

The hero is slain by a lone bullet fired by some terror-stricken novice in his first action, while the yellow-livered coward lives on in gilded safety. The cannon decimating enemy lines turns on its own, exploding, swallowing a whole platoon. The smokescreen parts in time to reveal the bayonet lunging at the guts, too late to parry. The battle wanes. Sides separate. The last to die, die, no quicker and no slower than the first. Fires are lit. Food and small comfort for those who've come through it all, who've made it through another day. Yet the very food bites back, poisoning, choking, dealing in death by degrees. A flesh wound rots and the bloodied saws sow gangrene where they sever.

It was so, is so, shall always be so. Out of the blue shall come destruction. Each day a small one. Maybe unnoticed at the time. But as years pass, the daily events of minor ruin pile up till the agony is realised. Too late. By then it's far too late. Too late for action. By then the whole edifice has been ravaged, undermined, fit only to topple.

Eric is at his greatest ease. His days are marked by rantings and signs of struggle, but not here. For old time's sake, he wages war at home and at school. But here, upstairs, with Wellington and his soldiery, and a bottle of Johnnie Walker whisky, there is no need. Here and only here he can lay himself open to the truths he has uncovered.

Eric's thoughts quieten. The whisper of each brushstroke can almost be heard. Tiny drips of paint nearly sound as they are squeezed from the overloaded brush.

'Mare see po toor luh ka-fay.'

"*De rien. Au revoir.*"

'Duh r'yen. Oh rev-war.'

"*Au revoir et a bientôt.*"

'Oh rev-war ay ab'yentoe.'

Eric strives to maintain the peace upstairs, but downstairs, the enemy, under cover of some as yet unfathomed plan, campaigns. In spite of EVERYTHING, Eric cannot sit idly by and be out-manoeuvred. That would be tantamount to surrender; to throwing up his hands and leaving the victory to Her. And that is unthinkable. So Eric is drawn to engage with the latest turn of events, this French business.

'Oh rev-war ay ab'yentoe.' Then in a rising pitch. 'Oh, rev-war ay ab'yentoe.' The phrase bounces up the stairs. 'Oh rev-war, ay ab'yentoe.' Mabel is on her way to the kitchen. Dickie patters after her and the plate.

Eric blows his nose, swishes his brush in the last of the turps, wipes it on a rag and seals the paint. The half-finished, half-started grenadier is left to dry.

*

For The Schools - 'Early Stages in French'
'Le voyageur anglais' – The Light Programme

'Dickie, mon petty shoe, now don't go wolfing it all down at once, Mummy's little greedy guts.'

Eric comes into the kitchen and heads for the cupboard under the sink, 'Have you seen the turps?'

Mabel aims and fires. 'Qwar? Pardon, may jhur ner parl par onglay.'

Eric is flummoxed. Even if he understood French, he can be excused for not being able to decode Mabel's version of the language.

'Parlay voo frarnsay?'

'What?'

'Qwar?'

'Look, have you seen the turps?'

'Qwar?'

'What are you on about? You sound like some duck or other. Kwar! Kwar!'

'Ay, voo parlay frarnsay!' Mabel beams, then lets lose another salvo. 'Doo vuhnay voo? Jhur v'yen dur Sharebor.' "Cherbourg" sends Mabel's heart beating double-time.

'Just skip the ruddy French and tell me if you've seen the turps.'

Mabel strengthens as Eric's sense of doom swells. 'Jhur v'yen dur Sharebor.' She repeats slowly and loudly. The man must be deaf. 'Sharebor, on Frarnce!' and she points through the kitchen wall. Eric follows the direction of Mabel's finger; he cannot stop himself. 'Common vooz appelay voo? Jhur mapell Monique.' Monique? Why not? Whyever not? 'Jhur v'yen dur Sharebor ay jhur mapell Monique. Ay voo?'

Mabel feels blessed with the gift of tongues. Possibilities crowd in, preparing to shower her in opportunities not to be missed. Cherbourg was always going to be fun, but now the whole adventure is revealing so many unforeseen joys. And though it is hard to believe, The Frog has no idea. Not an inkling. The Frog who fancies he knows everything that is to be known about Mabel-Monique; who said as much; who claimed she had nothing to say worth listening to. "Well, Frog," she thinks, "I'm boring, am I? You are tired of the same old me, hm?"

Eric has his back to the sink. Mabel-Monique lunges, pushing her face into his. 'COMMON VOOZ APPELAY VOO?'

'Mabel, for God's sake, what's got into you?'

'COMMON VOOZ APPELAY VOO?'

'All I want is the turps. After all is said and done, it is mine.'

'COMMON VOOZ…'

'Dear God, not again. Look, if you've used the stuff, just tell me. I can go and get some more.'

'COMMON VOOZ…'

'I know! I know! COMMON VOOZ APPELAY VOO.'

'QWAR?'

'COMMON VOOZ APPELAY VOO!'

'May voo parlay tray b'yen Frarnsay.'

'What?'

'Qwar?'

Eric senses the drain yawning wide behind him. He grabs the first thing to hand, a tin of Ajax. 'Look. Mabel. That's enough! Enough's eNOUGH!' He brandishes the Ajax. A scattering of scouring powder descends like dandruff. 'WHAT IS THIS ALL ABOUT?'

Mabel-Monique sways back. 'Qwar?' she asks, the sight of victory obvious in her squint.

'What is this French business about?'

She has done it? He doesn't have the foggiest. He's admitted as much. She's got him completely fooled and on the run. Boring old Mabel Dring, who nobody ever listens to because she's got nothing at all worth saying, has done the nasty.

She smoothes her hair and straightens a bra strap with some decorum. She draws a bead on her husband, The Frog, making it clear she is sizing him up. Her tongue rolls round in her cheek, pausing at a tooth where she sucks. Then she goes for the formaldehyde which she administers in a poisonous gush.

'ERN KA-FAY S'IL VOUS PLAY. OUI MADAME. AH ARN-REE, COMMON TALLEZ-VOUS? TRES BYEN, MARE SEE. ET VOUS? PA MAL. AR-SAY-YAY VOUS UN MOMMON, JE VOUS EN PRIE...'

For Eric that is enough. Still waving the Ajax he pushes away from the sink and makes for the hall. In spite of Mabel-Monique's improving accent, he is in the dark, and it is getting darker.

His wife lobs her final fusillade, peppering his retreat upstairs.. 'JE VOYAGE ON FRANCE APRES QUELQUES JEWERS SANS MON MARI!

Eric hears, but does not heed. Mabel's French declaration of intent sails clear over his head. He has been reduced to the condition of a Sandra or a Clive exposed to solving problems of filling baths with holes in them, or calculating the meeting points of two trains travelling from Land's End and John o'Groats. His head rings. His heart thumps. His whole being simply does not want to know.

In the kitchen Mabel hugs herself. She scoops Dickie up. In a hush she thrills. 'Who loves his wicked Mummy, hm?'

Dickie hangs limply overhead from Mabel's upstretched arms.

'Mummy's put the frighteners on Daddy, Dickie,' and she twirls him round. 'Wheee!' His tail and ears flutter with speed.

She stops and he drops to her chest. 'Oh, Dickie-Wickie, isn't Life so simply amazing! Who'd've thought it? Who would have thought it? It makes absolutely everything worthwhile.'

Mabel offers her cheek for Dickie to lick. 'You are wicked, too, you know. What a pair we are. You and me. We're as wicked as wicked can be! That's what we are. Wonderfully wicked. But, shh!' Mabel clamps Dickie's muzzle shut. 'That's our secret.' Her voice falls to a rasping whisper. 'We've got him just where we want him. Just like a nasty dead thing pickled in its own juices. But we mustn't let up. Not for a moment. If we do, he'll only try and turn the tables on us, and we're no having that, are we, Dickie?' He licks. 'No, we are not. At last we've put him in his place, and he's going to stay right there.'

*

'On Collecting Model Soldiers'
Tony Quinn talks about the practical side of the hobby – the paints and materials and cleaning processes involved – The Home Service

Eric places the tin of Ajax on his worktable with measured calm. Then with equal control he brushes the powder first from his right sleeve, then from his right knee. He sits down carefully, hitching his trousers as he does so. He prises off the tin lid and with an old cuticle stick stirs the thick enamel paint. He picks up his brush, smoothes the fine hairs to a point and dips the tip. It forms a tiny concave pool. Then the surface tension breaks. Eric raises the loaded brush, grazes it on the tin's lip to shed the excess and turns again to the half-finished, half-started grenadier. He picks it up for inspection.

A lovesick pigeon struts the window ledge outside cooing. The grenadier clatters against the glass and slides to the floor. Eric has hardly moved. So the arm swung and the hand blurred, but the man himself has not stirred.

Eric turns to the diorama. He picks up another grenadier. A soldier complete and stuffs it head first in the tin of paint that overflows. He gets up and leaves.

In the abandoned room a trickle of enamel paint is the only thing moving, catching the light as it creeps down the tin and on to the newspaper. The drowning grenadier then sinks a little deeper, before keeling over leaving his booted feet in sight; his booted feet and the base to which they are welded.

Outside on the windowledge the lovesick pigeon mounts its hapless mate again.

Even before Eric gets to the foot of the stairs he knows that Mabel is no longer in the house. He strides into the kitchen, and is soon out the back door.

Dickie is quite alone.

*

'The Personal Pain'

Dr Melzack, a physiological psychologist, argues that pain is much more than the mind's recognition of an injurious stimulus.
The Third Programme

'It's only me,' Rita Gordon announces herself at the shop door. 'You know, Mr Phipps, I've been meaning to tell you just how impressed everyone is by your "Professor Willard". It makes me wonder why you've not done more. Nan's pantomimes, for a start.' She approaches the counter. 'I can tell you're going to show us all a thing or two. And good for you. That's what I say. I really think that people like Bernard Williamson have had it too much their own way for too long.'

'Oooh.'

'You know. Bernard Williamson.'

'No. I was moaning.' Osbert is once again holding his side.

'Gosh'

108

Osbert pauses.

'Let me get your wife.'

'No,' Osbert releases the pressure on his side. 'No, I don't think I shall be needing her. I think the pain's easing. Yes, whatever it was seems to have passed.' That has done more of the groundwork, he feels sure.

'Oh, good. It was probably just indigestion.'

'But it could be something serious...'

'I'm always suffering from indigestion,' Rita buts in. 'It hurts like the very Dickens, doesn't it? And that's exactly the spot it gets me, too.' Rita points at Osbert's hand where it nurses a cushion of gut. 'But while you've got it, it feels as though someone's inflating a balloon inside, doesn't it?' There is no break for Osbert to reply. 'But then I get it particularly badly.'

Osbert is seriously contemplating a second, more stabbing pain.

'Why should I be surprised? You ask anyone about the Gordons and they'll all tell you the same. We are martyrs to pain and suffering, every one of us. Something to do with our biology. And doctors have been no use really. You, Mr Phipps, there's nothing really the matter with you. Your cheeks have the full flush of health in them.'

The flush of guilt more like. Faced with this litany of real ill-health Osbert is feeling the urge to sink to his knees and confess.

'Do you know, Mr Phipps, ever since the National Health Service started I've been on one type of pill or another. The doctors don't want to admit that they're in the dark when it comes to my problems. They don't have a clue. If I think about the bottles and bottles of medicine I've spooned into myself over the years, well, it fair makes my head spin just thinking about it. I've had medicine for my stomach, medicine for my chest, medicine for the other bits and pieces which I can't mention.' Her hand waves vaguely. Flicking fingers conjure up flailing tubes which Osbert doesn't wish to think about at all.

'If only I could go in for a swap. I'd love to be able to climb out of this body and into one that's worth having.' A laugh honks out of her. 'Talking of worth having, there's my blood. Several years ago I had some tests. Some new doctor was trying his best to sort me out.' A quick smile suggests the futility of such a scheme. 'He sent me to the hospital for them to take some blood. First, they couldn't find a vein. But eventually after a few false starts they got what they wanted. Of course, I passed out. No surprise. Anyway when the results came back, the doctor was at a loss. I could've told him. He had no idea how the stuff I had was keeping me alive. He said they'd never be able to use it in anyone else. It was as weak as water, to use his words.'

Rita nods like a hen with each new trial and tribulation, pecking her way through the seeds of discomfort, the crumbs of her suffering. If only she'd stop, Osbert could admit his falsehood and take whatever is coming to him.

'But as I say, it runs in the family. My father was always sick for years and years before he died. If it wasn't one thing, it was another. And he'd come through it all. Pneumonia. Gassed in the First World War he was. Always having bronchitis. Really bad chest he had.' Osbert sidles towards the stand of umbrellas, looking for something to do with his hands. 'We were ready for him to go every winter. Then he slips at work and falls into the vehicle inspection pit. That was the end of him. It was all so unfair. He'd always been so nifty on his feet. He was a whizz at a slow waltz. It knocked my mother for six. I mean, we'd all been prepared for him going with his chest. We'd never once thought he would go like that.'

The flap on the letterbox flicks open and shut. Neither Osbert nor Rita had seen it happen, but there on the shop's doormat is a flyer. Rita scoots over to the door and picks it up and gives it a look.

Osbert recalling the package that came through the door very recently and what that has got him into is reluctant to approach.

'Just look at this Mr Phipps.' Rita Gordon holds it out and as Osbert is not about to move away from his counter she crosses to him, reading as she nears, ' "Reject The Evil Thing Forever!" Goodness me!' She now pulls the flyer back to herself and skims the message blazoned in a large black type face. '"There is no real security in it, no decency, no faith, hope or charity..." ' before skipping ahead to read, ' "Life is going to be stark, elemental, brutal, filthy and miserable for the survivors." Oh, Mr Phipps, isn't that horrid? Such a horrid thing to put through your letterbox. "No survivors". I mean it's enough to give a person palpitations. And I'm prone to those, as I've said. I hope whoever put it through your door is not about to put it through mine, too. It's just the kind of thing that would have sent my Dad into shock if he was still with us. Thoughtless, I call it.' She looks at Osbert pointedly, holding the flyer in both hands. 'Shall I?' Rita Gordon takes Osbert's silence as agreement and tears the flyer in half, and in half again. 'That's the best thing for it.' She looks about for a waste basket. Osbert stoops to lift one up from behind the counter. Rita drops the pieces in. 'There's enough in the world to worry ourselves with without that, thank you very much. So much to cause upset without all that scaremongering,' and she points at the waste basket. 'Don't you think so, Mr Phipps?' But Rita doesn't wait for an answer. ' "No survivors",' and Rita shudders. 'I really hope that whoever is publicising that,' and again she points, 'realises the harm they can do.'

At last Miss Gordon pauses.

At last Osbert feels able to steer matters on to familiar territory. 'Wasn't there something you were wanting, Miss Gordon?'

Rita Gordon looks across the shop in the hope of recalling what had brought her in.

'Our sale is on. You may have noticed we have some high quality teatowels marked down. And other items of household linen, such as....'

Rita cuts in, 'Oh! Now promise me you won't go away.'

'I beg your pardon?''

She picks up her shopping bag. 'This is something far more important. That horrible flyer thing has fired a thought! A play poster! In that lovely big window of yours. Perfect to catch the eye of passers-by. I mean, we all want Dawlish to know about "Our Town", don't we? Bye for now.' The door bell sends Rita Gordon on her way.

Quietness is slow to settle.

The last puff of air oozes out of Osbert's day. Survivors? Who said there'll be survivors? Osbert seeks calm sorting knitting needles into size order.

*

Osbert has turned the shop sign to "Closed" and headed slowly upstairs.

John Clark is standing up close to the shop window, nearly touching. His hands are thrust deep into his pockets. Young Liddell is his Siamese twin. John looks casually right and left before planting a slobbered kiss on the glass. 'What I wouldn't do to you!' he pants. 'I could show you the time of your life!' Another smacker smears the window to dribble.

'Jeez! It just ain't FAIR!' Young Liddell empties himself of frustration. A final drool and the two lads peel themselves away. They have nothing more to say. Young Liddell has said it all.

The corseted dummy continues to thrust out her proud plastic breasts as across the town "Children's Hour" is coming to an end.

***

MONDAY, JUNE 2nd

'Woman's Hour'

Including: 'What makes a man attractive?' Some women attempt to explain; and Don Bannister with a man's-eye view of housework. - The Light Programme

Tom Trent is stirring his brush round and round in the murky water. He's been doing so for much longer than is necessary to clean it. He is looking at his painting. It doesn't look like a submarine at all. It isn't sleek and sheer. It isn't all hush and menace. It isn't surging through thick black polar waters. It isn't powering on, its engines a modern marvel. It doesn't excite or thrill.

Mary Bonfield, in her classroom at the Junior School, now in her role as Art Tutor at her Evening Class, claps her hands and waits. The class quietens much like her children do. 'Paint brushes down. It's time to tidy away. Don't go rushing now. You'll only spoil what you've done.' Mary sees no reason at all to change her approach from Eight-Year-Old to Adult.

The last brush is lowered. 'Can I have two volunteers to collect the paints?' Hands go up. 'That's what I like to see. Thank you. Kay and Josephine, please rinse the water colours that have become muddy, would you?' They nod. 'Fine, Now if Linda would deal with the water pots, and Tom deal with the brushes, we'll be done in no time.'

Mary slips into her stockroom to put the kettle on. She checks the biscuit tin. Thank the Lord there are some Rich Tea. Stepping back into the classroom clearing-away is in full-swing. Tom plunges a handful of brushes. 'You are making sure they are really clean, Tom, aren't you?' He holds a handful up for inspection. Across the width of the room Mary gives him the OK. She looks at her watch. 'While Tom's finishing off, who's going to show us what they've done.' A keen hand shoots up. 'Very well. Come along Josephine.' She swings between the desks. 'Mind how you go. We don't want you having an accident after all the hard work you've put in.' Mary moves a little to one side and looks round the edge of the painting Josephine Brooks is holding up to the rest of the class. 'It's not quite dry, is it?' A blob of brightest red trickles further. 'But not to worry.'

'I wanted it to trickle,' Josephine is very clear about that.

Mary looks harder. 'Very loud... A really bold use of colour.' She invites the class to agree. They do. 'Would I be right in seeing anger, Josephine?'

'It's war. It shows the industrial-military leviathan wallowing in the final bloodbath illuminated by the fireballs of a nuclear holocaust.'

All squint at the seriousness of the painting. Josephine's work is never lighthearted or pastel. The trickle of red has made its way on to her hand. 'I call it "Aldermaston".'

The Art Class doesn't ask why.

By the sink as Tom eases paint from bristles he asks himself why the Josephines of the world can't see that nuclear energy has the power for good. In fact it's probably the most important scientific development since the discovery of fire. After all, everyone wants cheap, clean electricity. Better to be a technical chap in a white coat than a miner crawling about underground is Tom's view. But looking at Josephine it is clear there is no point in him saying so. Instead he points out that the kettle is boiling. Wisps of steam are noticeably adding to the swirling images in the apocalyptic painting.

Mary drags herself away from the image of Hell and hurries to the stockroom. Holding herself very straight Josephine Brooks heads back to her seat, assured that she has again made a stand.

Mary returns. 'The tea will soon be ready. And there are biscuits.' She has nothing more to add. She is willing the tea to brew.

'May I show my picture? I think it may be among my better

efforts.' Linda Eaves comes to the front. She is never short of a title. The renaming of books at the Library occupies dull hours on wet days. 'It is "The Inevitable Upset: Can I Then Never Leave My Child?".'

Again the class applies its attention. Before them Miss Eaves holds up a carefully coloured-in outline drawing of a house in a pale wash. A path runs from the front door towards a garden gate. The path widens as it nears the foreground, that being Miss Eaves' only concession to the lesson on perspective. Drawing perspective is hard, but the class is finding it harder to get to grips with the picture, for unlike Josephine who always paints from fervent conviction, Miss Eaves flits from theme to theme without any warning whatsoever. And yet the content of her paintings never varies. A house. A garden. A garden path. Are they, the class, being taken up it? Is Miss Eaves an artistic tease?

'It reflects the views of Dr Bowlby.' This means nothing to anyone, but Miss Eaves is trying to help as usual. He is a recent read of hers. 'You see that the front door and the garden gate in my picture are both open wide.' At the sink Tom pulls the plug to release the slurry. Miss Eaves aims to lighten the class's darkness. 'Bowlby says, above all else, that the mother of young children is not free, or at least should not be free to earn.'

'So the Man gets to go out, making money, making war!' Josephine waves her declamation like a banner.'

'Not necessarily,' Miss Eaves remains calm. 'A man's place is also in the home in the Symmetrical Family as Young calls it.'

'Doing what exactly?' Whoever Young is, Mary is thinking of her Leonard.

'Nothing is strictly reserved for the husband, or the wife for that matter.'

'It's just that the little woman is confined to barracks while the man gets to leave. Is that it?' Mary exits for the tea leaving Miss Eaves to field that one if she can.

'Exactly,' Josephine jumps in. 'The woman carries the burden of childbirth and then is forced to remain on twenty-four-hour-a-day call for an indefinite term.' She ends not liking what she has said, after all a baby would be rather...

'In today's world men are to be encouraged to share in the pregnancy, the birth, and also the childrearing as part of Togetherness.' Only when she has offered that gem does Miss Eaves begin to realise that the water is deepening around her. Pregnancy. Birth. Childrearing. Togetherness. Not just deep water, but with dangers of whirlpools too. And she is not the only one present to feel so.

'Part of what?' says Mary coming back with refreshments.

'Togetherness,' Miss Eaves is mentally re-shelving Dr Bowlby. 'The T is capital.'

'Who's for tea?'

'Capital!' Tom's timing could not be better.

Mary now pours. 'What is to be the result of this wonderful modern Togetherness? Please don't expect me to believe that husbands are going to wash nappies.' That awful pail that had been full to overflowing for years looms back into view – a pail Leonard had never gone near.

Josephine is imagining a certain person "Togethering". In the kitchen, by the sickbed, with the first aid kit, changing rompers, at bathtime, pushing the pram...

'But with washing machines and spin driers nappies aren't a problem surely?' Miss Eaves is in need of some assurance.

'So are we saying that there's no prospect of Togetherness without gadgets?' Mary, pot in hand, is chairing the discussion admirably.

'We'll only get a bit of freedom from hard labour when men realise just what we have to do. First we get them "Togethering" and pretty soon we'll be getting ourselves a new foodmixer and the like,' Kay Trent, who has resisted up to now, winks at Tom as she moves away with her cup, nibbling on a Rich Tea.

'Is that the way to get men into the home?' Josephine sees

herself and A Certain Other in the nursery with the cot and the toys. 'What about love?'

'That gets you married, but it doesn't clean the carpets,' Kay is enjoying this.

'I do the carpets,' Tom announces.

'You have a Hoover?' Mary asks all-innocence. Tom nods. 'There we are then. Concrete proof. A scientifically-arrived-at piece of evidence. If there was a shred of doubt, it has been whisked away, along with the dust. Carpet + Dust = Filth. Man + Hoover = Cleanliness. Man + Woman + Hoover = Togetherness. Result: Happiness.'

Tea is sipped as the humour of Mary's equations is savoured. The wisdom waxes if anything as the tea refreshes.

'Can anyone find a mistake in my calculations?' It seems no-one can. 'I think it might well be we've stumbled on a law. The Hoover Law of Happiness. I see it becoming a guiding principle in the field of Social Satisfaction.' Mary smiles. 'And I'm not completely certain that I'm joking.'

'We thank goodness for dust, that's all we can say.' Kay makes her regal summation. 'Clearly society would fall apart without it.'

'Another biscuit, Your Majesty?' Tom bows. 'And whatever you do, Ma'am, be careless with the crumbs!'

***

TUESDAY JUNE 3rd

'Guided Missiles'
A study of the information at present available concerning the development, performance and possible employment of guided missiles for future warfare, together with their influence on international relations – The Home Service

There is a lengthening silence in The Hut. Hugh Dinsdale looks across at Josephine, urging her to think of another question, but to no good. Grace stares at nothing. Her head is churning.

'Well, as there are no further questions, on behalf of everyone I'd like to say how interesting and important your talk has been, Mr Bennington. For my part it has re-enforced my commitment to the struggle. The nuclear clock is ticking and we must act in order to stop it. We must act, and then drive the clock into reverse. It is our duty to open the eyes of our fellow Dawlishians to the cataclysmic threat of global disaster and to our government's role.' The jug of water wobbles on the card table. 'So, thank you once again, Mr Bennington, and we wish you well in your work.'

Hugh leads the applause, which sounds thin in this large space, even though it is enthusiastic. Mr Bennington nods his acceptance. Hugh gives Josephine the go-ahead. Up she springs in the way she used to do in netball matches, sending her pony tail swinging. 'Now there's squash and biscuits. No tea, I'm afraid, as the caretaker seems to have forgotten to leave the key to the cupboard where the boiler for the hot water's kept. Anyway, please help yourselves.' She flourishes an arm which would have laid low anyone within reach.

'Come along, Grace, you must have a biscuit.' Josephine stands in front of Grace with a plate full in each hand. 'Ginger biscuits or Nice?'

'I don't think...'

'Oh, but Grace you have to.' Josephine checks that Hugh is

deep in conversation with Mr Bennington, but still lowers her voice. 'I overestimated a bit.' Grace notes four other plates artfully arranged over on a side table. 'If only I hadn't gone ahead and opened them... so, anyway Grace, take a couple. Tuck them into your handbag for later maybe.'

Grace takes two at random. Josephine thanks her and speeds after Miss Jenkins who is in danger of leaving without one.

Hugh notices Miss Jenkins, too. From the stage he calls out bringing her to a stop just before Josephine manages to intercept her. Miss Jenkins spins around caught in the pincer attack of Hugh's voice and Josephine's lunge with her plates. 'Sorry!' she blurts. Josephine veers away, but the biscuits over-balance.

'Sorry!' ricochets several times between both the women before the first biscuit hits the floor; as they try to catch the falling Nice; as they try to reassure each other; as they stop to pick them up. Each time dosed with a 'my fault.' They are so eager to be allotted their due quota of guilt, that Hugh has to walk half the length of The Hut before they hear him. On realising he has been trying to get their attention, he is met with another fusillade of apology.

'Miss Brooks!' Those involved in The Biscuit Incident freeze. 'Josephine,' Hugh is quick to change his tone before she can start to weep. 'I just wanted to know if Miss Jenkins here has signed, so that we don't forget to keep her informed.' Josephine looks bravely at Miss Jenkins, who is on the point of saying "sorry" again.

Hugh hands Miss Jenkins the register clipped to a piece of cardboard, together with a pencil. 'If you could put your telephone number, too, if you have one that is.' He goes on to include everyone by raising his voice. 'As we never can be sure when we might need to get in touch with each other at a moment's notice.' The significance descends like lead.

The register does the rounds and comes back to Josephine. She hurries over to Grace who is stacking her chair away. 'There's no need for that, Grace.'

'It's no bother.'

'The caretaker can do that sort of thing.'

'I'm almost done.'

'Put it down!' Josephine pulls the chair away from Grace. 'You've got to sign this.' Josephine adds as if to explain her odd action.

'But you know me.' Grace takes the pencil.

'That's not the point, Grace. Look, please sign the thing. And put your telephone number like Hugh said.'

Grace takes the register, signs and hands it back. 'That's the shop number.'

Josephine looks about. 'That's everyone... I think.'

Grace watches Josephine carry the register like a communion plate to Hugh where he is talking further with Mr Bennington. Eight names in all. Eight names with three telephone numbers. But Grace is not thinking of that. She is thinking of Birmingham as it erupts in her mind's eye.

*

'The Sky at Night'
With Patrick Moore – BBCTV

Over Dawlish the evening is turning the colour of ink. In the west beyond Teignmouth today's light remains a short while longer. Bluebell is enjoying leftovers he collected after the Cookery Demonstration that had taken place earlier in the Marquee on The Lawn as part of Dairy Festival Week. He decides to save a bit of battenberg so he can be sure he has something to put inside himself when he wakes. He wraps it in newspaper and stashes it away in his coat pocket alongside a bruised apple left over from the few the greengrocer was getting rid of.

Bluebell watches the sky as the last of the day turns into night and the first bats are hunting. The birds have finally settled in the trees over his head and Bluebell settles himself. Staring up at the sky and its first stars Bluebell smiles.

***

FRIDAY MORNING, JUNE 6th

'The Daily Service'
"We saw thee not when though didst come." – The Home Service

Miss Hilton is already looking forward to this evening's play rehearsal but she has to stay focussed. Sitting at the piano in Assembly she and the children accelerate to the last chord. The children win, leaving the piano to echo alone, the notes falling at last to the floor to mix with the lingering scent of floor wax and the recently swept up disinfected sawdust.

After the hymn there has to be a massed fidget. There always is. The children can be still for just so long.

The Headmaster, Mr Newcombe, opens his book of Prayers and Good Thoughts. He has had no time before Assembly to make a choice, so he picks a tried and trusted one. He looks up and out. The fidget calms. 'Let us pray.'

He waits for the last eyes to shut tight and hands to come together. From where he stands Mr Newcombe looks out over downturned heads, hair mostly neatly parted or plaited. He knows this one well enough not to need the book.

Eric Dring doesn't appear to be listening. A girl near him is fiddling with a friend's pony tail. He taps her on the shoulder with his hymn book. The pony tail is immediately dropped as the girl becomes a statue. Mr Dring flicks back to his own thoughts. None of them Good Ones.

'Amen.'

'Amen.' The second choral one tripping over the heels of the first.

'Our Father…'

'Our Father who art in Heaven hallowed be Thy name…'

The formula is chanted.

Harold Newcombe nearly smiles. Coming to school as a five-year-old he'd been so proud to discover that he shared the name of Harold with God.

In her row towards the back Amanda's hands slip. Slowly they inch apart and drift down away from her chest. Through slitted eyelids she peeks to see if anyone has seen that she isn't praying. She hasn't prayed all week, but no-one has noticed a thing. Each day she's been showing her un-belief more openly. Today her lips hardly twitch. Soundless. She half-expected, half-hoped the first time she did it to be struck by a bolt of divine wrath. When nothing happened, she'd felt cheated. All that wasted devotion! The Power of Prayer fizzled out. And just to think that some time ago, when she'd been little, or rather when she'd been younger, she'd wanted to be a nun for a while. Not a nun for a while; she'd wanted, she supposed, - not that she can now remember exactly – to be a nun forever. She'd seen that film, the one with the nun in the War who saved airmen who crashed behind enemy lines. And she'd seen the one with the other nun who worked heroically to save lepers in Africa and had died. And she had cried. And she had felt warm all over inside. But now? Amanda's lips stop. She holds her breath. Not a single thing happens. Not a whisper of heavenly ire.

'...Forgive us our trespasses as we forgive those that trespass against us...'

Eric grinds his teeth, putting the new denture under severe stress. "You must be kidding!" he seethes silently. Something in his tense stance causes the boy nearest him to edge away an inch or two.

As the amen peters out Amanda is in fifth position, hands cupped, while Eric is running through details of his secret plan for the nth time.

*

'Junior Criss Cross Quiz'
Play for points; swap for prizes – ITV

Pencils are being sucked and nibbled, hesitating in mid-calculations. They are being sharpened; points being purposely snapped so they can be re-sharpened. They are drawing lines – for margins, under headings, making columns, under answers. Marks are being rubbed out, both correct ones as well as mistakes. Pens are dipped. Paper is being worn away; time, too. But not one child thinks to raise a hand, to ask Sir "Why?", to say it is lost, to ask for help. Sir has made it very clear, Questions 21 onwards are To Be Done. Nothing else. Just done. Examples are there as models to be looked at and learned from. Read and do. Because if not…

The class does not need to be told about the "if not". They can all guess. In fact, they don't need to guess. They know. As Dringaling sits at the teacher's desk shuffling paper, making brief notes, drawing his own lines and arrows, numbering and re-numbering his calculations, the children plod on through long multiplication. Not too quickly though. They know full well that after long multiplication comes long division or maybe even fractions. Or worse. Problems!

From time to time Dringaling looks up. Pencils scurry, pens scratch, urgently, stirred into life by Sir's gaze. Frowns deepen, advertising thinking of Einsteinian dimensions. Not that Eric is really looking. Looking, maybe, but not seeing anyway.

When he turns back to his notes, rubbers come out to erase, calculations are crossed out. The burst of activity slows once more; thoughts turn again to the world outside. Other children have gone to Manor Grounds to practise for Sports Day, preparing themselves for the rigors of sack races, obstacle races, three-legged races, throwing the cricket ball, hop-step-and-jump. That is Life. This is Arithmetic. Their time to run and jump and throw will come. This afternoon cannot come soon enough.

The class ends.

'Is This Your Problem?'

Members of the public present their problems dealing with, matrimonial conflict, erring husbands and much more. – BBC TV

'She's flipped.' Nobody is really listening to Eric, not that he is aware. 'She has. She's finally gone clean round the bend. What's more, if she keeps up this French business, she'll drive me round the bend, too. Everything's "bonjewer' this and "mercy bo-coo" that, I'm telling you it's like living in a madhouse!'

'*Une maison des fous*,' Mary Bonfield mutters, counting rows.

Eric goes back to his marking. His red pen jerks automatically at the foot of each page of each book. Tick. Tick. Tick. Just like time. Just like a time bomb counting itself down. 'And, you'll never credit this. Not in a month of Sundays. But last night she served up egg and bacon pie. Nothing remarkable in that. But she would have to have it that it was "keesh lorraine". I ask you!

'So there we were. Me not saying a word. Her babbling on in French, like some tap you can't turn off. And that stupid dog of hers pretending to understand every damned word.' Mary drops a stitch. 'It does. I swear it sits there with its long ears dangling, head cocked, looking so ruddy understanding it makes me want to be sick. And all this while there is some Frog radio station on!'

'She's probably getting into the swing of things, Eric.' Miss Hilton feels that on behalf of the staffroom she has to do something to bring a sensible perspective to things.

'Swing of things! Swing of things! I'll give her swing of things! A man can only take so much. He can only take so much garlic, too.'

'They say it's good for you.'

'Who does? You tell me his name and I'll show you someone who can't tell decent food from old socks.'

Miss Hilton seeks clarification. 'What are you going to do when you go to France?'

'ME!'explodes from Eric immediately triggering an equally explosive series of coughs drowning out anything else he might have been going to say.

Mary pauses in her knitting. Miss Hilton doesn't know what to think. There is some signal or other flashing ahead and neither of them is clear if it is green or red. To be safe, Miss Hilton proceeds with caution. 'Mabel sounds very enthusiastic.'

'Enthusiastic is not how I describe her scheme to drive me mad. Maybe they do things differently in Scunthorpe. (Eric knows full well that Miss Hilton is originally from Scarborough.) But let me assure you that in these parts what my wife is doing is not done.'

Mary makes a brave attempt to understand. 'She's just preparing herself, Eric.'

'I can see that. I'm not stupid. I can see further than the end of my nose, you know? She's getting herself prepared all right. But let me tell you, she's not the only one who can do that.'

'That's good to know.' Miss Hilton is on a different song sheet.

'It's not for me to say here and now what I plan to do, but rest assured that I'm making my own preparations.'

'I hope so Eric.' Mary is thinking of passports, travel guides, first aid kits and toothpaste. She's heard toothpaste is really expensive on the Continent.

'Things are in hand. Take it from me I shall not be found wanting. She may think she's stolen a head start, but I can tell you that Eric Dring is not one to be outmanoeuvred. I've not been twiddling my thumbs. As the chap in the Mikado says: "I've got a little list".'

Mary is still packing imagined luggage. Socks (four pairs), vests, pants, hankies...

'I'm satisfied I've not overlooked a thing.'

Mary would like to be sure. What about "Anthisan"? There's nothing worse than sitting at sunset being eaten alive by mosquitoes.

'It's all here,' Eric pats his top pocket. 'We shall see who is better prepared for what lies ahead.'

Mary focusses on her Fair Isle knitting pattern. Even though it's complicated it is much easier to follow than Eric Dring's intrigues. Is the man going to France or not?

*

| **'Eye On Research'** |
| *Up In The Clouds* - BBC TV |

Miss Hilton's class is busy practising sack-racing with a good deal of fun. Amanda and Susan are lying flat on the grass of Manor Grounds staring up at the sky. They are waiting for Mrs Thompson to get everything sorted. She's had to hurry back to school for a tape measure, leaving the Top Juniors to be good or else. Daisy-chain making is occupying the girls. The boys are trying to make rude noises blowing on blades of grass.

'So where is He, Susan? You tell me that. Where is He?' Amanda scours the blueness.

Susan is praying hard, deep down. She's not lying too close just in case God decides that enough is enough.

'Do you believe He's up there, watching what's going on down here, knowing what everyone's up to, who's being Good and who's being Bad?'

"I DO. I DO!" Susan silently declares.

'If Heaven's up there, why hasn't anyone ever seen it?' Amanda rolls over towards her friend. 'Answer me that.'

'Because it's such a long, long way up there, that's why.' Susan hopes she sounds really sure.

'Oh, yes? But scientists and people have got telescopes that can see for miles and miles and miles. And there's Sputnik.'

'So that just goes to show how far away Heaven is.' Susan is pleased with that. Amanda is not. She rolls back to watch the clouds. Slow, fat, heavy ones.

A face comes into view, looking down into Amanda's eyes. It is the boy with longish, blondish hair. 'Whatcha doing?'

Amanda looks up into his face, haloed against the sky. 'Trying to find God.'

Susan tenses ready for the shock. God's patience is being pushed to the limit.

'Can I join in?'

'If you like. But you must be quiet.'

'Why?'

'Cos it's not something you make a noise doing.'

'Right.' The boy drops to the grass and spreads himself out ready. 'What do I have to do?'

'Well…' Amanda is never slow when it comes to making up rules. 'First you have to lie completely flat so every bit of you is touching the ground.' The boy is already doing that but wriggles about to show he is willing and eager. 'Then you have to throw your mind up as far as you can.'

'Huh?'

'You have to throw your mind up into the sky, into space if you can. Like those people who can throw their voices; only you must do it with your mind.'

That sounds hard, but worth a try, the boy thinks. If he can go home and tell his Mum he's found God at school this afternoon, she'll be pleased.

So Amanda and the boy lie as flat as pancakes, eyes concentrating like fury on "far away", while Susan, eyes tight closed, prays for the best.

The slow, fat heavy clouds rank themselves as they file across the blue. Of course, they suggest animals and extravagant things like giants and monsters to the children. They wouldn't be clouds if they didn't do that. But Amanda in particular tries as hard as she is able to keep her mind on the job of tracking Heaven down.

So when she catches herself wondering if one especially beautiful cloud is more a rabbit than a flamingo, she gets quite cross and mentally pinches herself. Maybe people have never seen Heaven because the beauty of clouds gets in the way. Amanda switches her mind on to the furthest, bluest bit of sky she can find.

A silver dart spears the blue when two clouds drift apart. 'Look!' cries the boy flinging up an arm. 'Look! Is that it? That's IT!' and his voice drops to awe. Amanda sees the blinding spark, a twinkling star in the midday sky. Susan looks up, too, through her fingers. The children watch and watch, not blinking. Against the brightest blue the light blazes brighter than Christmas lights, sharper than a penknife. It doesn't move, it races. Three heads slowly swivel, releasing blades of grass to unbend as others are pressed down.

And the sun dips down behind another cloud, or a cloud puffs up to cover the sun, and the plane becomes a plane again.

'Oh,' says the boy. Just "oh". And he scrambles to his feet just as Miss Hilton calls.

'Right everyone in my class, that's it. You've got ten minutes play before we need to head back to school. Mrs Thompson's class, you can join in till she returns.'

A game of tag begins as if by magic and the boy runs off into the growing maze of chased and chasers. 'Bet you can't catch me!' he shouts.

Susan has sat up. The praying has taken it out of her. But it has worked. She'd wished God not to show Himself, and he hadn't. The idea of being face-to-face with Him is not one she wants to think about. Now she watches the boy, his longish, blondish hair bobbing. She wants to chase him. 'What's he called?' Amanda still lies, nailed to the ground, a child-sized doll washed up on a beach of flattened grass. The boy runs off further. 'What's he called?' Susan follows him with her eyes. He is "It". 'The new boy in Miss Hilton's class with the longish, blondish hair, who is he?' She needs to know ever-so-much and there is no-one else to ask but Amanda. 'Amanda, what's his name? You do know, don't you?' But Amanda is lifeless. The boy is getting away, chasing that Ann Mortimer.

'Amanda, if you tell me his name, I'll tell you my secret.' He has caught Ann. 'Did you hear? I said if you tell me his name, the new boy with the longish, blondish hair who was here, I'll tell you how I got to be so tall; how I got my long legs; how I got my long ballet-dancer legs. Only hurry up, or I'll never tell you! Never, ever!'

Amanda comes back from limbo. Susan can tell she's at last got through. 'All you've got to do is tell me his name and I'll tell you EVERYTHING!'

'Everything?'

'Yes. Yes. EVERYTHING. Now come on!'

'Cross your heart?'

A whoop from the game nudges Susan over the edge.

'Cross my heart! NOW TELL ME!'

Amanda pushes her few remaining thoughts of Heaven aside. 'When will you tell me?'

Susan is on her feet, coming and going, ready to let herself fly, 'Any time! After school! On the way home!... PLEASE!'

'Timothy...' and Susan flies. 'Timothy Unwin,' Amanda tells the sky above her head. Who could possibly have thought that Timothy Unwin would hold the key to a person's Absolute Happiness? So he has longish, blondish hair, but he chews lumps of coke from the heap behind the boiler house to show how tough he is. Ugh!

The clouds, the fat, slow, heavy ones trundle ever onwards above and across Dawlish. But transformed. Their fatness is not fatness, but layers of frothy net. Their slowness is Grace and Dignity. Their weight, not weight at all, but Presence.

The Corps de Clouds slow-motions against the sky-blue backdrop. Beautifully soft whipped cream. "Omo-ed" to brilliant whiteness. They swell. They slim. They swirl in layers of sugared paper-nylon petticoats. Soundlessly they shape-shift, pulling in their candyfloss while tossing off their mists. Their feathered heads arch up and away. Their feet as quiet as cotton wool now glissade, now all rise in perfect arabesque. Such unimagined elevation.

The sun bursts out in spotlight, throwing soloists into shade, briefly painting them in grey and gloom, before splashing them with joy.

And there she is, running, running, her face open with love, her arms like wings, her feet like flowers, running. Juliet running for Friar Lawrence. Across the silver screen. Across the silvered sky. Across Amanda's imagination.

There is a heaven!

There is a whistle followed by Mrs Thompson bringing the game of chase to an end. The children in Miss Hilton's class form up and are led away while Mrs Thompson instructs Derek Patterson on how to use the tape measure, not that he needs telling.

'Right, everybody. Form yourselves into a line. That includes you, too, Amanda Clark.'

'Coming, Miss.' And Amanda bounces up eagerly as if throwing the cricket ball was the very best thing in the whole world.

*

| **'Music While You Work'** |
| With *Cecil Norman and the Rhythm Players* – The Light Programme |

In the kitchen above the shop Grace switches the radio off. She doesn't need it. Not today. A trickle of soapsuds dribbles down the wireless. She turns back to the sink. Still Osbert's shirts to do and woollens and sheets. They are in a pile on the floor along with some of her things. She pauses at the sink and catches herself listening to the quiet popping of bubbles. Oily pinks and greens sheen, racing across the fragile surfaces. Water gurgles in the pipes. Should she turn the immersion off or not? She picks up the last of the woollens and eases it through the froth. It whispers loudly.

Her legs ache. The varicose veins in her left leg are twitching. She shifts her weight on to her right leg. There is a fly buzzing somewhere. Has she covered the leftovers in the larder? She decides to have a short sit-down. Just five minutes. Let the cardigan soak for a bit. It's still early. No need to start thinking about lunch yet. She dries and peels off the rubber gloves; spins them to trap air inside and squeezes. Finger after finger explodes right side out. Another spin is needed to force the thumbs.

Grace lowers herself on a chair, then massages her finger tips which have gone washer-womany, puckered. The rubber gloves lie on the table in front of her, lifeless in primrose yellow.

Grace rests forward on her elbows, cupping her heavy head, heavy with the facts and opinions, the ideas and possibilities she cannot sort. Since the café, since the meeting at The Hut and the book, Grace is piled high with bits and bobs, nameless whatnots which she has a vague notion might be the beginnings of thoughts, but they refuse to match up. Her head is filled with a mountain of odd socks as if she's been to an auction and come away with a miscellaneous job lot. Now she is faced with the thankless task of rummaging through them fearing she'll find that nothing seems to go with anything else.

Grace covers her eyes. She'll never get the hang of the facts. The names. When is an atomic bomb not an atomic bomb but a hydrogen bomb or a super bomb or…? That doesn't matter when the result is much the same. But maybe that isn't really true. Do they all slaughter millions, tens of millions or tens of tens of millions? A parade of zeroes marches past. Which one kills more people, more quickly? Which one wipes out places the size of

Birmingham or Manchester? Or San Francisco? Or Canada? Surely it can't be Canada? Canada is too big, isn't it? A place the size of Canada, however big it is, must surely be too big to be wiped out.

But surely doesn't come into it. Nothing is sure. Nobody is sure. Nobody can sort out the possibilities, so why should she be able to? Why should anyone expect her to be able to? If people who should know, who have so much knowledge about this, so much so that it is coming out of their ears, if they don't know, how can Grace?

The zeroes float up, neat and round, only to pop. Each tiny plosion wiping out another infant idea; inklings flutter back to earth, wings clipped, dying, dead.

The wrongness Grace clings on to. Why should she be made so frightened? Why should she have to live in a state of fright? Who has the right to make her wonder if each day might be her last? Who has that right? How dare whoever it is, wherever he is, wherever they are, play with her fears in this way, day by day. Who has given Them the right to do this? Those evil men in their white coats and evil men in their grey suits. Those fools. Grace tries to urge herself to anger. She wants to cry. She presses her eyeballs, trying to stop the questions from firing.

The last of the zeroes evaporate, to be replaced in a twinkling by an "if". Not just an "if", the "if". The fuse that ignites an avalanche of facts. At the talk at The Hut, Birmingham had been sacrificed. Since then it has re-staged its destruction time and again. The details confuse themselves, but even if they were other than true, it doesn't matter. The truth lies beyond the facts. The truth is in Grace's heart. "If a one megaton bomb detonated over Birmingham... total destruction up to two miles... no survivors... fires... all homes damaged in the whole city..." Is that right? "...radioactive fall-out... no services... one third of the people killed straight away or in the first two days... blasted, burned, crushed... the rest make the best of what is left..."

But what would be left? Behind her hands Grace again sees her kitchen curtains singed and shredded. She hears glass scrunch under foot. She smells fire licking at the walls.

Behind her closed lids, disaster. In front of her just-opened eyes the mangle grips the side of the sink, the water heater clings to the wall, and the net curtains still strain at the window. Grace blinks her eyes shut. Destruction. She blinks them open. Dawlish.

As she sits, her mind goes for a wander. Into the hall, passed the dining room, down the stairs, out the back entry, by the dustbins, across the yard, through the gate, up Queen Street, along High Street, down Strand Hill, round into Beach Street, passed the railway station, before heading under the viaduct and reaching the sea. All still there. As normal. As it should be. Ticking along. Tearing off the days from the calendar one at a time. No rush. No panic. Not getting anywhere special, but getting there all the same.

Days looked forward to, like anniversaries, picnics, treats and outings, visits from friends, and evenings when the wind blows and the windows rattle and the fire burns with a whoosh in the chimney and hot chocolate warms cupped hands and there's something happy on the telly, like "Billy Cotton's Band Show". Billy with his familiar summons: "Wakey! Wakey!" Grace would dearly like to wake up with all her worries gone.

Other days, ones not looked forward to, like stocktaking, quarter days, spring cleaning, visits from Osbert's relations, and mornings when the ice patterns the windows and the bedclothes have lost their warmth and the pipes have burst and there's no change for the meter.

But all of them, days on a human scale. Days which you know you can get through, even though there may be moments when you feel like throwing up your hands and giving in. But that is only a feeling. It's not as if you'd do it. Then again, even if you did do it, it wouldn't last.

Now? Good days and bad days don't count. In the scheme of

things, there are only days, and The End. Like at the cinema, those two words are waiting to slide on the screen. And nobody knows when.

"The End" descends bringing screams. Mayhem. Complete silence. Desolation. Over and done with. Nothing "Coming Shortly". Just time tick-tocking on alone.

Grace pushes herself up from the chair. Is it time yet to start thinking about lunch? Almost nearly, but not quite. She leans heavily on the sink. The cardigan is lying in the dregs of froth. The water has gone. The plug has somehow come out, and the water has leaked away. Frail foam puffs the soaked cardigan here and there. An arm lies twisted in the plug chain.

She lifts the heavy dripping weight out of the sink and lies it on the draining board. She shoves the plug back into the plughole and scatters some fresh soap flakes. They rustle, then stick to the wet sink. Little tissues. Tiny fogged leaded lights. The hot water beats down on them. In a moment they metamorphose into bubbles, climbing high up the sides of the sink. Grace has put her gloves back on and stirs them up.

She stands there palms pressed flat out of sight against the base of the sink. "If The Bomb drops," she thinks, "don't let it be just after I've done the week's wash. If it's got to happen, let it be now, before I do the sheets, before I get them out on the line. Now."

*

'Fashion Focus'

Iris Ashley highlights the gaiety in holiday clothes – BBCTV

Mabel hugs herself. She'd be hugging Dickie too, but he is downstairs. Her fingers piano-play upon her shoulders as she scans the neat, squared parcels resting in line on the counterpane. How much she absolutely loves the look of packages and parcels.

Especially ones wrapped in cellophane; cellophane smoother than water, which crunches and crinkles and gives off the essence of newness when touched.

Mabel counts them off from the foot of her bed to the head. They are all here, lifted out from their hiding places. Cork-soled sandals rest in a bed of tissue paper in their box. Pairs of stockings lie creaseless, peaking out through oval windows in their wrappers. Large paper carriers, folded edges still as sharp as if newly ironed, hold slacks and shelter a lightweight jacket with a double vent in a cotton mix. Tops in bold patterns come side by side. One with sombreros in white on green. One with bamboo leaves in blue on cream. One with polkadots in white on blue. One with zigzags, splotches and dashes in red and blue on white. All of them lovingly wrapped. All of them will make the most of Mabel's shoulders.

Then there is The Outfit. For the umpteenth time Mabel finds it hard to believe she has done it. She dares to peel back the sheets of tissue paper. She sees it again with disbelief. With fingertips she raises an edge and lifts it out away from the paper. She lowers it gently to the bed. She lifts another edge. Up comes more, its folds falling away. She places this too on the bed. As the material is spread, the single thread of white reveals its helter skelter route against the blue background. It seems the line goes on forever. More and more material is fanned out upon the bed. Always there seems more, until there is no more.

The Grosgrain Circular Skirt flares out, gently smothering the other purchases, wrapping them in its sky-blue drapery, promising to carry them all away, promising to carry Mabel away completely. She touches a pleat, lifts a fold, straightens a seam, traces the pattern, smoothes and smoothes the acre of blue. Then to complete the ensemble, there's a sweater, whiter than icing sugar. In angora, softer than a powder puff.

Mabel dares not ask herself questions. She knows the answers, but she isn't about to tell. More than anything she knows that The

Skirt is making no false promises. It reclines there in splendour, at total ease with its beauty. Not a smidgin of doubt is to be seen in the blue. The line spirals about, vanishing in the dips and folds, swelling over the rises, seeming aimless, but never once thinking twice. Thinking twice about anything is not something The Skirt does once. Mabel has that to live up to.

*

'Children's Hour'
"The Magic Fishbone" by Charles Dickens
"Tell the Princess Alicia, that the fish-bone is a magic present, which can only be used once; but that it will bring her whatever she wishes for." – The Home Service

'Why here?'

Amanda has led Susan to St Gregory's. The Church, low, grey and almost square, is tucked away. Its squat red tower pokes out above the rooflines of Barton Villas.

Amanda does a quick spin which becomes a pirouette before she almost trips and comes to a stop.

'Finished?' Susan is standing as tall as she can, doing her best not to look at the crowded graves.

'Finished?' Amanda mimics. 'Susan, don't you ever feel like having a good spin? Don't you do anything just for the fun of it? You're going to be a long time dead.' Having said which she grabs Susan and drags her down to sit on a hump.

Susan really doesn't want to think of what lies below. She catches sight of a carved name, Eliza someone, and quickly turns away. How can she leave?

With a fixed stare Amanda pins her friend to the spot. 'Stop wasting time. What's your secret, Susan? You promised. I told you about your boy friend, Timothy!'

'He's NOT my boyfriend!'

Amanda shrugs. 'Is or isn't, I don't care. So what is it?

She pulls the hem of her school skirt down over her knees before hugging them tightly. Her scuffed sandals line up toe by toe, heel by heel. She is all eyes, like a pointer, with Susan the quarry. Her secret to be flushed out.

Susan has that awful feeling, like when Mrs Thompson says: "Right, Class, today I want you to write a really imaginative story…" and Susan's imagination shrivels there and then. She now catches sight of herself in Amanda's eyes, trapped, with any thought of teatime a long way off.

It is because Amanda wants so much to know the secret of Susan's long ballet dancer legs that she is about to swallow the culinary rigmarole that Susan is about to concoct – a concoction which Amanda will not, in spite of its absurdity, question, for after all her ballet heroine, Ulanova, stews a bit of marrow each day as part of her dancer's diet. Amanda is set to be reeled in as Susan's concocted story brews moment by moment as imagined ingredients are added. If only Amanda realised that Susan is about to hear her own tale too for the first time as it bubbles into being to her own delighted amazement.

Amanda doesn't flinch at the appearance of The Gypsy Woman, who when Susan had been such a tiny baby that her Gran had wondered if she was ever going to fill her romper suit, had knocked on their door - before the Pearses moved into Second Avenue next door to Amanda that was. Amanda will go along with the sprigs of lavender (not heather) and the clothes pegs. They ring wonderfully true as far as she is concerned. Hanging the lavender in the wardrobe seems almost obvious, after all her Mum uses it to ward off moths. And getting lavender won't be a problem as they've got some three doors down. As for the clothes pegs for under the pillow of the reluctant grower, they'll be even simpler to get. Two or three won't be missed from her Mum's pegbag. No. Getting the lavender and clothes pegs was going to be easy.

Moving on Susan now shocks herself. She has a moment of totally unexpected inspiration. Something she's heard perhaps?

Pilchards. As soon as she dreams them up, there is a delicious twinge of wickedness. Who says she never has fun?

The shock which registers on Amanda's face warms Susan to the tips of her toes.

'If you need proof, here I am. It may sound odd but you can't argue, can you?' Susan rockets skywards. 'Look!' She stands with her head in the clouds towering over Amanda where she hunches over her knees, knuckles white, her stomach churning. 'I can't explain it, but it has all worked for me.' She spreads her hands in a ta-dah moment.

Amanda peers up knowing full well what she'll see. Susan is looming over her. Like Alice in Wonderland, Amanda is shrinking. Why pilchards? Why did Alice get that bottle with Drink Me on it, or that biscuit with Eat Me on it – both of which Amanda remembers as tasting perfectly all right - and she gets pilchards. The Unfairness of Life is there, crammed in a tin, shoulder to finny shoulder, coated in slimy oil, waiting to slither down an innocent throat.

'So there you are. I'm living proof of the power of pilchards once a week. I know you have to be a ballerina, and if it was up to me I'd willingly give you my long legs without all the fuss with the lavender, clothes pegs and pilchards, but that's not possible, is it?'

Amanda, now very small indeed, shakes her head.

Susan becomes very serious. She holds out a hand to pull Amanda up. It really is time for tea. Amanda stands in front of her. Susan hitches up her satchel before placing her hands on Amanda's shoulders. The final curtain is only a line or two away. Somewhere in a private corner of Susan's mind a camera whirs, viewing the scene from a high angle, the top of the Church tower maybe.

'I, Susan Pearse, give you, Amanda Clark, The Secret Of The

Gypsy Woman. May you use it wisely, and may your wish come true.'

The camera pulls away, leaving the two friends face-to-face among the wavy lines of gravestones. Cue music. Roll credits. Slow fade.

*

'For The Householder'

Designed to help people who want to do their own household improvements and repairs with Barry Bucknell and David Roe. – Network Three

---

Bluebell catches sight of two girls, the taller one striding out, leading the way from the graveyard, the shorter one trailing her, dragging herself along. Bluebell heads off to the pond in Newhay, a few minutes away, to find some peace and quiet among the trees.

Eric Dring's bicycle basket is empty. No books to mark. There are never any. What doesn't get marked at school doesn't get marked.

He always appears a touch cheery on a Friday evening. But when he tinkles his bicycle bell crossing Carpenter's Bridge, the black swans downstream on Dawlish Water interrupt their feather-care. It takes a swan to see to the centre of things. It takes a black swan to sense the darkness at Eric's heart. They ruffle their wings and paddle firmly away.

For no reason a memory swims back into Eric's mind – the scene some five years before, at the time of the Queen's Coronation. He'd somehow got roped in by Harold Newcombe to dance the Floral Dance through the streets. Not alone, of course. He'd partnered Mary Bonfield from school, and there had been no end of other dancers, too. Then there'd been a cycle race round and round The Lawn.

He swings across the road before hopping off and wheeling his bike away to the shed. At the backdoor he pats his pocket. A package is nested deep down inside. Eric straightens his pocket flap before adjusting his face and going in.

Eric is not the only one to hide things away. Not too long ago Mabel gave the bedroom the once over. She had uncreased the counterpane, tidied the pillows, removed a scrap of tissue paper and locked her wardrobe door. She had sworn Dickie to secrecy, not that he'd seen a thing, before turning on French Lesson number 24, "At The Post Office". That would serve to keep Eric at a distance when he came in.

Eric has had to come in the back door because he's yet to sort the front door out. The blade of the old key is still jammed in the lock. Eric has no time for DIY at the moment. Besides he gets pleasure from knowing that Mabel has to come and go the back way, too. Going out the back way in her town clothes hurts.

The babble of French is seeping under the sitting room door. Mabel and the record are lobbing the wretched language back and forth. Eric does his best to stop his ears, grabs some biscuits from the barrel and hurries upstairs, where he clears a space on his worktable before fishing out the package. From it he lifts out a small brown bottle, which he stands in front of him. He shuts his eyes in prayer. A sequence from The Scheme runs behind his closed eyelids. Faultless. He opens his eyes to find he has snapped one of the biscuits clean in two. Not an easy thing to do to a ginger biscuit accidentally.

*

Osbert Phipps is not feeling himself. Nor is the Professor, who is due to walk his few minutes on the rehearsal stage at the Old Forge in a little over three hours.

Osbert checks his watch again. Three hours and twelve minutes to be precise. Little beads of sweat dot his brow. An Actor Repents.

'Well, hello, princess. Mum's gonna murder you,' John Clark slips into falsetto even though his mother has a deeper voice than he does. ' "She knows it's the Beauty Contest tonight! She knows she's got to get ready!" '

'Ha... Ha... Ha.' Amanda dumps her satchel on the floor by the back door. She would slump on to a kitchen chair, but her mother comes in from the hall.

'And where have you been?'

'Told you,' and John edges towards the fridge. He doesn't mean to leave, though.

'Have you forgotten you're at the Contest tonight?'

'No, Mum.'

'Then maybe you wouldn't mind telling me where you've been till this time?'

'Just coming home.'

'Oh, and it takes you an hour and more to do that?'

'Perhaps she's been with her boyfriend.' John's eyebrows rise as far as they can in choirboy innocence. Amanda scowls. She knows she hates him. 'Been busy dancing with Johnny Hairpin, have you?'

'You shut up! You don't know anything!'

'Amanda, you're in enough trouble without making it worse. Now be quiet and say you're sorry.' Amanda KNOWS God does not exist. 'And you, John, if you want to go to the Contest, you'll say sorry, too.'

John doesn't have to think about that. He just says "bathing costumes" to himself. His eyes zoom in on a row of busts. His hands itch. He spoons out, 'Sorry, Amanda' sweetly, like malt extract.

'And you, Amanda. That is unless you want to be sent directly to bed. I'm sure they could get by this evening with just one princess.'

Amanda might've known that any Fate that could force pilchards down her throat wouldn't think twice about making her apologise to her brother. But she wouldn't mean it. As she forms the words, she sees John flattened by a ten-ton truck, and she doesn't wince at all. If only she knew how to drive.

'Now go and have a bath. The water's been on for ages. But hurry up, don't lie there like you usually do.' Amanda leaves without seeing her brother even though she has to push past him.

'Off you go, your Princess-ship,' and John tosses off a bow.

Amanda hauls herself up the stairs. With each step she stamps on John's grinning monkey face. Grin. Stamp. Grin. Stamp.

A kitchen drawer is pushed shut heavily. Amanda pauses mid-step, hoping against hope that the ten-ton truck has done its worst, or, if not, that Mum has clipped his ear. But probably she has just given him a no-nonsense look, and he's decided to stop; to save his breath for the next time.

***

FRIDAY EVENING, JUNE 6th

'Matters of Moment'

A question of current concern or interest will be argued or investigated. - The Home Service

Like a pair of ornaments Osbert and Grace sit at either end of their dining table with heads full of thoughts. Their supper plates carry the bright stains of fried eggs. Friday evening, for ease, is usually egg and chips with its echoes of childhood for Grace on her family's farm. On occasions it's fish fingers, or even a piece of steak. It's always chips. At least some things never change.

For them both nursing unexpected preoocupations it is by far the safest thing to focus on the wallpaper, the furniture, the carpet and the fire irons, the magazine rack, the table lamp and the low mosaic-inlay table where the gramophone sits. The scenery of Life. A present setting.

From dead centre beneath the light in the ceiling the room could be sent revolving through the quarters. Ahead over the sideboard the green-framed mirror reflects. A turn. The fireplace gapes back. The mantelpiece supports a run of the following, to use the inventory language of the establishment; from left to right. a small vase holds some of last year's statice, then a toby jug with a chipped lip, a clock in Sheffield plate, a glazed plaster figure of a Chinese fisherman with his rod, a pair of wooden birds which could be cranes, their heads thrown back reaching up. These things never change. To be dusted, of course, but always put back in that order from left to right. Sometimes the smaller bird is on the left, but more often it is on the right, for the sake of balance. A turn. The window wall. Looking out at another window of another building over the road, and further off, over that roof, the sky. A last turn. There they are still.

'Penny for them.' Grace feels she should really be doing something. 'Your thoughts.' Should she be clearing the things away?

'Sorry, Grace, but you'd be wasting your money. You really would.' Osbert has learned a lesson. Keeping a lid on his thoughts is best. Instead he runs some more of the Professor's lines.

'How have things been? The Sale's going well? Moved any of those flannels? We've not seen much of each other this week, have we?' Grace straightens her knife and fork.

'Mustn't grumble. Still early days, but we're shifting some ends of roll.' Osbert's shadow wavers across the angle of two walls, in danger of splitting itself in half. 'So can't complain. Though it'd always be good to see shelves emptying more quickly.' Osbert as himself is struggling to come up with his next line.

'How about those linen tea towels? The ones with the views of Widecombe?' Grace muffles her need to share her worries, gagged by Uncle Tom Cobley and All.

'One or two, dear. But we've plenty left.' From nowhere Osbert wallows in a stream of thought. All warm and comforting, safe and entirely inappropriate. His head is brimming with "Professor Willard".

'Just one or two?' Grace sees the attempted chit-chat cracking. Something is going to give.

'Though a woman from The Royal Hotel said she might be interested in some.' Can't the telephone ring to save them?

'Mrs Keeley?'

'Short woman with a bun.'

'Glasses and an Irish accent?' Osbert nods. 'Mrs Keeley,' And that is where the conversation dribbles to a stop.

Osbert pushes at a jellied smudge of egg with the tip of his knife. Almost as if he is about to pot it into some distant pocket. Grace stands up to clear the table; reaching out for Osbert's plate. Osbert lets goes of his knife, goes to pick up his plate to hand it to her – the fork begins to slide – Grace's hand goes out to stop it sliding – Osbert's hand goes out to stop it – The plate performs a somersault, clips the table edge, cracks itself, chips the woodwork, and falls floorwards watched by Grace holding her plate and Osbert holding his knife – The plate hits the floor in a way that both cracks it further and forces egg into the short pile of the carpet – Osbert's fork lies innocently on the table cloth.

'Never mind.' But Grace can hardly stop herself from flinging her own plate. 'Never mind. Accidents happen.' She holds her plate tight enough to hurt. 'Can't be helped.'

Osbert stoops slowly, aware of the pressure changing inside his head. A high-flying plane passes behind his lenses; the faraway sound of it. Gingerly with finger and thumb he lifts the rim. The plate cannot miss its opportunity. Without a noticeable sound it comes asunder, leaving only a portion of itself in Osbert's grip.

'I can fix it.' Osbert is now quick to pick up the pieces. 'I can fix it.'

'It doesn't matter.'

'No, I suppose it doesn't matter, but I know how much you like them. One of your mother's favourite set. I'll be able to put it together, I'm sure.' Osbert lays out the pieces on the tablecloth, even though it is in the way of these things that there'll surely be a chip or two missing. Then he could search all evening and not find it. This is clear even now before he matches the pieces together. Somehow a fragment will have vanished, meaning that the effort of sticking the plate together again is quite pointless.

'Look. There we are.' Osbert tries to overlook the chink in the patterning. 'Where's the glue?'

'Really, dear, there's no need to bother. It's just one broken plate. It's not the end of the world.'

And that is precisely where the can of worms is prised open and both Grace and Osbert know it. The reek of something rotten scents the room. Thoughts make their escape wriggling into the light.

'Do you know,' Grace begins, 'I feel like someone in a story.'

146

She stands quite suddenly. Osbert drops the pieces of the plate into the waste basket by the table and stands too. Straightway that feels wrong. He needs some direction. Where should he go? What should he be doing? Surely the stage belongs to Grace. He sits down in the nearest armchair. He longs to be out on the stage with the Professor.

'We should talk.'

Osbert's throat tickles and Grace takes his resulting slight cough as agreement which she straightway confirms, 'Yes, we should talk.'

Osbert's chair wraps its arms around him pinning him there. The living room door is fast disappearing. The carpet stretches away forever. He is in need of a prompt from somewhere off-stage. However, they are out here on their own.

Grace shakes her head shunting her thoughts into gear. Getting started is not easy. 'Osbert, have you read "On The Beach" by Neville Shute? The Australian?' Osbert manages to shake his head. 'It's about what you were talking about last week.' Osbert holds his breath. 'When you were talking about the way the World is going and… You do remember, don't you?' He now manages to nod. 'But never mind the book. It's not what all this is about.'

Grace's mind is firing falsely. Ideas and their words rattle around in bagatelle fashion to vanish through the holes before being able to score. Is she going to be able to make a point?

'Now, Birmingham. Take Birmingham. Do you know that if they drop The Bomb – the one you were talking about - on Birmingham the whole of the city, or at least everything from the centre out for two miles in all directions would be completely wiped out? Completely. Just like that.' Grace sees The Bright Light, hears The Complete Silence and feels The Loss.

'But why would anyone think to drop The Bomb on Birmingham in the first place?' Grace turns to the table that is still to be cleared. 'Why should they want to do anything like that? It's not as if the people of Birmingham have ever done anything that means they should be bombed.' She picks up Osbert's fork from the tablecloth. 'So why should they be bombed?' Her hands are sure as her doubts flow. She stacks the side plates. 'It's no good saying it's just an example, because that's just as bad. For it to be an example means that someone somewhere has thought that such a thing was on the cards.' Tea dregs are slopped from one cup into the other. 'And even if it never ever happens, the fact that it's been thought is horrible.' The salt and pepper, the ketchup and brown sauce are stood on the tray. 'It makes me sick just thinking that someone has thought that the destruction of thousands and thousands of people is possible.' The table is all but clear with just the tray and tablecloth to remove. 'Not just how can they bomb a city; how can they think about bombing a city? How can they come up with a plan or the possibility of a plan to destroy so many people with a snap of the fingers.' Grace fingers a blob of sauce. The tablecloth will have to go in the wash. She pulls it from the table and hugs it to herself as her worries play leapfrog.

Osbert is looking at Grace. He is looking at the place she calls her salt cellars, her collar bones, as she cuddles the cloth.

'I don't now.' Grace sounds beaten. She crosses to the window to shake the cloth out. It billows and its flapping applause draws a look from the man installing an aerial over the road. She shakes it again before yanking it back in.

'I bet you can't name a single solitary person who does know.'

Osbert allows his shoulders to relax. 'No, Grace, you are right. I can't.'

'And?'

'And I am not alone. Nobody can.'

'After all you said last week, is that it?' Grace pulls the window to, folds the cloth neatly before she remembers it is for the wash. 'Last week, you said...'

'I said a lot of things. But, dear, that doesn't mean I have an answer. I am sorry if I sounded as if I might. But saying a lot of things doesn't mean I have any of the answers. Not one.'

'At least you were trying to sort things out, trying to get to the heart of things.'

'Grace, those problems – the ones I was on about and The Bomb and all that are huge ones...'

'Which we must think about, Osbert.'

'Yes, we should think about them. I'm not saying we shouldn't, Grace. Course not. But we shouldn't expect to come up with any answers.'

Grace sits herself on the edge of an upright chair, the tablecloth still in her arms. 'Why not?'

'Because. Ordinary people like you and me don't have the necessary info.' His eyebrows shrug. 'You see that, don't you?'

'And why is that?'

'Because, Grace. Because we don't. That's all. I mean, I'm a draper, and you're you. How on earth can we know all we'd need to to be able to come up with... Answers?' Osbert capitalises.

He feels his glasses sliding and thumbs them back up his nose. The tray of cups and things is waiting to go out to the kitchen. 'Shall I...?' he offers.

For Grace the subject is not over and dealt with. Not at all. 'Why should anyone want to blow Birmingham to Kingdom come?' I'm not trying to understand Everything. I'm just trying to get one or two things straight. So, Birmingham is just a for instance. It could be Glasgow or wherever. The point is: "Is it right?"'

'No, dear.' Osbert sidesteps the spotlight, edging towards the wings.

'Is it right that anyone, people in Birmingham, Glasgow or Timbuctoo or anywhere should have to live with the fear that at any tick of the clock they might become so much steam and dust?'

'But, Grace, they don't spend their days worrying about it.'

'That makes it OK?' Grace pauses. 'They don't worry about

it, or most people don't, because they don't know.'

'No, Grace, they don't worry about it because they don't want to worry about it. Because they know there's nothing we can do. The whole thing is completely out of our hands.'

The clock chimes.

It takes a moment for both Osbert and Grace to react. He stands, accompanied by getting-up noises and looks about. She picks up his playscript from the coffee table and holds it out. 'You'll be wanting this.'

Osbert smiles thanks, pats pockets, finds a pencil that he waves before returning it to his breast pocket, and heads for the door. 'I shouldn't be too late, dear.'

Grace listens as Osbert hurries downstairs. The outside door closes. Grace is left to tidy up.

*

'Holiday Town Parade'
The contest for Great Britain's Television Bathing Beauty Queen, Fashion Queen and Adonis, hosted by McDonald Hobley. – ABC TV

In the ballroom at The Royal Hotel the royal party is grouped stage right surrounded by paper flowers. 'Smile!' encourages Susan in a ventriloquial whisper. 'Remember we're princesses.' She herself is radiant.

'Come on, Amanda,' puts in Kay Trent, the Violets Queen in her regalia. 'We've got to give them their money's worth. Is there anything the matter?'

Amanda's face greys further. Susan glows.

'...which one of tonight's beautiful contestants will go forward to the Grand Final at the end of the season when the magnificent sum of two hundred and fifty pounds...' Councillor Brewster as Chairman of the Holiday Beauty Girl Contest Sub-

Committee pauses for the audience to ooh, which it does, before going on, '...will be awarded to the winner together with the title of Holiday Beauty Girl of 1958! It only remains for me to wish all the lovely girls the very best of luck.' Councillor Brewster pauses once again to check if there was any reason not to move on.

'So, Ladies and Gentlemen, without more ado, let me hand you over to our Master of Ceremonies for the evening, our own, our very own Mr Stan Holman.' Councillor Brewster has been watching too much TV.

Robust applause and a shifting of backsides on chairs that have already turned uncomfortable cover the exchange of Councillor Brewster for Mr Holman at the microphone.

John Clark had not been able to eat much tea. Now he is sitting in the middle of the third row with a perfect view of the stage, wondering how much longer he'll have to wait to be transported to bliss.

'What is that you've got on?' Mr Clark asks from behind a wafting hand. There is no reply. 'That is you, isn't it?'

'Huh?' John gives his Dad a fragment of attention.

'That... smell.' Mr Clark sniffs closely.

'Be quiet, you two,' Mrs Clark leans across. 'I'm not having you spoiling our 'Manda's big occasion. If you've got to argue, save it for when we get home.'

'I wasn't arguing. I was just asking him what he's got on. He smells like...' but a look from his wife stops him before he can make any mention of Cairo. 'A man can't open his mouth these days.'

'Shh!' Mrs Clark pulls at her hem and pats her handbag on her lap. Her 'Manda is looking a picture. If only she would smile a bit, though. She has a really nice smile; the kind of smile that can charm the birds from out of the trees.

A banshee wail rips through the scene-setting, freezing every fidgeter in an instant. Up on stage Stan Holman is mouthing away.

'Feedback,' announces John.

'Static,' counters Mr Clark.

The scream rises in pitch to shatter itself in a chorus of crackles and whistles, leaving the microphone dead. Mr Holman taps the thing a couple of times before lifting it on top of its stand gingerly to one side. He goes on unfazed, 'You never can tell when technological wizardry is going to bite the hand that needs it, he announces to be rewarded with a ripple of polite laughter, which gives him a moment to peruse his notes.

In the pause Councillor Brewster, for reasons best known to himself, inches up to the edge of the stage and reaches up for the stand. It's not as if he's the most technically-minded person. He is most definitely not a Tom Trent, who is sitting in one of the back rows, wondering if he should step in.

Councillor Brewster has begun fiddling with the stand and needless to say every eye in the place homes in on him, as Stan Holman proceeds... 'Let me remind you that the contestants will be measured...' John sees himself, tape measure in hand. His hand which is sweating... 'for personality as well as for beauty.'

Very few people are attending to Mr Holman. Even he is finding it hard not to watch. In his efforts to be unobtrusive, Councillor Brewster is magnetic.

There is an increasing rustle out front as those who have failed to notice that the councillor's left leg is becoming snared in the microphone lead, are quickly put in the picture. Now with everyone aware, they can only wait for the inevitable.

Someone has to maintain the pretence that nothing unplanned is about to happen so Stan Holman ploughs on. 'It will be my very pleasant duty to ask our bevy of contestants one or two questions. Now it only remains for me to introduce our eminent panel of judges.'

Events suddenly accelerate.

Later, when those concerned reprise the catalogue of incidents over a cup of tea or something stronger, no-one is truly able to sequence them correctly.

Some allege that the electric flash came before the microphone hit the stage floor and indeed caused the thing to crash. They speak knowingly of overloads and blown fuses. Councillor Brewster is one of these, after, that is, he leaves the Cottage Hospital where he is found to be suffering from mild shock. Hardly surprisingly.

Others are adamant that the near-explosion resulted from the lead being yanked out of the wall, along with the socket and a chunk of plaster, when Councillor Brewster, snared by the lead, over-balanced and fell.

Some who share this view, among whom Stan Holman and Tom Trent can be counted, feel that the councillor's resultant nervous state arose from being revealed in a very public fashion as wearing a toupee, and had nothing to do with the electricity whatsoever.

Almost everyone has known for ages about Councillor Brewster's toupee. Maybe once upon a time it might have been convincing, from a distance, but since his real hair had steadily greyed, the gingery hairpiece has stood out like a.... like what it is, a toupee.

Over the years "Andre and Roma" have serviced the councillor's hairpieces. His particular demands are well-detailed in the salon's little red book along with the specific tonsorial requirements of others. How is this generally known? Councillor Brewster, the trusting innocent, has somehow overlooked the fact that council wives get their hair done by Mrs Owen, too; Mrs Lowe in particular. This means very few people are not in the know.

As the councillor's hairpiece parts company with its owner, a few other hands in the assembly surreptitiously check their own. However, in the near pandemonium they are quite safe from being noticed.

'Don't!' squeezes out Councillor Brewster in a strangled voice. Stan Holman takes the message at face value, and keeps his distance. Kay Trent does not.

'Don't!' Councillor Brewster appeals; he couldn't be more insistent.

'It's all right...' She cannot remember his name. 'I have training in this sort of thing.'

Councillor Brewster's face has gone ashen as if he's seen the Grim Reaper approaching. With The Violets Queen dressed all in white as she is, Kay Trent could pass for the Angel of Death. That is just wishful thinking by Councillor Brewster. The sounds of the audience confirm for him that this is not the afterlife. He is going to have to live through this. He now needs more than anything the services of a good hairdresser.

'Just don't,' he puts up a warding hand. 'Whatever it is you think you want to do, don't.'

'I think he's in shock, Mr Holman.'

'Of course I'm in shock,' the councillor hisses, crouch-walking to the nearest door, scrabbling all the way with his hairpiece. He finds some shelter and ministers to the wretched thing.

But he has not escaped. Kay Trent has followed.

'You'd be better off being seen to.'

'Haven't I been seen to enough for one evening?' Councillor Brewster fizzles. His words spurt. 'Why can't you go back inside and sit on your damned throne and do what you're supposed to do, namely smile and keep your mouth shut?'

Kay Trent is not going to rise to that. The man's clearly lost all self-control along with his ridiculous toupee. She regally returns to the stage and to her throne passing Stan Holman on her way.

'Ladies and Gentlemen, we need to be getting on.' He waits as a good MC does for quiet. He manages a calming smile and continues.

'We are most fortunate to have a most distinguished jury this evening.' The spectators are finding it hard to drag their attentions from what is going on out of sight, where Councillor and Mrs Brewster are exchanging words, but Mr Holman, with his years planning and presenting Entertainments, is the man for the task, to get things rolling. 'We have Mr Roland Tubbs who needs no introduction, Treasurer of the Bowls Club. Next we have Mr Len McCarthy, manager of The Royal Hotel. Last, but by no means least, Mrs Lowe, wife of our Council Chairman, and member of numerous committees in her own right.'

Kay Trent has resettled on her throne. Mr Holman checks for any signals that anyone might be giving him and sees none, so he invites the combo to start playing, and the evening's proceedings recommence with those on stage pretending nothing out of the ordinary has happened.

Stan Holman clears his throat and begins. 'Our first contestant is Miss Monica Hardman. Monica is 19 years old and is a sales assistant at Woolworth's.'

The delay has heated John's expectations to white hot. At the appearance of Monica he steams. He poaches and boils, roasts and fries. He steams in sweat. He poaches in lust. He boils in passion. He roasts in what he would do if. He fries in what she would do if. He is stirred to dissolution. He is whisked to a heady froth. Her stilettos spice his ardour. Her lips pepper his intentions. But her body, her figure, her form crack him apart, then stiffen him. He rises. He crisps. He browns. He is meringue, overloaded with sweetness, longing for Monica to sink her teeth in, offering himself for her indulgence.

'Monica, you work at Woolworth's, don't you?' She nods and smiles wider. 'Tell me, what do you like about your job?'

Monica knows the answer to that one. It is one of Mr Holman's standard ones. 'Meeting the public.'

John is public. John is volunteering to be met.

'And, Monica, what will you do with the money if you win?'

Monica smiles her widest. Two out of two. And this is her winner. 'Well, I thought I might like to go on holiday...' John is next to her on a towel on a beach. 'Or I might buy a Lambretta.' Monica pauses to let the audience respond. It also gives John enough time to seat himself up close on her pillion, arms wrapped around, holding on. 'But then I decided that if I win, I will give the money to the St John's Ambulance Brigade.'

In all his years Stan has heard some fairly blatant untruths, but this one surely takes the biscuit. Monica beams sincerity. The audience, that is the male section of it, warms to her. The women cool. They recognise a blatant ploy when they hear one.

The round of applause which comes as Monica teeters off the stage, is led by a pair in black and white uniforms standing by the exit doors. St John's Ambulance Brigade stands to benefit, so Monica gets their votes. They think of how many new stretchers £250 would buy.

Monica exits leaving John wondering what he's done wrong. No beach. No Lambretta. And there is no way he's about to join the Brigade. The sight of blood makes him throw up.

However, Monica is soon forgotten. Helen Gibbons, 18, a typist, Sandra West, 22, housewife, and the rest strut and smile. All eight get John's vote.

While the jury is in conclave, the combo lets rip. Not that the spectators pay much attention to them. It is time to stretch legs, have a quick fag, maybe get a drink from the bar, and as far as Susan's mother is concerned time to tear to pieces the young women who have paraded their figures for one and all.

Mrs Pearse was in full-flow before the last contestant had left the stage. 'That number four, Simone Scott, I am telling you for a certainty that she's not a 36. Never on your life. I mean, I should know. Wasn't it me that sold her that you-know-what for her last birthday. Now if you're saying she's developed that much in under a year, I'm here to tell you she has not. Look at her mother. Not a person I've got much time for in the normal run of things. Mrs Scott's chest is... well, let me say it's hard to credit she's a mother of three. Probably used Ostermilk. But there we are. So, what I'm saying is that her Simone is most definitely not a 36. Mine's the babycham.' The arrival of drinks allows Miss Eaves to get a word in.

'I was thinking how pretty Mrs Hardman's daughter, Monica, looked.'

Miss Eaves looks across to where Kay Trent is laughing at something. 'I think Mrs Trent handled herself very well when Councillor Brewster had his mishap.'

'I wonder, though, whether a woman with her colouration suits mauve.'

'She's a happy sort.'

'That's as maybe but I'm not convinced it's altogether healthy. There's not as much humour in the world as she seems to think. I've made that perfectly clear to my Susan. Take it from me, Miss Eaves, married women have their responsibilities, and first and foremost among them is not putting yourself about in public as a person who laughs at the drop of a hat. If there's one thing I want my Susan to get straight, it's that life is no joke. There's nothing wrong with a modicum of fun, but it must be kept in its proper place. And laughing out loud all the time only shows that our Violets Queen has failed to learn that one important lesson.'

'Laughing is just the medicine we need, surely, Mrs Pearse?'

'I couldn't agree with you more, Miss Eaves.' Mrs Harvey chips in. She with her husband, Jim, in tow, is just passing.

'We're always having a laugh, aren't we, Jim?'

'Too right, Cis. A day without a good laugh is a real waste.'

'I was just saying to Mrs Hardman, Monica's Mum, how really lovely her daughter is looking. Glowing. When I was looking at her and the other contestants too, I was struck by their confidence. It made me wish I was young again, but like them and not the quiet mousey girl I was.'

'Don't you go doing yourself down, Cis Harvey! I wouldn't have had you any other way. You were a real peach!'

157

'And you couldn't wait to pick me, Jim Harvey!'

The pair so recently voted The Couple Most Unlike Each Other bursts into hoots of shared laughter and heads off back to their seats.

*

'Amateur Theatre'
Dramatic Speech: talk by Fabia Drake – The Home Service

At the Old Forge Charles Burch is wondering if he has any aspirin at home. He finds he has been doodling while looming in front of him is the figure of Osbert Phipps.

'..."Of course, there are some more recent outcroppings, - sandstone showing through a shelf of Mezozoic shale..." ' Osbert stops again and stands unblinking again.

Harold Newcombe leans a little more heavily against a chair. His mind is wandering, going through a checklist for School Sports Day. Rita Gordon is quietly strangling twists of crepe paper which will never look like roses.

Osbert stares off through the furthest wall. Straining to see his next line, but it has conspired like almost every previous one to bolt with the speed of a rabbit seeking cover as it sees him coming.

Helen Bray looks up from under her fringe. She stopped giving prompts a good half-hour ago.

'Basalt, Osbert,' Charles lobs heavily. He has loosened his cravat. 'Devonian basalt, Osbert.' Charles sounds each syllable in an echo of his performance as "The Ice King" earlier in his am-dram career. His mouth almost vanishes beneath his neatly trimmed moustache. 'A shelf of Devonian basalt.'

In the following tiny silence the point of Charles' pencil draws attention to itself as it snaps.

It fails to draw Osbert's attention, however. He has set like concrete, or, as Charles has strongly suggested, something far denser, more massy and altogether immovable. Whatever fire blazed in Osbert's previous performance as "Professor Willard" hasn't only cooled, its temperature has plummeted to something approaching absolute zero. His descent to the thespian nadir seems endless to the small handful watching.

Rita hunches over her drift of tattered roses, scissoring with intent, blotting out the dismay. Alfred Tremlett, Richard Cornall, Billy Burrowes and now Osbert Phipps, and even her father when she really thinks – all much of a muchness. They all, in their different ways, let a person down.

They'd lead a person on. They'd get a person believing in them with their Ideas, their Schemes, and their Abilities. They'd sound off about emigrating to New Zealand, or starting a pig farm, or going to Bristol University, or taking a person on a cruise when they retired. Or in the case of Osbert, making a person think they had real acting talent. Each of them letting a person down by staying put, by settling for third best, for getting married to that Betty Crabb, by falling into a vehicle inspection pit, and now in the case of Osbert Phipps by proving himself to be just a dull draper. The scissors, the wicked dressmaking ones, with their chipped paint and spots of rust slice through the blood-red crepe.

From the brink of ossification Osbert stirs himself. ' "Of course," ' he begins hazily, his mouth sluggishly operating before his mind has refilled, ' "...there are some more recent outcroppings, - basalt..." '

'Sandstone,' Charles interrupts, as the mercifully blunt pencil jabs into his thigh.

For no obvious reason Osbert trips. He hasn't moved an inch. It's just that his right ankle hasn't been able to maintain the stillness any longer. At least that brings his attention away from the furthest wall to a point nearer, but not on, Charles.

'Sandstone,' Charles repeats like a man trying to kick-start a pre-War BSA.

Basalt and Sandstone perform some sort of magical metamorphosis within Osbert's mind. Are they one and the same and interchangeable?

'Sandstone, Osbert.'

Rita pauses in mid-slice. She fears for Charles' teeth. Their grinding can be heard from some distance. She knows about teeth. How she has suffered with hers. She catches herself wondering if Charles's teeth are his own.

' "Grovers Corners…" ' Osbert resumes.

Charles' head sinks.

Rita decapitates a just-completed rose.

Harold Newcombe is out the door before Osbert has completed that pair of innocent words. It is unlike Harold not to stay the course, but he has promised his wife, Dierdre, that he'd be home in time to look at package holidays to the Costa Brava before she goes to see Mr Nelson at the travel agents tomorrow. And she has made it clear that this year they both need a summer break, and it's going to be their first one abroad.

Helen Bray's finger crawls back to the very beginning of "Professor Willard"'s very first speech, again, knowing that this time like all the others Osbert will manage to recall less and less, so proving The Law of Diminishing Returns.

' "… lie on the pleiocene sandstone of…." '

'Granite.' Helen cannot stop herself. It has just popped out.

Rita snips the air, a Sweeney-Toddian.

Charles is no longer able to feel.

Osbert is at school, crammed into a desk in that room next to the boys' changing room. His trouser knees shiny, polished by the constant friction of kneecaps with desk bottom. "Granite" has spirited him back there. That time when Mr Spicer presented the class with the incontrovertible geological facts about the line somewhere east or west of Exeter, one of the two, where granite stops, where tors are no more, and where chalk starts. And it rankles afresh. Glastonbury is east of that line, but it has a Tor.

In the here and now, what had seemed to Osbert to be a magical conundrum, where Basalt became Sandstone and vice versa for no discernible reason, translates itself into a juggling trick. Where before there were two, now there are three; Basalt, Sandstone and now Granite, meaning the chances of being right diminish ever further. But then of course there is also Shale.

' "Grover's Corners…" '

It is quieter than is really possible, considering that four people are present. Three pairs of eyes pin Osbert to his spot with all the fascination of lepidopterists visiting a butterfly farm. Mouths dry like those of filmgoers at films like "Ice Cold In Alex" at the Scala when the management would turn the heating up to boost interval sales of pop.

Three minds set solid, achieving a firmness usually only achieved by hospital canteens on the days they prepare "shape".

Three visions shrivel. One sees his dream of local dramatic honour replaced by ridicule. One sees her faith dashed to pieces once more. One sees her boy friend who is probably already waiting by the bandstand.

Osbert stands on.

The Universe has jammed fast with Sputnik the only thing in motion.

'Prompt.' It doesn't register. 'Prompt, please.'

Helen Bray is unable to hurry. But she is the first to drift up out of her coma. Her finger crawls down the page and comes to a stop.

Charles shudders as he walks over his newly-heaped grave. A backward glance persuades him that on his gravestone is carved, "He produced Our Town". 'Helen!' he calls, breaking out of him like a nightmare cry.

Helen's eyes snap up from her copy.

Charles tries to smile.

Helen's lips pop open with a damp plop.

Charles Burch shouldn't have tried to smile. It has come out all wrong. Even he knows it. 'Please, Helen...Please.' "For all our sakes" is left unsaid.

'Mmmm...' Helen mmm-s.

Charles, who for a very short while thought that he was going to come through in one piece after all, begins to slide again. 'Sorry?' He is so incredibly sorry. For himself, naturally.

'MMmm...' Helen reprises with more emphasis.

Charles wonders if he turns he will see a pair of men in white coats coming to take him away. He is aware of looking for something to say. Without luck.

'Mmmm...That's it.'

Charles has no option. 'That's what?'

'It. The prompt. Where Mr Phipps has got to.'

'The pause!' And Osbert the Amateur Actor claps a hand to his brow.

'The pause.' Charles realises he is trapped. Roped into a scene which needs nothing more than a pair of French windows to remove him completely from reality.

'The pause,' Helen confirms, and nods.

'We've been waiting because Osbert forgot that he was meant to pause.' Charles announces to the ceiling or maybe to an agency further off in the direction of Heaven.

The door swings open and closed. Helen has caught a glimpse of her boyfriend, Jimmy. She is re-energised. 'Yes, Professor Willard says: "Grover's Corners". Then there's a dash while he thinks. Then he "mm"'s to show he's thinking. Then there's another dash. After the dash he says "let me see", and he thinks again, so there's another dash. Then to show he's been thinking he says "Grover's Corners" again before going on.'

'Thank you, Helen. I think that puts us all in the picture.' Charles closes his eyes briefly, but hard. 'So, Osbert, do you think you've got that?'

'After I say "Grover's Corners" I pause to think. Then I umm...'

162

'No, Mr Phipps, you don't umm,' Helen makes sure he's listening. 'You "mmm".'

'That's what I meant. I "mmm". And I think again before going on.'

Helen looks across to Charles as if to say "over to you", gets up, gathers her coat and hurries away.

It costs him so much but Charles manages to force back the desire to follow Helen's example. 'Very well, Osbert, in your own time.'

As Osbert re-starts once again, Rita at last feels able to relax her hold on the scissors She puts them down resting her hand on them before drawing it away. Away from temptation. Then without any hurry on her part, she reaches for her handbag, lifts her chair back as she rises, making no noise, and leaves. The roses can wait. Malcolm Hill can do them next time.

*

'Semprini Serenade'

Introducing old ones, new ones, loved ones, neglected ones by Semprini at the piano and his orchestra – The Light Programme

---

John lies nailed to his bed. He is a sacrifice waiting; waiting for the moment; for the moment when he'll give his all. His hands are the only thing limp about him. His knees are rigid. His neck locked. His mind glued shut. His eyes are fixed on the ceiling where the Parade parades again and again. There they are, whoever they are, 36", 22", 36", and 38", 23", 36", and 36", 21", 36". There is the black and white number, the blue one and the yellow one, the green one and the spotty one in orange and white. The faces blur. The elaborate hairstyes laboured over by "Andre and Roma" and "Carrolls" unrecorded. Even the legs taper off unremarked. But the gently uplifted, smooth twin mounds in matching sets are engraved in every detail. Especially Number

163

6's. They tilt a little prouder. They invite his eye. They magnetize his desire. They stop his heart and start his imagination. They squeeze his throat. They panic him deliciously. As they peak, so John's intention rockets. As they stir a little, John's fancy swells. As they leave the stage, John drags them back to bedazzle him, to tease him, to fluster him and delight him completely.

*

Amanda lies flat as a board. A hand reaches under her pillow where the clothes pegs nestle. Her mind reaches out into the darkness of her wardrobe. A sprig of lavender is there, tucked away out of sight.

She doesn't care to be a princess ever again. Each time that evening she had looked at Susan, she'd seen slimy, slithery, slick-grey fishy corpses, and her head had swum. As each bathing beauty had strutted by on legs that started just above sea level and went on forever, saltiness had welled in her throat. And not one of them needed such legs as they didn't need to be ballerinas.

Amanda hears the key turning in a gigantic tin. The lid rolls back, forcing her to see all the yellow-green bodies within. Transparent skeletons to be crushed by her tongue, maybe to find a hiding place between her teeth. Feather tails to whisper in her throat. Amanda presses her eyelids as shut as she can. In the darkness of her bedroom the lifeless scraps of nightmare swim by. She has nothing left.

*

Susan lies hugging herself. His longish, blondish hair brings a wider smile to her already smiling face. He says such funny things. When he does Dringaling it is a scream. He had run after her. He had run after her as fast as he could. He'd shouted that he'd catch her and he had. He'd tagged her twice. She hadn't had to slow down either. Not once, but twice. Twice more than Ann Mortimer, that was. What will they play on Monday? Susan curls up tighter.

She doesn't have her bedroom curtains closed. She likes the way the street lamp makes shadows on her wall with the strip of curtain that hides the rail. Susan watches as material ripples in the breeze from the just-open window. It throws figures, running figures scuttering along the picture rail, promising fun.

*

Bodies lie in pits, in heaps, in their uncounted thousands. Charred. Pieces casually missing. A hand in a glove. A stockinged leg. She is searching, rolling up the length of stair carpet, finding as she goes odd cups, odd saucers, unchipped, uncracked, unmatching. Nothing goes together. A torrent of odd shoes threatens her behind a half-closed door. A snowstorm of shredded books blows by telling snippets of numberless stories.

A mountain of washing is heaped up, soiled, stained and ripped, and as she sets about the task of folding it, tidying it, piling it up neatly, Grace stirs in her single bed, unable to come awake. She is struggling to match the corners, to find the edges of something too big to have a name.

*

Osbert half-lies, half-sits in bed. His uncovered feet a V at the foot. He can't stand having them covered. They are prone to overheat, and if they do, he doesn't get a wink of sleep. He looks across at the lump that is Grace. Her form stirs a nerve, a very small one, a twinge of guilt. Osbert turns back to his well-being. Snaps of the last several days present themselves. Osbert the Thinker. Osbert the Actor. He smiles as he tears each recent memory into tiny pieces and scatters them to the winds. No more. Enough of that. Over and done with.

He has managed against what seemed all the odds to shove Inspiration, that quixotic curse, back into the box from which it had sprung unannounced and unwanted. With it safely back under lock and key, and with the newly opened windows and doors barred and chained once more, Dullness and Ordinariness are free to walk the familiar ways of Osbert's mind. He had been wonderfuly weak. Perfectly awful.

Osbert shakes his head at the pathetic "Professor Willard". He really is a man to be pitied. Head crammed with facts and figures, shunting them back and forth, ordering them in as many patterns as glass chips in a kaleidoscope, vainly trying to sort them into Ideas, into an Understanding of What Made Things Tick. When, of course, there isn't one. No pattern. No order. Nothing to understand.

Osbert needs only a day or two and everything will be OK. Things will be going along nicely once more. The Professor has led Osbert a merry dance, but now it is Osbert's turn to call the tune.

*

The Scheme lies fully mapped out in Eric's dreaming head. But it's all hush-hush.

"Be like Dad, and keep Mum!" runs and re-runs through his sleeping mind. He is prepared "DYB, DYB, DYB. DOB, DOB, DOB"

He hasn't overlooked a thing. If those black swans on Dawlish Water could see him now! If they only knew.

*

"Je m'appelle Monique. J'habite à Londres Je suis une actrice dans un théâtre près du centre de la ville. J'ai travaillé avec tous les meilleurs acteurs, par exemple, Laurence Olivier, et les autres. Mon père est un homme très distingué. Il travaille dans le Corps Diplomatique. Maintenant, il se rend à Washington pour parler avec le président Eisenhower. Pardon? Non. Non. Je suis veuve. Mon mari est mort. Dans un accident. Por cette raison je voyage seule...."

Mabel's lifelines flow on.

*

And Grace turns again, under her weight of maybes, basting herself in sorrows.

*

And John can't find an inch of his bed that isn't as hot as hell.

*

And Susan is caught and caught and caught and…

*

And Eric's lips are sealed.

*

And Amanda pulls shut the coffin lid.
    "Choked to death on a pilchard," the mourners will weep.

*

Et Monique rêve.

*

And Osbert is just a draper again.

*

And Bluebell stares up at the clear night sky waiting for Sputnik III to pass.

***

ACT TWO

SATURDAY, JUNE 7ᵗʰ 1958

'Come Dancing'

Jack Watson invites you to look around the New Tower Ballroom, Blackpool and watch exhibition dancers Tony Traver and June Tyrell, Maurice Boyle and Phoebe Brindle, and The Stevenson Formation Team (of Cleethorpes) British Formation Dancing Champions – BBC TV

They have headed towards Dawlish Warren and arrived at The Langstone Cliff Hotel in their Rovers, Morrises, Vauxhalls and Standards, now parked up facing out over the extensive gardens towards the sea. It is not yet dark, but with the floor-length curtains in the ballroom already drawn, no-one inside is looking at the view.

Mrs Lowe is very aware of the heavy hand pressing lightly against the small of her back. Through her dress, through her slip, through her girdle she believes she can feel its meaty dampness. The hand does not move. It is doing its utmost not to be there at all, which is no surprise because it is attached to Mr Drummond, who is doing all he can not to be there either. Even though he has a hand spreadeagled somewhere out of sight on Mrs Lowe's knuckle-hard back, and the other stuck out stiffly in point-duty fashion, supporting Mrs Lowe's extended arm, Mr Drummond could well be standing a full football-pitch length away for all either party is showing by way of real warmth towards each other.

Of course they are smiling. After all this is the Dairy Festival Dance. Everyone smiles in a public fashion at the Dairy Festival Dance. Particularly as they are both Council; Mr Drummond being on it, and Mrs Lowe being married to the Council Chairman. Councillors and the wives of councillors always attend the Dairy Festival Dance, always smile, and always dance together, saving Mr Lowe, who smiles, but never dances.

*

'Any chance of a foxtrot, Mr Newcombe?' Mrs Jackson is on the point of putting down her drink.

'Later, Mrs Jackson. It will be my pleasure.' Unlike Mr Lowe Harold Newcombe loves to dance. He and his wife, Dierdre, met on a dance floor in Teignmouth at the end of the War. Nowadays at civic events dancing is a pleasurable duty for him, the best part of being an MC. A foxtrot or two with Mrs Jackson is to be looked forward to for she is still a nimble partner. Another more pressing duty is keeping the band happy; The Sylvan Dance Band can be difficult.

'Now, Mr Burch,' Mr Newcombe leans heavily on a chair. 'I expect to see you stepping the light fantastic out on the dance floor with Ginger Rogers here!' Harold indicates that Charles had better partner Miss Eaves or else the evening might just as well come to a full-stop here and now. He isn't to be ignored. Charles, tries not to think about "Our Town", offers his hand and a smile and leads Miss Eaves away. They worm their way through the throng of waltzers to the other side of the ballroom where the Harveys are sitting. Harold sees all this, but he has done his bit. Let them sit this one out. He can always descend on them again a little later if activity on the dance floor gets to look a bit thin.

People have said, more than once, that Harold Newcombe drives all before him in the Pursuit of Entertainment. But he always does it for the best possible reasons. People, some people, just need some forceful encouragement in order for them to have A Good Time. There is the type of man especially who needs to be dragged most unwillingly from his chair or corner, protesting a gammy knee, double hernia or worse, only to be dragged just as unwillingly off the dance floor some long time later. Or so Harold claims citing the case of a Mr X from Haldon.

For the time being, A Good Time is being had by the great majority and Harold is free to see how his wife is getting on.

*

Mrs Lowe is now being steered by Councillor Stephens. He is no more at ease than Mr Drummond before him. Partners have changed, but the smiles remain the same, as does the smallest of small talk.

Mr Stephens dredges up a topic, 'I'm told that Nestles will be sponsoring the Sand Drawing Competition at the Warren.' Mrs Lowe focuses briefly on him. 'On August Bank Holiday, that is.'

'I so hope it keeps fine for them. The children do love it so very much, don't they?'

'Indeed. Our Hilary did rather well when she entered more years ago than seem possible.'

Mrs Lowe slow-foxtrots off with Mr Stephens. His turn is almost done.

*

'I really don't know how a place built to further moral and social improvement can be thought of as a possible theatrical venue. There are still some people in town you know who were very keen members of the Christian Alliance of Women and Girls in their younger days. Times indeed have changed. But I for one feel the Shaftesbury Hall....' As the penny drops Mr Newcombe tunes out, leaving Mrs Brewster to preach to Dierdre Newcombe. Harold still doesn't have a drink.

'But you must admit by being on Brunswick it's in just the right place.'

'Mrs Newcombe, I admit no such thing! There is The Hut for those that need to prance about on stage.'

... which reminds Harold the band may be in need of some refills.

As he sidles up to the pianist Harold makes the signal recognised by pianists the world over. The boys of the band are most assuredly in need of refreshment, so Harold heads off for the bar.

'Harold, who's this "Dulcetto" fellow?'

'Ah, Stan, I gather Miss Gordon has been singing the praises of our very own dulcimer player. Apparently he does a very good "Harry Lime" theme. Rita calls him "cultural". Has she convinced you to book him for the Summer Show? Something to balance the high-stepping charms of "The Sparklets"?'

'She was talking to me or I should say at me with my Entertainments hat on. But she didn't have a chance to say much before she had to make a hasty exit to the powder room.'

'What can I get you, Sirs?'

The barman's query reminds Harold. 'A dry martini and seven pints of bitter, Paulo. And make sure they're in straight glasses.' The barman begins the job of pulling pints. 'And I'll need a tray.'

'…It came to me in a flash. I mean A Flash. Like that,' a man in the tight group to Harold's right makes a snap of the fingers without success. 'It is so right. In the normal run of things I don't have time for Carnivals and such like. But this is So Right.' All Harold can see without turning is the sleeve of a brown corduroy jacket. 'I'll be making a clear public statement, and waking this dozy old town up to what matters. Good God, Dawlish hasn't yet realised this is the second half of the twentieth century. You can be sure there'll be a legion of Tommy Steele impersonators, but I can tell you there'll be only one US Thor missile!'

'Seven pints and a dry martini, Mr Newcombe, on the tab.'

Paulo successfully causes Harold to lose the thread of his neighbour's strangely wonderful plan. Maybe he's heard the best part anyway. He gathers the loaded tray and heads off back towards the bandstand. Harold tunes in to the conversations he passes, collecting fragments en route.

'…I thought they did really well. Negro spirituals are notoriously difficult…'

Harold swerves managing to avoid any spillage.

'… Churn Rolling I understand, but whoever thought of staging a Milk Lapping Competition for Cats?'

Harold pauses briefly behind a pillar.

174

'…"Dulcetto". "Dulcetto". You haven't heard of him?'

Harold moves away, then pauses for a waltz to go by.

'…What sort of a play can it be without any scenery?'

The waltz moves on and Harold sets out across the no-man's land between dance floor and tables. An elbow nearly brings calamity.

'…Do you think she'll be there? Agatha Christie?'

An outburst of applause greets the final bars of a Glenn Miller medley from the Sylvan Dance Band. It seems remarkably well timed, but then the pianist has been keeping a weather-eye open, and, as Harold nears the bandstand, the medley has managed without the slightest hiccough to wrap itself up, leaving the dancers satisfied, and leaving the musicians with their hands free to unload the tray of drinks.

As the dancers drift off, their snatches of conversation are left to hang in the ether for a moment or two.

'…clean comedy and humour. Accordionists. That sort of thing.'

Harold has handed Dierdre her dry martini and is passing behind one of the columns to discover an informal council meeting in progress. '…a real Arts Centre, where Art could be exhibited in all its forms.' Harold tunes out the other nearby conversational channels and concentrates on Mr Stephens who is standing a little way away with his back turned. He has obviously passed Mrs Lowe on to a colleague. 'But up to now all other plans to replace The Hut have been like building castles in the air…'

'George, now don't go getting me wrong.' Mr Lowe never drops his role of Chairman. 'Like you I'm concerned. We're all concerned.' It always pays to share the load, even when it's only a case of sharing concern.

'All we need is for some old dear to be cheering on the goody in the panto a bit too enthusiastically and whoosh, exit like a baddy in a cloud of dust, straight down; probably, knowing our luck when it comes to these things, squashing a couple of youngsters who've crawled in the gap underneath to satisfy love's urge,' details Councillor George Stephens graphically.

Mr Drummond arrives at Mr Stephens' shoulder, dabbing at his forehead with his hankie. 'What's needed is a hall merely for entertainment.'

Mr Stephens turns on him. 'There's no merely about it, Arthur. Entertainment is a must. It's central to the well-being of the town.' Harold Newcombe cannot agree more.

'But we can't afford it.' Mr Lowe tightens the noose and throws the lever, springing the trap door.

Mrs Lowe is approaching, and though the band is still on its refreshment break, she is clearly on the look-out for a future partner.

'Now, gentlemen, I don't want to hear about nagging war wounds or lumbago, we're here to enjoy ourselves. All of us. So forget the Council meeting. It's a Dance, and at a Dance people dance. I'm not expecting a Fred Astaire.'

'Then how about Gene Kelly over there?' Mr Drummond volunteers Harold, who he has caught sight of.

Harold steps forward and proffers his hand, 'Shall we?'

'Indeed, we shall, Gene,' and Mrs Lowe places her hand in his.

'If I am Gene, then you must be Kay Kendall.'

'Oh, if only!'

Harold Newcombe escorts Mrs Lowe towards the dance floor. And in true film fashion the moment they reach it the band starts to play.

'So, Kay, let's show the rest how to have a bit of fun.'

'Yes, Gene, let's.'

Miss Eaves is not the only one watching wishing someone like Mr Newcombe would take them by the hand.

*

Miss Eaves takes her drink in both hands and sips. Two empty chairs flank the table. Then there is Charles Burch. She looks out over the rim of her glass, slowly scanning the crowd. For a moment everyone seems at rest, fixed as in one of those wall-sized paintings that are invariably attributed to the British School Mid-19th Century. Miss Eaves notes the relationships of figure and form, the minor points of focus, the artfully created shadows, and as she pans, she supplies one of those miniature outline versions with numbers and names that often hang next to the works by which the viewer can tell who is who.

In the quiet between musical sets a visual Kelly's Directory of Dawlish is at pose. To the left, from the artist's – and Miss Eaves' – point of view, stands the earnest group of Councillors, Messrs Lowe, Drummond, Stephens and Brewster with Mrs Lowe, who is clearly not listening. The sighting of Mr Brewster causes Miss Eaves to pause momentarily to note that his toupee is back firmly in place. The councillors stand against one of the pillars, a telling visual reference if ever there was, by the edge of the dance floor. They serve to frame the picture on that side. Moving right, in the background the Sylvan Dance Band relaxes with pints in hand, almost as if on the steps of an Edwardian Pavilion – during the interval of some village cricket match. In front of them and with his back to the viewer, Stan Holman of the Entertainments Committee is in conversation with a seated couple – him well-rounded, her well-rounded, too – Mr and Mrs Nelson from the travel agents. Miss Eaves cannot supply them with dialogue, so it could be that they're discussing Austrian dulcimer playing. Before the moment breaks Miss Eaves hurries on. At the next table, the blindingly bright acre-and-a-half expanse of whiteness draws her eye. It is the shirt front of Jim Harvey. Mrs Harvey basks in his shadow. Behind both of these tables a row of backs and half-backs line the bar, the lights of which illuminate some and silhouette others. Here stand and lean, sup and sip, a range of extras, among whom some characters draw Miss Eaves' eye. Hugh Dinsdale and Josephine Brooks are in conclave. He with a pint in a glass with a handle. Her with a half-pint in a glass with a handle. A nice touch that, Miss Eaves thinks. There are Mary Bonfield from school with her husband, Leonard, waiting to be served. And at the end of the bar, reaching out to pay, and incidentally neatly taking the eye back into the crowd, is Mr Haywood from the Chip Shop. Now that's a bit of a surprise, but his wife insists. It's the one evening of the year when she disguises the smell of cod with Chanel No.5 – no way she would use Devon Violets tonight – and manages to drag her hubby out. That is the bar. Miss Eaves has almost reached stage right. Here the dance floor curves out towards the foreground filled with pairs and posses of partying people waiting for the band to strike up again. Miss Hilton who is in the play as "Mrs Gibbs", is with Mrs Keeley from the Royal Hotel. Both are wondering why the men they came with are taking so long getting drinks in. Mrs Trent is in civvies tonight and is eager to be whisked on to the dance floor by Tom. They've only recently arrived and mean to get their money's worth. The babysitter was late. Then there's a scrum of people and half-people struggling to get on or get off the canvas, in front of all of them is Mrs Mavis Jackson, the Prettiest Grandmother, who is not about to let go of Harold Newcombe's arm now she has it. They're going to dance together, and more than once.

Another moment flips over, a miniature date on a calendar, and on cue, maybe directed by the musings of Charles Burch, who has been plotting a troublesome scene in "Our Town" in his head, everyone responds. "Action," they hear, and act they do.

'Sorry!'

'Sorry!'

'I was miles away. Sorry. What did you say?'

'Nothing. Nothing at all. Sorry.' Miss Eaves dips into her drink. The glacé cherry lies speared on its stick, waiting. It really is the nicest thing about drinking.

'I was....' they both say and clam up straight away. Charles calls "Cut" silently. This scene really won't do.

Miss Eaves realises she's being a Bennett, a Jane Austen figure, and doesn't care for it at all.

But Charles gives her no time to flick through her archives and come up with someone more her. 'After you, Miss Eaves.' And Charles pauses a lengthy pause.

Miss Eaves notices her empty glass and puts it carefully down. 'Well, Mr Burch,...'

'Do call me Charles, Miss Eaves.'

'Linda.' And she smiles.

'Do go on, Linda.'

'I was just going to observe that there are moments when Life, yes, even Dawlish Life, seems, only for a moment you understand, to mimic Art.' She holds her breath, waiting to be damned.

'Linda.' Her blood has surely stopped. 'How right you are! You'll never credit it, but I was thinking something not very different myself.'

'You were?' He nods. 'Well, I never did!' Her beads rattle as her lungs refill. 'And there was I thinking I was the only one who ever has such thoughts.' She picks up the stick and pops the cherry in. Perfect.

'Really, Linda, I've heard it often said that Art holds a mirror up to Life, but I incline to the opinion that Life when lived in truth and honesty and goodness is Art, or at least an art. It's that that I've been struggling with.'

Miss Eaves wonders if Mr Burch is talking Religion, because if he is, then she might be going to have a bit of a problem, which would be a pity all things said and done.

Charles picks up on Miss Eaves' unease. 'In the play,' he emphasises. 'I've really been finding it hard to get across to the cast that Art is not necessarily about action with a capital A.'

Miss Eaves agrees, pleased to learn that Religion is not the subject. 'Yes. Or that Life is Action, either.' Charles wants to agree, even though Miss Eaves has foxed him. She goes on. 'So many people poo-pooh common-or-garden everyday things and praise the Man of Action, don't you find? It's all very well, but where would we be if we were all Winston Churchills? For one thing, who'd deliver the milk? Answer me that.'

Charles is about to do no such thing. 'Acting is seen by so many people to be the activity of being busy. Of being theatrically busy. Of being entertainingly busy. Whereas, it's really about the demonstration of truth.'

'Like Life,' Miss Eaves adds, satisfied that she is keeping up.

'And truth can be so simple…'

'Just like Life.' She's got the hang of this.

'Yet when it's simple, why should it be so difficult?'

That jars. 'Difficult?' Miss Eaves savours the word, not committing herself to ignorance.

'You'd have thought that simple truths would be the easiest to demonstrate; that acting simply would in effect be simple. But no.' A pause lengthens. Nobody is in hailing distance. Everyone is busy. 'Let me get you a drink, Linda.' Charles gets to his feet. 'Sweet martini?' He is off towards the bar whether she wants one or not. Miss Eaves is left hoping that Charles will think to ask for a cherry.

*

The Councillors are not to be dragged away from their pillar and their debate.

'We're going to have to do something.' Mr Stephens will not relent.

Nor will Mr Lowe. 'Doing something will cost.'

'Doing nothing will cost, too.'

'I'm talking a penny or maybe tuppence on the rates.'

'I'm not talking money.'

'That's all very well, but we have to live in the real world. And in the real world money is always the main consideration.'

'We might not be talking money, but certainly money talks.' Mr Drummond likes the well-turned phrases of the "Daily Mail".

'Surely you see that with the Shaftesbury Hall there could be a Junior Repertory Company for instance, to provide a continuing flow of talent to bridge those awkward years between school and some degree of maturity?'

Attention has slipped away from Mr Stephens, and around the dance floor conversations have quietened for even the non-dancers at the Dance have picked up on a musical change. The seamless chain of tunes to waltz and foxtrot to has made way for something rarely heard at Dairy Festival Dances. On "Come Dancing", yes, but not here at the Landsdowne Cliff Hotel. The Sylvan Dance Band has – maybe only for a short time – headed down Mexico way! Or even further south to Argentina. With a sense of fun perhaps fuelled by the pints Harold has been providing them the Band has fired up the sultry strains of tango much to the disbelief of many and the delight of a few.

Harold approaches Dierdre. They smile. She laughs. He leads her out into the space, holds her close, wraps his right arm around her, pulling her even closer. Married men watching become anxious. Married women suppress sighs. Dancing cheek to cheek Harold and Dierdre flick and turn, crossing and re-crossing, alone together.

But not alone entirely.

Other hands lead other hands, bringing partners from their tables, from the bar, from the watching crowd, none more shocked than Miss Eaves and Josephine to find themselves on the move. None more surprised by their nerve than Charles and Hugh.

The band plays and couples tango. More than could be expected. With some reserve, of course. Palms find themselves placed in unfamiliar places.

Feet try hard not to kick or trip. There is concentration. There is fun.

Charles is no longer "The Ice King", but instead in his

imagination dressed in a suit of lights, in silk and satin, richly beaded and embroidered in gold and silver. Not the accounts manager he is by day, but the matador he saw last year on holiday in Valencia.

Hugh is no longer the apprentice draughtsman with ink-stained fingers, but instead a speed merchant, a Stirling Moss driving his Aston Martin, taking every corner at maximum speed, roaring to victory.

Josephine and Miss Eaves are beyond knowing who or what they are, other than bubbling with something called happiness.

Mrs Lowe has not found herself a partner on this occasion, but then she has not been looking. She has found a spot from which to watch. She is not in this particular moment but instead back at a dance in 1944 weeks before D-Day when along with best friends, Ruby and Peggy, they had jived with Americans, who had thrown them about, sending them flying with no fear of falling. Everyone was alive. Mrs Lowe has not thought of any of this in years.

*

'Well, I never did. And that is so true in more ways than one. I never knew you had it in you, Charles. And I've most certainly never had it myself. The tango, I mean. As for your partner, well, Miss Eaves, you really should dance more often. You looked to be in your real element out there.'

'Thank you, Vicar.'

'Linda and I were talking about Life and Action and, well, when the music began it just seemed right to put them together and Act! And we did, didn't we, Linda?'

'We did.'

'You most certainly did. Both of you.' The Vicar glances away and catches sight of Mrs Lowe. 'Excuse me, won't you? I feel a dance coming on.'

'I feel we deserve some refreshment, don't you, Linda?' She smiles. 'Another martini?'

After the slightest of pauses, 'Why not?'

'That's the spirit.'

Miss Eaves watches Charles Burch head towards the bar, engaging with others on his way. She has never ever been called Linda so often in such a short space of time and in public. She is glowing.

*

Out on the dance floor the Vicar and Mrs Lowe are foxtrotting.

'Not quite a tango, Mrs Lowe, but it's as much as I can do.'

'You never know, Vicar, you might have a tango in you. If you looked.'

After a brief thoughtful pause the Vicar smiles. 'I suppose we all may have a tango in us. That is indeed something to think about. I wonder if I could take that as a theme for a sermon. What do you think, Mrs Lowe?'

'I for one would hang on your every word, Vicar.'

*

Josephine has not let go of Hugh since the Sylvan Dance Band brought the tango to its glorious conclusion. Her right arm is linked through his left leaving his right free to raise his pint and when not taking a drink free to make expansive gestures.

'It couldn't have rained more if it had tried, could it Josephine?' But Hugh goes straight on, knowing that she will agree, now more than ever. 'Talk about bitter, too. And the fields, it was like those pictures of the trenches back in the First World War. Yet, in spite of it all, in spite of everything that the mindless lackeys of the Tory Press printed, there were five thousand of us all marching together, united. Marching those last few miles to Aldermaston in complete silence.' Josephine is nodding, but also feeling on the brink of tears at the same time. Her day could not get better.

'You could hear the rain and feel the spirit. It didn't matter that the weather was the worst it had been for forty years. Nothing mattered besides the fact that we were telling the World exactly where we stood. We were telling them that this madness has to stop.' Hugh plonks his glass down on the bar for effect. 'And it damn well will!

'We've only just begun, Mary, Leonard.' Hugh underlines the names. 'Believe me, we've only just begun. If they won't listen to us; if they think they can just ignore us and we'll go away, they are deluding themselves. I mean, who do they think they are? It's not their world for them to do what they like with. It's Our World. But if we let them carry on going over our heads, then there won't be any world at all – Theirs or Ours!'

'I see.' Mary comes up for air.

'Of course, you see, Mary. Any sensible person can't help but see. It's as clear as day to any person blessed with any degree of common sense; and that's 99 percent of humanity. It's just that the other one percent, the criminally insane and the mindless idiots are not safely locked away in asylums. Oh, no. Somehow or other they've got hold of the keys and got themselves into Whitehall, or the White House or the Kremlin for that matter, and they've got the run of those places.

'Now maybe in the normal way of things that wouldn't matter. As long as we know where the psychopaths are we can breathe more easily. But now, the ground rules have changed. Now all it takes is for one of the lunatics to press the red button and "Farewell Humanity! Hello Doomsday!" '

Hugh's torrent has forced both Mary and Leonard back against the bar where as one they pick up their drinks which they sorely need.

Josephine's admiration for Hugh has doubled and redoubled and shows every sign of trebling. She must be dreaming. How can she have Hugh as her boyfriend? Thinking about calling Hugh that, if only silently, causes all sorts of emotions to spark. As a result her heart is in every danger of blazing.

*

'Mr Newcombe, you and your wife, where did you learn to dance like that? Your tango was something very special.'

'Should you and Mary here want some tips, Dierdre and I would be happy to give you some pointers. Say, a session one day after school?'

Leonard Bonfield, though not moving, is backing away at speed. Mary steps in before he actually flees. 'Thank you, Mr Newcombe, but getting Leonard waltzing is as much as I can expect.'

Leonard Bonfield breathes a little more calmly, offers to get drinks in if that is acceptable, which it is, and exits for the bar, leaving Harold and Mary to share a knowing smile.

'I realise it's not the done thing to talk shop at these dos,' and Harold Newcombe dons his hat of Headmaster. 'I am wondering how everything is going with regard to the Stonehenge trip. We really don't want a repeat performance of last year, do we? In hindsight I can see the funny side, but it wasn't a laughing matter at the time, was it? Leaving a child behind might be considered almost par for the course, but returning with one more than we took with us took a great deal of explaining.' There is a pause while both remember that unbelievable moment when, counting children off the coach, the stowaway was discovered.

'Before last year there had never been more than us there in all the years we have been going. Fingers crossed that we have Stonehenge to ourselves again.'

'That would be ideal, Mary. Then all we have to do is not lose one of ours,' Mr Newcombe points out and both teachers nod. A fresh drink would now be most welcome, but Leonard can be seen in conversation.

'Who is your husband talking to? The young man in the corduroy jacket.'

'That's Hugh Dinsdale. A former pupil of ours.'

'Hugh Dinsdale? Am I right in recalling a rather quiet, serious lad, father a butcher?' Mary nods. 'He's grown up to become far more outgoing it appears.'

'A very committed pacifist and advocate for CND. Not to mention having a talent for the tango.'

'It is rewarding to see a child flourish in adulthood.' Harold recalls how hard it was to get a peep out of Hugh in class. 'He certainly seems to have discovered his voice.'

*

'But he was ever so good. So musical. Everyone said that. It would raise the cultural tone of the Summer Shows no end.' Rita Gordon hiccoughs before going on, 'It's just so unfair, Mrs Harvey. We must get a petition together to make those fools on the Entertainments Committee see sense.' Rita splashes the drink in her glass.

Naturally Mrs Harvey smiles. 'He was that good, you say?'

'Absublotely!' Rita briefly doubts herself.

*

'Mrs Lowe,' Mrs Brewster takes her arm. 'Mrs Lowe, you remember C.A.W.G, don't you? The Christian Alliance of Women and Girls?' Mrs Lowe shows that she does. 'I've been trying to tell Mrs Newcombe here...' And Dierdre Newcombe steps out from behind Mrs Brewster's large floral print, '... that the idea of using the Shaftesbury Hall, "Our Room" as it was called, goes counter to all that worthy organisation stood for.'

'Isn't it rather small, Mrs Brewster?'

'That is not my point, Mrs Lowe.'

'No, Mrs Brewster, but it is mine.'

'Mrs Lowe, you can't possibly be saying that you would accept the performance in "Our Room" of pantomimes with all their distinctly crude humour.'

'I am saying that the Hall is so small that there is no danger whatsoever of any pantomime, crude or not, being performed there. I have fond memories of cheering on the goodies and booing the villains over the years which might surprise you, Mrs Brewster, but you can rest assured that there will be no restaging of the shipwreck scene in "Dick Whittington" at the Shaftesbury Hall.'

'More's the pity,' chips in Dierdre Newcombe. 'Both my boys loved being pirates.'

'Is it true that someone from the Theatre Royal in Exeter came backstage to see how the shipwreck was handled?' The Vicar has a thing about legitimate theatre.

'Indeed they did, Vicar.' Mrs Lowe turns back to Mrs Brewster. 'So Mrs Brewster, if your complaint is against pantomimes and musical comedies, you could do no better than support the proposed use of the Shaftesbury Hall as a theatre. That would be a surefire way of seeing the end of them in the town, in the light of the wretched state of The Hut. And to echo Mrs Newcombe here, more's the pity.'

*

Harold Newcombe gives himself a moment to savour the scene. The glitter ball turns and turns, flashing its signals in shattered morse code, scattering its sparkles across the faces of the dancing partners. They twinkle by, dipping into the dark, wheeling away the evening, flickering as briefly as so many thoughts. Harold receives another signal from the pianist which he acknowledges. The Sylvan Dance Band beams, sending up its music in clouds to drift. Music and cigarette smoke and coloured lights and chatter. Couples circle the floor. A human carousel. Up and Down. Up and Down. Round and round and round.

Harold weaves his way to the bar once more overhearing scraps and oddments of conversation as he goes. Once there and having given the barman the band's final order he gives

Councillor Lowe the nod. 'Ten minutes.' Councillor Lowe raises his glass to confirm the message is received and understood.

*

After a roll on the drums and a cymbal crash; 'Ladies and Gentlemen, if I could have your attention, please.' Standing as he is in front of the band, Harold Newcombe might well be wondering about breaking into song. Something by Perry Como? How about his latest, "Magic Moments"? But, no. Mr Lowe is edging towards the stage. A small paper is being popped back into his top pocket, and he's checking that all the flaps on his jacket are out.

*

It takes Mr Lowe a few moments to climb the steps and reach centre stage. Looking out he sees his council colleagues are still standing close to the pillar where they have spent much of the evening. Though nothing has been decided, the fate of The Hut has been aired. It now really needs to be resolved.

In the crowd looking stagewards Mr Lowe sees nothing but smiles.

The vision of an all-walking Thor missile is striding across Hugh Dinsdale's inner eye. Josephine hangs on his arm so happily.

Miss Eaves, Linda, toys with her beads and with an idea she is already wrapping in tissue paper to keep it safe. Charles, quite unaware of being so cosseted feels that maybe, just maybe, he can see a way to bring natural simplicity and Art together. He's actually looking forward to the next rehearsal.

And Mrs Brewster smiles, too. She now sees those hideously common pantomimes are as good as over and done with.

*

Having delivered a long list of thanks Mr Lowe steps back to lead the applause for Councillor Holman and the Entertainments Committee's sterling work getting the Dance to be the roaring success it has been. And while Harold Newcombe has a quiet word in the pianist's ear and some people edge away from the back of the crowd to get to the bar for one final drink, the glitter ball still twinkles.

*

'Allow me.' Harold offers his arm and leads Dierdre off in a slow foxtrot.

Conversations surge. Laughter blooms. Hands reach for hands and tug them towards the dance floor just once more. There's really so little time left.

***

TUESDAY MORNING, JUNE 10th

'The Army Game'

Conscripts in the Army are determined to dodge duty and derive maximum fun out of every situation. – ITV

With rubber gloves on Eric Dring releases the catch on the pantry door. It drops with a click and he freezes. In the crack-of-dawn hush the blood in his ears drums a tattoo.

He carries the dish gingerly out to the table and sets it down. Then he remembers to breathe. From his dressing gown pocket he draws the small brown bottle and a pencil. For a moment the kitchen blurs. Eric steadies himself with a damp hand on a chairback. Military Service hadn't prepared him for anything like this.

The kitchen comes back into focus. Here is the last serving of Shepherd's Pie, made from the leftovers of Sunday's joint. A Last Supper, and Eric smirks.

A blackbird in the lilac tree outside the kitchen window announces the unscrewing of the small bottle, and trills as a trickle of green-brown crystals scatter on to the pie. There they lie like measles, till with the tip of the pencil Eric nudges them out of sight. "Out of sight, out of mind", thinks Eric and he chuckles way down deep. Mabel will never know until it is too late.

Eric returns the dish to the pantry shelf, adjusting it with a window dresser's eye, and shuts the door, quietly. He recaps the bottle, slips it back into his pocket and removes the rubber gloves which he puts back by the sink. He wipes the pencil on the edge of the coconut mat and puts it in his pocket.

When it comes down to it Eric can teach those SAS types a thing or two. He gives the kitchen the once-over. Everything is as he found it, so he leaves.

Early morning light is grey back in the bedroom. Back in his bed there is an echo of body warmth. The alarm clock ticks smugly. 4:28am. In her bed Mabel lies as still as a corpse. Eric grins.

*

'Ask Me Another'
General knowledge contest – BBC TV

The blackbird from the lilac tree takes wing, lifting up and over the house heading towards town from the back garden where the lilac grows, its blooms already turning brown.

The centre of town might seem deserted. Of course there is no-one about, but the shrubberies and trees flanking The Lawn and along The Brook are filled with the calls of birds. Some warn of approaching cats. Cats who swear at their discovery. Cats who melt through the bushes. Cats who twitch the tips of their tails at the smell of feather and the tell-tale cheeps of nests still full of fledglings. The heart of the town is alive. The prospect of quick and skilful death is in the air.

Bluebell opens his eyes, unsure as he often is. The hardness of the slatted bench and the angle of the panelled roof place him. Both belong to a shelter on The Lawn. He doesn't want to move. The bench is hard, but his body has numbed to the aches. To shift position now would stir them up.

He lies still under a mound of newspaper; newsaper from the stash kept out of sight in dry hidey-holes about the town. The day is lightening and soon enough he'll be disturbed. So he stays, savouring the peace and the birdsong and the flight of seagulls that pass overhead.

He groans. He tries to ignore the message. He closes his eyes tightly willing it to go away, but the message is repeated. He swears, 'Bleeding typical.' Even though he knows he is quite alone he swears quietly. He doesn't swear a lot, in spite of appearances.

Even at this time of day, with a dew on the ground, the newspapers crackle as Bluebell shoves them off. The true value of quality broadsheets. He heads for a shrubbery.

The sudden scurry of a cat causes him to splash his boots. If he had a hand free, he'd lob something. He doesn't like cats, and they're not fond of him. The steady stream steams between the bushes. He never does it in flower beds. He has standards. He knows how small children can't resist picking the scarlet salvias or the heavy-scented stocks.

The sun is turning the sky the colour of clotted cream. Bluebell readjusts various layers before rebuttoning his heavy blue-grey-black-brown coat. He backs out of the bushes, scuffs loose earth from his boots and slowly straightens up, testing the nameless bits of his creaky skeleton. A raucous cough erupting from the depths rattles him, making his head ring with a flash of headache, and silencing the birds.

Bluebell looks back at the bench, but there is no way he's going to get another kip. It'd be much better to go find a doorstep where the milkman has already been.

Bluebell is crossing the length of The Lawn heading in the direction of the Bandstand when he comes across the first curved line on the hard standing. Focussed on reaching the doorsteps of Brunswick before the milk bottles are taken in he crosses the line without really noticing it. It's when the second line curves into view under his boots that he stops and turns. The first and the second are linked. The joined chalk-white line trails in a double sweep first to the right, then when he turns again, to the left. He looks further off to see other markings. Moving to them, they remind him of a TV aerial, almost a giant aitch. Beyond that the hard surface stretches blank grey.

It is too early in the day to think. Besides, that bottle of milk needs to be tracked down. Bluebell just notes the white lines, turns and heads off towards a footbridge that will take him across The Brook to Brunswick.

He does not get far. Not far at all. Another pattern, an outsized V for Victory, but with a cross-bar, now passes under his boots. He catches himself stringing the shapes together. The H. The S. The almost V. His brain has woken up and he walks on. Next comes a pair of pyramids, or an M. An idea is triggered. It has to be a message.

Bluebell looks around believing someone must be looking, but no-one is about to step forward with the explanation. He scrawls the letters on his inner eye. Furthest away was the H followed by the S. Then the V that isn't quite a V. That niggles. He shuffles back to the letter in question to give it another look.

Light dawns. He turns and sees the letter for what it really is, an A! He's been reading the darned thing upside-down. Not H, S, V, but A, S, H.

Bluebell stands for a while warmed by the feeling of satisfaction.Then, he recalls the M further away. He clumps over to it, knowing it for what it will be before he gets there. There is more satisfaction. It is indeed a W. So not ASH but WASH, which as he walks on becomes EWASH, then TEWASH, ITEWASH, HITEWASH, WHITEWASH.

Time for the milk.

*

'Cookery Club' chosen by Marguerite Patten
Including liver ragout, caramel of eggs, nut roulade and unbaked coffee marshmallow – The Light Programme

Mabel Dring is sitting on the side of her bed, slipping her feet into her mules. She throws a look at the lump that is her husband in the other bed, pulls her dressing gown from the foot of her bed and begins to hum "*Je ne regrette rien*", though she has one major proviso.

The curtains run back, the hooks sticking where they always

stick. Mabel hums a little louder and yanks them apart. Sparrows are chirruping in the guttering, and Mabel pads out of the bedroom, pulling the door to with no regard for her husband.

Eric rolls over on to his back. He still has ten minutes before he has to move, but he wants to catapult out of bed. He forces himself to lie there, flicking looks at the alarm clock. A look when he hears the toilet flush. A look when he hears the letterbox go. A look when the first sub-aqua sounds of the wireless drift upstairs.

Hovering before his mind's eye is the Shepherd's Pie – the Shepherd's Pie with the "little something extra" – ticking away, a bomb waiting to… Eric jack-knifes in alarm when the clock goes off. His hand flashes to silence it and he lies back, grinning from ear to ear. "Is everyone sitting comfortably?" the sing-song sings in his head. "Then it's time to begin."

Flinging back the covers Eric is up and out the bedroom door as if it is a Saturday in August, not a Tuesday in June.

*

As he fixes his bicycle clips Eric hears Mabel crooning.

'Oo's a lickle diddums den? Oo's Mummy's wicked naughty lickle boy? You are. You are you know.' Eric can't be sure who is nuzzling who. 'I could love oo to deaf!' Eric pauses. The Shepherd's Pie hovers again – a UFO.

On his way to the shed he has to, he just has to do it – a step better executed by Gene Kelly, but never with more heartfelt pzazz. Out of sight he leaps as high as a teacher of arithmetic can, and kicks as high as a painter of toy soldiery can be expected to be able, spurred by the knowledge of a Plan in Action.

As Eric wheels his bike from the shed, Mabel clears the breakfast table.

' "Keep young and beautiful. It's your duty to be beautiful. Keep young and beautiful, if you want to be loved." She sings while Dickie waits for anything that might come his way.

Eric cycles away down Oak Hill, his adrenalin pumping.

*

'Counterspy'

*Security Officers Greg Vaughan and 'Rocky' Mountain in their
latest assignment, 'The Chandos Affair'* – The Home Service

Bluebell has come back from Brunswick and is watching the
comings and goings of various Suits and Ties from his bench.
He's already folded his paper in case he'll have to move on
sharpish. With these Official Types around it won't be long before
one of them takes exception to him being here. Not that he's
particularly niffy. He makes a point of keeping himself clean, just
like he makes a point of having a sense of humour and a dry place
for his papers. They'll move him because there won't be much
else for them to do. Once they've seen the writing from all angles;
once it's been measured and a sample has been taken for testing;
once they've ummed and aahed, and have taken all their photos,
there won't be much else left but move Bluebell on.

As for the testing Bluebell could tell them not to bother. He
could tell them – if they thought to ask - it's that thick chalky
liquid they use to mark out things like tennis courts. He could tell
them this because he had heard a clanking noise during the night
and yesterday council workers had made their accustomed early
start marking out the pitches for the stalls and stands in the
Carnival Fair some weeks hence. So it doesn't take the brains of
an Einstein to put two and two together.

The Suits and Ties stare at the message a while longer. It is
time to call in the council workers to Do Something; to wash and
scrape, maybe scrub like Mrs Mopp. Bluebell grins at the thought
and at the knowledge that these Official Types along with the
Coppers haven't got the foggiest what it all means:
"WHITEWASH".

'It could mean what it says, couldn't it?' The young man toting a clipboard stands clicking his biro.

'Is that supposed to be helpful?' The older man has turned his back on the whole thing and is rummaging for something in his coat pocket, patience maybe.

'It's white and it looks like whitewash, so maybe that's all it is.'

'If you've got something worth saying, say it.'

'I'm just suggesting that the thing doesn't mean anything at all. It says whitewash, because that's exactly what it is. Whitewash.'

"Is that what we pay our rates for?" thinks the police constable who's been told to stay until told otherwise, in spite of the fact that it is way past the end of his shift.

The older Suit and Tie is finding his search fruitless. He stubs out his cigarette. 'If that's all you've got to offer, I'd best go and report to Councillor Lowe. He'll want to know.' The young man doubts he will. 'And, constable, if you've got nothing better to do, do something about that.'

Bluebell has been proved right again. He is already stacking his arms with papers before the constable has moved.

*

| **'Parents and Children'** – Network Three |

'For goodness sake, Amanda, get a move on. It's almost half-past. You're going to be late.' Mrs Clark is collecting the milk from the front doorstep. 'Did you hear me?'

The sound of running water in the bathroom stops. The bathroom door opens and Amanda makes an entrance, preparing to walk to the gallows. She clumps downstairs, each tread a muffled drum beat.

'What is the matter with you?' Her mother is now rubbing the banister with her pinny. 'What's got into you? Don't tell me you're sickening for something?'

She feels Amanda's forehead. Amanda stands unprotesting until whatever her mother intends to do with her is done.

'Let's see your tongue.' Amanda pushes it out. Mrs Clark feels the glands at her throat. 'Have you got an arithmetic test today?' Amanda shakes her head. 'Well, whatever it is, shake yourself out of it. I can't stand around all day while you play half-dead.' She glances at her watch. 'Now, look at the time. Here's your satchel. Oh, and hang on a sec.' Amanda remains rooted on the last stair. 'Here. Eat it on the way.' Amanda takes the toast. It is now or never.

'Mum.' Nothing more.

'Well, what is it?'

'I was wondering.' Amanda's toes peek over the last stair's lip, ready to dive.

'Out with it. I haven't got all day.'

Amanda steps off. 'Could I have pilchards for tea?' She clamps her throat shut as the floor jams up against her feet.

'Pilchards? Pilchards for tea?' Amanda manages a nod. Mrs Clark wrings her pinny. 'Is that all? Pilchards you want. Pilchards you can have. Now, be off with you.' She flicks a lick of hair out of Amanda's eyes and bundles her out of the house.

St Amanda, Martyr to Terpsichore, drifts off to school. Her last day on Earth may prove to be a very long one.

*

'Mainly for Women'
'Just Your Size' – fashion for the fuller figure – BBC TV

Mabel hurries to shut the dining room door. 'Now stay there, Dickie, it's all alright. There's nothing for you to worry about.' She checks her hair in the hallstand mirror.

Mrs Rudge is standing with her case before her when Mabel comes into the front room. 'Please, Mrs Rudge, have a seat. Would you like a cup of coffee? It's instant.'

'That's very kind, Mrs Dring, but I find that foundation garments and refreshments don't mix. One's hands are so often occupied, if you get my drift.'

Mabel poses herself on the edge of an armchair. Mrs Rudge tucks her case to the side of her armchair and looks around the flawlessly neat room. At this point the training manual advises expressing warm regard for some item of décor or furnishing in order to create the correct atmosphere for the Consultation. Yet there is really so little in the room to remark upon; the chunky three piece suite, a cane-seated stool, a wall mirror, a spider plant dead centre on the window ledge, a mantel clock with a pair of dark wood candlesticks and a family group of china dogs, and that is about it. 'This room is so tasteful, Mrs Dring. It tells me you are an artistic person who likes balance. Did you do it yourself? Such a clever use of colour.'

Mabel looks around the room uncertain what Mrs Rudge sees that she doesn't. 'My husband is the one with the paint and brush.' She pulls her hem down over her knees.

'That's as maybe, Mrs Dring, but what do men really know about colour schemes? If they had their way we'd all still be in shades of brown and dark varnish. And would there be pelmets? I hardly think so.' Mrs Rudge smiles conspiratorially. Mabel smiles back her public smile. 'When I think of the years we had to put up with all that drabness.' Mrs Rudge's eyebrows are encouraging Mabel to commit herself, but she waits in vain. Mabel is finding it hard enough not to laugh. Not at Mrs Rudge. No. She is just picturing herself in the Grosgrain skirt if only Mrs Rudge would get on with it. 'And the china dogs are so cute. Is yours a spaniel?'

'Dickie's a dachshund.'

'Aah!' Mrs Rudge sounds as if she couldn't keep from

hugging him if he was there. 'Such little gentlemen, aren't they? Dachshunds.'

Ice, if not broken, has melted to a degree.

'Now Mrs Dring, we could either draw the curtains or maybe adjourn to your bedroom. Whichever is more convenient.' Mabel scampers to pull the curtains to. 'Now if I may turn on the light,' and this Mrs Rudge promptly does, 'we can see how Spencer can be of service to you, Mrs Dring.'

From her case Mrs Rudge produces a notepad and pencil and soon discovers what it is that Mabel needs. The why is not forthcoming. It isn't necessary. Mrs Rudge knows about the trip to France. She won a casserole dish in the draw herself.

Mrs Rudge sits nursing the Spencer Modelling Garment. 'With its many lacings and its hook and eye adjustments it may look rather complicated, but it is the proven way to get the most exact measurements, Mrs Dring. All that remains is for you to slip out of what you are wearing and we can begin.'

Mrs Rudge, a woman of the most repressive respectability, all but levers Mabel out of her clothes and into the Modelling Garment with a look. She adjusts laces. She smoothes panels. 'Take an uplifting breath, Mrs Dring.'

Mrs Rudge begins one or two eyelets above the holding knot to take up the slack to the pull-loop. 'Do you feel that grip around the pelvis, Mrs Dring?' Mabel does indeed feel that grip as Mrs Rudge pulls the garment well down to aid in the anchorage. Mabel cannot imagine where her flesh is going.

'There now,' Mrs Rudge says stepping back to admire her handiwork.

Mabel expects to see beads of sweat and at least one loop of hair out of place, but no, Mrs Rudge won't allow herself to show anything as common as the effects of strain.

Mabel stands, an unfamiliar figure in her own front room.

'See how it bends in all directions, Mrs Dring.'

Mabel ventures to lean and is surprised that she can move and breathe at the same time. She feels rather like the lid of a kettle drum, and she is uncertain how far she can trust the stays. She wonders if they might suddenly spring on her, skewering her in a hundred ways. A gruesome image of an Indian on a bed of nails comes to her.

'The elastic is thoroughly resilient, Mrs Dring.' Mabel has no doubt that it is. 'How do you feel?'

Mabel doesn't want to put her feelings into words. If someone tapped her, she'd ring like a bell, she might say, or possibly something far less musical. It is then that the suggestion of an itch teeters on the brink of revealing itself embarrassingly, in a place of unspeakable inaccessibility.

'I'm going to have to think about it, Mrs Rudge.' Mabel begins to finger one of the laces.

Mrs Rudge makes no move to assist Mabel. 'You can have the 204 in pink, cream or white, full-length or mid-length with cutaways.' She presents Mabel with a picture of some sylph in a mid-length 204.

Mabel's fingers are those of an infant struggling to tie its shoes. Panic is not that far away, spurred on by the itch which is nearing all the time. 'I really am going to have to think about it, Mrs Rudge, and let you know later. But now...' and she searches for a suitable lie, 'I must hurry to get my husband's lunch. If it's not on the table when he comes in, there'll be no point in having a corset. Corpses don't need them.'

Mrs Rudge realises that though Mrs Dring has not committed herself to a selection of material and style, she'll have to release her. Whatever the manual says to the contrary, there comes a time when the consultant must use her discretion.

Mabel becomes aware of an easing of tension.

Mrs Rudge is opening laces out of sight. 'There, do you feel your hips spread, Mrs Dring?' Mabel senses the return of flesh from where it had been forced to flee. Mrs Rudge begins to unlace the front. 'Feel that drop of your flesh and organs, Mrs Dring?'

Mabel fears that unseen parts are in danger of landing in an unsightly heap on the carpet. As she hurries to cover her oh-so-white body in her still-warm clothes, Mrs Rudge goes on, 'That comfort and support you felt, Mrs Dring, is assured with the 204. In either pink or white it would bring you all the confidence you might wish for.'

Mabel nearly tears the curtains off their rail in her desire to let some light in, and, if possible, drive away The Corsetiere.

Pleasantries between the two women cover the next few minutes, an exchange to mask silence.

Mabel leads the way along the hallway, into the kitchen. She had explained to Mrs Rudge when she had made the appointment over the phone about the need to use the back door and had no intention of referring to it again.

'I hope you manage to get your front door sorted soon, Mrs Dring.'

And Mabel closes the back door having offered a thin smile and a 'Me, too.' She waits awhile facing the door, thankful to hear the sound of Mrs Rudge's footsteps walking away.

*

'Mainly for Women'
'Keep Fit' with Eileen Fowler – BBC TV

The ash on her third cigarette snakes like a pipe cleaner. Mabel taps it into her hand before it can drop. She gives the roller towel on the back of the kitchen door a long stare, then grinds out the cigarette and rubs at the nicotine stains. She'll have to pumice her fingers well before getting on the boat to France. The tune of "*Sur le Pont d'Avignon*" refrains, but in a desultory fashion. It fades out completely by the end of the second line.

'Nothing but flab,' she tells the kitchen what it probably already knows. Mabel pictures Eric sitting here troughing away for all he is worth, stuffing his face and never putting a pound on. He could still get into his demob suit if he had a mind to.

'Look at me, Dickie. Just look at me.' He does so with liquid eyes. 'No, don't! How can you love your fat, flabby Mummy? How can you? My boobs droop. My spare tyre's got a spare tyre.' She pats her chins. 'And just take a shufti at this.' She raises a large arm and shakes it. 'With muscles like these I could take on Brian London. I mean, have you ever in all your life seen wings like these?' She clenches her fist. Her bicep swells. 'It's not fair.' From many years ago Mavis Whittaker's face presents itself – the same blurred image as always. As always it is slipping.

Mabel thumps the table hard and Dickie backs away. 'It's never been fair. Life's always dealt me the bum cards.'

Mabel's size dominated whole albums of childhood snaps. From bonny babe to chubby infant to big-for-her-age child to podgy girl. She grinned happily in the early photographs, on days out, or wrapped up well for wintry expeditions in the woods, like a barrage balloon.

But more and more as the years passed she slid to the edges of snaps. She could move at speed over short distances, especially when the Box Brownie came out. She was often the palest pink blob half-off and smudged. More than once her presence on a photo had gone unnoticed, quite a feat for someone of her girth. That is not to say that she was invisible. Far from it. Just that she was not seen for who or what she was. Auntie Alice had been the first to say something like: "Lovely photo. Shame you got your thumb in the way, though." Of course, Mabel had been that thumb.

After about the age of ten Mabel's increase went unrecorded. She was then big enough to throw her considerable weight about, which she could do with remarkable results. She had been instrumental in her father putting two discs out.

Her mother had consulted friends, but without success. It wasn't as if Mabel had a big appetite. After all the War was on. It wasn't possible to have a big appetite. It was simply that anything Mabel did eat seemed to go into immediate store against a time when rations ran out. Her body, counter to all her wishes, had no intention of letting one calorie go to waste. Mabel had mushroomed.

Then, when it had looked as if she might never cease enlarging, much of her fat reshaped itself. Her plump, roly-poly roundness nipped and tucked itself here and there revealing a figure. But, true to the unfairness that ruled Mabel's life, it was not a trim one, nor a fulsome buxom one; not Ann Shelton. Naturally, it was never going to be a Jayne Mansfield either. Mabel's body took the limitless reserves of fat and in little over a year turned it into muscle. What had been pudding was reborn.

It had been inevitable that someone would pay the price. Having been called names since she was old enough to be hurt by name-calling, Mabel had a lot of venom stored up along with what had been fat.

During the spring of her fourteenth year most of her legion of tormentors had the good sense to redirect their cruelty. After all, there were other blimps to be prodded and called Humpty Dumpty. Not to mention the skinny ones, the spotty ones, the smelly ones and the ones who were skinny, spotty and smelly. That it had been Mavis Whittaker who hadn't the wit to lay off had surprised her friends when they had come round ostensibly to console; when Mavis was able to receive visitors that was. They might have tut-tutted and intended to offer sympathetic advice, but the sight of her leg in plaster and her jaw wired shut had pushed wise words out of their heads.

After that, Mabel had been left alone. This had been almost as bad as being ridiculed. At least she had been noticed when she was a blimp. Now that she was a carthorse, and a carthorse that could kick, she was ignored. She dissolved from school rather than left it.

As each week passed between spring and summer Mabel was

at school less and less. She became fourteeen and passed that notable benchmark upstairs at Grannie Nicholson's.

Her Grannie was out at work, doing her bit. It was in her Grannie's back bedroom that Mabel came up with a disguise, or the idea of a disguise. The heavy wardrobe was chock-a-block with outfits. The chest of drawers was stuffed with accessories. Grandad Nicholson had never come back from Ypres, but it hadn't knocked the stuffing out of his wife. Quite the opposite; it had been the making of Grannie. And on Mabel's fourteenth birthday it had a hand in the making of the future Mrs Dring.

Mabel spent that day and many others trying things on, wrapping herself in layers, shoving her hair up inside hats, pulling gloves on over her chewed fingernails, daring herself to inch in front of the mirror to see.

Now from off-stage upstairs in the house on Oak Hill all these years later, an outfit calls. Mabel pushes back her chair and takes herself up to the bedroom, knowing what she will find hidden carefully away, but needing to see it all the same. Dickie shadows her to the foot of the stairs, and settles.

The Grosgrain circular skirt trumpets The Continent. Foreign words, words foreign to Mabel in everyday life, banner in her head. Disque Bleu. Balcony. Cocktail. Couture. Coiffure. Her hand tugs gently at the flesh at her throat, finger and thumb rolling a fold. A shiver runs through her. Sitting on her bed it is as likely she will go to France as fly... Unless. She smoothes the near-silken skirt. She cannot give up on it.

*

'Whack-o!
Weekly school report starring 'Professor' Jimmy Edwards. – BBC TV

Mary Bonfield and Christine Thompson can't help but watch. A forkful of gravy-soaked mush passes into Eric Dring's smiling mouth. Children are still lining up to get theirs.

'What has got into you, Eric?' Mary has seen more than she can take. She raises a spoonful of pudding, then lowers it. 'Eric, did you hear me?' Her spoon unloads itself on to her plate. She gives Christine a quick look. She shrugs unhelpfully. 'Hello. Is there anybody in there?'

Eric's jaws, tongue and gums press and push the mouthful about. An inevitable tray hits the ground by the serving hatch. If anything Eric's smile burns more brightly. It is not nice.

'That's it, Eric! What's going on? What do you know that I don't, but really should do if that look on your face is anything to go by?'

Another forkful is meticulously loaded, a dollop of this and a blob of that welded together with a slap of something that is becoming ever thicker as it cools.

Mary has an awful idea. 'It's Stonehenge, isn't it? You've heard something, haven't you? Somebody has told you something about the trip to Salisbury Plain. What is it, Eric?' She turns to face him full on. 'There is another school party visiting on the same day after all?' Eric continues chewing. 'You've heard that the Army is on manoeuvres. Is that it? They'll be blowing up tanks or going through their game plans for World War Three just when I'm pointing out the standing stones in a gale force wind and driving rain. Hm?'

Eric's knife is steadily sawing through an anchored greyish brown wodge.

'Eric. Is that it? That or something worse.' And something worse than The End of The World brought about by Thor missiles straight way presents itself to Mary. 'Oh, please! You're not telling me that Rita has said she'll go.' She swings on Christine. 'Fifty kids are enough; with their brown paper bags filled with squashed bananas and warm egg sandwiches. But Rita'll be throwing up before we've got out of Dawlish. Little did that poor coach driver know on the trip to Plymouth when he invited Rita to sit behind him at the front.' Christine recalls only too well how that scene played out.

Eric pauses in his final chewing of the morsel he's persuaded to part company from the wodge on his plate. He then focuses on Mary, but instead of quelling her fear he lays knife and fork together and gets up, sliding his chair back under the table and leaves with his tray.

Mary turns to Christine. 'Isn't it bad enough being told that I've only got four minutes warning to get ready for the hereafter...' A Thor missile hoves into view.

Eric's smile is hushing children as he passes.

**

TUESDAY AFTERNOON, JUNE 10th

'The Invisible Man'
'Secret Experiment' - ITV

As Josephine Brooks pushes open the shop door something crashes. She pauses in mid-stride. A single large brown button rolls to meet her. 'Hello? Everything all right?'

'Sorry. Sorry. Just a bit of an accident. Nothing really.'

Josephine picks the button up and comes in.

Grace is on her hands and knees struggling with the button display stand. 'It's not the first time. We are making a bit of a habit of it really, upsetting the button display.'

'Here, let me give you a hand.' Between them they manage to get the stand upright. 'It still looks a bit wobbly if you ask me, Grace. I think it needs its nuts tightening.' Josephine gives the stand a last look, then swings her full attention on Grace, setting her ponytail scything. Her excitement is about to burst out. 'Now, Grace,' She pauses for effect. 'You must have heard!' She now pauses in disbelief. 'Don't tell me you haven't!'

Grace is still focussed on the buttons.

'Leave them, Grace.' Josephine's disbelief swells. 'You haven't heard then? You can't possibly have heard or you wouldn't be able to fiddle around sorting silly buttons.' Josephine stops, letting the tension rise like mercury in a thermometer, finally forcing Grace to attend. 'Direct Action has been taken!' She nods and bobs defying any doubt Grace might be about to expess. 'Yes! Someone, and I'm not at liberty to say who – though, of course, it doesn't take very much for those of us in the know to guess – well, someone, this unknown heroic someone, has made a decisive public statement of the most telling kind.' She now needs to breathe and does so. 'You haven't heard, have you? I cannot believe it!' And Josephine saws the air with her arms, flapping them at the unimaginability of Grace's ignorance.

'You've not the slightest idea what I'm on about? Oh, Grace, it's what we've been waiting for! It's what we've been working towards for months. At last, at long last Dawlish is being made to face up to facts!' Josephine's sense of purpose is palpable.

'As soon as I got wind of what had happened I hot-footed over to do a recce, very low-profile, naturally, There's no need to draw attention to oneself at a time like this. In fact it would be most unwise. I mean the powers that be are running around like so many headless chickens, desperate for answers to all the wrong questions. And they'd home in on the first activist they could find. You know how these types think.'

Grace needs to sit down.

Josephine follows her over to the counter. 'Well, I think it's brilliant. Absolutely brilliant. This enormous message, screaming WHITEWASH to the world. And WE know what that refers to, hm?' She taps her nose. 'WHITEWASH, written all across in front of the Bandstand on The Lawn. Goodness knows how he, or whoever,' she adds quickly, 'managed to do it.' She flushes. 'Oh, Grace, I am so proud. But, Grace, now that you know, though of course I've not said a thing…' and she has to wink, '…you mustn't, on any account, breathe a single solitary word to anyone. Also, whatever you do, don't do anything out of the ordinary. Lord alone knows who'll be brought in to deal with it. It could easily be Special Branch. I wouldn't be surprised to get a visit in the next few days. I mean, my sympathies are well-known locally.

'What's more I bet our meetings are monitored. I don't want to name names, but I've got my suspicions. I'm not convinced that everyone who comes is entirely with us. And, Grace, at times like these if people aren't with us, they're against us.'

Grace is like a cushion that is being sat upon. Everything Josephine says squeezes more and more air out of her. What has she got herself into? And, what is more to the point, why does she feel excited?

'Now, Grace, I can't stay any longer. I've taken a bit of a risk coming here as it is. It's just that I needed to be sure that you knew.' She throws a look at the door, expecting a rush of blue uniforms. 'For the immediate future we'd best not meet. You-Know-Who has already gone to ground, I believe. I tried phoning The Person In Question without luck. It was only afterwards I started wondering if, in the present situation, we can trust telephones. You know what I mean. They do tap them after all. So, Grace, if you need to get a message to me, leave a note for me at the counter at the Library. In a sealed envelope, of course. Now I have to get back to work. We must all go about our normal routine. Saying that, you can give me a set of those blue buttons. They'll do for my duffelcoat.'

A couple of minutes later Miss Brooks, holding a paper bag in front of her, leaves the shop. She has insisted Grace put her purchase in a bag so justifying her visit to anyone who might be watching.

Outside the shop she tries not to look around, but heads off, ponytail swinging, ears peeled for the clanging of a bell on a distant police car - the picture of normality, while deep inside she sees herself swapping stories with Bertrand Russell.

Grace is in need of a coffee. She looks at the clock. Osbert will be back down soon to take over after his lunch. Then she can hand over and go upstairs to have yet another think.

*

| **'Woman's Hour'** |
| *Including 'Keeping a Small Shop'* – The Home Service |

'Good afternoon.' The greeting formula fades. It might be the white crocheted gloves, or the coat or the hat with the brim, or the whole combination, but something doesn't ring true. There is a chink in this customer. And Osbert, his drapery career built on assessing people before the shop bell stops sounding, has already sensed that all is not what it would like to seem. Hands in white crocheted gloves should nip handbags in their fingertips, not throttle them. Osbert moves ever-so-slightly from the counter. 'How can I help you?'

Mabel Dring purposefully scans the shelves behind Osbert's back. He cannot catch her eye, not that he really wants to. One white-gloved hand rises to her cheek. Osbert's Adam's apple jiggles. When, with a frail explosion, Mabel tuts, 'It's silly of me,' Osbert's spine tingles. She peers down into the glass-topped counter cabinet. Here is a person, thinks Osbert, who wouldn't use elastic in her catapults. She'd use catgut. The real McCoy. From cats. Cats caught and gutted by those white-gloved hands of hers. 'I feel so silly.'

This cannot be allowed to go on. 'Can't you see what you're looking for, madam?'

Mabel flickers little looks at Osbert over a half-turned shoulder. 'Oh... Sorry... It's just that... I was wondering if you... Is there Anyone Else?'

'Sorry?' And Osbert is. For himself.

'Sorry. Is your wife in by any chance?... Or, you know, Someone Else?'

'I beg your pardon.'

'Sorry... After all this is 1958.'

Osbert can only agree and wonder if he'll soon be needing a telephone.

'I mean, we can't have any secrets left after that Kinsey Report thing, can we?' And Mabel smiles.

Osbert, who defends his secrets with vigour, feels suddenly very alone.

'So, I suppose I should just go ahead, shouldn't I?' and Mabel ploughs on. 'You see, Mr Phipps, it's like this. She takes a deep breath...'Iwanttoseeoneofthefoundationgarmentsyouhaveondispla yinyourshopwindow. Gosh! There, I've said it. What must you be thinking of me?' He could not have answered.

For the first time Mabel looks at Osbert directly, sending him almost sprinting to the shop window with Mabel close behind.

He slides back the panel before clearing his desert-dry throat. 'Which garment would you care to see?' he asks, addressing himself to the display which blurs before him.

Peeking round Osbert Mabel leans forward. 'That one. If it's not too much bother.'

'No bother at all.' Osbert reaches in, lifts the torso in question out of the display and backs away from the window. He swallows to settle himself. 'As you can see it is a full-length model with reinforced panels at the sides and across the front. Perhaps more a corselette than the traditional corset which some clients find too restricting...' Mabel recalls her sense of gruesome entrapment in the Spencer 204, which had caused her to send Mrs Rudge packing, as Osbert patters on. 'It is lined throughout and fastens in the usual manner. I am assured it is most comfortable affording as it does maximum support without limiting movement.' His blood is pulsing.

'My, but you do know your foundation garments, don't you, Mr Phipps?' Mabel admires. She could be flirting, but if so it is with the genteel skills of a commando in Osbert's nervous opinion.

'Well, madam, I have been selling such garments for quite a few years.' Osbert is keen to reclaim some professional territory.

He adjusts a hook and eye, and manages to trap a flap of flesh. Mabel is about to help, when Osbert jerks himself free.

'I must say it does look very comfy, not too restrictive, but really it's not possible to say without trying it on, is it?'

Osbert's fingers refuse to unfasten the next hook and eye. Instantly horrors assail him. He sees it all. Swinging doors; half-clad figures; consorts and better-halves popping up out of the woodwork – the complete obscenity of farce.

'Do you know Mrs Rudge, Mr Phipps? She's the Spencer Registered Corsetiere.' Mabel fingers a gusset. 'No? I thought you might, being in the same line of business.' She twiddles with a suspender. Osbert holds the translucent pink torso firmly between himself and this woman. 'In strictest confidence I don't think I quite need the full corset.' And once again the memory of the Phantom Itch is rekindled, causing Mabel to shiver.

'You could take it on approval, madam,' Osbert manages to say. 'Then you could try it on in the privacy of your own home.' But before Mabel can reply Osbert's attention is arrested by a squashed tomato against the shop window.

Not so much a tomato, rather a puckering mouth drooling its youthful lust on the glass. Exactly that. John Clark has returned. Rolling eyes. Hands miming the urges of desire.

The scene misses a beat. Cogs temporarily jam leaving Osbert, his right hand in mid-fiddle with yet another hook, while his left uses the torso's chest to get a better purchase; leaving Mabel Dring crushing her compact, comb, spare hankie, safety pins and cigarettes in her strangled handbag; leaving John imagining things he'd do to Brigitte Bardot if only he ever gets the chance. BB or Contestant Number 6.

Time hates freezes. It wants to run. With a swift jolt the cogs re-engage and the scene lurches forwards. Osbert is noticeably the third one to react. Mabel and John dead-heat for the honour of equal first.

Like one of The Furies, Mabel, sheds her meekness in a trice, whoops, and barges her way to the door. A white crocheted glove flops to the floor. The revealed hand flashes palely, nail varnish chipped.

Outside in the street John is rivalling whoever it is who holds the land speed record.

Mabel flings aside the door, crashing the blind and bell. Heads cannot fail but turn as Dame Dring bursts from the shop, rampaging.'YOU DIRTY MINDED SQUIRT!' She clears the pavement like bleach in a toilet bowl.

Osbert hurries outside. Visions of headlines in the local press are bannering themselves. He pulls up short. Mabel Dring swings towards him, fuming. 'FILTHY BEAST!' she misfires, before she can stop herself.

In a trice the buttons of her disguised life are popping, pinging across the pavement. Mabel has exposed herself. Her ungloved hand thrusts itself too late into her coat pocket. It has been revealed. Most certainly it has been seen for the heavy, broad-knuckled, thick-fingered, nicotined thing that it is. As much as it might try to hide itself deep down in the mix of fluff and old shopping lists, Mabel knows that it has brought her close to disaster. Is this Mavis Whittaker's long overdue revenge? Mabel dares hardly breathe.

Osbert is still embracing the torso which has revealed more plastic than is decent. He now fears that much like iron filings in that oft-presented experiment much loved by science teachers, the Good People of Dawlish are patterning themselves around the pair of them. They are definitely being watched. Dawlish is tuned in and everything else is on hold. This is Theatre for all.

The wide open shop door offers an exit from the street-stage The racks and stacks, the rolls and haberdashery call to Osbert who responds to its promise that "all can be well". He heads inside and makes for his counter where he places the torso at one end of the glazed top before moving behind it to the other end. Mabel has followed him in desperate to be out of the public eye, closing the door firmly behind her.

There is no need or wish to comment. Neither one of them has any intention of referring to what has just happened and read the silence as mutual agreement. Mabel veers towards some bolts of curtaining material where she pauses allowing "shop-life" to be resumed.

'Mr Phipps, do you do this in beige?' She is holding a swatch of velveteen. 'Or… light… tan?'

Osbert straightens his shoulders before leaving his refuge behind the counter. 'Is this what you mean, madam?' Osbert offers a length of material for inspection.

'No. Not quite. Have you not got something more coffee-ish, cafe-au-lait-ish. You know?'

Osbert reaches up. 'There's this. It's not as fine a velveteen as the cinnamon, though.' With each passing moment normal service is being more firmly re-established.

'Have you got any cushion covers?'

'Over by the chintzes.' Osbert moves in that direction.

Mabel pulls a pair of cushion covers out from a pile.

'Do you think these go, Mr Phipps? I think they might, but I can't be sure.' Mabel has put together the cushion covers and the bolt of curtaining. 'Maybe they clash ever-such-a-little. Do you think they clash? I think when it comes to browns and yellows I must be that teenie bit colourblind. I can tell red from green. No, I've never had any problem at all telling red from green, or green from red for that matter. But, when it comes to a dark yellow and a light brown, that's quite another thing altogether. I got some formica for a trolley which I was sure was corn yellow, but when I got it home you won't be surprised to hear it was a gingery brown.' She has never spoken so much about so little, and without doubt never ever in the public domain. If only she could stop herself, she would.

'Now you're sure that it's golden yellow, aren't you?' Osbert nods professionally as he measures out six yards of velveteen. 'You do like it, don't you?' Osbert is scissoring. 'You do, don't you?'

'It's very summery.'

'Yes. Summery. Light and summery. I honestly think summer is THE season. It's the only time of the year when you can have a bit of fun.'

Osbert does not care for the sound of that at all. He gives the torso a glance. 'Will you be taking the... garment, too? On approval, naturally.'

'*Naturellement*!'

'Excuse me?' There is a wave of exhaustion ready to crash over Osbert.

'Oh excuse ME, Mr Phipps. That was French. Don't you think French is just so Continental?' Osbert strips the torso and wraps the corselette by way of reply. 'The very sound of it is... we just don't have words to describe it, do we?'

*

'The Manner of Learning and Training'
Discussion chaired by John Clarke Stobart - The Third Programme

The whole class is sitting with their hands on their heads, saving Clive Webster and Thomas Jennings. They are stood in the corners; one facing the book cupboard; the other one a blank wall. All Dringaling's walls are blank.

'Right, you lot, when I say three you will lower your hands. What did I say?' A finger flies at Wendy Wetherall in the middle of the front row. Her face stays as blank as the walls. 'You!' The finger fires again elsewhere. 'Tell her.'

'When you say three we lower our hands, Sir.'

'Exactly!' Clive Webster looks over his shoulder. 'Not you two. I don't want to see your faces at all. So, when I say three, you'll lower your hands, put your books away quietly - quietly, mind you. That does not mean your usual idea of quietness. It means si-lent-ly. And when you've done that, you will sit without making a noise until we are all released. Do I make myself clear? Wendy, do you think you've got that?' Wendy is about to nod when Dringaling springs another one of those hideously frightening smiles that have been the root cause of everything that has gone wrong this afternoon. Wendy's head locks on her shoulders. Dringaling seems satisfied though.

'Well then. One. Two. Three.'

The first braver hands slip from various heads. On Eric's face the most recent smile simmers on, ready to flicker back into a chortle for no reason that any of the children can fathom. He idles with the hairs in his left ear as desks are cleared and children settle to wait out the last long minutes.

The clock on the classroom wall reaches Hometime. Not a child moves. It is most definitely not a day to move. Who knows where moving might land one of them.

Eric rubs a smear of wax between finger and thumb. 'Now, everyone, I hope you all have a really nice evening. To make it nicer, do you know what I'm going to do?'

The Frighteners stamp through the desk-bound statues.

'Go on, guess. How am I going to make your Tuesday evening really special?'

They are all trying as hard as they can to blot out their guesses. None of which bode well.

'I asked you to guess.' His smile becomes a grin. But he doesn't look happy. Yet then he laughs.

In that very instant conditions that will manifest themselves later in the lives of Robert, Brenda, Sheila, Martin and Maureen spark into being. Heads of hair that may never have turned grey now probably will.

'Can it be that not one of you is able to suggest how I might make your evening..' he pauses, '... nice?' Three bladders are near to bursting.

The last of the running feet of children from other classes pass the classroom.

'Well, it seems I'm going to have to tell you, aren't I?'

"PLEASE!" choruses the class wordlessly. Anything is better than imagining.

'I have decided that because it's Tuesday and because I feel in the giving mood and because I had jam roly-poly pudding with chocolate custard at lunch, I have decided that tonight you will have........ no homework!'

216

One of bladders breaks there and then. No-one is aware, not even its owner. Faces flush. A few find it hard to breathe momentarily.

Eric Dring half-expects a cheer. After all he's not given them a night off since he can't remember when, and here he is giving them the chance to indulge themselves in whatever it is that the young of the day do when they have the opportunity. But he doesn't mean to give it a thought. He needs to check up on The Scheme which through the day has been playing itself out at home. 'So, do you think you can remember <u>not</u> to do any homework?' He has stood, hands empty as per usual. 'I'm sure you can.'

At the door he turns with a snap. 'Did you get that, Clive?' Clive squints around, 'Make absolutely sure you don't do any homework whatsoever, or there'll be hell to pay,' and he sniggers.

Eric has reached the bike shed before the last of his Top Juniors have raised nerve enough to get up and go. Wendy leaves last of all. She has to. It is her bladder that hasn't been up to the strain.

*

The hour is fast approaching when St Amanda, Martyr to Terpsichore, is to be tested. She floats away from school a little behind and above her corporeal form as it makes its slow way home. She notes the regular scuffing of her shoes. She admires the degree of slouch. The sense of doom, of unavoidable suffering, advertises a soul about to be weighed in the balance. Spirit purrs at the prospect of Trial. Body blanches at the likelihood of failure. But what has to be has to be. She thinks there's a song about that.

Amanda pauses at a kerb. "Go on." urges Spirit. "Go on. This is Pain. Pain is necessary. Remember Pavlova. Remember Ulanova." Amanda points a foot and steps off the kerb. Home is slowly reeling her in.

*

Eric is riding home at pace, head down, fuelled by eager anticipation. He has already shot downhill along Hatcher Street with its blur of red terraces, swung sharp right at the T-junction avoiding the blank cobbled wall dead ahead into Park Road, and is now in Old Town Street where mothers tug their Infants to safety as he roars on. As a man possessed of the greatest need to know how things stand he is pedalling for all he is worth, a veritable Reg Harris, renowned cyclist whose ferocious will to win pales in Eric's mind when compared to his own drive to do Mabel down. Reg has collected gold medals from his multiple victories, but Eric knows Reg has never been pitted against a woman of Mabel's ever-maddening nature. Reg has had it easy.

Eric pumps his legs harder as he crosses Carpenter's Bridge and begins the long climb up Church Street. So he is not reaching the speeds achieved by Reg when he set his world records, yet for an unfit middle-aged man on a bike with a basket at the front Eric is certainly setting new figures for his journey from school to home. He cuts across the end of Barton Crescent before weaving through the narrow Z bend by St Gregory's. He is slowing but still pumping away with determination.

Coursing adrenaline is countering his allergy. If he was aware, he would note that he has not breathed more clearly or so sweetly for weeks. Delight at the prospect of a load so soon to be lifted is welling up. Each revolution of his flying wheels sends his racing heart into ever faster overdrive.

He is almost there.

There are only yards to go.

Eric, grinning widely, looks up and straight away brakes hard, so hard he almost comes a cropper. And coming a cropper was to be Mabel's fate today, not his.

For the briefest moment Eric disbelieves his eyes.

Mabel is approaching home.

This is wrong. So ruddy wrong. Nothing could be more wrong. How can it be? According to The Scheme Mabel should be in no fit state to be walking, let alone carrying bags of shopping. What has happened? Eric had been meticulous in his planning, but it would seem that the best laid plans can go awry. Most definitely Mabel does not give the impression of someone who has eaten Shepherd's Pie with the added mystery ingredient.

Knowing her robust constitution Eric had not stinted when it came to administering the dose of greenish-brown crystals, so the only thing must be that she has not eaten it. And if that is the case, he may need to come up with an excuse and be quick about it, if she presents it warmed up for his supper.

His Scheme has not succeeded, but then again it hasn't failed either. It simply hasn't been implemented. Now he needs time to sit down and think things through. His campaign is far from being over.

Mabel lets the side gate swing back in his face. But two points to him; it doesn't so much as touch him or his bicycle.

She pushes open the back door and puts her foot in it as soon as she steps in the kitchen. The stench hits her very soon after. 'Dickie!' Mabel's care echoes out of the kitchen and along the hall.

She wipes her shoe on the mat but then notices that the mat is dotted with little packages, oozing their odour along with their nuisance. 'Dickie! Where are you, my little darling? Where's Mummy's sick little boy?'

There is no sound.

Mabel puts her purchases down on the kitchen table before tossing the fouled mat into the yard. It greets Eric as he comes from putting his bike in the shed.

Mabel reaches out the door with her soiled shoe and drops it. She launches a look at Eric, before turning back indoors. Eric doesn't need to go in anyway.

Mabel begins to hunt for Dickie. Piles and pools are awaiting her, some more obvious to the eye than others. The smell is everywhere, rising and falling like a noxious sea. Mercifully the lounge door is closed, so one area has escaped Dickie's most unaccustomed fall from grace. Mabel gives the front doormat the briefest inspection. It will have to go in the bin. Coconut matting doesn't come cheap.

She has an awful thought. This isn't evidence of a tummy upset. This is something much worse. 'Dickie! You must tell Mummy where you are. She's not cross. Mummy wants to help, but you must help Mummy first.' She takes out a hankie as much to wipe away tears she fears at any moment she will shed as to cover her nose.

She is at the foot of the stairs. There's a waft of stink. 'Dickie are you up there? Mummy's coming.' A few stairs have smears of slurry trickling from riser to tread. She pushes away the imagined sight of his little black and tan body crumpled up.

Now on the landing she sees that all the doors are open or ajar.

'Dickie?' She goes from door to door. No Dickie. She then edges the door to the front bedroom open.

The Scream.

Eric drops his cycle clips. He involuntarily makes to hurry indoors, but moves only inches before settling back on the dustbin.

The Second Scream makes the first seem nothing more than a weak and watery rehearsal. Curtains press themselves back against window panes. Wallpaper fades. Cobwebs fall from bedsprings. This Scream rings around the house battering at the wainscot.

Dickie is lying, a shivering wreck, wrung out. His nose is dry as Winalot. His fur matted with his suffering.

Another Scream ricochets off the vanity table, off each and every wobbling knick-knack - the glass elephants, the Wade walruses, tigers and pomeranians, the line of miniature china liquer bottles. This Scream lashes out. It snaps the nerves of the Easter-flowering cactus. It destroys woodworm in the back of the chest of drawers. It knocks the stuffing out of the bolster; crazes the glaze on the Coronation plate; unravels a section of the cane chair and warps a photo of Mabel's parents with him in uniform.

The Horror of The Bedroom eats through Mabel's hope and into her spirit in her first glimpse. Details are fragmented, but it only takes the splinters of event to build up the overall.

In that first intaking of breath, breath needed to give vent to the Scream after nudging the door open, the room fixed itself in her eye. Foul stains on the bedside rug where a fluffy mule sits spattered. Dickie, hardly more alive than a fox fur, lying against the window wall as if thrown there. Her dressing table stool on its side. The arrangement of dried flowers in the grate disarranged, a shattering of seed heads, tissue-thin. Honesty adrift. Mabel re-records each still life. The mule. Dickie. The stool. Honesty.

With her Last Scream still echoing through her; with her hands rending her perm; with her stockinged feet unable to budge, Mabel's organs, so recently lifted by Mrs Rudge's corset, falter. She sways, her hand reaching out to touch, but not to touch.

How could she have left it out? A sharp inbreath threatens to fire another blazing scream. Her reaching hand clamps back over her mouth damming her voice. A shudder sets her gasping. She looks and looks away and looks again. The mule. Dickie. The stool. Honesty. The Grosgrain Circular Skirt.

It is lying half off her bed, crumpled, patterned with yellow-brown paw-prints. Both yellow and brown and neither one nor the other. The thread of white that had scored itself, a vapour trail against the sky-blue, dream-blue skirt, now links mocking stains. With the rose wallpaper looking on, among the most familiar pieces of furniture, the worm of nightmare eats away in the full light of day.

Dickie whimpers. He has nothing more to give. Mabel

approaches him, one hand to her throat prepared to stopper another scream. She will not voice her pain again. 'Dickie,' she says in a tone just above silence. She kneels by him. Guilt wells in his eyes.

In the yard Eric stubs out a cigarette and drops the small brown bottle of laxatives in the dustbin, pushing it down deep out of sight. It has gone awfully quiet indoors after those screams. Maybe he should go in and see. Though she's had it coming. After all it is her fault. She started the whole thing with her French. So it wasn't her that ate the pie. Very well. But this must teach her something. Her dearest Dickie has severely blotted his copybook. Maybe he, Eric, will get a bit more care and attention as a result. It isn't as if he goes around doing his business on her linoleum.

Perhaps he should call upstairs. Perhaps he should just call to see if there is anything he can do to help. He should show concern. Then, when he learns that Mabel gave Dickie the Shepherd's Pie, the pie she had made, he could say something like: "Just think what might've happened if you had eaten it, dear." No, not the "dear"; that would be going too far. He'll have to get it right. He mustn't let her start wondering. First he must see which way the wind is blowing. Dickie could be dead. A heady mix of glee and worry bubbles up inside.

Mabel carries Dickie into the kitchen wrapped in a towel from the bathroom. Eric catches sight of them through the open backdoor. The Dead March starts playing in Eric's head, but he needs to know to be sure. Looking round the door he watches Mabel lower Dickie's still body on to the draining board. A swaddled cocoon. Eric comes in and closes the door, before taking up a position by the larder.

Mabel lets the water run for a while. She ties on her pinny. When it is running warm she puts the plug in and leans against the sink as it fills, facing the window but looking at something deep inside. When she is satisfied she pulls on a pair of old rubber gloves and gingerly uwraps Dickie. Maybe it is because the door is now shut, but most likely it is just the sight of the dog that gusts the stench back.

Dickie moves.

That settles that, thinks Eric.

*

'Wives and Daughters' *by Elizabeth Gaskell*

The Home Service

Life for Amanda is over. On June 10th, 1958, Miss Amanda Clark, aged 11, has died in the company of a pair of pilchards and a mother who doesn't understand her. As she places the knife and fork on either side of the slice of toast where the fish lie, Amanda lays down her Art, too.

'If you've finished playing around in there, bring your plate through and I'll get you something else.'

Amanda carries the plate before her into the kitchen as if it is bearing the head of John the Baptist.

'It's a crying shame wasting good food, Amanda. We're not made of money, you know. And think of the starving millions in Africa. There are people there who'd give their eyeteeth for some pilchards as well you know. You should be grateful I don't serve them up to you tomorrow.' Mrs Clark gives the fish a look. 'It's not even as if we've got a cat I can give them to.' She scrapes them into the bin.

Amanda watches as her Life is so casually tossed away.

'Now what about some scrambled egg?'

Amanda is standing by a kitchen chair unaware she is swinging a leg.

'Amanda, whatever has got into you? You were a misery at the Beauty Pageant, then you go asking for something we both knew you'd never eat. Now to cap it all, you've gone deaf.'

Amanda offers her mother a face of hurt resignation.

'Don't try that on me either. I've had my heartstrings tugged until they've snapped. So, what's it going to be? Scrambled egg or cheese on toast?' It is in fact tears. Tears and Running Feet. 'What is it, Amanda? Don't just rush off like that.

'Look, 'Manda, I didn't mean it about the Pageant.' Mrs Clark's voice is steadily rising as she calls from the kitchen. 'If you don't want scrambled egg or cheese on toast, what do you want?' A bedroom door slams. ''Manda! You've got to eat something... You're a growing girl!'

*

'Woman's Hour'

Including 'He likes to be surprised': Jeanne de Casalis tells a story with a moral and a recipe. - The Light Programme

---

Grace finishes turning the sausages and slides them back under the grill. 'From your description, Osbert, with the white crocheted gloves, that was Mrs Dring. She has always been a bit distant on those occasions I've seen her.' She turns the heat down under the potatoes. 'Perhaps not so much distant as closed in. Private.'

Osbert finishes buffing up his left shoe and picks up his right one. 'I could not fathom her, Grace. She appeared to be seething just below the surface.'

Grace pauses on her way to the larder to listen. Not to Osbert. Just a moment to listen.

Osbert is applying polish to his second shoe.

Having collected the ketchup Grace is turning the sausages again and pauses midway. 'Was that the door?'

Osbert listens, shakes his head, and continues polishing.

'You say she bought the corselette, as well as some material.'

'The material, yes, and three cushion covers. But she took the corselette on approval.'

'Let's hope it fits.' She tests a potato with a knife. 'Are you positive that wasn't the door, Osbert?'

'Do you want me to go and see?

'No. No, don't bother. You do your shoes, but mind where you're putting the polish. If it is someone, they'll knock again anyway.'

'Is something up? Has something happened?'

Grace turns the sausages one last time. 'Something's always happening, Osbert.'

'Don't tell me, Birmingham's been vaporised!' Grace swings from the cooker fork in hand. 'That was a joke, dear. A joke.'

Grace turns back to the sausages and stabs one hard. 'It's no joking matter.' She pushes the grill pan back under the heat. 'You seem to have jokes on the brain lately.'

'But I thought you liked jokes, dear.'

'Not when they're not jokes I don't.'

Osbert threads the lace back into his second shoe. 'Let me tell you that what happened in the shop today was not exactly a joke, dear.'

'But it ended all right, Osbert, didn't it?'

*

'Did you get these from Dinsdales?'

'Why? Don't you like them?'

'No. I mean yes, I like them. They're different though, aren't they?'

'Are they?'

'They taste a little different, yes.'

'But you like them?'

'Hm.'

'They're the same as I always get.'

'They may be the same, but they just taste different to me.' Osbert chews his mouthful of sausage carefully. 'Different, but nice.'

'Shh!' Grace flaps a hand to keep Osbert quiet. Their cutlery pauses. 'It's nothing.' Grace loads her fork.

'What's nothing?'

'I just thought I heard the phone in the shop.'

'Grace, anyone would think you were expecting a call from Her Majesty the Queen. I'm sorry to say but her birthday has been and gone and we've both been overlooked again.' Grace manages a small smile. 'That's better. I was worried you'd forgotten how to.'

*

'Tinned peaches or pears?' Grace is holding both.

'I don't mind, dear. Whatever comes?'

'We've got both. Which would you like?'

'What needs eating? I really don't mind, Grace. Whichever is easiest.'

'They're both easy, Osbert. It's only a case of opening a tin after all.'

Osbert swills the plates under the tap while Grace opens a tin and serves up.

'Pears. My favourite.'

Grace plonks her spoon down. 'Then why didn't you say, Osbert? Why didn't you say you preferred pears?'

'But I really didn't mind if we had peaches.'

'But pears are your favourite, are they?'

'Well, yes, I suppose they are.'

'Either they are or they aren't. Which one is it?'

'You're quizzing me as if I've done something wrong. Have I done something wrong, Grace?'

'And you're avoiding the question again.'

'Does it really matter which one I like?' Grace answers by loading her spoon. 'I have done something wrong, haven't I?'

'You've not done anything wrong in particular. But why when there is a choice can't you make it and be ready to stick to it?'

'What is that supposed to mean exactly?'

'It's supposed to mean that when I ask you if you want peaches or pears, you say: "Pears, please." '

Grace concentrates on her bowl of pears. Osbert is simply confused. Why are some days such a struggle?

***

FRIDAY, JUNE 13th

'How to Manage Men'
A light-hearted programme in which women of experience give advice to women whose menfolk are sometimes difficult. This week's male guest, Kenneth Horne. – The Light Programme

When the driers are on it isn't possible to have a quiet conversation, and difficult to hear all that is said.

'Another five minutes,' announces Betty, laying a copy of "Woman's Realm" in Mrs Lowe's lap.

Mrs Lowe's primped and newly permed hair is setting, coiled on its rollers, gripped between its crocodile clips, inside its net. She has decided to have a rinse, too. 'That message in front of the Bandstand was one thing, but painting bodies by the Floral Clock is vandalism pure and simple. It gave Mr Tucker a very nasty turn, and he wouldn't harm a fly.'

Mrs Newcombe pulls the wad of cotton wool away from her ear. She is overheating. She's been trying to get Mrs Owen to turn her down a tad, but without success. The hairdresser is currently occupied with Mrs MacAskill's shampoo and set.

'It's definitely you, Mrs MacAskill.'

Mrs MacAskill turns her head to check in the mirror if it really is her. 'Do you think you could soften this a little?' She fingers a tightly wound curl at her temple. 'It makes me seem hard.'

'Do you really think so?' Mrs Owen appraises Mrs MacAskill from a distance.

'I'm not a television announcer, you know.'

'Oh, no, of course not.' Mrs Owen begins to work life back into the offending curl.

Mrs Lowe continues to explain to Mrs Newcombe who is now better able to hear. 'My husband is doing his best, as you'd expect him to, but there appears to be no getting to the bottom of it. And the police are completely stumped, though that doesn't come as a real surprise. They ought to call Exeter in to sort it all out. After all it only takes someone to act the goat and before you know it the whole thing has snowballed and everyone is being put out.'

'Heaven only knows where it might end,' chips in Mrs MacAskill.

'At least our mystery painter, The Phantom of the Floral Clock, has given us something to talk about.' Mrs Trent has emerged from under her drier and is ready to join in. 'I was beginning to wonder if anything newsy ever happened in Dawlish. After Woking it's so quiet.'

'Things like this happen in Woking then, do they?' queries Mrs Lowe feeling sure that she has made a most definite point.

'Lots of things happen in Woking, Mrs Lowe. You'd be surprised.'

'It's in the stockbroker belt, isn't it?' Another point is chalked up.

Mrs Trent's smile does not waver. 'Dawlish needs to be jolted into the modern world. You must agree it is rather dozy.'

' "Dozy" is a bit harsh, Mrs Trent. Change is all very well and good, but there's no need to rush into it.' Mrs Lowe looks around her. 'Dawlish does not need to be jolted into anything.' She invites the other women to comment as a well-versed committee chairwoman should.

'This modern world they talk about is fine in its own way. Like I said to your hubby, Mrs Trent, on the occasion of your coronation, which was lovely, wasn't it ladies?' There is full agreement from everyone. 'But I do worry. Progress needs to be thought through. It doesn't have to be made at the cost of what we have.'

'Well said, Mrs MacAskill.' Praise from Mrs Lowe counts and Mrs MacAskill will definitely be telling Miss Wilkes later on. 'What do you think the modern world has that Dawlish needs?'

'A coffee bar.' Betty chips in uninvited, getting herself a look from her mother, Mrs Owen, that sends her off to sort out refreshments.

'Aren't you keen on Dawlish then, Mrs Trent?' Mrs Newcombe has now cooled off.

'Please get me straight. I love the town. I really do. And I've got nothing against anybody. It's just that there are some people who still think it's 1920-something. We've got to move with the times or we could get left behind. This is a modern technological world we're now living in after all. You've only got to look around.'

Mrs Lowe does just that. 'I'm not at all sure that this technological world of yours...'

'... It's not mine, Mrs Lowe.'

'Point taken. I'm not sure that this technological world we are heading into is the one I'm really ready for.'

'Me neither.' Mrs MacAskill can't agree more.

Mrs Lowe opens up further. 'I do feel we are being pushed into it against our will.'

'Hear. Hear!'

'Perhaps it's just that it's full of things I don't feel able to get to grips with.' And Mrs Lowe who is not accustomed to confessing inadequacies pauses while Mrs MacAskill if only she was not restricted by the gown she is draped in would give a round of applause.

'Excuse me, Mrs Trent.' Mrs Owen edges in to remove all the bits and pieces that go to construct Mrs Trent's BeeHive. 'Now, you'd best close your eyes while I spray.'

With eyes shut Kay Trent sits in a drift of mist. 'Mrs Owen, I've been wanting to ask for a while but haven't got around to it; the name, "Andre and Roma", is there a story behind it? It sounds as if there should be.'

Mrs Owen stops spraying, and in the pause the shop goes quiet, for even those who have heard the story before want to hear it.

'My hubby, George, God rest him, when he came back from

the War he was not in a good way. He had served from the start. You name a place and he'd fought there, but for him the War ended in Italy at Montecassino where the fighting was just awful. He'd never speak about that sort of thing, but he had fallen for the country, its countryside. The destruction of the hill-top monastery was vandalism in his eyes. It was in the main attack there that he was wounded and got his ticket home.

'Anyway, moving on. Five years ago this business came up for sale. It was a hairdressers, owned and managed by Mrs Dewhurst. She only did basic stuff. She did it well, mind you, but like I say basic. And the shop – it couldn't call itself a salon – was simply called "Dewhursts". Lots of people over the years pointed out that Dewhursts were butchers, but Mrs Dewhurst didn't see any reason at all to change. So "Dewhursts" it was when we bought it from her.

'The first thing that had to go was that name. But what to? Nothing came to mind straight away.' Mrs Owen pauses but only briefly.

'Now George and I always went to the Cinema. We hardly ever missed. Whenever the programme changed at the Scala we'd go along. Didn't matter what it was. Even if we didn't end up liking the film, it was a night out. We must have seen hundreds over the years. No exaggeration.

'So in a way it was inevitable. One week they announced in the "Coming Shortly" that the following week they were showing "Roman Holiday". I could say that the rest is history. The programme changed on Saturday and we were there. We were also there on Monday, Tuesday, Wednesday, Thursday, and Friday. We were smitten. There is no other word for it. I fancied myself as Audrey Hepburn. A bit unlikely I grant you, but a woman can dream, can't she?'

Every woman there agrees wholeheartedly.

'The sight of Audrey with Gregory Peck on a Vespa riding round Rome was, well, perfect. And her hairstyle was so modern, so different to what Mrs Dewhurst had been providing. So that and George's memory of Italy was what gave us "Roma".'

'And "Andre"? Who was he?" Kay Trent asks on behalf of Mrs Owen's audience.

'Nobody. Nobody at all.'

'Nobody?' Kay would rather like Andre to have his own story.

'Nobody real. But there were the Appleyards.'

'I beg your pardon.'

'Husband and wife team, Ian and Patricia Appleyard, were in the news back in 1953. In their Jaguar they had just come second in the Monte Carlo Rally and George was one for Jaguars. We'd have had one if we could have afforded it.'

'We would, too, Mrs Owen! Tom would die for an open top Jag. So where did "Andre" come from?'

'To us it sounded just like someone who would live by the Mediterranean with the palm trees and the blue, blue sky. Very Monte Carlo. And as we live on the English Riviera...' Mrs Owen drifts to a halt. Her story told. A final spray of Kay Trent's BeeHive and she heads for the counter to consult her appointments diary. She really has fallen a little behind.

'I would love to be behind the wheel of a Jaguar, with the top down, roaring across Europe on those wonderfully long empty roads you see in the films. Roads edged by mile upon mile of poplar trees. Roads tying the continent together.'

'Do you actually drive, Mrs Trent?'

'I actually do, Mrs Lowe.'

'I leave the driving to my husband.'

'Why?'

'Well, I've never learned.'

'They do say "it's never too late to learn", Mrs Lowe.'

'They also say "you can't teach an old dog new tricks".'

'There is no trick to driving. Perhaps you should give it a go.'

At that point Betty brings Rita Gordon's dripping head up out of the basin.

'Mind my neck!'

'Pardon?' Betty unwraps some of the muffling towel.

Rita tests her neck gingerly. 'Can't you hear that? The grinding?'

If Betty can, she isn't saying. 'How is the Play going?'

'Still two weeks to go before first night.'

'We've already got our seats. It's our Christopher's first time on the stage.' Betty is rubbing Rita's hair dry.

'Betty, please! My neck!'

'He says Mr Phipps is in it. His shop's round the corner in Queen Street. Funny really, I've never put him down as being one for the stage.'

At the counter Mrs MacAskill forgets where she is with her money. 'I really think that some people lose control and take dramatics too far, don't you, Mrs Owen?'

'I suppose they do, Mrs MacAskill.' Though for the life of her Mrs Owen cannot think of anyone there and then.

Mrs MacAskill is savouring the prize of having what seems to be private knowledge crying out to be shared. 'Has no-one told you, Mrs Owen, about a public incident involving a certain shopkeeper and the wife of a certain teacher?' Mrs Owen slowly shakes her head. 'That is difficult to believe.' Difficult but thrilling. Mrs MacAskill now raises her voice sufficiently enough to increase her audience. 'Suffice it to say that the wife of the certain nameless teacher exited from a shop, a shop which among other things sells items of clothing of a personal close-fitting nature, and was heard – indeed it was impossible not to – she was to be heard yelling at the very top of her voice in a way suggesting that someone had been trying to take advantage of her.'

Rita claps a hand to her mouth knocking the comb from Betty's hand.

Every other client is agog. Images of Audrey Hepburn on her Vespa with Gregory Peck holding on are fast fading.

'But what had been going on, Mrs MacAskill?' Mrs Owen has decoded the name of the shopkeeper, but cannot fathom the storyline.

'What indeed? All I can say is what I saw, Mrs Owen. I wasn't the only one let me add. The street was not empty.'

'And what did the woman shout?' Mrs Newcombe calls for any available evidence to try and understand what seems incomprehensible.

'I wasn't too near, but it sounded to me as if she said, or shouted rather, something like: "Get away, you brute!" I could be wrong, but it was something like that.'

'Brute!' Rita takes in a large breath and goshes.

'And there was I saying that life in Dawlish was dull.' Mrs Trent shakes her head. 'I can tell you, Mrs Lowe, nothing like that ever happened in Woking.'

'Are you telling us, Mrs MacAskill, that...' and Mrs Lowe, like Mrs Owen, has had a light bulb moment, 'this shopkeeper, let's call him a... draper...'

Rita is aghast.

'... had shown attention to this woman, in broad daylight... during opening hours when anyone could have entered the.... drapery shop.' Her eyebrows rise. She sees she has scored. 'Isn't it possible you were mistaken, Mrs MacAskill? It is unlike the person in question.'

'I am only saying what I saw with my own eyes and heard with my own ears. Nothing more.'

'There has to be some explanation. Perhaps you misheard, after all it can be hard to hear over the calls of seagulls and the like.'

'I may be of advanced years, Mrs Newcombe, but...' and Mrs MacAskill stops abruptly.

The ringing of the salon doorbell had gone unnoticed momentarily. But now a wave of panic wells up in all the women when they realise who has just come in.

'Good morning, Mrs Owen.'

Mrs Owen is wringing her hands while at the same time smiling. 'Good morning to you...' there is a slight pause, 'Mrs Phipps.'

Mrs Trent picks up on the pause. A pause that has surely delivered a message. But what? She is being provided information of the most pertinent kind. She is also aware that all other conversation has dried up, as if the driers have done their worst. Like Mrs Newcombe and Mrs Lowe she seeks refuge behind her magazine. Rita is between seething and tears.

'Good morning, Mrs MacAskill.'

Mrs MacAskill manages a nod and a smile as she runs and re-runs the tail end of what was being said before Mrs Phipps came in. What could she have heard?

'And what can I do for you?' asks Mrs Owen, ever the professional.

'I've just dropped in to cancel my appointment.'

The pages of magazines stiffen.

'Oh... I see. I hope there's nothing wrong?' Mrs Owen prays as the assembly of minds in the salon conjures up a host of cans of worms on the brink of being prised open. Mrs Owen not only prays, but bites her tongue. Why had she asked?

'It's just that with one thing and another I haven't got the time.'

'Busy at the shop, are you?' Mrs Owen can't help herself; it is the curse of the chatty hairdresser.

'Well, it is our sale.'

'Yes. Yes. Of course it is.' Mrs Owen hears the rush in her own voice. It must be clear as day to Mrs Phipps. 'Now when exactly were you going to be coming?'

'Tuesday. At 10.45.'

Mrs Owen flicks pages in her appointments book. For some reason her fingers and her eyes are not able to work in tandem. Tuesday seems to have vanished.

The drone of the driers fills the quietness that is flooding the salon. There sit the women, magazines up, empty tea cups, heads swallowed by the hoods. And Grace sees them skeletal, among the burnt-black debris, charred to a frazzle. The bomb-domes squat, sucking the women dry. Ears stuffed. Heads netted. Brains pulped by the latest serial; by romance with Rodney or Clive or Nathaniel.

'Here we are.' Mrs Owen flattens her hand on the page lest it should vanish again. 'I knew it had to be here. Mrs Phipps: 10.45. To cancel, yes? Will you be making another appointment instead?'

'No.' Grace moves a little away from the counter. 'No. I'm not sure when I'll be able to.' She needs to leave. Now.

'I hope...' Mrs Owen speaks to Grace's back. She already has the door open. 'I hope the sale goes well.'

For a few moments after the door closes the salon holds its breath, while all eyes watch Grace passing the window.

'Oh, the poor, poor woman!' Rita's nerves rattle loudest. 'What a brave face!'

'Men!' Mrs MacAskill fires the word at point blank range. 'What we women are put through.'

'Did you see how she is suffering?' Rita thrums.

Mrs Lowe sits quiet with a sense of unease. Even if Mrs MacAskill has misinterpreted what happened, and Mrs Lowe really wants to believe she has, it awakens a worry, showing that even the most stable applecart can be so easily upset, even if totally unintentionally.

Mrs Trent cannot wait any longer. 'Who?..'

'That was the Wife of the Draper! Of the brute!' Rita hisses.

Mrs Trent does a bit of mental note-making.

With the lid now off that piece of information Mrs MacAskill feels no need to keep the rest of the cast list to herself. 'The Wife of the Teacher is Mrs Dring. Her husband being the Teacher, naturally.

Heads not held firmly in the driers are shaken. But not Mrs Newcombe's.

'I have known Mr Phipps for ages. We all have. And do you all honestly believe that the Mr Phipps we know would actually lay hands on a customer, let alone a woman. I am sure that each and every one of us has been in his shop over the years and always found him to be a gentleman. A bit aloof. A bit cold at times maybe. But always keeping his side of the counter, so to speak.'

'Mrs Newcombe, I heard what I heard.'

'But, Mrs MacAskill, did you see all that was to be seen?'

Mrs Owen needs to get on. She has a salon to run. She can't stand around all day worrying about the ups and downs of her clients' lives, much as she might like to. 'Will you be doing the refreshments at the play interval, Mrs MacAskill?'

This drags Mrs MacAskill's attention back to the matter in hand; finishing paying for her shampoo and set. 'The WRVS have offered their services to the Festival as per usual, yes, Mrs Owen.'

'It wouldn't be the same without you and your helpers. Shall I book you in for an appointment in a couple of weeks, then?...'

Whatever else Mrs Owen is about to say freezes as the doorbell rings in a new client. She blinks from the face to her appointment book for confirmation that she isn't imagining things.

For Mrs MacAskill with this new arrival whole possibilities bloom. Yet there appears to be no way she can sit and have her hair done again in order not to miss out on potential developments.

'Be with you in a minute... Mrs Dring.' Various sets of jaws lock or else they would have dropped. 'Be with you in a minute, if you wouldn't mind waiting.' Mrs Owen is wondering if this morning is ever going to end.

Mabel Dring pulls a "People's Friend" from the pile of magazines and sits.

'Shall we say a week on Wednesday, Mrs MacAskill?'

'I've not got my diary with me. I'll pop in next week to confirm.' Mrs MacAskill homes in on Mabel Dring. 'Getting your hair done for the trip, are you?' Mabel looks up. 'When are you off?'

Betty, who has handed Rita over to Mrs Owen to finish off, swings a chair round by way of inviting Mabel to come across, tracked by the other women.

Though ignored, Mrs MacAskill leaves the salon thoroughly satisfied. She has got so much more than enough to tell Miss Wilkes.

'What can I do for you, Mrs Dring?' Mabel pulls out a picture of Simone Signoret cut from a "Picture Show" magazine 'My word, you're going to look the bee's knees with that and no mistake.'

"C'est vrai", thinks Mabel-Monique.

Mrs Lowe and Mrs Newcombe are finding it hard to cope. Never before has so much happened at the hairdressers.

'I think it needs another five minutes, Mrs Lowe.' Mrs Owen is determined to move things on. 'You've got such lovely glossy hair and so much of it.' She now includes Mrs Newcombe. 'Would either of you like another cup of tea?' She gets two small shakes by way of answers, before checking on Rita and returning to her counter to take stock.

Mrs Lowe searches for something to say to bring back a touch of normality. 'It says here in "Woman's Realm" that tea goes straight to your hips. Apparently it has something to do with the minerals in it.'

'Well, I'd best stop drinking the stuff,' chortles Kay Trent, winking at Rita, who is finding it hard to re-think things. 'If there's one thing Tom especially likes, it's my hips.' Mrs Lowe, Mrs Newcombe and Miss Gordon, who has been left for her setting lotion to set, don't know how not to show what they are thinking. 'When I'm at the sink doing the washing up and he's doing the drying, he finds it hard to keep focussed on the job in hand.' The Draper and the Teacher's Wife dim.

'You don't let him...' Mrs Lowe speaks deliberately in order not to be misunderstood.

'I've not got much choice with my hands covered in suds, have I?' And she laughs as the memory warms.

'No, Mrs Trent, let me finish. Do I gather that you let your husband help you with the housework?'

'Let him? He's got no choice.'

Mrs Lowe turns to Mrs Newcombe. 'What do you make of that? Does your Harold do likewise? I mean housework, not the other.'

'He has been known to push the vacuum cleaner over the carpets.'

'Really? Well, you surprise me. I wouldn't let Fred get anywhere near my appliances. Anything electric I will let him have a look at, if a fuse goes or something like that, but I'd much rather know he's out of harm's way in the garage or at some meeting or other.'

'My father, God rest his soul, never did so much as boil an egg.' Rita puts in.

'As it should be, Miss Gordon. Men aren't supposed to work about the house. Goodness me,' Mrs Lowe chortles, 'you'll next be telling me that he washes the nappies and embroiders.'

'And what'd be wrong with that if he did?' Mrs Trent shifts in her chair. If only she could remember the name of that man Miss Eaves mentioned at Art Class.

'He doesn't, I take it.'

'No, he doesn't. But what'd be wrong if he did.'

'What'd be wrong? He's a man, my dear. Men are men, and women are women.'

Mrs Trent feels stumped.

'Look, housework calls for planning and application, and they're just not up to it. They're all very good at schemes and ideas and pie-in-the-sky projects, but they're simply not practical. If your husband washed nappies, they'd not be really clean now, would they? And what's more they've not got the stomach for it. They go weak at the sight of blood, don't they? Can you honestly imagine one of them going through childbirth? Can you?'

Of course, the married women can't, and Miss Gordon doesn't want to think about that at all; it'd make her cry.

'No. There's only one thing that you can't really do without them.'

The women dare not believe that Mrs Lowe is about to put IT into words. Though Kay Trent is eager for Mrs Lowe to do so.

'And that's… ballroom dancing.'

The women don't know whether to feel relieved or let down.

Kay Trent is most dissatisfied. 'But why should they be allowed to keep on getting away with it?'

'What do you mean? Getting away with what?'

'Why should it be us women, Mrs Lowe, who wipe their noses for them when they're boys, and wash their socks for them when they're men?'

'What would you rather do?'

'I'd like the chance to choose.'

'There is no choice to be made. If we want men, we have to take care of them. It's made clear to us every day that they can't do for themselves. That's the way it is.' Mrs Lowe could not be more certain.

'Harold quite often offers to help.'

'Do you let him?' Mrs Lowe looks down over glasses that aren't there.

'Sometimes I do.'

'So he can think he's making himself useful?'

'Well, yes,' Mrs Newcombe confesses.

Kay Trent simply shakes her head at her, forcing her to go on.

'It's just that it takes me twice as long to explain to him how to do something as it'd take me to do it myself.'

'There we are.' For Mrs Lowe the matter is nearly sealed.

Not for Kay Trent. 'You'd only have to take the time once.' She is finding it hard not to explode. 'Then the next time he could do it without all the explanation.'

'Yes, but I like it done in a particular way. I mean, I know where everything goes for a start.'

'The home belongs to us women,' Mrs Lowe decides to step back in before Mrs Newcombe can weaken. 'Men have their offices and the like.' She rolls a piece of wadding in her hand as she decides to take the women into her confidence. 'You know, I'm never happier than in those few minutes after Fred's gone off to work and I know I've got the place all to myself.'

Kay Trent is trying as hard as she can to argue reasonably. What were the points she should be making? 'Taking that into account, why do we put ourselves through it? Why do we let them into the house in the first place?'

'Some of us like looking after them.'

'But if all you want him for is ballroom dancing, why don't you just hire a man for the evening when you go out? Get yourself an escort.'

'A home wouldn't be a home without a man.'

'Oh, I see. He's like a TV set? Quite entertaining and looks good when you've got visitors.' Mary's "Hoover Theory" might need some amendments made but it seems to be standing up well in its first real-life test.

Mrs Lowe, with all her committee experience knows when she is winning the argument and can afford not to be irked. 'I'm not sure Fred's ever looked good.'

'But he's useful in the winter, hm? A warm place to put your cold feet?'

Mrs Lowe laughs in such a way as to encourage Mrs Newcombe and Miss Gordon to join in.

Kay Trent is unamused. It isn't possible to argue when the other side isn't willing to fight.

It isn't necessary to argue when the other side has so clearly lost, thinks Mrs Lowe.

The debate runs on listing the pros and cons of The Other Half, restating their failings, their foibles and their fancies, welling like a sea, at times running through the pebbles of Mabel Dring's daydream, nibbling at the sand trapped between her toes, though never disturbing her mind. It is set.

'I think you're ready to go under, Miss Gordon.' Mrs Owen tests Rita's hair with the back of her hand. 'Regulo 5, I think.' It is her regular joke. Rita braces herself. Not that the others can possibly know, but she really and truly hates the drier. It is silly of her, but there it is. Ever since she saw "The Quatermass" on the TV, she has had this feeling that driers might do something to her, might addle her brain and leave her like a toasted marshmallow, not that she's ever seen one outside the pages of a glossy magazine with all their talk about fondue dinner parties. In their own different ways Rita and Grace share a similar vision. That would surprise them.

Before the hood heats up a question pops into Rita's head and before she knows, it pops out, 'Why did you get married?'

The women are not sure who is being asked.

Kay Trent comes to Rita's rescue. 'Because I loved Tom and I still do.'

Even Rita can tell that there is much more to those simple words than is apparent.

Ding, ding. Round Two.

'I love my husband,' Mrs Lowe pauses to clear her throat. 'He's a good man in his way. When I married him I knew I could depend on him.'

'Depend on him for what?' Rita needs to know.

'Not to meddle in the kitchen for a start.' And Mrs Lowe finishes with a flourish.

'Tom is the kind of man I couldn't possibly not love.'

'Meaning?'

242

'He's 100 per cent lovable.'

'Really?' Mrs Lowe banners her doubt. 'I find it hard to believe that there's any such beast.'

'Harold's sort of 70 to 80 per cent lovable. I suppose it'd be greedy to expect the rest.' Mrs Newcombe leans towards Mrs Trent. 'How come your husband is perfect?'

'Oh, Tom's not perfect. There are some occasions when he's quite the opposite. But that doesn't make him any less lovable in my books. It makes for fun. Fun and games. Salt and spice.' Her eyebrows dance.

'How long have you been married, Mrs Trent...if you don't mind me asking?'

' Four years.'

'Ah...' "Need I say more" does not need to be said.

'And you, Mrs Lowe... if you don't mind me asking?' Kay Trent bats the query back.

'As it so happens we had our 25th wedding anniversary in March. I was such a young bride. That was usual back then. Fred was my first and only love.' Mrs Lowe goes dewy-eyed, or as dewy-eyed as it is possible for her to go.

'Did you have a do?' Rita asks, delaying the coming of the drier a bit longer.

'We most certainly did. We had champagne, smoked salmon, vol-au-vents... those are little pastry shells filled with tasty things..., profiteroles... those are really wicked, with cream and chocolate. We had the lot. A cake, of course. It was in fact a copy of the top tier of our wedding cake.'

'That is so romantic,' gushes Rita. 'And did you get anything special by way of presents?'

Before answering Mrs Lowe checks that everyone is attending. 'Fred gave me a washing machine, a Hotpoint Plus 6 Countess which comes with an adjustable wringer.'

Kay Trent is going to have to report back fully to Mary and the rest at Art Class next week.

'How very useful.' Mrs Newcombe thinks of her sink and mangle.

'It's a godsend. I couldn't have asked for more.' She had in fact asked for precisely that.

'It says a lot,' and Rita, feeling she is never to be the proud owner of such a modern machine, sighs.

'I've always been able to count on Fred.'

'And what did you give him?' Kay Trent wickedly draws up a mental list. She is betting on it being a lifetime's subscription to the "Practical Householder Magazine". Either that or one of those sets of spanner gadgets which can undo every type of nut and bolt in existence. Then again it could have been a car ramp with accessories, or something really thoughtful, a petrol-driven lawnmower so he could mow with pride every Sunday morning.

'Well, you'd never guess in a thousand years,' claims Mrs Lowe in an approximation of girlish glee. 'I still can't be sure where the idea came from. But it was just what he needed. In fact he almost said as much... after I gave it him, you understand. He didn't have an inkling beforehand, of course.' She draws in the attention of all the women in the salon, save Mrs Dring. 'A six-month course at the Vernon and Daphne Croxley School of Dancing, with,' she emphasises, 'made-to-measure evening wear from Hockins on The Strand, single breasted with satin lapels. He looks a dream in it. Like someone out of "High Society". I can't wait to get him on the dance floor.'

'How far's he got?' Rita, now under the drier, asks loudly. Now, however, it seems that Mrs Lowe cannot hear.

'I was really clever. I took his best suit, the one he uses at all the annual functions, to Hockins, and they arranged for a tailor to make it up. I doubt if Fred even noticed the suit was missing.'

'How's he doing?' Mrs Newcombe like Miss Gordon wants to know.

'He does have two left feet, but I've known that as long as I've known him. So I'm not expecting too much too soon. The

Croxleys are being very patient with him, but even they can't work wonders overnight.'

'He started in March, then, did he?'

'April, actually. He said he couldn't possibly get started till the new financial year.'

'So he's been going to the Croxleys for almost three months.'

'Two-and-a-half,' Mrs Lowe corrects.

'Right. Two-and-a-half months.'

'So he's not yet half-way through the course.'

Mrs Newcombe seems satisfied.

Kay Trent at last feels able to speak without giggling. But her sense of fun is hard to disguise. 'What will he be able to do at the end of six months? Waltz? Foxtrot? Rumba? Cha Cha Cha? A passable Paso Doble?'

'The Croxleys aren't making any promises, of course.'

'Of course.'

'But they are holding out the hope that he should be able to manage a Viennese waltz, a Valeta, and perhaps, if he works at it, a slow foxtrot.'

'And is he working at it?'

'He says he is.'

'I didn't notice him on the dance floor at the Dairy Festival Dance.'

'As I said, Fred is still not half-way through the course. And he's got such a lot on his plate. Some people think that being Chairman of the Council means sitting around all day drinking cups of tea, but let me tell you that's not the case at all. What with The Hut – you must all have seen the state it's in. It could blow down in the next strong wind. And now there's this business with the whitewash. If whoever's responsible knew how things like that affect Fred, I could hope it might make them think twice. But that's unlikely to happen. So, what with one thing and another, he really hasn't got the time to put in the practice he needs.'

There is a chorus of understanding nods.

Over with Mabel Dring a pair of treacle-coloured eyes look into her mind. Eyelashes that could give the gentlest butterfly kisses batter shut, then open, then shut. Mabel shudders.

'Sorry, did I pull?' Betty apologises and works on.

A pink fringe of tongue peeks out as Dickie's jowels sag. Mabel's heartstrings snap. Again and again. The vet had left them together. It had been all for the best, he'd said. There was nothing he could do for him, he'd said. Little Dickie's tummy had ruptured from the effort. He was an old dog. He'd had a good innings. A good run for his money. Mabel had been beyond feeling hurt by the pat words. Besides, Dickie looked lovely. His black and tan glossed. The feathers of his legs, ears and tail traced themselves where he lay, a dachshund couchant. Almost dormant. Only his peace betrayed his death. Dickie no longer dreamed. His ever-flickering feet were still.

The treacle-brown eyes look deep again into Mabel, giving everything that there is to give.

'There we are, Mrs Trent.' Mrs Owen stands back from the construction that is the BeeHive. The mirror she is holding up swoops from side to side. Mrs Newcombe admires. If only she had the nerve.

'Right, Betty. If you come over to Mrs Trent to finish off with another good spray, I'll see to Mrs Dring.'

Mrs Newcombe glances across and silently asks herself "Why does Mabel Dring have to attract comment as she does? As she always has." To say she knows Mabel Dring would mislead. But for anyone, or rather any woman of a similar age who grew up going to school in the town, Mabel is known; and so many of them, if they admitted it, carry a feeling of unease for what they did then or in Dierdre's case failed to do.

Avoidance now works both ways. Excuses can of course be made for the misdemeanours and thoughtlessness of youth, but surely now as mature women they could and should try to build bridges.

The stinging smoke made by the Grosgrain skirt swirls as it burns again. Mabel watches once more as it stains, then chars, then holes and flares among the flaming towels. The coconut mat roars. The honesty crackles and is gone in a flash of sparks. Only the mules had refused to dissolve themselves, instead becoming lumpen things, shrivelled, and set hard.

'Goodbye.' Kay Trent balances her BeeHive under a loose-fitting gauzy headscarf. 'And good luck with the Quickstep.' She couldn't have left without saying something of the sort. 'See you at the next highlight of the social season.' She sways out of the salon.

A final spray from Betty encourages Mrs Lowe up and out of her chair and back on with her coat, a grey and pink herringbone with half belt. She turns from her reflection to Mrs Newcombe. 'Have you made our appointments for next week?

Mrs Newcombe is having her net removed and smiles a "yes".

'I do so enjoy having my hair done. It's such a relief escaping the daily chores for an hour or two and being pampered. But now I'd best be getting back to see what crisis has come up while my back's been turned.' At the door Mrs Lowe fingers a wave with her gloved hand, a small hand in a small neat glove.

'We're getting there, Mrs Dring.' Mrs Owen steps back. 'Not quite done though. We need to take just a little off here and here.' Her quick hands conjure. 'Sweep this up and away like so.' Another pass with her hands. 'And then we'll really see what's what.'

Mabel focusses on her reflection as Mrs Owen, taking half-noises for agreement, moves back in to perform her promised tricks.

As Betty teases Mrs Newcombe's unclipped and ungripped waves and curls with her comb, Mrs Newcombe allows herself a further out-of-the-corner observation of Mabel Dring. An ungloved hand rests half clamping the chair arm. Mrs Newcombe isn't aware of thinking how easy it must be for Mabel Dring to wring her weekly wash. She'd need no mangle. Even blankets would give up, lugged from the sink dripping their weighty bulk, dumped onto the draining board and then methodically strangled into submission into a pail.

Mrs Newcombe shakes the thought away as she twiddles with her wedding ring, rolling it against her flesh. It is not the one she got married with. That was a thin gold band, nothing more. This ring, which she calls her wedding ring, which she supposes now really is her wedding ring – after all, the other one is somewhere among the tangle of jewellery at the bottom of her box - this ring has a diamond in a raised claw setting.

The setting grasps and upholds the stone for all the world to see that here is a wife with a husband who not only cares but has the wherewithal to show his care, to show it even if he had been short of money at the time he bought it.

Mrs Newcombe's gaze switches back to Mabel's hand and she knows why it had drawn her first. It isn't its size or its strength. It is a married hand without a ring. She does not know what to think.

*

'Woman's Hour'
Including 'What makes a man attractive?' - The Home Service

'Can I join you?' The café is quite busy.

Josephine Brooks looks up, but her spoon continues stirring its circles in her cup of tea.

'Are you waiting for someone?'

'What do you mean?' Josephine lets go of the spoon sending a wavelet of tea lapping into her saucer, her customary bounce missing.

'Are you all right? If you'd rather be alone, I'd understand.'

'No, Grace... it's just... oh, when you think you really know somebody... and then they... you find... Look, Grace, please sit down.'

Grace sits. 'You are looking down in the dumps...' Grace looks about before going on in a whisper, 'What about last night?'

'What?' Josephine chokes on a mouthful of tea, before in a smothered whisper of her own she fires, 'What do you mean by asking a question like that?'

Grace leans back before moving in. 'I was only referring to... it.' Her whisper is now conspiratorial.

Josephine dies a death. 'How do you know?' She accuses in a hush.

It is Grace's turn to fluster. 'Well... I heard about it.'

'Dear God. Who from?... You must tell me Grace... I have a right to know, after all.'

'People. They were talking.'

Josephine is rigid. 'Is nothing private in this town?'

'They were saying the bodies were very lifelike.'

'Lifelike!... Lifelike... Of course, we... What the devil is that supposed to mean?'

Grace has no idea how to rephrase what is already crystal clear. 'I'd've thought You-know-who would've already told you.'

Josephine feels the tea wanting to come back.'Told me? Told me what?'

'Why, about the bodies... the bodies painted by The Floral Clock... Last night.'

Grace is now registering a raft of emotions as they flicker and fade across Josephine's face. Most of them flash across so fast as to escape recognition, yet chief among those that linger briefly are Relief and Heartbreak in fairly equal amounts.

Josephine steels herself. 'Mr Dinsdale did not tell me about those bodies, for one good reason, he was elsewhere... He did not do them. He was... busy. He was... Well, there is no need for you to know how I know, but you can believe me when I tell you that Hugh Dinsdale is not our... activist.'

Grace can only sit twiddling with the strap of her handbag.

'So, there you have it.' Josephine pushes herself away from the table.

'You going?'

Josephine tidies the front of her duffel coat. Toggles slip into their nooses. 'Take it from me, Grace, he's not our man.' She stands, her thoughts adrift. Last night scrabbles at her memory like a rat in a trap.

Grace's thoughts are quite clear by contrast. If Josephine knows it wasn't Hugh Dinsdale, will she set out to discover who the whitewasher is. Should Grace offer some names? Not that there are many likely candidates.

Josephine taps the table in a sense of purpose. 'There's no point in sitting around. Our Secret Activist has set us all an example to live up to. The struggle continues, Grace, and tempus is fugiting. The eleventh hour has been and gone, and if Little England is going to be shaken awake, it's going to have to happen soon. So, see you Tuesday evening, Grace, if not before.'

Grace watches Josephine swing across the road, her pony tail sweeping from shoulder to shoulder. Her gloom replaced by the need to act.

'Don't you want anything then?'

'Oh, sorry, Mrs Speller, I was miles away. I think I'm in need of a Horlicks.'

*

Grace cups the flared mug in her hands, not that it is a cold day. She needs the comfort it provides.

Each day these days has more than its fair share of high steps to trip a person up; high steps, and low beams to crack your head against. Almost as if the world is shrinking that little bit more every day; like something that has been left steeping in hot water too long. Yet the stains are still there.

And now there isn't room enough to move about. There is no way to turn without coming up slap-bang against another subject she needs to have an opinion about, to show concern about.

Grace is trying hard to focus her meagre efforts, but she feels herself squeezed. Major worries are pressing in on her. Even though, in her own way, she has been taking steps, something more is called for.

***

'Journey Into Space – Operation Luna'
After travelling through time could Jet Morgan and his crew be bound for home at last? - The Light Programme

'Aren't you gonna come and play?' Wendy Wetherall shouts through cupped hands against the wind whistling round Stonehenge. She is standing on the brink of the dip. She's been running round the ring, stomping on each concrete disc as she goes. Beyond her are most of the rest of the children weaving in a never-ending game of chase round and round the gigantic standing stones.

From where she's sitting in the lee of the Heelstone, Amanda shakes her head in one exaggerated sweep from left to right. Wendy doesn't really expect Amanda to come and play. After all she's been a misery for days.

'How about you, Derek? You coming?'

Derek Patterson is not to be drawn from reading "Our Friend Jennings". He has reached the part where Jennings and Darbishire are attempting to stage their masterpiece, "The Miser's Secret", at Linbury Court public school. Derek is in that other world.

Wendy throws up her arms and whee-es down into the hollow. Arriving, she turns back on herself, and, with arms flapping, begins a circuit of Stonehenge, but this time anti-clockwise.

Amanda hunches back against the Heelstone. The massive sandstone boulder leans forwards over her, shadowing itself across her. Craning back, Amanda fancies that this stone wears a serious expression; jaw firmly set, teeth pressed hard together. This is not one of the bashed-about and mauled stones that stand oh-so-properly in their ring-a-ring-a-roses. This is a wild one. Amanda presses up closer to its smoothed roughness, forcing the bumps and sticky-out bits into her shoulders. She feels its weight. She toys with the thought that she is helping it to stand the test of time. If now she moves away of a sudden, the hugeness of the stone could crash. She has a responsibility for it.

*

'Timothy,' Susan opens her lunchbox. 'Would you like an egg sandwich?'

Timothy Unwin is sharing a Stone with Clive Webster.

'I've got more than I want.' She peels one open. 'They've got cress in.'

Timothy and Clive continue to blow bubbles into their drinks through straws.

Susan nibbles at her softly-warm sandwich.

'Just think, Clive, how many people had their throats cut. Millions and millions.' Timothy draws his straw across his own throat. 'If this place is as old as people say it is, they must have sacrificed, well, thousands anyway. See this stain here? That's where they used to collect all the blood so they could drink it after, I bet.'

'And over there,' Clive points off with his bottle. 'Over by that huge Stone, I bet, that's where they cut the bodies open.'

'After they drained the blood here.'

'Yeah, after they drained every drop of blood out of the bodies here, they cut them open over there and probably cut the bodies up so everybody could have a bit.'

'Yeah. And then they probably used the insides in their ceremonies.'

'To tell the future. They'd wave them around,' and Clive spills some pop as he shows what he means. 'And chant. Like Red Indians.' In a moment the boys hop up whooping, waving imaginary tomahawks, before falling into giggles.

'Timothy, would you like my crisps?' Susan's lost her appetite as the boys have chattered. 'They're Smiths and they're not soggy.'

Timothy has turned his straw into a peashooter and aimed a

pellet which hits Clive fair and square. He races off before Clive can retaliate.

'If you don't want them, I'll have them,' Clive offers. Susan rips the bag open and stuffs a handful in her mouth. 'You said you weren't hungry.'

'I never said any such thing, Clive Webster,' she mumbles, mouth full.

'Did, too.'

'Well, even if I did. They're my crisps and I can do what I like with them.' This includes nearly choking herself.

Clive thinks about that. 'Tim said I can sit next to him on the way back.'

The crisps turn to blades in Susan's throat.

Clive finishes off his drink at speed and races off arming his straw as he goes.

'I wouldn't give them to you, Clive Webster,' Susan shouts after him, 'if you were starving to death... I'd give them to Wendy Wetherall long before I'd give them to you!'

'Whatcha giving me?' Wendy shouts just as loud. Susan twists round. Wendy is balancing on one of the discs in her route round and around the ring.

'Nothing! Not a thing! I'm not giving anything to anyone!'

Wendy shrugs and starts off again running, jumping and stomping. She is having fun.

*

'Whatcha doing?' Amanda ignores Thomas Fowler, but he just stands there. 'Whatcha looking at?' Amanda still ignores him.

'Tim told me you were looking for Heaven at school. Is that what you're doing?' Thomas looks off in the direction Amanda is looking. 'It's big, isn't it? The Stones.'

The pair of them watch Stonehenge as if expecting it to do something.

'Whatcha think it was for?'

'Go... a-way!'

'But..'

'Can't you see I'm busy?'

Thomas stares at her as Amanda carries on with her vigil. 'Whatcha doing? Why won't you tell me whatcha doing?'

Amanda slowly swivels to focus on Thomas. 'You wouldn't understand.'

'How d'you know I wouldn't?'

Amanda gives him what her mother calls an old-fashioned look, and sighs significantly, 'Because.'

'Because what?'

'Because I just do, that's all. You're a boy after all, aren't you?'

Thomas delays a moment. 'Yes.' He is worried that there's a trick here somewhere.

'There we are then.'

Thomas squints.

'You wouldn't understand... because... you haven't got any imagination.'

'Have, too.'

'Have you?' Amanda announces her scepticism.

Thomas nods firmly.

'Prove it, then. Prove you've got imagination. Show me... Go on.' She settles herself, with a look that says she is all ears.

Thomas scours the cloudy sky. 'What should I imagine about?'

'You tell me.'

Thomas scours the sky a bit more. 'This is stupid. Course I can imagine. Anyone can.'

'Fine. If you say so, then it shouldn't be difficult, should it?' Amanda warms as Thomas's head empties. 'Look... perhaps I can give you a bit of help.'

Thomas is not fool enough to think that there isn't a trick now. He's been ready for one for a while. Still, as long as he's prepared, it won't harm to go along with whatever Amanda is on about. Besides, Thomas likes Amanda, in spite of the fact she doesn't have time for him. She doesn't snigger when Dringaling makes him stand in the corner.

Amanda reads Thomas's agreement. 'Right, here goes... What do you imagine Stonehenge was for?'

'That's not fair. I asked you that first.'

'Ah yes, but you're the one who says he's got an imagination.' Amanda smiles; a picture of murderous innocence.

Thomas feels exposed. He'd been one of the slow ones off the coach. In all truth he doesn't mind too much being stood in the corner during Arithmetic. Now, however, he is faced by the wide-openness of Salisbury Plain. 'I think...' Amanda's eyebrows rise inquiringly. She hugs her knees, all-attentive. Thomas's mind is a stew. 'I think...' And then it comes, with a bit of help from "Dan Dare, Pilot of the Future".

'I think it was built by Men from Mars who visited Earth thousands of years ago on a trip through the Universe. They had these enormous rocket ships, you see, and they built Stonehenge. They built Stonehenge so they could park their rockets – like a spaceport. That's what it was, a spaceport. When they built it, it had a dome-thing over the top, but that's gone. It was probably made of some sort of plastic and it blew away.' Thomas's ideas flow on with surprising detail.

'Now, those big spaces in between the Stones were where corridors led off – like... like... like corridors do – they led off to the parking areas, where the rockets waited to pick passengers up. And that ditch was where they had a fence, or a wall even, to keep the wild animals out, like sabretooth tigers and mammoths and bears and all. Oh, and right in the middle, dead centre, they had a huge fire burning all the time, so that rockets could see it from Space and know where to land.'

Amanda and Thomas stare at the ruined spaceport. Thomas sees monster machines on their tail fins, pencil-pointing the heavens. Amanda sees Martians in bubble helmets hurrying about on their sticky-out legs.

'Now you.' The Martians fade. 'Now it's your turn. What do you reckon Stonehenge was made for? I've told you what I think. And what's more it could be true, you know.'

Amanda is finding it hard to balance six years of being in the same class with Thomas Fowler with what she's just heard out of his own mouth. She's never heard him say so much. And, for sure, she's never had any reason to listen to him before.

'Well, it could have been a Martian Spaceport like you said...'

'You can't copy what I imagined, 'cos I imagined it. You've got to imagine something different... Go on.' Thomas relaxes enough to sit down on the grass. He is ready to be told.

'So,' deep breath, 'you know that place in Rome where gladiators fought lions and Christians.'

'Yup.' Thomas nods encouragement. He even manages to stop himself picking at his fingers because he knows that some people can't stand it, and he doesn't want to spoil things.

'Maybe Stonehenge was something like that. Mind you it wasn't for killing and fighting. It was a theatre...'

'Like The Hut, you mean?'

'Oh, no. Something much, much bigger and greater than that. People from all over the country, from places really a long, long way away, like Wales, would come and watch and act, too. There were extra special shows on particular days of the year.'

'Fr'instance?'

'Fr'instance, at this time of the year, summertime, there was a show with Pixies and Elves and Fairies and Magic.'

'Wow!'

'Then at Christmastime – not that they had Christmas 'cos this happened ages ago, before Jesus was born, before all that...' And Christianity is dismissed. 'At that time, in the middle of winter, there was another type of show, like we have pantos. Then at springtime they had the biggest, most important show of all.'

Amanda's imagination rushes ahead.

'People from all over spent months and months practising what they were going to do. Of course, before that they had auditions to pick the best. When they'd picked the best dancers, because it was a Festival of Dancing they had at springtime, when they had picked the quickest, the cleverest, the most graceful, and the most beautiful, they had lots of rehearsals. Oh, and each year they had a special theme, like "Heroes" or "Rain". - You've heard of rain dances, haven't you?'

'Course.'

'At last the time would come for everyone to set out from wherever they lived. The ones who lived a long way away had to leave home weeks before or else they wouldn't get here in time. There weren't real roads then, were there?' Thomas is with her. 'So travelling was pretty tricky.'

'Well they didn't have trains or cars or things, did they?'

'And... there were always those fierce animals.'

'Yeah, sabretooth tigers!'

'On the way, people from different villages met and so bit by bit crowds built up, all on their way to Stonehenge.

'Now, one year, one of the crowds from Wales found a huge rock had fallen down a hillside and blocked their way. Because there was a lot of them they managed to move it quite easily. But that wasn't all. They decided to take it along with them because they thought that the people at the Festival wouldn't believe what they'd done without proof.' Thomas is convinced.

'At last everyone arrived, including the Welsh group with their rock. Quite a lot of people made fun of them and called them rude names. Not for long though because that year the Welsh danced brilliantly, and everybody agreed they'd never seen dancing like it; they danced like angels.

'Which one is theirs, do you think?' The question halts Amanda in full-spate. 'The rock. The Welsh one. Which is it?... I think it could be that one there.'

'Yes, that's probably the one.'

'Wow!'

'`Cos Wales is over in that direction, I think.'

Thomas jumps up to see. He stands on tip-toe and isn't disappointed to see just more grass.

As Amanda goes on creating living breathing dancers out of words, the beat of their feet pound through her. 'They danced as if they'd never stop. When everybody else collapsed, they just kept on going, twirling and jumping and kicking and spinning and leaping. They did amazing tricks and everything they did was perfect. They were so good that people cheered and clapped and even cried.'

Amanda basks in the warmth of her fancy, and she hops to her feet to do a big spin. She stops of a sudden as the story goes on. 'The very next year when the Welsh group came to the Festival they brought another rock with them. This time nobody laughed and nobody called them names. And that year they were even better. When this happened for the third year, some other groups from other places made up their minds they were not going to be beaten by the Welsh again. So, the fourth year, quite a few groups turned up with their own huge rocks and they stood them up pointing in the direction they came from... and that was how Stonehenge started to look like it does.'

Amanda just has to spin again. Stonehenge flicks by in a blur. Sky. Sky. Stonehenge. Sky. Heelstone. Sky. Sky.

She slows giddily, shakes her head and makes a successful grab for Thomas's nail bitten hands. He squeezes out a 'Wh..?' before being spun at speed and at arm-wrenching length. Amanda's hair streams. Thomas's nose, too. They lean away back and back, staring at the revolving sky, sending clouds pirouetting, setting their brains afloat. They 'Wheee!' as one, holding on to each other, flying loose from the earth.

One hand snaps free and the pair race over the dip into the theatre-spaceport. Off they roar round the wheel of Stonehenge.

Children flash on and off through the gaps.

Wendy Wetherall stops on one leg as Thomas and Amanda dash on. 'Whatcha doing?' she yells as they pass. Thomas grabs for Wendy's hand and yanks. Off they go together.

As the three children sweep around the Stones, others are drawn in. Clive and Timothy and Susan and almost all, even Derek. Amanda senses the stones hurtling by in the other direction. It is hard to be sure who is going quickest, the children or the stones.

Amanda's fingertips brush the giants as she races. Then with a heave she leads the string of whooping children through an arch and onto the stage. She threads them between and about the fallen stones, then slips her hand from Thomas and spins.

'Come on!' she yells. And they do. There are no second thoughts. They spin in ones, windmilling, arms slicing the air, fingers grasping at clouds. They spin in twos, hanging on for dear life. They spin in rings, feet tripping, dust puthering. They spin like corkscrews and revolving doors. Eyes open, smudging Stonehenge in chalky colours. Eyes shut, reeling with the Universe.

'Stop that at once!' Miss Gordon panics. Just watching makes her feel queasy. Yet the children spin still faster. Collisions breed amalgamations. Near accidents create happy chances. Rings snap open sending singletons careening and carouselling. Lone spinners orbit. Pairs link into twizzling chains cometing across space. Spinning is endless. A galaxy of variations.

'If you don't stop it…' Rita Gordon's voice is lost.

Skirts balloon. Shorts flap. Socks fall. Sandals and plimsolls hardly touch the ground. While the stones stand as still as ever, or chase each other at undreamt of speed, nimbly bearing their mass in dance.

*

Kneeling up on the back seat Amanda watches Stonehenge slip

for the last time below a rise in the road. Yet it is still there, a roundabout turning in her mind's eye with her holding on.

'Sit down at the back there. You'll make yourself sick.'

Wendy sits slumped up against a window, her thumb resting on her lower lip within sucking range.

Jennings and Darbishire have failed to stage their masterpiece in favour of "Henry V". Derek reads on.

Clive and Timothy are playing battleships, sinking the might of each other's navy.

Susan is munching slowly away through egg sandwiches. She looks at each one as another nail in her coffin. She has managed to lose her flask, the new one she pestered her mother into getting, so there is really nothing for it, she has to finish the lot before she gets home. She looks back from her seat to where Amanda is now sitting, a smiling statue.

Amanda becomes aware of Susan and turns her smile on her friend full-force. Susan swallows a wodge of bread and egg. Guilt goes off like a banger on Bonfire Night. She splutters soggy pellets.

'Ugh!' Clive is staring at a lump threatening to ooze its way through one of his unsunk subs. 'Whatcha do that for?!'

'She didn't mean it, did you, Susan?' Susan's hand is clamped to her mouth. 'Besides Tim knows where your sub is anyway.'

'He does not!'

'He does now!' Amanda moves forward to where Susan sits alone. 'Budge over.' Susan, one hand still over her mouth shifts before offering her lunchbox once Amanda has settled. Amanda takes a sandwich and a light flickers on in Susan's gloom.

'Hasn't today just been the most amazing day in your whole life? I've never ever had such a wonderfully marvellous time. Never ever in the history of the world has there been such a fantastic school trip! I mean, hasn't it been amazingly amazing?' Susan wrings a smile out of her withered spirit.

The girls sit quiet, Amanda with her head thrown back against the seat; Susan with her head confused by Timothy Unwin and also by the missing flask. 'Can I have another sandwich?'

'Sure.' And the dark lightens further.

'Do you know, Susan, I'm never going to forget today. Not in a thousand years. Not if I live to be a million.' Amanda laughs for joy and hugs her friend hard, as hard as best friends can.

'Have you got any sandwiches left, Susan? Any that you don't want.' Susan watches a hand as it removes her very last sandwich from her lunchbox. She'll never ever in a zillion years forget today. Timothy Unwin has had her last sandwich.

***

WEDNESDAY, JUNE 25th

'Amateur Theatre'
'On Stage' – Network Three

Osbert Phipps once more fiddles with the sticks of make-up, lining them up parallel to each other, tidying the gilded paper where it has been stripped away, removing a whisker of cotton wool. They lie like so much live ammo on the folded towel.

The men's dressing room is still as empty as when he arrived. Though now there are increased noises off. Outside doors bang shut. Something heavy is being manhandled. Feet hurry by in the main body of The Hut. In the other dressing room voices protest about the size and style of costumes. The Dress Rehearsal is not about to begin any time soon.

Osbert stares at his empty face. Most unhelpfully it stares back.

'Rita!... Oh, it's you... Seen Rita?' Osbert's blank look is interpreted by Charles Burch. 'No?... Where is the woman? Never around when you need her...' The closing door gusts a piece of crepe hair away behind the radiator. Osbert clutches after it, too late. He plonks the Cremine on what remains.

'Rita!' Charles calls again stoking anxieties in others, tweaking the nerves of those within earshot.

Osbert turns in the collar of his shirt, rolls up his cuffs and forces the lid open on "Professor Willard". It is time to paint that face upon his own, to transfigure himself.

*

The door barges open. 'Seen Rita?' Malcolm Hill knows straight away that Mr Phipps is of little use. 'Charles is after her blood. And now I've got to find something to mend the Junior Fresnel Spots with. Whatever they are, they're apparently both kaput.'

He dives for a cardboard box under one of the trestle tables to emerge almost at once. 'Have you seen any straw or pale gold gels by any chance?' It is a waste of time asking, but he can't very well ignore Mr Phipps entirely. 'Or lavender for that matter?... You know? Filters.' Malcolm Hill is aware of quizzing Mr Phipps like a foreigner, slow and loud.

'We've got enough pea green ones to sink a battleship it seems.' Osbert is saying nothing. 'Do we need pea green? Apparently not.' Malcolm has to be going. He shoves the box away and yanks the door open. 'How the lighting people are meant to come up with what Charles wants with a handful of blue and red, and a stack of pea green...?' He slams the door to behind him rather harder than is necessary and leaves the query to crash land.

Osbert settles himself and reaches for Leichner No.5. He tears a little more of the protecting paper away and applies a streak across his high forehead. He then streaks each eye socket, his nose, his cheeks, his neck either side of his Adam's apple. To finish, he draws a line on his chin from lip to tip. Watching himself in the shaving mirror unblinking. He swallows and then pauses, the fingertips of his right hand hovering, unwilling to commit themselves further.

'How, Kee-moh-sa-be!' Chris Owen is holding his hand up in Red Indian fashion. 'Me, Tonto.' Osbert forces a smile. Chris moves into the room over to the costume rail.

Osbert touches his forehead as if it might break and begins to spread the colour. He smoothes it up into his hairline and along his worry lines. Little by little the streaks blur into each other as his face changes. The corners of his angular face send his fingertips backtracking. They gather confidence on his cheeks. They flourish across his jawline. They swoop down Osbert's long neck. His ears are not forgotten, nor his nostrils. He sits back briefly wiping his hands on the towel.

'When you've done, would you hear my lines?' Chris is nursing his script. But before Osbert can reply, a light voice outside magnetises Chris, who speeds from the room.

Osbert daubs some No.9 on the palm of his left hand, dips a finger and starts to create. A dab, a smudge, a smear all serve to bring some health to the Professor, but not too much. No.7 is applied to the eye sockets. A few lines of it are brushed underneath the eyes and the outer corners. An artistic shadow is drawn on the temples and the cheeks, and from the nose towards both corners of the mouth, and along the edge of his lips. Osbert smoothes each mark with a fingertip. His forehead needs no attention. It seams with enough age already.

Osbert gives the Professor the once-over. Does he have a drink problem? He hasn't thought of that. Maybe that is at the bottom of the Professor's vague muddle headedness.

The carmine and lake glint invitingly in their unopened wrappers. His hands itch. The peeled paper reveals a wink of wine-red. A faintest smudge of blood appears in the Professor's cheeks and on his nose. Osbert is persuaded. Carmine No.1 is replaced by No.3 and he highlights the highlights.

Now the shadows look a little thin. Lake is the answer. The shadows deepen, sinking the cheeks, hollowing the temples. The sticks hurry through Osbert's hands. No.20 is rubbed into his eyebrows against the line of the hairs, leaving them rough and bushy. Dots of carmine sit in the corners of his eyes. His hands are attended to. No.7 shades the flanks of each and every finger. No.5 highlights from nail to base. Veins are emphasised in grey. The spaces between the fingers are shadowed in No.7.

As Osbert sits his stoop increases with the Professor's added years. His fingers all but claw with arthritis.

*

There is increasing activity in the dressing room. Men peel out of shirts and trousers, scenting the room with their day's work and their nerves. Most hurry to cover up their underwear and white skin with empty chat. Costumes are held up, are ummed-and-aahed over, are wondered about. Though nobody says as much, there are several who give the provenance of what they are to wear more than a second thought. Who died in these trousers, and did he have a problem with his bladder? What is that smell, mothballs or mould or something else altogether? The sudden cold dampness of air trapped in trousers baggier than usual lowers confidence. Fingers which have lost the knack of doing up cufflinks fumble. The falling clicks of links and collar studs punctuate proceedings. And no-one offers anyone else any help. Although the chat patters on, the room is quieter than a church.

'Are you lot decent?' There is a flurry for trousers interrupted by Rita who pushes the door open. 'Thirty minutes, everyone. Thirty minutes.' She delays a moment before exiting.

'Better watch out, Henry. She's got her eyes on you.' Philip Bray, playing "Howie Newsome" chuckles before Henry Carey thumps him.

The powder settles and Osbert blinks his eyes open. Somebody stares back, Is this "Professor Willard"? It might just be. But not quite yet. Osbert now teases at the heap of crepe hair, borrowed from Mr Lennox, who has used it to good account for nigh on twenty years. Osbert sets his jaw. Most certainly a moustache will decide his accurate presentation of "Professor Willard". Then, and only then, will the old man materialise before Osbert's mirror.

The moment of truth is fast approaching. He unscrews the spirit gum. A whiff of resin wafts up to thrill his acting blood.

Through the fringes of reflection in the mirror flit half-dressed forms, seen in a blur as trout beneath a stream's surface. Sleeves and shirt-tails flap like fins as limbs struggle, arms and heads pushing for the right openings. Figures hop by, mimicking overgrown eight-year-olds in three-legged races, tracking down wayward socks or boots, toes stuck in trouser turn-ups, trying to pause long enough to hitch up braces.

Accusations of theft are rife. Grander crimes are hinted at.

Revenge is bandied about. Coat hangers clink endlessly on the rails. Ties refuse to be tied; shoes refuse to be untied. Hats don't fit. Seams split. Buttons pop.

Out of shot lines murmur, chanted but soon forgotten. In corners characters fall unnaturally quiet while others explode about the place, dislodging dust, trampling on the nerves of one and all.

And the door swings open. 'Fifteen minutes.' And the door bangs shut.

The action cranks into a higher gear. Ties are yanked into nooses. Zips trap flesh. Nerves tinkle like expensive glass.

*

The Face isn't Osbert's. It isn't him etched in the circle of the shaving mirror in an essence more corrosive than acid. It most certainly isn't Osbert Phipps who's pinned there, fixed for display, a common-or-garden, dullish-brown specimen, Draper Dawlishiensis. But then again, and here is the rub, it isn't "Professor Willard" either. Whoever that transient gentleman might be, however he might be imagined to be, this hazy muddiness, this crazed greasespot with all the charm of something that a dog might throw up and hurriedly leave on the hearthside rug is not him. This is no character. This is a kedgeree, a stew made flesh. The larder had been laid bare in order to come up with an undercooked, over-seasoned set of slops.

'Five minutes, everyone.'

That starts Henry Carey. He erupts. He bays and whinnies. He barks. He clucks and cock-a-doodle-doos.

'Shut up, Henry.'

Henry caws.

'I said "shut up".' Vernon Barry, playing "Simon Stimson", throws his script at the crow.

Henry ducks and quacks.

'Henry, for all our sakes, please give over,' urges Harold

Newcombe as he tries another angle for his grey felt hat. 'If you really have to go through your entire menagerie, how about going outside?'

Henry pauses. 'It's all very well for you lot, but if I get just one of them wrong, if I cluck when I'm supposed to whinny, or grunt when I should be quacking...'

'But, Henry, you're not called upon to grunt,' Harold points out, before deciding to leave the dressing room for a quieter spot to run his lines.

'You don't grunt, or quack,' Vernon Barry puts in.

'You know what I mean. Don't go pretending you don't. As I was saying...'

'As you were quacking, you mean!'

'As I was saying... if I don't get my sound effects right, it's not me that's going to look a fool out there. I could scupper the whole thing by clucking instead of chirruping. What would happen if the milk horse barked? Hm? Answer me that!' Henry looks around. Then, satisfied no-one has an answer, takes a breath to crow.

'Henry! Henry!' Henry wonders if Vernon is about to come up with an answer after all. 'Has anyone ever told you?'

'What?' Henry is all suspicion.

'Has anyone ever told you that you bear an uncanny resemblance to Robert Helpmann?...' Vernon makes sure the room is attending. 'The Ballet Dancer.'

On cue Vernon, Chris Owen, and Philip Bray go up on their toes, arch their arms above their heads and twirl.

Henry flaps his arms at them, as if shooing cows. 'Just you stop that! You hear? You stop that!'

The trio twitter round Henry. 'Ooh, Henry, don't you love us any more?' Philip puckers. Henry flails. The smack echoes as Vernon trips backwards over a box of shoes.

'There was no call for that.' Vernon rubs his cheek, not that it is hurting half as bad as when his Mum used to hit him years ago.

'Can't you take a joke?' The other ballerinas are waiting to see what Vernon will do, when Rita settles matters.

'Act One Beginners.'

There is a final flurry of activity, much of it pointless, as the dawdlers and ditherers hurry to do up buttons, pick up hats, almost put on the wrong jackets and desperately ransack their memories for their first lines.

Harold Newcombe pats his pocket for the "Stage Manager"'s pipe. The dressing rooms empty. Out troop real life father and son Alan and Derek Patterson as "Doc Gibbs" and "Joe Crowell"; Alan with the doctor's bag and Derek with the paperboy's bundle of newspapers to deliver.

'Remember to project.'

'Yes, Dad.'

' And there's no need to rush.'

'No, Dad.'

'Move along, you two.' Henry Carey is keen to get to his spot, followed by Chris Owen, and most of the rest of the menfolk of Grover's Corners, merging with the women and girls in bonnets and aprons. Chris manages to smile at a face framed by shiny plaits, and his first line as "George Gibbs" comes back to him. He snatches at it and chants it voicelessly, lips moving, running it over and over head to tail, again and again, nodding in time to keep it from disappearing into the dark.

As the dressing room door swings closed a light bulb pops. Osbert blinks, and now he knows why the face worries him. It is The Blazer's face. It is the face the headless dummy that year after year stands sawn at the waist and neck in a blazer or sports jacket would have if it had one; the dummy that screens its wounds amid a clutter of socks on sawn-off tip-toeing feet; the dummy that thrusts out its manly celluloid chest anonymously among rosy-lipped and brilliantine-slicked heads in blandest pink parading hats, each head cravatted for taste, cravatted for decency. These heads register none of the shock of the recently guillotined, are unable to plead for the sympathy deserved by the gruesomely dead. They half-smile, half sleep. Their open eyes, unblinking, never focusing, never allowing themselves to be any trouble at all. Open and blind. With all the features and none of the feelings. Only gently oozing a scent of manufacture when the window heats up on sunny days. Imperceptibly fading with the seasons.

The shadows and lines Osbert has drawn do not speak of age or experience. They say Leichner numbers this and that. He has fabricated the Professor, who he had come to feel deserves more than this. And the result is that Osbert has set alarm bells ringing - is he fabricated too?

*

'Stop! Stop!' A chair grates in the darkness out front. Philip Bray does as he's told.

'Something wrong?'

'Didn't we say that Bessie must stay your side of the chair?' Philip looks for a chair. 'The one behind you! The one in the Gibbs' house.' Philip waves an arm at the chair and peers out into the gloom to where Charles is. 'Yes, that one. You've led Bessie straight through the wall and into the kitchen.'

'Well, it does say Bessie's all mixed up about the route.' Philip shares this thought with Alan Patterson.

'So, if you lead your horse out of the house, I think it'd be best, hm?' Philip lingers. 'Do you think you could do that? Do you think you could?'

'I was just wondering if anybody's going to notice. After all, it's not as if Bessie is really here, is she? No-one's going to be able to tell exactly where she is, now, are they?' Philip's sister Helen cringes with embarassment over her prompt copy. An intake of breath from Charles is all the answer Philip is going to get from that quarter. 'It's just a thought, but couldn't I just as well leave Bessie over there for instance?' Again Philip waves an arm. This time towards what passes for the wings, stage left, not far from one of the stoves where Rita and Malcolm Hill are standing to attention by the props table.

'Get on with it, Phil,' Helen hisses, but Philip isn't finished.

'Just a thought, Charles. Only it would make it much easier to remember where she is.'

'I don't think we need any more thoughts, thank you, Philip.'

'Charles?' Henry Carey now pokes his head round a drape. 'Since we've stopped, how do you think the whinny was?'

'Fine, Henry.'

'Not too loud? I mean it says she's going on seventeen. Pretty old for a working horse. I'm not making her sound too fit and spry, am I?'

'Henry. Bessie is spot on. Now, can we please get on? Hm? Let's go back to... ' Charles refers to his script, '...Doc Gibbs' "Going to rain, Howie?"'

'That before Bessie whinnies, Charles?'

Harold Newcombe catches himself thinking about an Infant Nativity Play. Henry is very much in the mould of a Third Shepherd. Malcolm Hill reaches out and tugs Henry off stage.

*

The pages turn on Rita's script more slowly than the Play demands. The combination of costumes and lights has shaken several members of the cast so that nothing they can do is right. It is as though the Play has become something altogether different from the one they have rehearsed.

Yet, somehow, the pages turn. For Rita progress is marked by the sound effects. Henry, on her right, goes through a lip-wetting and neck-stretching before each one. While on her other side Malcolm Hill stands with his array of milk bottles in racks, klaxon, whistle, crockery, school bell and the ecetera of Thornton Wilder's imagination. Clock-watching has already started.

Malcolm raises his eyebrows as the newcomer sidles in. Mr Phipps looms. Malcolm replaces the school bell on the table and

271

mouths 'Very nice!' Mr Phipps doesn't twig.

Why did he ever say he'd do it? Some people just aren't cut out for it; standing up in front of a lot of people. Maybe once, but not now. Not like Mr Newcombe, who is so at home out on stage.

Malcolm twiddles an imaginary moustache above his own lip and re-mouths, 'Very nice'. This time Osbert gets it and smiles back weakly. Somehow he is just going to have to get through it.

Henry begins to cluck excitedly as out in Grover's Corners "Mrs Gibbs" feeds her chickens. Henry has been observing Rhode Island Reds for weeks. 'Break a leg', Malcolm Hill encourages in a theatrical whisper.

"If only", hopes Osbert half-heartedly. Moving off into the light.

"If only", Rita's unforgiving mind is racing. The account Mrs MacAskill gave at the hair salon of his behaviour reverberates for her and will not go away. If only she could cause him to come a cropper. That would serve him right. For all women who have been mislead and treated thoughtlessly by men she needs to act.

*

'The Silver Lining'
A message of comfort and cheer for all in trouble – The Home Service

Osbert nudges the bedroom door open, crosses the rug and lowers himself on to his bed. The hiss of escaping energy is almost audible. But, like a much-punctured tyre there's really nothing left to give. Just a dribble.

He brushes his spectacles from his face, and pinches the bridge of his nose till it hurts. His fingers come away greasy. Thank goodness it is dark in the bedroom for he is saved from seeing a smear of red, carmine No.3. The smell of Cremine is bad enough. He thinks to go to the bathroom, but the thought wilts. He

272

toes his shoes off one at a time, pulls up a foot, peels off a sock and takes a breather before dealing with the other. He sloughs off his braces. And, bit by bit, he undresses. His clothes melt into each other. One moment he's shedding, then the very next he's putting on. The clerical grey trousers become flannelette pyjama bottoms. There is no break between the undoing of flies and the tying of a pyjama cord. The vest is pulled off, flicking his ears, before the striped pyjama jacket is buttoned up. A blur of white with hairs and a birthmark.

Osbert settles himself, wishing that his weary head might sink into the pillow forever. The sheets are a blessing. They remind him of Grace. Osbert looks across. The hummock of her is in relief, backlit by the streetlight through the curtains. It's a great shame to rumple a fresh bed, a great shame but also a joy. Osbert urges his toes down to the foot of his bed where they unmake the tucking.

The bed takes Osbert to itself. The mattress cossets him. The pillow puffs itself up, holding his worrying head between its feather-filled muffs. He lies, willing sleep, eyes shut. Yet, behind the lids, all is light and action. He tries. He tries. But there is really nothing else for it but to think things through.

A sudden quietness is added to the quietness of the room. Two breaths are being held. Grace has waited. She cannot wait any longer. She has to go.

The landing light slices under the bedroom door. Osbert tracks Grace to the toilet in his mind's eye. Only to the door.

A script begins to write itself for him. "When she comes back I'll ask her what she watched on TV. I'll ask her, and she'll ask me how things went. And what's more I'll tell her. I'll tell her and then she'll say something. Something like, 'Put your mind at rest, Osbert. There's nothing to be gained by worrying yourself sick. You see, it'll all be all right in the morning.' That's what she'll say, or something like it. If I go on a bit, she might suggest a cup of something, tea or something, or a glass of milk. A glass of milk and perhaps a biscuit. She'll ask if I had supper, and I'll say I had something, and there's no need for her to worry on my account. And then she'll go and bring me a biscuit or a sandwich. I'll tell her she shouldn't have. She'll say it wasn't any bother. The whatever it is, the meat or whatever needed eating up anyway. I hope there's some of that ham left. Some of that ham would be just what the doctor ordered. She'll tell me not to go getting crumbs in the bed; that she only changed the sheets today, and she'll smooth them and tuck in the sheet at the bottom of the bed, and fold her arms over her dressing gown, one hand toying with the flesh at her neck and..."

And Osbert is asleep.

*

'It's My Opinion'

A platform where members of a West Country audience have one minute to express their views for discussion. - BBC TV

'They'll catch you.' Grace freezes by trees on the Brunswick side of The Lawn. 'Take it from me, they'll catch you.' There is a rustle of dried leaves, but then it can't be leaves, not in June. 'You'll not keep on getting away with it. Third time unlucky? But don't you mind me, though. You go right ahead.'

Grace can't stand fixed to the spot all night. She slowly lowers her old shopping bag she's using to carry the tin of "whitewash", all the time looking off into the dark. 'Who's there?'

'Me? Nobody.'

'Are you the police?' There is another rustle of leaves that cannot be leaves. 'What are you doing?' Grace's anxiety is rising.

'Sitting up.' The voice strains as the body moves. 'If we're gonna chat, it's not right to stay lying down while a lady stands.'

'You're not the police then? Or anything like that.'

'Quite right. I'm nothing like that.' Grace backs away to get behind a bench in case. 'What was it going to be tonight?'

'Never you mind,' just pops out.

'Me, missus, I don't ever mind. It doesn't pay, minding doesn't.' Bluebell humps his body out of the bushes where he has a nest near the footbridge. He totters into the lighter darkness, his weight carrying him forwards before he is properly upright. Grace pulls her coat firmly closed.

'What were you doing in there?'

'Watching you passing the Bowling Green, among other things.'

'You've got no right spying on people…'

'I've got no right spying on people who've got no right splashing whitewash about the place.'

'It's not whitewash as a matter of fact. It's chalk I've mixed up at home.' Grace only now wonders why she has explained. 'Besides it's my business what I do.'

'Too right. And I don't want any part of it. If there's one surefire way to end up in trouble, it's getting mixed up with people who go around in the middle of the night with pots of chalk,' Bluebell underlines the "chalk". 'You got a licence for this sort of thing?'

'Don't talk nonsense.'

'Pardon me, missus. But I thought I'd best check you weren't employed on some official scheme to paint the town white. You never know these days.'

'Anyway, what about you?'

'What about me?'

'I bet the police would be interested to know about you.'

'Them? Interested in me?' He has to smirk. 'They know everything there is to know about me, they do. And they don't care tuppence.'

Grace edges round the bench. 'You had no right scaring me like you did.'

'For a person who goes on about rights, you seem to be overlooking something…' and he looks meaningfully at her bag.

Grace is drawn into looking, too.

'What are you going to do this time?'

Grace flusters. 'What?'

'I've seen you before. I saw you paint those bodies.'

'Shh!' Grace expects the bushes to reveal the hidden forces of the constabulary.

'Very well done they were too. Very artistic... It was you, wasn't it?'

'You said you saw me.'

'I saw someone, and unless there's more than one crackpot going around...'

'Crackpot?! Look who's calling who crackpot?!'

'Settle down.' Bluebell waves a calming hand. 'So you're not a crackpot. Now, for Pete's sake lower your voice, unless you really do want the coppers to come.'

Grace finally sits heavily, in part to quieten her nerves. An owl chooses this moment to call. The night seems quieter afterwards. 'Look, I'll have you know I'm no crackpot.'

'Of course, you're not.'

'I... am... not.' Grace wants to be sure herself.

'Didn't I just say that?' Bluebell peels his tongue away from the roof of his mouth. It comes away stirring the taste of rough cider.

'I suppose you're wondering what I've been up to.'

'I don't have to wonder, missus. I was there.'

Grace picks at a blob of chalk that has dried on the cuff of her old jumper. 'That's as maybe.'

'There's no maybe. Believe me I was there, with a good view of the Floral Clock.'

'Do you want to know why?'

'Not especially.'

'I might've guessed. Here I am willing to explain things to you and you don't care. Typical. I bet you think you're not like the rest, living like you do, but you are. You are.'

'What you do in the middle of the night is your business. Nobody else's.'

'There, you're wrong. You're completely wrong. What I do in the middle of the night, as you say, isn't just my business. Far from it.'

'So, what is it?' Bluebell sits on a nearby bench

'Now you want to know, do you?' Grace expels a brittle laugh.

'You gonna tell me? Yes or No? 'Cos if you're not, I'll turn in and catch up on my beauty sleep. Which you disturbed. I'll just push off and leave you to paint all of Dawlish, if that's what you want.'

'Believe it or not, what I'm doing is for your benefit.'

Bluebell looks unconvinced.

'In part it is.'

'I suppose I should thank you, then?... How?'

'This could take some time...'

'I'm not in a hurry.' Bluebell stretches, making himself more comfortable on his bench.

Grace from her bench prepares herself and begins, 'Up to now I've taken action on two different occasions...'

'By the Bandstand...' Grace's heart rushes into double-time. 'I heard the marking machine.'

'You did?'

Bluebell nods.

'Well, on the first night I painted "whitewash" – though it wasn't, but that's neither here nor there – in front of the Bandstand. Then on the second night... '

'By the Floral Clock.'

'I painted those bodies.'

'Tonight I'm planning to do a giant egg-timer by the Putting Green.' Grace now waits for a reaction.

Bluebell thinks before smiling. 'I see.'

'What do you mean, "You see"?'

Bluebell clears his throat. 'I imagine you're trying to draw attention to the threat of some sort of atomic disaster. Hm? Atomic disaster or nuclear disarmament or atmospheric testing or something like that.' Bluebell can see Grace's reaction even in the dark. 'I can tell you're surprised. Ask me about most things, the Hungarian Uprising or this year's sandbuilding contest at The Warren, and I know. Though I could probably tell you more about Hungary. The quality papers last a darned sight longer than "The Gazette" let me tell you.' The rustling of leaves that weren't leaves echoes in Grace's memory. 'Whitewash, bodies and now an egg-timer? An egg-timer that measures the time it takes to boil an egg and the time we've got to prepare ourselves for oblivion. Eh? Hoping to wake Dawlish up before it's too late, aren't you?'

'Not just me.'

'No. Not just you. You and a handful of others.'

'There you're wrong.' Grace is finding it hard to keep up with this ragged man. She needs to score some points and fast. 'There's Bertrand Russell and Barbara Hepworth and J B Priestley and...'

'But here in Dawlish there's you and one or two others. Right?'

Has this man been lurking by The Hut during CND meetings? Grace is nervously wondering if he is her own Guardian Devilkin. 'We've only just started to mobilise.'

'Mobilise?'

'It's all very well for you to scoff. Doesn't it worry you?'

'It scares me to death.'

'So?'

'So I drink. I drink and I sleep in the bushes.'

'You're just an ostrich.'

Bluebell shifts position. 'If you're gonna be like that, I'm going back to sleep. I get all the insults I need during the day without you coming along here after dark. What would you say if I came to your house uninvited and started making rude comments about your wallpaper?'

'Sorry, but you should face up to things.'

'Give me one good reason why.'

'Because as you say, you know what's happening.'

'Missus, just because I'm possibly the best-read person in town doesn't mean I've got to worry myself silly about things. So I know all the facts the papers print, but what good does that do? I can care till I go blue in the face, but there's nothing I can do that'll make one scrap of difference. If the world wants to blow itself to pieces, that's exactly what it'll do. Sooner or later.'

After so much said Bluebell has a bout of coughing. Grace gives him time to recover and for her to come up for air. First Osbert, now this man, both chipping away at her need to feel that action is possible.

'You're wrong. You're so wrong. You must be wrong. Do you want the world to blow itself up?'

'It doesn't matter what I want.'

'Of course it matters! How can you sit there and say it doesn't matter?'

'In the real world people like us don't count.'

'That's because we believe we don't.'

'And we're right.'

Grace inspects chalk stuck under a fingernail. She is not about to give up. 'If you could change anything, anything at all, what would it be?' Bluebell rolls his head. Grace senses his eyebrows rising. 'It might be wishful thinking, but what's wrong with that. Don't you ever remember thinking wishfully?'

'Course, I do. When I was a kid... A..long...long time ago.'

'And?'

'That's what kids do. Pretend and stuff.'

'Yes. And it doesn't hurt, does it?'

'It can. You can get let down.'

Grace backtracks. 'Can I make a suggestion?'

'It's a free country.'

That nearly sidetracks her. 'I've got plenty of paint. Why

don't you paint something too?'

'You're loco, you are! I might be an ostrich like you say, but I'm not round the twist!'

'That's no answer'

'You're gonna get caught, missus, And I'm not about to join you in the clink.'

Having almost been sidetracked, having backtracked, a new track now suddenly appears before Grace. 'It's all very good what I've been doing undercover, but I should stand up in order to be counted, like you say.'

'Don't you go saying I told you to do whatever it is you're gonna do! I'm as happy as Larry. Not a care in the world, me. Not a cloud in the sky.'

Ignoring Bluebell's protest, Grace goes on, 'Let's forget "The Phantom Painter"…'

'Oi, there's no "let's" about it. It's none of my business so just leave me out of it, missus.' Bluebell rummages in his pocket as if he might find a way out of this mad woman's scheming.

'But you're right. Stand up and be counted you said…'

'Stop saying that!'

Grace's mind is made up. She is determined. Grace Phipps has started her personal countdown.

***

ACT THREE

THURSDAY JUNE 26th

"OUR TOWN", FIRST NIGHT

'Where England Begins'
A plea for a resurgence of English provincial life – The Light Programme

The Hut, or to give it its full title The Hut Concert Hall is not full, though there's still time. Two years before, 400 packed in on the canvas chairs with another 115 standing for a record-beaking performance of "Dick Whittington". "Our Town" is a different kettle of fish, but with all the members of a large cast selling tickets to friends and families tonight's audience is a sell-out. With every light on, the cream and green paintwork looks as good as it can. Besides, tonight isn't about noticing The Hut's dilapidated state, but feeling the community warmth that is building up inside its wooden walls. One or more of the high windows might have to be opened during the evening to let some of it out.

Councillor Lowe moves along between the row of knees and the row of chair backs, one hand splayed across his paunch, the better to get to his place the far side of one of the stanchions that hold up the roof.

The Hut is continuing to fill. Councillor Drummond ushers his wife along the row behind. She nods their thanks to Tom and Kay Trent. It is clear to Councillor Drummond that Tom Trent is a very lucky man.

Councillor Lowe makes a show of putting the cushion he has been carrying on the chair next to him before pulling his jacket across his girth and sitting.

Councillor Drummond leans forward. 'How are things at the Floral Clock?'

Councillor Lowe dismisses the efforts of those trying to get to the bottom of it, council workers and the police, with an extended shrug.

'And how are the lessons going? Tripping the light fantastic?'

Councillor Lowe looks round. 'Enough of that if you don't mind.' He turns back and catches his neighbour's eye. 'How are you, Miss Wilkes?'

Miss Wilkes smiles and touches her hat. 'Quite on top of the world.' The councillor has no answer for that.

Councillor Drummond squints up at the roof. In this light it doesn't look half-rotten, but he's seen the reports. The felt has gone and the louvres let in a lot more than fresh air. Bird droppings on the rafters are evidence of that.

Mrs Lowe has finished looking about her, reviewing who's here, and is readying herself to sit. 'It's no good, Councillor Drummond,' she is patting her cushion prior to settling. 'I really and truly think that it's too much for even Him to save.' The councillor is at a loss. 'Praying won't do. The time for divine assistance has been and gone.' She points a precise finger aloft.

Mrs Lowe then airs a smile which descends on Miss Eaves, who smiles back before lowering her eyes to her programme.

When Mrs Lowe has taken her place, Councillor Drummond leans forward once more and slips into tea-shop talk. 'A little bird tells me, Mrs Lowe, that Fred is doing very well at the military two-step.'

The set of Councillor Fred Lowe's shoulders signals that he has most definitely done no such thing. Rather than engage he occupies himself attending to Mrs Owen sitting in front of him, who is complaining about the state of the stoves. It is the duty of the Chairman of the Council to listen to an elector air her views, even when there is not the slightest chance of taking the kind of action favoured by this woman with a pink rinse.

Councillor Lowe then shifts back into his seat, and tries to push away the thought of two hours and more on a canvas chair.

*

'Fifteen minutes, everyone.' Rita looks around. 'You seen, Mr Phipps?'

Harold Newcombe looks towards the costume rail where the Professor's outer self still hangs.

Rita darts a look behind the door. Just a cardboard box of unused garments. 'My, oh my. I suppose Charles should know about this.' She chews on the inside of her cheek and exits.

Outside the dressing room Rita checks her cardigan pocket. The key to the metal cabinet meets her touch. She gives it a pat and nips off to pass on the bad news to Charles. She knows she will find him out front with his friends from Teignmouth Amateur Operatic.

*

'Six pennorth of chips and a piece of plaice, Mr Haywood – er… salted and battery.' Osbert enjoys his pun. 'And how is your good wife faring?'

'She's taken herself off to the Show. I'm not one for plays and the like myself.' Mr Haywood slips the fish into the welcoming fat. 'Besides someone has to stay behind and man the fort.'

'Indeed.'

'Someone told me you are in it, Mr Phipps.'

'Me, Mr Haywood? Yes, I am most certainly in it.'

'I'd best get a move on, then.' He picks up the fish slice.

'I've time to spare, Mr Haywood. No rush. Some things are far too good to hurry.'

*

'Thank you, Mr Hill, that'll do just fine.'

The boiler is exactly where Mrs MacAskill needs it. 'All we need now is the crate of milk, if you would be so kind.'

She now focuses on her helpers as if she might begin a clean-hands inspection. 'Ladies, the Rich Tea go on the blue plates, the wafer biscuits on the white with roses, and the sponge fingers can stay where they are.

'Now, keep the sugar bowls to the back and, unless someone especially asks, put only one lump of sugar per saucer. We've got sufficient stock for four performances, but keep the other packets under the counter. If they see them, they'll be sure to ask for two lumps, mark my words.'

Mrs MacAskill flicks and re-folds a tea towel, hanging it just so over the rail. 'Mr Burch has told me he will pop out when there's ten minutes to each interval – remember there are two – and give us the go-ahead, so there really is no need to start boling water before then. There is nothing worse than over-boiled water. It picks up the taste of the boiler and loses so much of its goodness. There's orange squash for the children. Don't go giving them tea, even if they ask for it.

'I need two volunteers to wash up between the first and second intervals…' she pauses and two hands go up. 'Finally, there's the milk.' With admirable timing Malcolm Hill has just finished lining up the bottles on the counter top, and is ignored. 'Everyone has their own way, but to avoid disappointment, pour the milk first and one pint should do a tray of cups. It's always done so in the past, so there's no need to think that anything will be any different tonight.

'One more thing, teapots are to be warmed. I prefer using steam from the boiler. That way we don't waste water. Anything else? Tea? As per usual I'll be in charge of spooning the tea leaves, so there's nothing for you to go concerning yourselves about on that account.'

*

'Penny for them?' Grace's handbag slips from her lap. Josephine Brooks swoops to pick it up. Grace stoops to do the same. The women almost bump heads. For a moment there is the possibility of a tug-of-war as both have their hands on the bag. But, like a hot brick, Josephine lets go and springs back up, enough to make the blood pound in Grace's head out of sympathy.

'You must've been miles away. You were looking right at me when I waved, but you couldn't have seen me.' She dips down to whisper. 'I've been thinking about... the bodies.'

Grace has her handbag in a sort of armlock. 'Sorry. Sorry. What?'

Josephine whispers even more quietly. 'The bodies by the Floral Clock.'

Grace seems almost tearful.

'Is there anything the matter, Grace?'

'No.' She tries a smile. 'Did you come alone?'

'Oh, No. Hugh is here...'

'I thought that you and he..'

'Yes. Well. We talked and now... And now he's over there. He likes to say that theatre is very middle class...very bourgeois. But I know that bourgeois or not he rather fancies the idea of treading the boards... Yes, he's over there telling Mr Grafton about Direct Action. He's an accountant. You might know him?' Grace manages to shake her head. 'No? Well, I don't see him as a fellow traveller.' She places a comforting hand on Grace's shoulder. 'There's no need to worry yourself...'

Grace's worry instantly flares. She fingers her glasses back up to the bridge of her nose.

'Mr Phipps is going to do fine. Just you wait and see.' She looks across at Hugh, still lecturing. 'It's not as if he's one of the leads, is he?' Another head shake from Grace. 'There we are then. He'll do his best, and none of us should expect anything more than that. Oh,' and here Josephine dips back into undercover agent mode, 'if you have any ideas about our You-Know-Who, you will pass them on, won't you?'

Grace manages to nod.

*

'There you are.' Harold Newcombe is juggling the "Stage Manager"'s hat.

'Here I am indeed.'

'We thought you'd might not make it… in time, that is.'

'Time enough. Five minutes and sixteen pages to be precise.' So saying Osbert heads to the dress rail and with professional ease removes the Professor's attire without jangling a single coat hanger.

He slips the shiny, dark blue serge double-breasted jacket on to the back of his chair, then flicks the similarly shiny trousers over it like an angler landing an eel. The taste of fish is still on his lips. He then sits down and removes his watch which he places face up on a loop of strap. As if for the last ever time Osbert begins to untie his tie.

Harold runs his hat by its brim through his eager fingers. He simply has to make himself turn away from Osbert's measured preparation.

'Act One Beginners,' announces Rita. She sees Osbert sitting in front of his shaving mirror. She thrills. Very, very soon his panic will detonate, sending splinters of himself deep into the woodwork. Tucked in her cardigan pocket, her clammy hand grasps the key.

*

'Take your hands out of your pockets!' Mrs Clark tugs at John's right wrist. 'And do buck up.' She hurries along towards the front. Amanda and Susan are standing in the aisle showing they've found the seats. Amanda is fighting the urge to go up on pointe. What with such an audience, it is a chance not to miss.

'No, you don't!' Susan hisses.

'What?' Amanda poses innocently.

'You know what, so don't!'

'Are you sure these five are ours?' Mrs Clark takes the tickets from the girls to check. The two-minute bell goes. 'Ooh, where is your father? John, go and tell your father to get a move on. No, on second thoughts, don't.' John hasn't moved a muscle. 'Just sit down. And take your hands out of your pockets! Girls you sit nearest the gangway.' Mrs Clark nudges John into the row. She follows. 'Uph!' she goes as she sits. If only she could slip her shoes off. They are already pinching and sitting down for a couple of hours always makes her feet swell. She now licks a couple of fingers to tidy up John's Elvis quiff. He ducks away. She feels she should explain to the lady on John's other side, but Mrs Brewster tucks her coat further over her knees and stares ahead at the red stage curtains.

*

The one-minute bell brings Mr Clark, Mr and Mrs Stephens, and Mr and Mrs Nelson scooting in. The ladies from the kitchen whip off their aprons, straighten their hems and along with Mary Bonfield from school squeeze in towards the back, just as Charles Burch gives the nod for the double entrance doors to be closed.

As the seconds tick away, as lips mouth 'Good Luck', as those backstage steel themselves to pull back the curtains and throw light switches, as Mrs Jackson has a minor coughing fit out front, and as Mrs MacAskill re-arranges a plate of biscuits before checking the water boiler again, Chris Owen gets a peck on his cheek and LOVE blitzes him.

The Hut dips gently into a kind of darkness as the lights are switched off, leaving summer to slip in where it can through the chinks that on wetter days and windier ones let in "the weather". Hands reach out to hold others. Bottoms shift in a last hope for comfort. Younger voices giggle and are shushed. There are last minute whispers concerning programmes, sweets, putting coats and bags under chairs, taking hands out of pockets for the last time, and 'Sorry' for arriving late, 'Sorry' for making people move. 'Sorry'.

*

Bluebell settles himself under the raised floor, in more comfort than anyone seated above. He tries not to miss any of the Shows. First Nights he especially likes. There are usually some good pickings to be had after the audience has gone away. He nestles down among his newspapers ready to share the evening's entertainment through the cracks and knot holes. If people "upstairs" had any idea what he could sometimes see if he puts his eye up close to the floorboards, it would set tongues wagging and no mistake.

Tonight Bluebell has stationed himself towards the "front", Plays being harder to follow than Concerts. He hopes they've all been told to speak up. He has a slurp from a bottle and decides to save the rest for the intervals.

*

Charles's fingers are crossed. Mrs Owen is praying. Chris is adrift.

In the dressing room Osbert is sitting holding the gaze of "Professor Willard", who is sitting holding Osbert Phipps's gaze just as firmly. They are both ready and waiting.

*

The red curtains swing apart.

"...It was hell all over the city. I don't think I can describe a ten-thousandth of the reality by... telling a story. I think only those who experienced it can understand. Black rain was falling..." The handbag holding the notes is pressed hard against Grace's stomach. Her mind reels on and on, winding and rewinding what she has to say, coming back and back to doubt; her doubt at making the reality real enough. "Many were killed instantly. Others lay writhing on the ground screaming in agony from the intolerable pain of their burns. Everything was annihilated. Hiroshima ceased to exist..."

Facts and figures line up, jostle each other aside, avalanching through Grace's memory, but it is the Black Rain that speaks loudest. It is Evil made visible. It is Death scattering its seeds indiscriminately. A piece for you and a piece for you and a piece for you. Fair shares of dying for all.

And all Grace can do is sit and wait as the Black Rain falls and falls in her mind's eye, dusting, filming, coating, choking Dawlish, draining away the colours as it steels Life little by little.

Characters troop on and off the stage and through the hall; the people of Grover's Corners go about their lives bathing the audience in nostalgia for a time and a place that has never been, at least not in this part of Devon. But, in all truth, for Grace, this is like TV, flickering away, filling in the background, while she is over-flowing with the need to act.

*

Malcolm Hill sounds the factory whistle. Next to him Rita gives her copy of the script a quick look. 'Be back in a jiffy,' she mutters. Malcolm gets himself ready with the school bell.

*

Rita clutches at the key in her pocket through the material. All the men who've not lived up to her expectations slip across her memory like slides in a projector. She has been misled so many times.

The school bell rings on stage.

Rita pauses outside the dressing room door. She adjusts her face, putting on a mask of sympathy. She dries her palm on her skirt before reaching for the handle just as the door flies open.

"Professor Willard" stands, handle in hand. This is not how she has planned it. 'Oh,... Mr Phipps... I thought I'd best... you know, it's not very long now... but...' She has to say something about it. She simply has to. 'Whatever's happened to your magnificent make-up... to that moustache and... and all that characterisation?'

'I don't need any of it, Miss Gordon. It came to me. A minor revelation. The Professor is a bit of a windbag, but he deserves the best I can give, and... this is it.'

Osbert tugs a lapel and adjusts the Professor's spectacles. His face is clear of make-up. No carmine, no lake, no numbers 9 and 7 and all the rest. And, no whiskers. Just his own worry lines, his own bald head, his own pasty face. 'All the greasepaint and stuff was pure cartoonery. This is what "Professor Willard" is like, Miss Gordon. Just like this.'

'But, Mr Phipps... it's you.'

'That's it in a nutshell!' Osbert the Professor almost pats Rita on her arm. 'Do you know, Miss Gordon, the dear old man loves Grover's Corners, actually loves the place, probably more than all of the others put together.' Osbert exits for his entrance.

Rita enters the empty dressing room. The table top in front of the shaving mirror is clear of towel, make-up and, of course, Mr Lennox's false hair. She replaces the key in the cabinet door and leaves, pulling the dressing room door shut and heading back to the props table.

As she slips into her place by Malcolm her defences are back intact. It will be later, after the show, after she makes herself a late night hot chocolate she'll face things, and possibly come up with a rewrite.

'Don't go forgetting the drinks for the cast at the interval.' Malcolm doesn't need reminding. 'Helen and I can really manage the wedding without you.'

*

When "Professor Willard" enters the light very few are aware of Harold Newcombe's slight double-take. This is most surely not the Professor he introduced at the Dress Rehearsal, and he fixes Osbert hard, in the hope he might read what is in store. In the very back row Charles Burch's fingers are crossed in knots.

"Professor Willard" settles, scans his audience to allow them all to focus their attention. "Yes, it really is me," Osbert announces silently to them all and to himself. Then, he speaks. He speaks to Mrs Newcombe. She is wearing cultured pearls. He speaks to Mrs Haywood from the Chip Shop, to Councillor Stephens and Councillor Drummond together with their wives neatly sandwiched. He explains clearly so that Mrs Jackson can hear. He delivers the long words with relish, so that the children can hold on to them. He sends them ringing through their heads – "Appalachian", "mezozoic", "anthropological", "precipitation". He notes that "precipitation" causes the slightest of murmurs. "Bra-chio-ceph-alic" bounces of the rafters of the old place. He knows for sure that never has that word ever been uttered here over all the years since The Hut came from Salisbury Plain soon after the First World War complete with its soldierly graffiti. Those had been other words altogether – some quite technical and detailed anatomically-speaking, so soon painted over -, not one of them had had the resonance of "brachiocephalic".

The Professor gets an understanding nod from Miss Eaves in the front row. He senses he has got a gold star from Mary Bonfield sitting with her husband, Leonard, and fellow teacher, Miss Hilton, and a slap on the back from Mr Harvey.

Grace watches Osbert leave the stage, having delivered himself of those neatly-parcelled facts. Her own shopping list of doom still crams her head. For "Appalachian" she can offer "conflagration"; for "mezozoic" she has "radioactive"; for "anthropological" "mutually assured destruction"; and for "precipitation" she has "Black Rain", which continues to fall.

Come the final curtain she must be ready. She is unaware of the bag of sweets offered by Mrs Harvey.

*

Ding-dong ding-dong! Ding-dong ding-dong!

Bluebell splutters awake. What with the cider during the afternoon and in the first interval, together with the closeness of the evening and the comfort of his newspapers, he'd dropped off. Now he is left wondering where they've go to "upstairs".

Feet crowd overhead. Then, after a moment's peace, a more regimented parade of footsteps. The bells ring on, then stop. Bluebell belches before he can stop himself. It echoes around the joists, before being drowned out by "Handel's Largo" on an organ.

'Must be going to have a wedding,' Bluebell tells himself and kicks away a cat that's got too familiar.

Up above some lads tease as two pairs of slow-stepping feet pass immediately over Bluebell's head. The organ strikes a chord and the choir launches itself into "Love Divine, All Love Excelling". Bluebell looks off to where the cat is licking itself. He shoves it something wrapped in stained paper.

Something slips through from above to patter into the dust far enough away from Bluebell to be hardly heard. Heavy feet have caused a floorboard to give it up, whatever it is. He's given no time to go and see. "Blessed Be The Tie That Binds" takes off, reverberating.

*

'Sorry, but have you put the heater on, Mrs MacAskill? Second Interval is imminent.' Charles gets no more than a nod to confirm and dismiss. 'Where would we be without you?'

He smiles, and hurries out as Mrs MacAskill removes tea towels from the re-stocked plates of biscuits. She had nipped out of the hall as soon as all that wedding nonsense had begun.

*

From down below Bluebell is certain he's not really imagining this. He feels the smiles on faces. He hears hands hold and fumble for hankies, twiddle with rings, and clasp themselves with contentment, past, present and future intended. Some clasp themselves out of loneliness, each hand only having its partner to

294

hold. But for the most there is warmth or the memory of it.

*

The organ and choir and bells now let rip.

"Mendelssohn's Wedding March" sets the floor vibrating, puthering dust, sweet wrappers, fag ends, old raffle tickets like so much rain.

*

'Just one more minute, ladies,' Charles tells the WRVS in the kitchen.

*

'Ready with the curtain,' Rita tells the lads with the ropes.

*

'It's nearly the interval,' Mrs Clark tells Susan who needs to go.

*

'I'll come back for the teas,' Malcolm picks up the squashes.

*

"How much longer?" Grace squeezes the last breath out of her handbag.

*

The Moan, The Gasp, The Clatter, The Thump, The Grating of Chairs, The Raising of Voices.

Bluebell cracks his head very early in the chain of events that is playing itself out above, not that anyone above knows or cares. They are very busy caring in another direction. He coughs as a downpour of dust scatters itself from floorboards shocked and strained. He presses an eye up to the nearest knothole. Blocked.

He shuffles on his behind to another one. Blocked like the first. He pokes a finger through, but draws it back as it has come up against something firm but soft, something warm and, well, a bit like clothed flesh. More cautiously he feels into a crack between boards. Nothing. He presses up close, gets something in his eye, wipes it on his cuff.

Now there is Weeping, much Advice, Calls for Water, for Help, for Air. One voice is calming, reassuring, no-nonsense, taking charge. Quite close. Really just the other side of the floor. Bluebell peeps through the crack, wary of more falling dust. He is a bit slow to register what it is he's looking at, but he has every reason. He's never been so close to the back of a man's ear before. Close enough to notice the hairs, to smell the brylcreem, to be aware of the odd colour.

The calming voice is very near. 'Would you keep everyone back. There's really nothing to see. Would someone take over here, please... Yes, just hold his feet up. Perhaps someone could rest them on a chair... He's going to be fine, Mrs Harvey... We must loosen his tie. Mrs Harvey, do you think you could loosen his belt a bit?... There. He's coming round... Now, where's that water?... Here, Mr Harvey, take a small sip. It'll make you feel better... There now... In a few minutes do you think I could have some hefty fellows to help Mr Harvey to somewhere a bit private where he can have some peace and quiet?... You, I'm sorry I don't know your name, could you put down that tray and organise that?' Her face comes into view, as her hand rests gently on Mr Harvey's forehead. But Bluebell has known who it is for a little while. She is smiling the softest smile, lines crinkling around hazel eyes. Bluebell knows it is not for him; he knows he is cheating, almost thieving, but he takes a share of it. Besides, the face clearly shows that now, just now, it is capable of much more care than Mr Harvey needs.

'I should've known Jim wasn't right when he turned down afters.'

'Now, don't go worrying and blaming yourself, Mrs Harvey. Mr Harvey's just had a funny turn and fainted. That's all. What with the place jam-packed as it is, it's hardly surprising. All he needs is a quiet ten minutes and a breath of fresh air. And as luck has it, it's the interval or as near as makes no difference, so if those young men of yours are ready?'

'They are. They are.'

'In that case, I think, Mr Harvey, if it's alright with you, we'll make our move.'

*

'She was in the Queen Alexandra's Nursing Corps in The War, I hear.'

'She was?'

'That's why she knew just what to do.'

'She certainly did.'

'I was telling our Harry I'd never have thought it of her.'

'Me neither. Not in a thousand years.'

'A dark horse and no mistake.'

'We'd best hurry or there'll be no time for a cuppa.'

Mrs Scott, Mrs Hall and Miss Hilton head off to join the queue.

*

'He looked a goner. Didn't you think so? All white and clammy. And do you know? I had a feeling something was going to happen. I did. Call it what you like, but I had a sense. It makes me shiver now, just thinking about it.' And Mr Nelson shivers.

'She drove an ambulance during the Blitz in Exeter, like Ena. Doing that sort of thing a person learned to cope in an emergency. You can't help but wonder as to some of the sights she must've seen. I dare say she could tell you a tale or two fair fit to turn your stomach. Not that she would, mind you. Mrs Phipps is not one to rake up the ashes. What's gone is gone is her motto.' Mrs Nelson, who is acquainted with Mrs Phipps by way of both being "in business", leads the way to the queue for tea, her husband and Mrs Haywood in tow.

*

'Amanda, did you see the way she gave Mr Harvey artificial restoration?'

Susan now knows for sure she's going to be a nurse.

*

'Osbert Phipps is a lucky man. It's not every man with a wife who can be relied upon like that in a crisis,' comments Mr Liddell, whose wife is off in the kitchen helping.

'You're telling me. You should see my Win. When it comes to housework, cooking and that sort of thing, there's not a woman, and I don't mind who you care to name, yours included, Jack - yes, I'd go so far as to say that there's not one of them whose a patch on my Win. But, when it comes to people having heart attacks and that sort of thing, heart attacks or attacks that look like heart attacks, well, when it comes to that, she's neither use nor ornament. She is. I'm sorry to have to say it, but she is. She only stands around all of a dither. That, or cries.' Mr Carey, Henry's father, gets several nods from the men around him.

'And where were you when the trump sounded?'

'I beg your pardon, Vicar?'

'I was simply wondering, Mr Carey,' and the Vicar drifts off, tea cup balanced, plate too, well practised in the Art of Taking Refreshment.

*

'Amanda! Amanda! It's him. It's him again!' Amanda is leaning over the stage lip. Susan pinches her shoulder.

'Whadya do that for?'

'Well, look, then!'

Amanda turns her swan like neck, if not Odette, then perhaps Isadora Duncan. 'Where?'

'Over there. With an orange squash... It's Robert Helpmann.'

Amanda almost sets off, but brakes straight away, 'Him? That's not Robert Helpmann. That's Henry Whatsisname – he's in the programme. He's the one doing all the animal noises. How could you think he was Robert Helpmann? Look at his turn-out for a start. Honestly, Susan, after everything I've taught you!'

*

'Grace?' Osbert is standing quite close to where Grace is sitting in the vestibule with a cup of tea and a slice of unwanted cake. 'Are you alright?' Osbert stoops to straighten her saucer. 'You're all right, aren't you?'

Grace slowly looks up, but her eyes won't focus on him. They slip away scanning the wall.

'Grace, I'm so proud of you. People have been telling me – Mr Hill for one – just how wonderful you were. And you were, you know? You were absolutely wonderful. You did the right thing. Even Dr Wallis says he couldn't have done any better himself. You did exactly what was needed. And Jim Harvey is singing your praises in there.' Osbert points towards the dressing room. 'He swears he'd be pushing up the daisies, to use his phrase, if it wasn't for you.' Osbert swings an arm enthusiasticaly, but stops and at last sits himself. 'What is the matter Grace? There's something the matter, isn't there? Are you just feeling tired? It's only natural to feel drained after what you've done.'

'But I've not done a thing.'

'How can you say that, Grace? There's Mr Harvey who's as sure as can be that you saved his life. Now, that's not nothing.'

'All I did... '

'Was the right thing.' Grace shrugs her shoulders. She offers the cup and saucer to Osbert. 'Would you like another?' She shakes her head.

One of the WRVS pokes her head into the passage. She sees Osbert and mouths something. He makes no attempt to understand and hands her the cup and saucer together with a smile and a nod. Back she goes with material for another chapter in The Grace Phipps Story.

'You were very good. Your "Professor Willard" was... oh...'

'Fine?' Osbert's voice tries a little skip.

'Oh, more than just "fine". Honest. That's it. Honest. The Professor had no way with him. He was speaking from the heart... Very like you, really, Osbert.' Grace smiles the smile that Bluebell saw from under the floorboards. It's a smile Osbert has forgotten she has.

Grace wants to pull a thread from his jacket cuff.

'You amazed everyone... and I do love you. I do. Honest... From the heart...' and Osbert tries to catch and hold the quick gaze she gives him.

Her hand reaches out for his. Not the cuff. She takes his hand in both of hers. 'Osbert I really had hoped I was going to do something important.' He squeezes her hands over his. 'I had such plans.'

'Dear?'

'I had plans.'

Osbert misunderstands. 'But you can still have plans, Grace. We both can.'

'I wanted to stand up and be counted. But here I am... here we are... outside, sitting in a passage... much like always.'

Both Osbert and "Professor Willard" are bemused. Grace is clearly tired. Both men pat her hand. 'Do you want to see the end of the play?... Or shall we go home?'

Grace looks towards the door back into the hall. 'I don't need to know how it's going to end.'

'So, it's home then.'

Osbert stands. 'We could go for a stroll by the beach, if you'd like to? If you're not too tired.'

Grace picks up her handbag with the unused notes. 'Yes, let's do that.' She stands. She can hear one or two bones crack deep down. 'Maybe the tide'll be out.'

Osbert follows Grace out the double doors, while in The Hut the Dead of Grover's Corners debate Death, which, they decide, is not such a bad thing after all.

Once outside, even though the evening is not cold, Grace pauses to put her coat on. Osbert helps with the sleeves.

'Fainting can make people think really funny things, Grace. Leastways I suppose that's the case. When I popped in to see if there was anything I could do, when Dr Wallis arrived, Jim Harvey was going on about the rain. Now it's not rained for days. I never would've thought that fainting made you imagine such things. Not just common-or-garden rain, mind you. Dear me, no. Black rain. That was it. Black rain. Did he mention it while you were with him, dear?'

Behind her bi-focals, beyond her hazel eyes roller blinds spring up, whirring on their poles. 'Black rain, dear?' Grace's mind is letting in the light, casting doubt aside and scuttling along at breakneck speed.

'Yes, that's it. Black rain. But he didn't say anything of that to you?'

'Can't say he did, dear. I'm sure I'd remember someone saying something about Black Rain.' Grace takes a peek inside herself. Her beliefs are blooming. Without doubt they must be tended, nurtured, then offered matter-of- factly, whenever the time was ripe. A bunch of them handed over with a smile, over a cup of coffee, during a chat, at a time when people can listen.

Outside The Hut Osbert straightens his hat. 'Black rain... Not a very nice thing to think about.' The sky doesn't have a cloud in it. 'Shall we go the usual way, dear.' Osbert offers his crooked elbow, like at the end of a film.

'Yes, dear, let's go our usual way.' Grace loops her arm through his, and they begin the walk back down through the town, along Brunswick by the stream where the black swans are asleep, where the coloured lights sway gently in the evening breeze. Red, green, yellow and blue spangling the water, flickering in the trees – a chain of rainbows.

***

AUGUST 1958

'Frontiers of Science: New Moons'

Since last October six artificial satellites have been launched across the frontiers of space. What information are they sending back to earth? -BBC TV

Every one hundred and six minutes every day of the month as it has done since being launched on May 15th at Baikonur Cosmodrome in the Soviet Union, Sputnik III passes over Dawlish, crossing the sky above the town in a little less than five minutes. A cone measuring 1.73metres across its base and 3.57 metres at its tip, it orbits at an angle of 65degrees to the equator, rising over the horizon in the south-west and heading off over the horizon in the north east, rising over Dawlish from beyond Oak Hill and a handful of minutes later dropping out of sight past Dawlish Warren. It carries various instruments to perform geophysical research of the upper atmosphere and near space. It also carries a large on-board tape recorder, but this unfortunately failed soon after launch and is of limited use.

The Space Race is on. The Future is getting closer. Down on the ground which Sputnik flies over that prospect is being met with varying degrees of enthusiasm and worry, but only among people who actually give the future a moment's thought.

*

Friday, August 1ˢᵗ

Hugh Dinsdale is busy in his uncle's garage at the bench building the Thor missile's pencil-shaped framework from bamboo canes. Josephine is indoors sitting at his aunt's Singer sewing machine in the back bedroom. She is no natural seamstress, and at times she is almost driven to tears when the spool runs out, a thread snaps again or when the old cotton sheet gets caught in the foot. Worst of all when a needle breaks as it has just done.

Thankfully the allegretto of Beethoven's Symphony No.7 is playing on the wireless, coming live from the Royal Albert Hall, lyrical, swooping, growing in majesty, carrying Josephine, who sways and calms, as a daydream of family life re-surfaces.

*

Tuesday, August 5th
'It's been going on for the last twelve years and all the plans we've come up with over that time are like castles in the air, which I know is something I've said before,' says Councillor Stephens again.

'We must get down to brass tacks, decide on a site and bear in mind that something in the region of £10,000 must suffice for the job,' says Councillor Lowe, always focusing attention back on the money.

'We just need four walls and a roof,' chips in Councillor Drummond.

'The present condition of The Hut is disgusting as anyone who attended "Our Town" must have noticed. The toilets alone are a health hazard. It's time to take up the cudgels on behalf of the public hall. Three years ago we were almost in agreement and the plans had only gone back for alteration for about the seventh time when the Credit Squeeze started,' Councillor Stephens is refusing to let go.

'We must make a decision and stick to it.' Councillor Brewster has had more than enough

A brief pause before Councillor Lowe as Chair draws a line under proceedings. 'We need to call a Public Meeting.'

*

Wednesday August 13th
"Variety Fare" has attracted a mixed crowd of locals and holidaymakers to The Hut.

'I come every Wednesday during the season. But this one's

going to be really special.' Rita Gordon can hardly wait.

Miss Eaves is looking through the programme. She is not sure she is going to warm to Our Freddie described as "Chocolate Coloured Coon". She has really only come because Miss Gordon got her to promise she would at "Our Town". She feels the world should have moved on. She had caught the first of "The Black and White Minstrels Show"'s on TV in June and had had to switch it off. It seemed so wrong of the BBC. She now becomes aware that Rita is still talking.

'…he plays the Austrian dulcimer with such heartfelt emotion from lullabies to folk tunes and so much more. I feel it's down to me that "Dulcetto" is appearing in these shows. You'll love him, I know you will. Like I do.'

*

Wednesday August 13th
(106 minutes later with Sputnik's return)
'Young woman, I feel such energy coming off you.'

Susan inches herself away from Amanda. It never pays to sit at the front and draw attention to yourself. That's a lesson she's already learned. Not Amanda, though. Quite the opposite. Susan sees Amanda is almost pulling "Mystery of the Mind" – such a weird name, she thinks – to focus on her and nobody else.

'Let me ask you to focus on the most important thing in your life.'

Susan and anybody that really knows Amanda can read her mind on that subject without any special mind-reading skill.

'I am sensing it is not a place…' Amanda shakes her head. 'No, and it isn't a doll or a teddy.' Amanda rolls her eyes as "Mystery of the Mind" smiles at the rest of the audience. 'Of course it isn't, not a young woman like you. Childish things are all in the past. Almost.' He brings his fingers to his temples. 'I am hearing music. Not what I might expect. Not The Everly Brothers. Not "All I've Got to Do is Dream". Though you are definitely dreaming. Not "Volare", though flying is in there somewhere. I know what it is. It's Tchaikovsky...

And Amanda gasps.

'It's... Swan Lake.'

She gasps again.

'You have a dream. And your dream is to be......' a lengthy pause for deeper thought for the vision of swans to glide by, 'an animal collector like David Attenborough.'

*

Friday, August 15th

A Sousa march is blaring, but still the ruddy pigeons can be heard at it on the windowsill. Eric Dring concentrates very hard and dips the tip of his brush, the very tip of it into the enamel paint. A grenadier waits for his buttons to be painted in. Lines of near-identical others stand drying and dried on the newspaper. Sometime, sometime really soon, Eric will be ready to stage the set pieces of the Peninsula Campaign, but there's no rush.

Sousa sends brass thundering up and up and clashes to a halt. The whole house takes its fingers out of its ears. Even the pigeons are for the moment quiet from exhaustion. Eric senses a sneeze coming on, clutches for his hankie, smothers his nose and softly pants. It goes away. But his right eye itches and waters. The saltiness stings the tenderness round hs nose. "God, how I'm made to suffer," he thinks. "Why must it always happen to me?" But he knows he is no longer convincing. After all now he can go to the Chip Shop any night of the week and bring them back and spread the smell of them and their vinegar through the house and stuff the paper in the bin in the kitchen and have brown sauce on them and leave the dirty plate on the draining board.

Eric pours himself another scotch. These days he can do what the hell he likes.

*

Saturday, August 16th

The shopbell sounds.

'Hello, Charles, this is a first.'

'Hello, Osbert.' Charles Burch looks around at this unknown territory. 'Trade is going well?'

'I cannot complain.' Osbert is immediately struck by the novelty of that phrase coming from his mouth.

'I've been meaning to call in to let you know how impressed I was, how much we all were, by your Professor.'

'We both thank you,' and Osbert dips his head, a small theatrical bow.

'I wanted you to know that you... both,' and all three men there smile at that, '...were seen by 857 people, which is up from last year's 785. And from a financial perspective we made a profit of £16 14s, which is not to be sniffed at.'

'Certainly not.'

Charles is wondering if he should go on or not. A look at Osbert persuades him. 'Having triumphed with your Professor....' Charles quickly raises a hand to delay Osbert's protest. 'Having triumphed with such a telling performance, I was hoping you might consider being a regular with the Repertory Company in the future.'

Osbert doesn't flinch or even blink, but smiles wider. 'I'd be pleased to.'

*

Saturday August 16th, Carnival Week Procession

(Two orbits or 212 minutes later)

'Oh, Grace, doesn't he look heroic! Like a Norse God for today,' Josephine Brooks is gushing.

Grace is not as tall as Josephine and is finding it hard to see anything through the crowds lining the route three to four deep in places. She can however see the top section of Hugh's pencil-pointed Thor Missile as he passes by among the other fancy dress contestants; any number of Queens and Tommy Steeles, Batmen and Smurfs and one Paddington Bear.

'He really looks the part.'

Josephine beams. 'We both worked so hard on it, Grace, because we knew there was this magnificent opportunity to present to the people of Dawlish the threat that nuclear missiles pose.'

When a breeze catches Hugh causing him to lean one of the Smurfs starts to cry. But one of the Queens leans Hugh the other way and the Procession heads onwards through the town from The Avenues towards its destination, the Bandstand on The Lawn.

*

Saturday August 16th, Carnival Week Procession

(One more orbit or 106 minutes later)

'He was amazing! That missile was brilliant. He really should've won. Really.' Timothy Unwin, holding his cup, and Clive Webster, two of the Tommy Steele lookalikes are passing with their cut-out guitars. Susan is agog.

'You see, Hugh, everyone thinks it should've been you.' Josephine feels the need to console Thor.

'I knew I wouldn't win when I saw who was judging. That gaggle of Tory councillors' wives weren't about to choose me, were they? Best mates of Mad Macmillan, Monty and their merry band of maniacs. But that was not why we did it, Grace. We did it to get people thinking. You see, time will tell. Sanity will prevail.

Josephine leads Hugh away, weaving through the crowds in search of refreshment, dodging Dawlish Civil Defence waving from a Green Goddess fire engine, leaving Grace by the Bandstand.

Looking down there isn't a trace of the whitewash that wasn't whitewash even though it said it was. Grace is thoroughly resolved to make the world safer, one person at a time.

Saturday August 16th, Carnival Week Procession

(One further orbit or 106 minutes later)

'On behalf of the Pleasure Ground Committee I think you will agree that this Carnival Week has been a plucky effort, especially when it is taken into consideration how chancy the weather is and coupled with the present unsightly upheaval in the main part of town caused by the laying of the new sewers on Tuck's Plot. The deluge that stopped the Opening Ceremony a week ago and caused our admirable Violets Queen, Kay Trent, and her charming retinue to take refuge along with others on the Bandstand certainly dampened proceedings and a lesser town might have thought of calling the whole thing off. But we Dawlishians are not like that. We are used to weather!' Councillor Brewster pauses to encourage the applause and shouts of 'Hear! Hear!' which he duly receives.

'It only needs me to utter those immortal words, 'See you all same time, same place next year, when we will do it all over again!' The applause and cheering redouble.

*

Wednesday, August 20th

'Vera, Could you come through into the lounge.' Fred Lowe, lowers the needle on to the record with perfect timing, for as his wife comes in the first notes of Strauss's "Blue Danube" begin to play.

He knows he has made an impact for Vera stops, taking it all in. The three piece suite pushed back. The ceiling light off. Just the two wall lights on. And Fred standing dead centre. Fred in his brand new suit looking like Clark Gable, or better, his arms held out inviting her to him. 'May I have this dance, dear?' Mrs Lowe steps in. Fred takes hold and they waltz.

'Ohh, Fred.'

'Don't speak, Vera. Just dance. Besides, I can't talk, I'm counting.'

Sunday August 24th

(105 miles away from Dawlish in Cherbourg Sputnik can be seen after dark every "*cent-six minutes*").

Mabel just knows she's never going to get over these coffee-making machines. The process does things to her insides. What's more there aren't any words in English for the bits and pieces. *Le peuple anglais* have never had words for them. *Quelle surprise!* There's the cute little saucer-shaped thing with the short handle which Lucien uses to collect the ground coffee from the dispenser. Real coffee; nothing instant. Then he taps it, or presses it to make sure... to make sure... Mabel must ask him why. She has so much to learn. Then he locks it into place with a flick or twist and a final nudge. And every time he does anything he tickles the machine with his cloth, flirting with it, teasing it to release the thick rich dark bitterness which drops like sweat, or tears of pleasure into the cups.

Mabel eases the straps of her top an inch or so further off her shoulders. Lucien never fails to admire them. And they are so *admirable*. He's not the only one to think so, she knows.

Mabel sits at her table. The machine drips more slowly and stops. Lucien performs the last stages of the ritual; clinking the cup on to its saucer; resting a spoon there; tossing, not putting, a couple of sugar cubes; arranging the cloth over his arm with its tattoo; tapping the counter as he eases from behind the bar, exchanging a few words with a regular before he descends on her. The coffee all but floats from neat round tray to table.

'*Voilà, MaBelle...*'

She melts each time. That's how he says it. That's how everyone calls her. *MaBelle. MaBelle.* Every time it rings, her beauty chimes.

'*C'est tout?*'

Oh, no never! Never ever *dans un mois de dimanches* would it be all!

'*Merci, Lucien*' She isn't ready to stop saying "thank you".

Lucien admires her shoulders and sashays back to the bar carrying his weight lightly.

"I'd only have to click my fingers..." Mabel sips the coffee. It's still too hot. She rests the cup back on its saucer. Let it cool. She has all the time in the world.

Time to learn the secrets of the coffee machine.

Time to become a regular.

Time to practice clicking her fingers.

*

Bank Holiday Monday August 25th

The tide is out at Dawlish Warrren. The beach is packed. There have been 227 entrants for this year's Children's Sand Drawing Competition, the reporter from the Gazette has been told.

'Say Cheese.' Thomas Fowler is already grinning fit to bursting. Kneeling on the sand. Hands holding the small silver cup and box of chocolates in front of himself.

'Age?'

'11.'

'Can you tell me a few words about it, Thomas.' The reporter needs a caption.

'It's the Future.' Thomas turns to admire his sand picture. 'A Spaceport with rockets, all pointing to the stars.'

'Thanks, Thomas, you've got a great imagination and a real eye for detail.'

Thomas glows.

'I bet you'd like to be Dan Dare.'

The reporter moves off to capture the other prize-winning pictures before the tide turns and washes them away.

106 minutes later the beach is clear.

*

Bank Holiday Monday August 25th

(Two orbits or 212 minutes later)

Outside, Dawlish is in full holiday mood, all flagged and festooned. Indoors in the small bedroom that is Eric Dring's workroom the diorama is complete. It is 1812. After so long Eric is finally ready to lead his army in his own version of The Battle of Salamanca and thrash the stupid French, who made the fatal mistake of underestimating him and his English troops. Eric's infantry stand in serried ranks ready for their commander's call to "Charge!"

The house on Oak Hill had been full of tense expectation, prepared to let battle commence.

By the top stair there is a ruck in the carpet.

Below the bottom step there is the body of Mr Eric Dring and the scent of whisky.

The house is at peace.

***

EPILOGUE

THURSDAY, SEPTEMBER 15th 1988

The Epilogue
A quiet moment of reflection at the end of the day – BBC Radio 4

It is already gone 10:00pm. Biscuit crumbs filter down into the cracks of settees, the crannies of armchairs where coins, pins and fluff are stored. Teabags sit by sinks to drain. Duvets are making encouraging come-hither noises. Dogs want to go out for one last time. Cats make up their own minds. And the People of Dawlish look back.

10:00pm is a time when a high proportion of those still able to recall or reconsider do so. It's a time when there's a bit of peace, when nobody with any sensitivity phones. In the weeks after high summer evenings become ever quieter as the light seeps away.

Time has passed. It no longer ticks on mantelpieces. Clock keys are no more to be found tucked away behind letter racks. Now time glows. It flicks its numbers. Sometimes it clicks. In an empty room it half-whirs, half-hums. It's driven onwards by batteries or the mains in clocks with no apparent workings inside. And it gives no warning when it's going to stop. No tired hands moving more slowly around circular faces. No lengthening pauses between the chimes. The mantelpieces themselves are being boxed in or even pulled out.

*

Tim and Susan Unwin are sitting on their new IKEA sofa with its padded roll arms all in a brown print, admiring their even newer black stack CD player, an AIWA pulsing its volume like flickering columns on a bar graph, maintaining its balance with ease, bouncing Bob Dylan's "Blonde on Blonde" against the magnolia walls.

'The sound quality is just as good as people say, hm?' Tim goes over to give a control a tweak.

Susan looks again at the lyrics and sings silently along with Bob.

She has discovered that fun can be had if only in moderate amounts.

Tim's hair is no longer longish and blondish, more shortish, mousey and receding.

'Who sang "Concrete and Clay"?' she asks.

Tim turns from the equipment, "Unit 4 Plus 2". But he's a bit unsure. 'Or "Hedgehoppers Anonymous"?'

'Good.' Susan transfers the question from her draft list to one of the cards she's preparing for the upcoming Conservative Association's 60s Quiz Night. If Tim is uncertain, Tim who can rattle off the lyrics of "Lieutenant Pigeon"'s "Mouldy Old Dough" and name the female drummer of "The Honeycombs" and so much more, if he is not immediately sure, then the question is a cert. Susan moves on to "The Beach Boys"' "Pet Sounds".

*

The last of the audience are leaving the Shaftesbury Hall having had a good night being entertained by The Repertory Company in their autumn production of Alan Ayckbourn's "Joking Apart". Cars are pulling away.

Looking from outside through the windscreen of her Austin Metro it is as if Miss Gordon and Miss Eaves are on TV. Around them most other cars have left. Headlights sweep through the glass, glinting off rain and spectacle frames. 'I'm not leaving till Brunswick has cleared.'

Linda Eaves is content to wait. She turns the programme in her hands. She'll be adding it to her very extensive collection in her archives at home. A lifetime at the Library, though now over, means that cataloguing is deeply ingrained and indeed gives her real pleasure. 'Do you know, Rita, I'm never sure with Ayckbourn. I'm left wondering if his view of life is a sad or a funny one. As always he dares us to laugh at ourselves.'

Rita Gordon's hands grip the steering wheel. 'But poking fun at the misfortunes of others is cruel.'

There is a shared thought, one unsaid.

'Everyone is to be praised for doing their best.' Rita's hands relax a bit. 'Derek Patterson is always good.'

'So talented. I remember him being always in the Library as a lad. I wonder he never went on the professional stage... Would you like a mint?'

Rita takes one. 'My favourites.'

Sucking on her own mint, Linda is in full agreement.

'What are they doing next?'

Miss Eaves flicks the programme over to see, but looks up when a reversing Cavalier swings a bit too close for comfort. The lights cause the two women to blush bright red.

The Cavalier pauses as it reverses from its tight parking space. Hugh Dinsdale looks right and left while his wife weeps. The Kleenex is a wodge in Josephine's scrunched hand. Hugh manoeuvres out and heads off. The coloured lights along The Brook are swinging in the wind.

'I didn't know. Why hadn't anybody told me?'

Hugh manages the tricky manoeuvre of digging out his hankie from his trouser pocket and offering it. 'I didn't know either.'

'We should've known.' Josephine sobs. 'Just think, all afternoon I was baking for The Green Fair. Those stupid date and walnut slices, the apple and cinnamon loaves. I was happy listening to "Midweek Theatre"...' The hankie smothers an upwelling of guilt.

*

'... the 29th or 30th would be possible. Shall I make them both provisional for the time being for 2:30pm? It sounds from what you tell me, that there shouldn't be any problems with the necessary paperwork.' The Vicar of St Gregory's pencils the dates in the church bookings diary and ends the call after a few pleasantries.

Harold Newcombe puts down the phone at his end, returns to his chair and picks up the threads of the memorial address he started soon after he got the news yesterday. If Dierdre were here she'd tell him he was too old now to keep taking on such responsibilities. But as she isn't, he feels not only obliged, but that keeping being there for others helps to keep him going. He will have to do some checking to make sure of his facts. It was after all such a well-stocked, well-lived life, crowded on the small scale.'

*

Mrs Brace, as Amanda Clark has been since marrying Peter in 1970, has had a shock. She has recently closed the door to the police, who have been quite understanding. She had readily accepted their offer to drive her home to Marston Close from answering questions and making a statement which they recorded. She had to explain how she found the body on The Promenade. Now for the time being she can try and settle herself before Jess comes home from Ballet. Peter won't be home from work till later. She has wondered if she should phone him to let him know, but the news can wait. So for now the house is hers for her to reflect on the day.

'I was walking along looking out to sea, looking out at nothing really, just looking at the waves. I like the sea, but then, so do a lot of people. There was no-one else about – no-one except a couple and their dog further down the beach. I suppose there were other people but I just didn't notice them. They could have been up above on the railway station waiting for a train. But on The Promenade there was just me and... Well, like I said I was walking along watching the seagulls when I noticed her.

'That's not to say I really saw her. I mean, I wasn't paying any attention. You don't, do you?, not when you're going for a stroll to blow the cobwebs away. She was sitting on one of those benches. Sitting upright looking out to sea. Sitting with her shopping by her side. I didn't think anything. Well, she was doing what I was doing. We were both there looking out to sea. Though, I do remember looking a bit harder – at the sea, I mean. She was so intent that I thought perhaps she'd seen something I was missing. I slowed down a bit and really looked. Up to then I'd just been watching with only half an eye. Anyway, I looked to see what she was looking at. So silly really. After all she wasn't looking at anything, was she? Maybe she had been, but she wasn't any longer.

'I was getting nearer. Nearer to her, that is. I remember deciding to comment, to make some remark about the sea, to see if she had seen something that I had missed. Only when I got up to her, or quite close anyway, I felt something was wrong. I mean when you get near someone there's always some reaction or other. don't mean they look or speak, but there's just a sort of signal which tells you you've been noticed. Anyway this didn't happen. straight way thought she might be deaf - she hadn't heard my ootsteps over the wind. But then my shadow crossed her face and there was nothing and I knew.

'I've never seen a dead person before, but it was clear she was dead, I didn't have to do anything. It was clear there was nothing I could do. I'm not sure why, but I sat down on the bench, too. I sat down on the end and I leaned back against the wall. It was hard. It was really hard, very hard, cold, and a bit bumpy. I sat there and looked out at the sea, just as she was doing. Or as she had been doing. But she was still looking, after all her eyes were open.

'It set me wondering if the image of the sea was still moving in her eyes. If, even though she was quite dead, the waves were still rolling in there. I couldn't think of a reason why they shouldn't have been. Why shouldn't they have been? I'm sure they were.

'We sat there together. Her and me. Both looking out, but her seeing so much more. After all she had caught the sea in her eyes. And I started to feel really happy. I sat there, looking far out to sea, feeling so happy.

'Then, it might have been the tide turning, or the wind changing, or nothing at all, but I was sure I could sense the woman's memories unravelling themselves. I had this picture, I still do, of a lose thread being drawn, undoing the hours, the days, the years, and I was being taken along with it, as her mind was emptying itself, like an hourglass.

'I stood up. We must have been sitting there some time because it had come on to rain. It hadn't looked like rain earlier, but now it was raining, falling just the other side of the overhang, falling on to the sand, falling on to the sea. I stood up. I put a hand out into the rain, to feel it. All the stones on the beach were perfect. Each one a solid shiny bubble. Perfect. Unblemished. And I danced. On The Promenade, looking over the beach to the sea while the rain fell just out of reach, I danced for Mrs Phipps.'

*

'...we watched her dance. The tide was coming in. Rain was falling. It was magnetic. We oughtn't to have been there. I'm not sure she knew we were there. She was beautiful...'

*

'...I was with my dog. I thought she was going to fall. She leant so far out into the rain...'

*

'...we went to the beach to mess around. There's nothing else to do. Not after the summer anyhow. Soon as we went under the Viaduct we saw something was up...'

*

'...as I'm going away for a couple of months I went to see the sea. I need to each time before I go away. Even if it's only for a week say. I sort of mentally charge my batteries. I was walking along

The Promenade from the direction of The Warren. As I got nearer
I had this odd feeling that I was in a film. Knots of people in ones
and twos and more were standing around. Still. Not many people
in all. But since it was raining it was quite a lot to be standing.
Maybe fifteen. Perhaps a few more. They were all watching.
Some from quite a distance. It's rather worrying, I find, to come
upon people watching. You want to half-know what it is that's
attracted them. On the other hand you're not sure you want to get
involved…'

*

'…I don't know how long. Quite long. Quite some time…'

*

she danced with such freedom. Like a child…'

*

then she stopped. Not all of a sudden. She drifted to a stop,
anding with her hands out into the rain…'

*

…the rain was the kind that falls effortlessly. It didn't splash.
Like silk, it was. I don't even recall it pattering on my anorak…'

*

'…the rain didn't make a mark. Not really. It didn't have any
effect on the sea. It was a haze, a veil. Falling and vanishing…'

*

'…then she stopped…'

*

'…at last she finished…'

*

'…she reached out into the rain and didn't dance any more…'

*

'…she turned to the bench where someone was sitting. I hadn't noticed her till then. I'm not sure why. Maybe because she was in shadow. She took a step or two to the woman and stooped. I think she was telling her something…'

*

'…I think she said something…'

*

'…it looked like she was trying to hear something. Somethin quiet…'

*

'…she tucked away a wisp of hair…'

*

'…I wasn't far away. Possibly the nearest. She stooped to clo Mrs Phipps' eyes…'

*

'…I was on the beach…'

*

'…we were at the bottom of the slope…'

*

'…we were by the breakwater…'

*

'…I was on The Promenade near the lifebuoy…'

*

'…most people we on the beach, on the sand below the stones…'

*

'…she moved from the lady on the bench and walked away…'

*

'…I watched her walk away…'

*

'…we all watched. Every one of us…'

*

.I couldn't take my eyes off her…'

*

was over…'

***

due course Betty Liddell (née Owen), Chris Owen and his wife, ichola, Wendy Marcus (née Wetherall), Charles Burch and Bernard Williamson with their labrador, Bruno, Mrs Stephens and Mrs Brewster, Mr Nelson, Malcolm Hill and his wife, Hilary, (née Jenkins), Monica Trewis (nee Hardman), Mr and Mrs Haywood, Clive Webster and his sons, Steven and Tom, along with Rich, Simon, Mike and Andy all left…

And Osbert? He's been dead almost ten years. Cancer. The shop is a boutique now, "Glitz n' Glamour". Owner and Manager is Mrs Trent. Doing very nicely. Her husband, Tom, is on the Council. It's his turn to be Leader next year.

***

Acknowledgments:
Sincere thanks are long overdue to Val Gale, Liz Wedlake and Cyril Shorland who many years ago shared their memories of The Hut and the grand shows they put on. Thanks to Liz Botterill of Dawlish Museum for arranging viewing of the Dawlish Gazette with the gems it contained, and to Mike Trigger and Marion Trigger of the Dawlish Local History Group for fielding questions and for putting me in touch with current Dawlishians Bob Baker, Chris Grayling and Cindy Gloyn.

Many thanks too to Amanda F who has been so happy to lead me through life as a child who wanted nothing more than to dance. Unlike Amanda Clark, she turned her dreams into reality. Without the encouragement and many wise words of Chris F I ould never have brought my novel to its end, something I naged in the writing room Patricia B let me use.

More thanks to Chris F and Brian H who both stepped in with h needed technical support that has helped me make my k a reality.